About

Barbara Hannay ha... novels and has won the... Times Reviewer's Cho... Romantic Book of the... yen for country life, ... on a misty hillside in beautiful Far North Queensland where they raise pigs and chickens and enjoy an untidy but productive garden.

Cursed with a poor sense of direction and a propensity to read, **Annie Claydon** spent much of her childhood lost in books. A degree in English Literature followed by a career in computing didn't lead directly to her perfect job—writing romance for Mills & Boon—but she has no regrets in taking the scenic route. She lives in London: a city where getting lost can be a joy.

Margaret Barker has enjoyed a variety of interesting careers. A State Registered Nurse and qualified teacher, she holds a degree in French and Linguistics, and is a Licentiate of the Royal Academy of Music. As a full-time writer, Margaret says, 'Writing is my most interesting career, because it fits perfectly into family life. Sadly, my husband died of cancer in 2006, but I still live in our idyllic sixteenth-century house near the East Anglian coast. Our grown-up children have flown the nest, but they often fly back again, bringing their own young families with them for wonderful weekend and holiday reunions.'

The Single Dads
COLLECTION

July 2019

August 2019

September 2019

October 2019

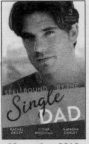

November 2019

December 2019

Captivated by the Single Dad

BARBARA HANNAY

ANNIE CLAYDON

MARGARET BARKER

MILLS & BOON

First Published in Great Britain 2019
By Mills & Boon, an imprint of HarperCollins*Publishers*
1 London Bridge Street, London, SE1 9GF

CAPTIVATED BY THE SINGLE DAD
© 2019 Harlequin Books S.A.

Rancher's Twins: Mum Needed © Barbara Hannay 2011
Saved by the Single Dad © Annie Claydon 2016
Summer with a French Surgeon © Margaret Barker 2012

ISBN: 978-0-263-27560-5

0719

MIX
Paper from
responsible sources
FSC™ C007454

FSC
www.fsc.org

This book is produced from independently certified FSC™ paper to ensure responsible forest management.

For more information visit: www.harpercollins.co.uk/green

Printed and bound in Spain
by CPI, Barcelona

RANCHER'S TWINS: MUM NEEDED

BARBARA HANNAY

I'd like to thank Anne Gracie, for her wonderful
insights into adult literacy, and Elliot,
my live-in bush poet.

CHAPTER ONE

THEY were asleep.

At last.

Holly held her breath as she closed the storybook, then backed out of the children's room with the stealth of a special ops soldier.

The caution was necessary. Really. These kids could sleep soundly through the familiar blast of car horns and sirens from the busy New York street below, but the tiniest squeak from within the apartment could rouse them to instant panicking wakefulness.

This evening, to Holly's relief, neither child stirred. They lay perfectly still in their matching bunk beds. In striped pyjamas, one dark head and one fair, they clutched their favourite fluffy toys—a kangaroo for Josh, a koala for Anna—and their eyes remained blessedly closed.

Holly reached the doorway without a mishap and quickly flicked the light switch, plunging the room into darkness. For once there were no responding squawks or protests. Just sweet, blissful silence.

She tiptoed down the hall…and the silence continued.

Fannnntastic. With a little luck, tonight would be a good night. No wet beds. No nightmares. In the past month there'd only been a handful of good nights. But, before

Holly could even think about letting out a sigh of relief, her cellphone rang.

No-o-o!

With the speed of a baseball short stop, she dived across the room, snatched the phone from the coffee table and darted into her bedroom, closing the door quickly but softly behind her.

The phone's screen identified the caller. Her boyfriend, Brandon. *Wonderful.*

'Hi, Brand,' she whispered.

No squeaks emanated from the bedroom down the hall and she sank gratefully onto the bed.

'Holly, why are you whispering?'

'I've just got the twins to sleep.'

'Oh, right.' Brandon gave an audible sigh. 'How are they coping this week?'

'A little better.'

'That's great.'

Great wasn't quite the word Holly would have chosen to describe the small improvement in the children's progress, but of course she wouldn't correct Brandon. He'd given her fabulous support during the funeral and its aftermath.

'I got your message,' he said.

'Right. Thanks for calling back.' Holly took a moment to relax into the pillows and she deliberately lightened her tone. 'So, what do you think? Can you wangle a leave pass for this weekend?'

She crossed her fingers as she waited for his answer. *Please come, Brand. I need you.*

Brandon's family owned a dairy farm in Vermont and his dad's health wasn't the best, so the responsibility of running the enterprise had fallen squarely on Brandon's shoulders.

So, yes—it was asking a lot to expect him to get away to New York again so soon. Last month, after Holly's cousin Chelsea's sudden and tragic death, he'd taken almost a whole week off to be with her and to help with the children.

That was pretty amazing, actually. Holly had been touched and surprised. Since she'd moved away from Vermont to study in New York, she'd come to accept that if she wanted to see her boyfriend it was up to her to make the effort. She'd grown up on a dairy farm, too, so she understood the demands and she'd been prepared to be the one who did all the travelling. Even so, she'd only been able to see Brandon a handful of times in this past year.

If he came this weekend, she would make sure they had time alone together. She and Brandon had been an item since high school, almost six years. Very soon now, she would be finished with her studies, Anna and Josh would be settled in Australia with their father, and she was looking forward to going home to Vermont to settle down with Brand.

She could so easily picture their lives together—Brandon with his dairy herd, while she worked in the local school, the two of them balancing their day jobs with their life at home, and eventually, with a family of their own—copper-haired children like their dad.

Holly was very happy with that picture, and thinking about her boyfriend always made her feel cosy and safe.

Admittedly, most girls might not place cosiness and safety high on their wish list when it came to boyfriends, but Holly wasn't looking for a guy who spelled excitement and passion. Her cousin Chelsea, the twins' mother, had taken that risk and the result had been divorce and heartbreak.

'I don't know if I can get away this weekend,' Brandon said suddenly.

Holly suppressed a sigh. 'I do understand, honey, but—'

'Do you?' His voice bristled with unexpected impatience. 'Because I *don't* understand why you're complicating this, Holly. The children's father is on his way at last, so why do you need me? Why do you need my help if he's going to be there, too?'

'It would just be good to have your support. I've looked after the twins for a month and now I have to say goodbye.'

Holly suppressed a sigh. She needed to be calm and composed when she talked with Gray about his children, and she would have liked a little backup from Brandon. She needed to explain to Gray about Anna and Josh's schooling needs, their eating habits, their fears…

The twins had been at home on the day Chelsea had collapsed, and it was six-year-old Josh who'd courageously dialled 911. They hadn't only lost their mommy; they'd suffered a terrible trauma. Anna's nightmares were truly terrifying.

Holly needed to explain all this to their estranged father, but it would be so much easier if her steady and reliable boyfriend was there as well. As a buffer. An anchor. A safety net.

'Actually, Holly, I can't come this weekend.'

The sudden nervousness in Brandon's voice penetrated the whirl of Holly's thoughts.

Why was he nervous? Brandon was never nervous. Was something wrong?

'There's…um…there's something I should tell you,' he said.

'What is it?'

'It's really hard to explain. I…I don't know how to say this, but…'

Holly's insides froze and she was gripped by a terrible deer-in-the-headlights fear.

Brandon cleared his throat.

She forced herself to ask, 'Brandon, what's the matter?'

'I didn't want to tell you before—because of Chelsea and everything…'

'Tell me what?' she almost screamed. He was scaring her.

Brandon cleared his throat again.

Holly gripped the phone tighter, squeezing her eyes to hold back threatening tears.

Was Brandon trying to break-up with her?

No. No. Surely not.

Like someone drowning, her mind flashed back through precious memories. The school dance when they'd first met. Brandon helping her with algebra homework at the big scrubbed table in her mother's cosy kitchen. The familiar, comfortable texture of his lips. The ruby heart locket he'd given her on Valentine's Day three years ago. The way she liked to bury her nose against the warm freckles on his neck when he held her. The cosy sense of safety that she'd always felt with him…

Now, suffocating panic filled her throat.

She couldn't bear to think about losing him, especially not when she'd just lost Chelsea. Fear pulled tight knots in her stomach.

Brandon said, 'You have to agree it's not really working for us.'

'What do you mean?' she bleated.

'We only see each other a few times a year.'

'But I've almost finished my studies.' Her voice was shrill now. Pleading. 'I'll soon be home for good and we can—'

'I'm so sorry, Holly. You see, the thing is…I…I've met someone else.'

CHAPTER TWO

As THE taxi pulled into the kerb on West 69th Street Gray Kidman was thinking about the first time he'd arrived at this red-brick apartment block. He'd been a bridegroom then, fired with love and certainty and hope, with no premonition of the heartache that lay ahead of him.

This time he knew what he was in for, knew the challenges and the very real chances for failure. Right now, as he stepped onto the pavement and looked up to the level where his children were waiting, his stomach felt like a jar full of jumping grasshoppers.

His hand was actually shaking as he pressed the security buzzer.

The children answered immediately.

'Daddy!'

'Hi, Dad.'

Gray closed his eyes, momentarily stunned by the emotion his children's voices aroused. For three long months he'd been waiting for this. First, the wet season floods had held him up, then a broken ankle after a desperate attempt to cross a raging creek. Now, at last, he dipped his head to the speaker phone. 'G'day, scallywags.'

Anna squealed, 'I'll press the button to let you in.'

'I've already pressed it,' shouted Josh, full of self-importance and equally excited.

A wry smile tilted Gray's mouth and the glass doors slid open, allowing him access to the apartment block's foyer. He hefted his duffel bag over one shoulder and strode with only the slightest hint of a limp across the blue-tiled floor. As he pressed the lift button, he reminded himself that he must remember to call this an elevator now. His kids would be quick to correct him.

His kids…

His stomach jumped like crazy.

Taking sole charge of Anna and Josh was a huge task, probably the toughest challenge he'd ever faced. He wanted the very best for them. If it was in his power, he'd give his children the perfect foundation for their lives—a safe and comfortable home, a loving family network, and the best possible education.

The irony was that they had all of the above right here in New York City. This apartment block was secure and modern. His ex-wife's teacher cousin was a first-rate nanny, and the children's doting grandparents were nearby. The school they attended had won all kinds of awards for educational excellence.

Although it had nearly killed Gray to let his wife walk away from his Outback cattle property, taking their children with her, he'd been forced to accept that Anna and Josh were better off here in New York than in his home in one of the remotest corners of Australia.

He hadn't given in without a fight but, despite his heartbreak, he'd eventually let his family go.

Yet, tragically, here he was, reclaiming his children and taking them halfway across the world to the very situation their mother had fled from.

Gray had no other option. Running a cattle station was his only income-earning skill. Jabiru Creek Station was the best he had to offer. It was all he had to offer.

He was very afraid it wasn't enough.

The elevator arrived and shot him quickly to the third floor, and when the doors slid open his children were waiting for him.

'Daddy!' Anna launched herself, like a small torpedo, straight into Gray's arms.

He let his duffel bag slip to the floor and lifted her high and she clasped him tightly around his neck.

'Daddy! My daddy!' She buried her face into his shoulder and her silky fair hair smelled wonderfully of flowers.

'Hey, Dad.' Josh was standing close, looking up expectantly.

Crouching, Gray juggled Anna onto one knee and hugged his son. What a fine little fellow Josh was. Gray had been moved to tears when he'd heard that his small son had been brave and quick-thinking when his mother collapsed at home, rushing to dial Emergency.

Now…how good it was to embrace them both. At last.

They seemed fine. Gray had been worried he'd find them pale and pining, but they looked happy and healthy and bursting with energy. It was such a relief.

'That's some welcome,' a voice said and he looked up to see a young woman with dark hair and dark shiny eyes standing in the apartment's open doorway.

Holly O'Mara, Chelsea's young cousin. Gray sent her a smile that felt crooked with emotion. He winced at the twinge in his ankle when he stood once more.

'Holly,' he said, holding out his hand.

'It's good to see you, Gray.'

He didn't know this young woman very well. On the rare occasions they'd met at family gatherings, Holly had always been shy, keeping well in the background, as if she preferred her own company, so he'd never gone out of his way to chat with her. Besides, she was training to be an English teacher, which meant she was as well educated and cultured as his former wife, another woman destined to remind him of his inadequacies.

But he couldn't deny he owed her a great deal. She'd been sole carer of his children for three long, difficult months.

With the twins skipping at his heels, he followed Holly inside the apartment. It was then, without warning, that he was sideswiped by a new emotion—the realisation that his beautiful bride was gone for ever.

It was crazy to feel like this now. Truth was, Gray had already lost Chelsea three years ago when she left him. He'd done his grieving then, and in time he'd moved on, eventually finding comfort in a healthy cynicism for the married state.

Now, suddenly, the finality of her passing hit him like a physical blow. A sense of loss descended like black, suffocating cloud.

Don't break down. Not now. Not in front of the children.

He heard Holly say gently, 'You've had a long journey. Why don't you go through to the living room? Take the weight off. I have coffee brewing.'

Gray was grateful for the normality and everyday ease of her welcome. 'Thanks,' he said. 'Thanks for everything, Holly.'

Their gazes met in an unexpected moment of connection. Holly was smiling, but Gray thought he saw tears glistening in her dark eyes and he felt a painful tightening in his throat.

He spoke more gruffly than he meant to. 'Come on, kids, show me the way.'

* * *

Holly told herself to keep smiling as she watched Gray and his children head down the hall. Alone in the kitchen, however, she was fighting tears as she filled the coffee-maker.

It was two months now since her break-up with Brandon, but Gray's arrival *at last* brought it all back—memories of the horrible phone call, the heartbreak in the following weeks of anxiety, of hoping against all hope for another call. *It was all a mistake, Holly. I really do love you.*

But on top of that pain…she felt so tense, so conflicted about this reunion.

Oh, she was very happy for Anna and Josh. She knew how much they needed their father, and it was wonderful to see how thrilled they were. But she wasn't sure she could bear to let them go all the way back to Australia.

Of course, Gray had every right to take his children home, and there was no denying that he loved them.

Just now, when he'd hunkered down in the corridor to hug them, Holly had seen the way he closed his eyes and held them close against his heart. She'd watched the concentrated emotion in his face, and she'd been so moved she'd almost spoiled the moment by weeping.

Until then, she hadn't realised how fragile she was after the emotional pressure cooker of the last three months.

She and the children had been through so much together, and they'd grown incredibly close. When Chelsea had died so suddenly, the very foundations of their world had been shaken and Holly had needed to dig deep, discovering a sensitivity and wisdom she hadn't known she possessed.

Even though Chelsea's parents lived close by in a luxury Westside apartment, they'd been too shocked and grieving to be of much help. They'd gladly handed over their grand-children into Holly's full-time care until Gray Kidman arrived to claim them.

Looking back, Holly wasn't quite sure how she'd managed. In a cruelly short space of time she'd lost Chelsea, her cousin and her best friend, and then Brandon. Filled with despair, she'd wanted to crawl away and hide for a decade or two, and she might have done exactly that if Anna and Josh's needs hadn't been even greater than hers.

To give them the love and attention they'd needed, she'd been forced to put her own heartbreak aside.

So…in a way the children had saved her. But right now, she was finding it hard to accept that her role as an integral player in this little team was almost over. She couldn't imagine living without them.

'Look, Daddy.' Anna lifted her top lip.

'Wow. You've lost a tooth.'

The little girl grinned proudly, revealing the gap. 'I left it under my pillow and the Tooth Fairy came.'

'Lucky you.'

'Josh hasn't lost any teeth yet.'

His son's lips were tightly pressed together, and Gray caught a flicker of embarrassment in the boy's eyes. Clearly, sibling rivalry was alive and well, and no doubt Josh felt left behind in the race to shed baby teeth.

'Josh must have extra tough teeth,' Gray suggested.

The boy sent him a grateful smile.

To change the subject, Gray unzipped a pocket on the outside of his duffel bag and drew out a small packet.

'Is that a present?' asked Anna, eager-eyed.

'It's a game to share with your brother. A card game. Snap. With pictures of the Outback on the back.'

'Your Outback?'

He smiled uncertainly. 'Yes. My Outback.'

The twins had been three when they'd left his home—he doubted they'd remember it.

They knelt at the coffee table as Gray fanned the cards onto its smooth glass surface, showing bright photos of kangaroos, pink-flowering gum trees and wide red plains shimmering beneath sunburned skies.

'Is that where you're going to take us?' asked Josh.

Gray nodded.

'Is your house like this one?' Anna picked up a card that showed a faded, shabby homestead with a broad iron roof standing alone in the middle of a sparse red desert.

'More or less,' Gray admitted with some reluctance.

The little girl stared with large worried eyes at the rather ugly house and stark forbidding landscape.

'We have more trees than that and quite a decent garden,' Gray amended, feeling rather like a real estate agent trying to sell inadequate property. 'My homestead is painted white, and there are lots of extra buildings.'

'What kind of buildings?'

He realised now that he should have brought proper photos of Jabiru Creek Station, instead of these generic tourist images. 'We have machinery sheds and storage sheds and houses for the ringers.'

'What are ringers?'

'They're stockmen.'

'Cowboys,' added Holly cheerfully as she came into the room with a coffee pot and two black and white mugs.

'Except that in Australia we don't call them cowboys,' Gray amended with a smile.

'Can we ride horses?'

The animated excitement in Josh's face was a stark contrast to the sudden fear in Anna's dark brown eyes. Gray's chest tightened. His daughter looked so much like her mother. So beautiful, like a delicate flower, and right now, so worried and sad.

'I have a nice little horse that you can learn to ride,' he

told Josh. For Anna's sake he added, 'But you don't have to ride if you don't want to.'

He tried to cheer Anna with a smiling wink. She wouldn't remember how she used to love to ride in the saddle in front of him, while he kept one arm around her and one hand holding the reins. To his dismay, her lower lip trembled. Damn. He had so little experience in handling kids. The simplest thing could suddenly become a huge problem.

Holly, who'd made herself comfortable in an armchair, leaned forward and picked up another card—a picture of blue sky reflected in a large pool of water at the bottom of a steep red-walled gorge.

'Look, Anna,' Holly said. 'Isn't this beautiful?'

Over the children's heads, her expressive dark eyes sent Gray a silent message. They needed to change the subject.

'Do you have beautiful places like this on your ranch?' she asked him.

'Sure. We have a fabulous deep gorge and a sizeable river.'

'Can you swim there?' Holly asked with an encouraging smile.

Not unless you're willing to risk being eaten by a crocodile.

Sidestepping that question, Gray said instead, 'There's a dam near the homestead where you can swim.' *When it's not too hot or muddy.*

He tentatively touched his daughter's arm. Her skin was soft and smooth and perfect and his heart lurched. He hated to think of her being muddy or sunburned or in any kind of danger from the harsh environment that was his home.

Would he be able to take proper care of her? He hunted for something positive to tell her.

'Do you like puppies, Anna?'

She nodded solemnly.

'I have a nice kelpie and she's going to have babies very soon. By the time we get home there might be puppies.'

'How many puppies?'

'Maybe three or four.'

Anna's eyes widened. 'Are they all in their mommy's tummy?'

'Yes. They're growing fat and wriggly and they're almost ready to be born.'

'Like Josh and me? We were together in our mommy's tummy.'

Gray tensed, expecting his daughter to burst into tears now that she'd inadvertently mentioned her mother. His skin grew clammy. His heart picked up pace. Hell. What should he do and say now?

Holly spoke for him. 'That's right, Anna. The puppies are just like you and Josh, all together in their mommy's tummy.' She said this smoothly and calmly, as if nothing awkward or dangerous had happened. 'If there are three puppies, they'll be triplets. If there are four they'll be quads.'

To Gray's surprise, Anna grinned, clearly pleased with Holly's answer.

'Why don't you two have a game of Snap while your dad drinks his coffee?' Holly suggested next. 'Take the cards through to your room. I'll call you as soon as lunch is ready.'

'Is Dad having lunch with us?' Josh asked.

'Of course. He'll be staying here with us for a few days.'

Satisfied, the boy began to gather up the cards and the two trotted happily off to their room.

As they left, Gray sent Holly a surprised smile, shaking

his head. 'They did exactly what you asked. Are they always so obedient?'

She laughed. 'Heavens, no. Although they're getting better all the time.' She poured coffee into two mugs. 'Here's your coffee. Drink it while it's hot.'

'Thanks.' He relaxed into the sofa and took a deep sip. The coffee was indeed hot and strong and of very good quality.

Over the rim of his mug he stole a closer look at Holly O'Mara. Although he'd only met her a few times, he was sure there was something different about her. He tried to decide what it was. Was her face thinner? Was that why her dark eyes now looked larger, her mouth more curving and lush, her cheekbones more defined?

Or was there something different about her expression?

The change was hard to pin down, but he sensed a depth in Chelsea's young cousin that he'd never been aware of before. He knew these past three months must have been very hard on her. No doubt she'd had to grow up fast.

Whatever it was about Holly that was different, the change seemed to suit her. *And* she'd clearly done a very good job of looking after his children.

'I hope you realise how very grateful I am,' he said. 'Honestly, the way you've taken care of the twins has been amazing. Fantastic. It can't have been easy—being dumped with everything after…after Chelsea…'

Holly nodded. 'There have been some grim moments, but each day gets better.'

Gray wondered, somewhat anxiously, about the 'grim moments'. He sat for a bit in silence, wrapped in worried thoughts as they drank their coffee.

'How's your ankle?' Holly asked politely.

'Oh, it's fine.' He pulled a face, remembering the

exasperation of the floods, and then the further frustration of his accident. 'You have no idea how maddening it was not being able to get here any sooner.'

She let out a soft huff. 'I'll admit it wasn't easy at this end, either, trying to convince Anna and Josh that you were held up all that time by floods.'

'I'm sorry.'

She shook her head. 'No, you couldn't help it, and you did the right thing when you asked me not to tell them about the accident. They'd just lost their mom. They would have been devastated if they'd heard their dad was hurt, too.'

'I wouldn't have been much use to them on crutches.'

'Imagine your journey home,' Holly agreed, smiling. 'Twenty-something hours on a plane and trying to manage six-year-old twins while you're hobbling on a cast.'

'Exactly.' Gray sat forward, eager to voice the question that had been plaguing him. 'So—how do you think Anna and Josh will cope with going back to Australia with me?'

He hoped she would answer with an easygoing shrug and a quick reassurance.

They'll be fine. They're over the worst now.

To his dismay, she dropped her gaze to her coffee cup and twisted it in her hands.

His throat tightened uncomfortably. 'I thought my place—somewhere completely different—might help them. Might be a...a distraction.'

Holly looked up again and, when her dark eyes met his, she was frowning. He saw no hint of reassurance.

He spoke again quickly, needing to strengthen his case. 'This apartment must hold so many sad memories for the children. Won't it help them to get away?'

Her mouth opened again as if she was going to reply, but then she hesitated.

Gray's entire body tensed. 'You agree, don't you?' He forced an awkward shrug. 'I admit you know my children better than I do. I'd value your opinion.'

She responded with a faint smile. 'I certainly hope they'll be fine, but I can't promise it's going to be easy, Gray. I'm no expert, but from everything I've read—'

'Everything you've *read?*' He felt himself tense. As a cattleman who'd always relied on purely practical skills, he was sceptical about the glorified merits of the written word.

Perhaps Holly sensed his doubt. Her cheeks flushed deep pink but, when she spoke, she lifted her chin and her dark eyes narrowed. 'I've never had any first-hand experience of grief, certainly not with helping children who've lost a parent. So I consulted a GP who referred me to a psychologist, and I've done some reading, too. After all, the books are written by experts.'

The skin on the back of Gray's neck grew hot. Not quite meeting her gaze, he said, 'So what did the experts have to say?'

Holly set her coffee mug on the table with exquisite care, as if it were a rare antique. 'It seems that children who've suffered a loss can benefit from a predictable routine and structure. The familiarity of a routine helps them to feel secure.'

A predictable routine.

Structure.

Security.

Gray's heart sank. Predictability and security were scarce commodities in the Outback. Cattlemen and their families lived at the mercy of the elements, or at the whim of fluctuating markets. Daily, they dealt with the problems caused by isolation and vast distances.

He recalled all the things his ex-wife had hated about his lifestyle, and he thought about his experience over the past three months—being cut off by the floods, almost running out of supplies, busting his leg in a flooded river.

Doubts crowded in. What was he doing here? How could he take his kids away from this safe and secure world that they knew and loved?

Abruptly, he stood and strode to the window where he dipped a slat in the blinds with one finger and stared down at the crowded pavements and busy traffic below.

Without looking at Holly, he said grimly, 'If the experts in your books are right, the last thing my children need is another big change.'

Unhappily, he folded his arms over his chest and his jaw jutted belligerently. 'I'm planning to drag Anna and Josh halfway across the world to a place that's completely different from here, and your book-writing experts are telling me it's the worst thing I can do.'

CHAPTER THREE

FOR a moment, Holly was seriously tempted to tell Gray that yes, his children would be much better off if they stayed right here in Manhattan. Of course they'd be happier if they were allowed to continue in this familiar environment—living in this apartment, going to their highly acclaimed school, playing with their select circle of appropriate friends.

For three months she'd been trying to follow the psychologists' advice. She'd built little rituals into the children's days so they always had something to look forward to.

She'd carefully planned mealtimes around their favourite nutritious foods, and she'd scheduled regular after school treats. Of course, she'd made sure that bedtime was special with their favourite stories. And plenty of hugs.

But she couldn't suggest that Gray would not be able to meet his children's needs. She'd witnessed his deep emotion when he'd first greeted his children, and she could see the incredible tension in his face right now as he waited for her answer.

Gray wasn't just a proud, possessive male reclaiming his rights. He was a man who loved his children very deeply. Chelsea's parents had told her that over the past three years he'd made the arduous journey from Australia to America several times a year, just to see them.

Holly knew that her possibly selfish opinions about the benefits of staying in America had no place in this conversation.

She drew a deep breath. 'Anna and Josh want to be with you, Gray. You're their father.' After a beat, she added gently, 'They've missed you very much.'

His face softened a fraction. 'But it's still going to be hard for them to leave here and to make the change, isn't it?'

She couldn't deny this. 'You should probably be prepared for one or two tricky moments.'

'I was hoping that if I stayed in New York for a few days, and gave them a chance to get used to me again—'

'I'm sure that will help. And, while you're here, we can both talk to them about what to expect on the journey and when they arrive in Australia.'

Gray nodded, and let his thoughtful gaze fix on the row of windows on the opposite wall, as if he was seeing far into the distance. Then he sent Holly a slow smile.

Despite the fact that Holly was thinking about Gray's children and not his looks, something very odd happened to her insides. She dropped her gaze from the sudden flare in his light blue eyes and found safety in the tan leather duffel bag, dumped on the floor by the sofa.

It was the sort of bag that would look at home on a dusty homestead veranda, or in the back of a battered pickup. Here, in this city apartment, however, the scuffed leather holdall looked out of place, almost like a symbol of everything that had been wrong about Gray's marriage to her cousin.

Chelsea had rarely talked about the problems that had sent her scurrying home from Jabiru Creek to New York. It was clear to everyone that her decision had been painful— that she hadn't stopped loving Gray, but that she'd loved her

ballet and choreography more. There'd been no jobs for a
choreographer of Chelsea's calibre in Outback Australia
and, in the end, she'd found it too difficult to relinquish
her city life and her career.

She'd told Holly once, 'It was a fatal attraction. Gray
and I were wrong for each other and in almost every way.
I think we both sensed from the start that our marriage
was doomed, but our feelings were so intense we still had
to give it a try.'

Now, sitting mere metres from Gray Kidman's intensely
masculine presence, Holly was all too aware of the force
that had urged Chelsea to take that risk. He was still
disturbingly attractive. Looking at him, the word *manly*
seemed to take on new meaning.

Abruptly, she jumped to her feet. 'If you've finished
your coffee, I'll show you to your room and you can stow
your things away.'

She charged across the room, feeling a need to put a
sudden distance between them.

'Holly, before you go—'

Slowly…she turned.

Gray offered a dangerously shy smile. 'I know I'm probably old-fashioned and you're a contemporary New Yorker,
but I just wanted to make sure you're completely okay with
having me stay here in your apartment.'

'Of course. It's perfectly fine.' Holly tried to sound off-
hand. 'It makes sense.'

'And your boyfriend? Is he cool with it, too?'

A horrible knife-in-the-heart pain pierced Holly, the
pain she always felt whenever Brandon was mentioned.
After two months, the shock was still very raw—especially
the painful discovery that Brandon had been seeing Maria
Swain for six whole months before he'd found the courage
to tell her.

Somehow she forced a breezy smile. 'That's not a problem. I'm between boyfriends right now.'

Not wanting to see Gray's reaction, she hurried on to the spare room. 'It's important for you to stay here, Gray.' She tossed the words over her shoulder. 'You need to maximise your time with the children before you set off.'

'Thanks. I appreciate that.'

At the doorway, she stepped aside to let him into the room. 'It's nothing special, but I guess it's adequate.'

'It's terrific.' Gray dropped his bag onto the rug at the foot of the single bed. Holly was about to leave when he said, 'What about you, Holly?'

'Me? Oh…my room's…um…just down the hall.'

Gray looked a tad embarrassed and scratched at the side of his jaw. 'I wasn't asking where you sleep. I meant—what are your plans now—once the children are off your hands.'

'My plans? Oh…' Holly gulped. Talking to this attractive man about bedrooms must have scrambled her powers of thinking. 'I've just finished my final exams, so I've started sending out job applications. Who knows where I'll end up?'

With luck, anywhere except Vermont.

Taking three quick steps backwards, she added, 'Right now, I need to fix lunch.'

'Anything I can help with?'

'No, thanks. It's only chicken salad. You go and see the children. Join in their game.'

Gray suggested a trip to Central Park after lunch. He always felt more at ease entertaining his children in wide open spaces with grass and trees and blue sky overhead, instead of pavement and department stores and hurrying crowds.

This time, Holly came with them.

Initially Gray hadn't invited her. He'd assumed she'd be keen to grab a few hours of freedom to paint her toenails, or go shopping, or whatever city girls liked to do when they had time to themselves.

Just as the children and he were about to leave the apartment, however, Holly had handed him a pamphlet.

'This shows you everything that's going on in Central Park,' she'd said.

Gray had dismissed this with a quick, 'We'll be fine.'

Even though he was only familiar with a tiny section of Central Park, he could find the zoo, and the carousel. Anna and Josh had never complained. 'We'll play it by ear, won't we, kids?'

Holly looked surprised and she tapped a brightly coloured centre page. 'But this pamphlet lists all the children's activities. And there's a puppet theatre.'

'Puppets!' Anna and Josh both squealed in chorus. 'We want to see the puppets. Please, Daddy, please!'

Holly was still pointing to the printed page and Gray felt the first squeeze of panic. The words on the pamphlet danced and jumbled before his eyes and his chest tightened as frustration and inadequacy—two foes he'd been fighting all his life—surfaced.

'Why don't you come along with us?' he asked her then. 'And bring your pamphlet.'

Her cheeks turned pink—a very pretty pink, a perfect foil for her dark eyes and her shiny dark hair. The blush surprised Gray. Perhaps she was shyer than he'd realised.

'Yes, Holly, come with us,' Anna was pleading and grabbing her hand. 'Please, come. Please!'

Holly shook her head. 'But this is your special time to be with your daddy.'

However, she didn't need much convincing.

'Would you like me to try for last minute tickets for the

puppets?' she said next and already she was pulling her cellphone from her pocket.

They were in luck. There were four tickets available for the last performance that afternoon and when they set off for Central Park Gray noticed that Holly's shyness was quickly evaporating.

It was soon clear that she genuinely *liked* to spend time outdoors with his children. She laughed a lot and her eyes shone, and she looked somehow just right in slim blue jeans and a simple grey T-shirt, with her dark hair tied back in a ponytail and her face free of make-up.

He thought, uneasily, that his children were really going to miss Holly when it was time to leave. He couldn't help noticing how totally relaxed they were with her. Affectionate, too. Josh was perfectly happy to hold her hand when they crossed the busy streets, and Anna, all excited after a super-fast slippery slide, exchanged ecstatic high fives with Holly. The gesture was so automatic and natural Gray knew they'd done this many times.

And Holly's pamphlet proved to be a great asset. It showed where the really cool playgrounds were, like the Ancient Playground based on the Egyptian Temple of Dendor, with model pyramids for climbing. And after the children had climbed and run and explored the zoo and thrown Frisbees and eaten ice creams, they all headed off to the puppet theatre in an old Swedish cottage.

The show turned out to be lively and hilarious, full of drama and excitement and silly pranks that were impossible not to enjoy.

All the children in the audience were encouraged to call out advice and warnings, so they practically lifted the roof off the ancient cottage. So very different from the serious, respectful hush of the audiences at the ballets Chelsea had dragged him to.

At one point, Gray glanced over Anna and Josh's heads and caught Holly watching him. Her dark eyes sparkled with amusement and he realised he'd been laughing out loud.

Strewth. When was the last time that had happened?

They emerged from the theatre in the late afternoon, and together they strolled through the park in the softening light of the late spring evening. The children skipped ahead, wide smiles on their faces as they imitated the Big Bad Wolf, playing hide-and-seek behind tree trunks.

His kids were okay. They were happy. And Gray discovered that he was completely and totally relaxed. He hadn't realised how tense he'd been, but now, for the first time since he'd received the shocking news about Chelsea, he was conscious of having truly unwound.

'You shouldn't have to cook again tonight,' he told Holly. 'Why don't we eat out? My shout.'

She laughed. 'I was going to suggest grabbing a meal on the way home. We have a tradition of eating out at our favourite diner on Saturday nights.'

A tradition? Gray wondered uneasily if Anna and Josh would miss these traditions. Would they be willing to help him create new traditions? He couldn't take them to a diner near his Outback home. The nearest café was a hundred kilometres from Jabiru Creek. Could a campfire on a riverbank be a reasonable substitute?

As they pushed through the swing doors of the diner on 81st Street they were greeted by laughter and happy chatter and the appetizing smells of frying bacon and coffee. The waiters recognised Holly and the children and welcomed them warmly.

Gray was introduced.

'My dad from Australia,' Josh said proudly.

They slipped into a booth with Gray and Anna on one side, Holly and Josh on the other. The waiter handed out menus.

Gray barely looked at his. 'I'll have a hamburger.'

Holly shot him a surprised glance. 'What kind of hamburger? There are at least six varieties.'

He shrugged, cracked a careless smile. 'I've worked up an appetite. Whatever's the biggest.'

'That would be the Mighty Mo,' the waiter told him with a grin.

'Thanks. Sounds perfect.' Gray turned to his daughter. 'What about you, princess? What would you like?'

He watched Anna study the menu, following down the lists with her finger.

'A grilled American cheese sandwich,' she decided.

'And I wanna hot dog,' said Josh.

'I'd like a hot dog, please, Daddy,' Holly reminded him.

'I'd like a hot dog, please, Dad.' His son sent him a cheeky grin.

'You're both excellent readers,' Gray said.

His children smiled politely, as if they were thinking—*Of course. It's only a simple old menu.*

He asked quickly, 'What are you having, Holly? Let me guess. A Greek salad?' This had always been Chelsea's choice and, judging by Holly's slim build, Gray assumed she was equally diet-conscious.

'Actually,' she replied with a raised-eyebrow smile, 'I rather fancy nachos with cheese, guacamole *and* sour cream.'

It was hours later, close to midnight, when Holly woke to the sound of high-pitched screaming. Her heart pounded as she leapt out of bed. Anna was having another nightmare.

She hurried through the apartment, not bothering to turn on a light. She was so familiar with the route from her bedroom to the children's room that she could easily dodge furniture and find her way in the dark.

But tonight, halfway down the hall, she ran into a solid object. Six feet three inches of near-naked male. Gray's warm bare chest and arms. His shoulders, bulky and smooth. His sculpted, cow-wrangling muscles. And he was only wearing boxer shorts.

'Gray.' She was suddenly breathless and flushed and—

'What's the matter with Anna?' he demanded, stepping past her.

Holly came rapidly to her senses. 'She's having a nightmare.'

As they hurried into the children's room, she gave herself a mental slap. Okay, so having a close encounter with this man's partly naked body was likely to send almost any female into a tizzy, but what had happened to her priorities? What about poor Anna?

In the children's bedroom she switched on a lamp and the room was illuminated by a soft pink glow. Anna was huddled in a tight ball in the middle of her bed, sobbing, 'Mommy! Mommy!'

Gray looked appalled and helpless, but Holly was sadly used to this scene. Kneeling on the bed, she drew the little girl into her arms. 'There, there. It's okay.' She stroked Anna's silky hair. 'It's okay, honey. You can wake up. You're all right.'

She felt the mattress dip beneath an extra weight. Gray was sitting on the other side of the bed, his eyes fierce and filled with concern. Lifting a shaking hand, he touched his daughter's tear-stained cheek.

'Anna,' he whispered. 'Anna, baby.'

'Daddy!' The little girl lifted her head from Holly's shoulder, then turned and hurled herself into her father's arms. Within minutes her shuddering sobs calmed and she buried her face into his chest.

Holly couldn't blame her. What little girl wouldn't want to be held safe in those big, strong, manly arms?

Just the same, she couldn't help feeling rejected. After weeks of comforting Anna during these middle of the night crises, Holly had suddenly become redundant.

She looked across to Josh's bed. In the early weeks he'd been the first to jump up, trying to calm his sister. Lately, he'd been more inclined to lie quietly, wide awake, knowing that Holly would come, that Holly knew what to do and that the storm would eventually pass.

'Hey there, champ,' Holly whispered.

'Hey,' the boy returned softly and then he yawned.

'You go back to sleep.' She leaned over to drop a kiss on his warm, still baby-soft cheek. He really was the greatest little guy. She adored him.

Adored them both.

When she turned back to see how Anna was now, she found Gray watching her, and it was then, in the warmth of his gaze, that she remembered that he wasn't the only adult in this room who was half undressed. She was in her thin cotton nightie—little more than a long, baggy T-shirt with a trail of dog's paw-prints stamped across her chest.

She tried to shrug off the intimacy of this situation, of being here with Gray, both in their pyjamas, tending to his children in the middle of the night. But the intimacy seemed even greater now after their afternoon in the park and their shared meal. Almost as if the four of them were a little family.

Good grief, what am I thinking?

How could she betray Chelsea with such thoughts? Very

soon she would be waving goodbye to this father and his kids. In the fall, she would embark on an exciting new career.

Enough already.

Determined to be sensible, Holly said softly, 'I think Anna will be okay now.'

In the early weeks, she'd taken the little girl back to sleep in her bed, but lately she'd been weaning Anna out of that habit.

'Perhaps she'd like a drink of water.' Holly handed Gray a glass from the nightstand and watched as Anna took a few sips. 'We can leave the lamp on for five minutes,' she said.

'Okay, princess?' Gray gently eased his daughter back into bed.

Holly pulled up the covers and tucked her in. 'Night, night.'

The little girl looked peaceful again, curled on her side, eyes closed, golden curls gleaming softly in the lamplight as she clutched her favourite fluffy koala.

Gray gave his daughter a kiss and his son a gentle shoulder thump.

''Night, Dad.'

When Gray and Holly were safely down the hallway once more, Gray let out his breath with a whoosh.

'My God,' he said quietly. 'That scared the living daylights out of me. I'd rather hear a crocodile growling at my elbow than my own daughter screaming.'

'Anna's screams are heart-rending,' Holly agreed.

'Has this been happening all along? Ever since Chelsea—?'

Holly nodded. 'It was worse at first. She's getting better. This is the first nightmare in a while.'

'Maybe she's had too much excitement for one day.'

'Perhaps that's it.'

Gray let out a heavy sigh. 'I'm sure I'm not going to be able to get back to sleep.' He ran stiff fingers through his thick dark hair. 'It's two o'clock in the afternoon where I come from. Would I disturb you too much if I made a cuppa?'

'No, not at all. Go right ahead.'

'If I make tea, would you like a cup?'

'Tea?' She laughed. 'English tea?'

He shrugged. 'English, American...I'm not fussy.'

'I'm afraid I only have green tea or camomile.'

He pulled a face. 'How about wine, then? I bought a couple of Australian reds in the duty-free.'

No, thank you.

Holly was sure she should get straight back to her room. Right now. She should not sit around in the middle of the night in her jammies having cosy chats and glasses of vino with her charges' scarily handsome father.

'I...I'd love a glass. I'll...um...just grab a wrap.'

Okay, I'm a bird-brain, but I do have a good excuse, Holly consoled herself as she hurried away. Gray needed to talk about his children. He needed to debrief after the scare he'd had with Anna.

By the time she came back into the kitchen, safely covered by a tightly knotted kimono that ended well below her knees, Gray had, mercifully, pulled on jeans and a T-shirt and he was freeing the cork from a bottle.

CHAPTER FOUR

GRAY was extremely grateful that Holly was prepared to sit and have a drink with him at midnight.

His daughter's screams had shocked him and, even though Anna had calmed quite quickly in his arms, the experience had left him feeling shaken. Anxious.

Now, more than ever, he was aware of his lack of skills. There was so much he didn't know, didn't understand about his children. He wouldn't be able to read the experts' books on psychology and grief and yet, very soon, Anna and Josh would be completely in his care.

Suddenly, his excitement over having them back in his life was mixed with terror. All his failures came back to haunt him—all the problems stemming from his childhood that had tainted his marriage.

Hell. How could he be a good single father? How could he be a role model for his kids? He'd let his parents down, let his wife down. Would he let his children down, too?

Worries chased each other, snapping like dogs at the heels of his thoughts as he and Holly sat on the corner sofas next to plate glass windows with views of the city.

They left the lamps turned low and the curtains open so they could see the black towers of the skyscrapers dotted with squares of lemon light. From below came the non-stop honk and roar of traffic. New York, the city that never sleeps.

It was a wonder anyone could ever sleep here with that constant racket, Gray thought wryly.

Holly was now wrapped in an elegant dressing gown of jade-green silk with a pattern of graceful white cranes. She sat with her bare feet tucked to one side, slim fingers curled around her glass of wine.

'It's a Margaret River red,' he said. 'Should be good. Cheers.'

She smiled faintly as she raised her glass. 'Cheers.'

They sipped the wine and shared satisfied smiles. The wine was very good.

At first they talked about practical things, about the kinds of clothes the children would need immediately in Australia, and what could be boxed for posting. There were toys to be sorted, too—favourites to go with the children now, some to be sent to charities, others to be shipped.

'How will Anna and Josh feel about leaving their friends behind?' Gray asked.

'Their school friends?' Holly shrugged. 'I don't think that will be a problem. Little kids move on. Friends come and go.' She smiled. 'Don't look so worried, Gray. Josh is cracking his neck to get to your ranch.'

Somewhat reassured, Gray had to ask the question that really bothered him. 'About Anna's nightmares—'

'Yes?'

'Do you know why she has them? Could it be because she was with Chelsea when it...when the aneurism... happened?'

'There's a good chance.' Holly dropped her gaze to her glass. 'Chelsea collapsed when she was in the middle of making Anna a peanut butter sandwich.'

It was almost too awful to imagine. Poor Anna. Poor

Chelsea. For a moment he couldn't think past the horror of it. How helpless and terrified Anna must have felt and, quite possibly, even guilty.

He sighed heavily. 'Does Josh have nightmares, too?'

Holly's dark hair rippled as she shook her head. 'I think Josh is naturally more resilient than Anna. But he rang for the ambulance, so he knows he did everything he could. I'm sure that's helped him, even if it's only at some sub-conscious level.'

It made sense, and the reminder of his son's quick thinking caused a small glow of pride. But poor Anna shouldn't feel guilty. 'There must be so much I need to understand. Is there anything else you should warn me about?'

Frowning, Holly took another sip of wine before she answered. 'I actually wish Josh showed more signs of grief. He's been bottling it in and I'm sure a good cry would do him good.'

'He probably thinks crying is for girls.'

'Probably. My brothers would agree.' Holly sighed. 'He probably needs to be encouraged to talk about it.'

Gray grimaced. *Talking about feelings? Sharing emotions with others?* That was so not his scene. Weren't women supposed to be so much better at it than guys? All his life, he'd been a man of action, not words.

Watching him, Holly said, 'I guess you must be very busy running your ranch. I assume you've hired a nanny to help with the children.'

'Ah...' Gray drew a sharp breath. 'So far, I've organised a team to look after the mustering, so that frees me up quite a bit. My plan was to wait till I saw Anna and Josh—and saw how they were. I thought I'd take them home, help them to settle in first, then look around for someone suitable.'

He set his empty glass on the coffee table. 'There wouldn't be any point in hiring a nanny they didn't like.'

'No. It will need to be the right person.'

Holly looked away quickly as if she didn't want him to see her eyes, but Gray was sure he'd caught a glitter of tears and his throat tightened. He'd expected her to be anxious to be free of his kids, but was she upset at the thought of saying goodbye to them?

It was so difficult for a family to span two hemispheres. There was always someone who missed out.

She turned to him again, her eyes extra-wide. 'So will Anna and Josh be involved when you choose their new nanny?'

'They'll be consulted.' Gray thought this was only fair. 'Do you have any advice?' he added, trying to be diplomatic.

'I...I'll give it some thought.' She shifted her position, uncurling her legs.

He couldn't help watching. Her legs were long and shapely and her toenails were painted a deep sexy red. In her Oriental dressing gown, with her dark hair shining in the soft light, she made a charming picture. Like a painting.

Girl at Midnight.

He thought how perfect it would be—from his children's point of view, of course—if Holly could continue on as their nanny. She understood them so well, far better than he did, and they clearly loved her. Added to that, she had teaching skills and, with her help, the transition to Australia would be almost painless.

It would never happen, of course. Holly had already told him she was about to start a new career in the US. Why would she give that up and go all the way to the Australian Outback?

She was a city girl. She was his ex-wife's cousin, for crying out loud. She was educated and cultured, just as

Chelsea had been. If she hated his place the way Chelsea had, her attitude could rub off on his kids.

Gray realised that Holly was already on her feet.

'Thanks for the wine,' she said.

'Would you like another glass?'

She shook her head. 'I need to hit the sack. Tomorrow is another day and all that.'

Her voice was tight, so tight it almost cracked. Without another word, she set the wine glass on the kitchen bench and hurried away.

She was upset. Had she been able to tell what he was thinking?

In bed, Gray lay wide awake, his thoughts running amok, trailing through the events of the day, and inevitably through the dizzying highs and lows of his romance with Chelsea. He'd met his children's mother while she was travelling in North Queensland with a touring American dance troupe, but he'd made so many mistakes...so many wrong turns...

He'd never seen a girl so delicate and fair, so perfectly beautiful in every way. He'd never looked into a woman's eyes and fallen from a great height.

It had been a classic case of love at first sight, with all the usual symptoms—the thunderbolt to the heart, the obsession.

With the recklessness of youth, Gray had followed Chelsea back to America. In New York he'd courted her with the single-minded passion of a young man desperately in love. A hasty engagement, a wedding in Central Park and a blissful honeymoon in Paris...

Then back to Jabiru Creek Station. To the Outback.

Within the first month, Chelsea had realised her mistake. She'd loved Gray—about that there had never been any doubt—but in the Australian Outback his precious bride had wilted like a flower without water.

His throat ached now as he remembered the tears streaming down her face as she'd confronted him.

We've made a mistake, Gray, haven't we? Don't you think we should separate now, before this gets too complicated? You're a good man. I should have been more honest. I didn't want to hurt you.

Of course, he should have given in then. It was so easy now to look back and to see how foolish and blinded he'd been—how he'd kissed her tears and begged her shamelessly.

You must stay, Chelsea. Please, please give it a go.

It was only a few weeks later that she'd realised she was pregnant so, of course, she'd stayed...

'You wake him up.'

'No, you.'

Childish giggling penetrated Gray's sleep. *Damn.* Was it morning already?

It had taken him hours to fall asleep and he felt absolutely stuffed, unable to move, like an elephant paralysed by a stun gun. Perhaps, if he lay very still, his children would creep away again and leave him to sleep.

Not a chance. Already small hands were poking and shaking him.

'Dad! Dad!'

He groaned in a low protest.

'Daddy!' That was Anna's voice, now suddenly panic-stricken.

His eyes snapped open, then he cringed from the bright daylight flooding the room. 'Good morning,' he groaned. 'What time is it?'

'It's really late,' Josh told him. 'We had breakfast ages and ages ago.'

Gray struggled onto one elbow, yawned and rubbed a hand over sleep-bleary eyes.

'Are you all right, Daddy?' Anna still sounded worried.

'Yeah, chicken. I'm fine.' He yawned again. 'Just sleepy. My body thinks it's still in Australia.'

He swung his legs over the side of the bed and sat for a minute, elbows propped on his knees, holding his dazed head in his hands. Jet lag was taking its toll.

'Holly said to tell you she's made a fresh pot of coffee,' Josh announced.

Bless Holly. Coffee was exactly what he needed. As soon as he'd had a shower.

Gray ruffled his kids' hair. 'So what have you two got planned for today?'

'Packing!' they chorused.

'You're kidding?' How could they look so excited? 'Don't tell me packing's fun?'

'Sure, Dad. It's great fun. Holly's playing a new game with us. We're putting all our toys in a magic rocket box, and it's going to take off for Australia all by itself.'

'Wow. How about that?'

Gray had to hand it to Holly. She sure had a way with his kids. Damn pity she wasn't coming home with them.

As the hot water in the shower streamed over him, he reminded himself why he mustn't put any pressure on Holly to help him out. She'd already gone above and beyond for his children, and now she had a life of her own to lead. Holly was a good sport and she would never let on that she was cracking her neck to be free of her commitments here. But he knew she must be keen to get on with her new career and to start dating again, find a new boyfriend.

He wouldn't appeal to her good nature…couldn't exploit her genuine affection for his kids by trying to talk her into coming with them. That would be nothing short of emotional blackmail.

Just the same, Gray wished he felt more confident in his ability to raise his kids.

Their education was his major worry.

For all kinds of reasons Gray's own parents had totally stuffed up his schooling. Just thinking about his lack of education triggered unwelcome memories of his parents' harsh and heated bickering. He found himself remembering his mother's fits of crying and his father's sulky, blustering anger and his innards twisted.

Truth to tell, his formal schooling had finished almost as soon as it started, around the same time as his parents' divorce. However, it was only much later in his adult years that Gray had fully understood the handicap he carried. By then he'd developed a tough veneer and he'd managed to bluff his way through most challenges, never realising that his failings would come back to bite him, that he'd let his wife down…

And now he was in danger of letting his kids down…

No. There was no way he would allow Anna and Josh to grow up with the limitations he'd endured. But if he wanted to give them the very best chance, he needed help. He needed someone exactly like Holly.

If only she was free…

We've done well, Holly thought at the end of a full day of packing and, thanks to Gray's involvement, it had been relatively painless. Gray's sense of humour—a side of him she'd never really seen before—had saved a few awkward moments when decisions over toys might have ended in tears.

And then he'd surprised her further by cooking dinner.

'Because you've been working so hard,' he'd said with an endearingly shy smile that sent her stomach fluttering. 'And only if you like spaghetti bolognese. I'm afraid there's a limit to my kitchen skills.'

Spaghetti bolognese was absolutely fine, Holly assured him. Unfortunately, anything seemed fine when he sent her those smiles.

Except she didn't want to be susceptible to his smiles, did she? She was simply grateful for the chai latte he'd brought her from the drugstore two and a half blocks away, as well as the chance to soak in the tub and change her clothes before dinner, and then enjoy a meal she hadn't had to cook.

Over dinner, Anna and Josh talked about Australia. They were very excited to hear that Gray had an airstrip on his property and that his mail and supplies were delivered by aeroplane.

'We'll fly to Normanton,' Gray explained, 'and then we'll drive home to Jabiru from there.'

We'll drive home to Jabiru...

Holly pictured Gray and his children in a big SUV, skimming over wide red plains towards a distant homestead, and she was swamped by a wave of loneliness.

What was wrong with her? She'd known all along that this would happen. But she still couldn't help feeling miserable. Everyone who was important in her life was being taken from her—Chelsea, Brandon, and now Anna and Josh.

I'll start again and build a new life around my new job.

Right now, it was hard to feel happy about that.

Suddenly she realised Josh was asking his dad about their new school.

To Holly's surprise, Gray's ears reddened. He looked pained and cleared his throat. 'The school in the Outback is a bit different from what you're used to.'

'How different?'

'It's called School of the Air.'

'School of the Air?' This time it was Holly who butted in. She couldn't help it. Her interest was thoroughly piqued. 'How does that work?'

Gray smiled crookedly. 'It's like a normal classroom, but the classes are held over the radio. There are children living in homesteads scattered all over the Outback and each homestead has a special transceiver. They send messages back and forth. The teacher can talk to all of the pupils and they can talk to each other.' He shrugged. 'It seems to work really well.'

'School over the radio? Wow. That sounds totally awesome.' Josh couldn't have looked more excited if he'd been told there were pet baby dinosaurs at his new school.

'It sounds amazing,' Holly agreed, thoroughly intrigued. To her surprise, she felt quite jealous of the nanny who would mentor Anna and Josh as they came to grips with this unorthodox schoolroom.

She shot the children sparkling grins. 'Aren't you two lucky?'

Josh, twirling spaghetti onto his fork, nodded enthusiastically.

Anna, however, looked uncertain. She turned to Holly. 'Will you still be our nanny?'

Holly held her breath, not trusting herself to answer this question without giving her feelings away.

To her relief, Gray answered for her. 'Holly can't come

to Australia, Anna. You know that. But we're going to find a nice Australian nanny.'

Anna drooped. 'I want Holly. And I like my school here. Why do you have to live in Australia? Why can't you live in New York?'

Holly saw the sudden bleakness in Gray's eyes, the wavering of his smile. Even though he'd sounded confident about finding a *nice Australian nanny,* he was obviously worried by Anna's reaction.

She'd been determined to keep out of this conversation, but her heart was melting at the sight of Gray's discomfort and she felt compelled to jump to his aid.

'How could your dad live in this apartment?' she asked with a deliberate smile. 'What would he do with all his cattle?'

Anna shrugged. 'Put them in storage?'

'As if.' Josh groaned and rolled his eyes.

An awkward hush fell. Gray continued to look worried and Anna looked as if she might cry. Her lower lip trembled.

Watching her, Josh began to look anxious, too. 'It's going to be great living with Dad,' he urged his sister softly.

'Not if Holly can't come with us.'

Holly saw Gray's shoulders stiffen at the same moment she felt her face flame.

Then Anna burst into tears.

'Hey,' Holly said, quickly drawing the little girl onto her lap, and not daring to catch Gray's eyes again. 'How can you cry in the middle of this lovely dinner your dad has cooked?'

Anna's response was to cling to Holly tightly, sobbing louder than ever. 'Why can't you come with us?'

It was a truly difficult moment. Holly knew Gray was anxious about his ability to care for his fragile daughter and now her tearful reaction would only deepen his apprehension.

But, despite this, Holly couldn't help feeling electrified, too, as if she'd touched a live wire. Anna had innocently brought into the open the very question that had rattled around in her head all day.

The thing was—school in the US didn't start again till the autumn, which meant she could spend June and July in Australia helping the children to settle in to their new home and school, and she'd still be back in time to start her new teaching job.

And now that she'd heard about this School of the Air, the idea was especially intriguing.

Of course, it wouldn't be plain sailing. After the past hectic months she would have liked a proper vacation and, if she went to Australia, she'd still be 'working'. She'd have very little chance to catch her breath before she had to start in the new school.

Then again, she didn't have any particular plans for the next few weeks—and she certainly didn't fancy going home to Vermont, where she'd spend her time either avoiding Brandon or being showered with sympathy from family and friends. And she *was* intrigued by the set-up in the Outback—and, of course, she would love to see Anna and Josh happily settled.

The only negative factor was the silly frissons that danced over her skin whenever Gray Kidman came too near—but Holly was sure she'd soon conquer that foolish tendency.

For heaven's sake, there wasn't any danger she'd actually fall for poor Chelsea's ex when the pain of being dumped by Brandon hadn't even healed. She planned to be mega-cautious around all men in future—especially the attractive ones.

* * *

'Why don't you tuck the children into bed and read them a couple of stories?' Holly suggested to Gray after dinner.

To her surprise, he looked unhappy, as if she'd asked him to help with some horrible chore like cleaning the toilets with a toothbrush.

'But won't they expect you to do it?' he asked.

His obvious nervousness puzzled Holly. Perhaps Anna's tears at dinner had upset him more than she'd realised. She tried to reassure him. 'Anna and Josh will love it if you read to them tonight.'

When Gray still looked worried, she added, 'They need to get used to small changes, and this would be a good first step.'

He swallowed uncomfortably. 'I guess.'

'Their favourite books are stacked on the nightstand.'

'Okay.'

As he left the kitchen, heading for the children's room, Holly saw a deep red tide that was *not* sunburn staining the back of his neck. The sight of it caused an ache right in the centre of her chest. Was he nervous about being alone with his children? Was he afraid Anna would cry again? Should she have offered to be there, too?

She almost called out to him, but there was something about the resolute straightness of his shoulders and the purposeful length of his stride that stopped her. He was like a soldier marching off to war. No, she was being fanciful.

And in the end everything was fine.

While Holly cleared the table and stacked the dishwasher, she could hear the deep masculine rumble of Gray's voice and the bell-like tinkle of the children's laughter. They were clearly having a great time.

With the kitchen tidy, she went into the living room and tried to relax, curled on the sofa with her current paperback novel. As soon as Gray was finished with the bedtime stories, she would talk to him about Australia. She only wished the thought of their conversation didn't make her feel so inordinately excited.

It was quite a while before Gray returned, however, and he was smiling, his blue eyes reflecting relief and a new contentment.

'That seemed to go well,' Holly said warmly.

'Yeah.' He stood in the centre of the room, hands resting lightly on his hips, and he grinned. 'Seems like I passed my first test as a single dad.'

'That's great. I suppose Josh pressured you into reading the pirate story.'

'No, actually. I told them a completely different story tonight.'

'Oh, right.' She couldn't help asking. 'Which one?'

Gray shrugged. 'I made one up. About Hector Owl and Timothy Mouse.' He shot her a shrewdly narrowed glance. 'Your experts wouldn't object, would they?'

'N-no, of course not. I'm just surprised. Amazed, actually. I've loved stories all my life but, even if you paid me thousands, I couldn't make one up on the spot. Anna and Josh seemed to love yours.'

Still standing in the middle of the living room carpet, Gray shrugged again and scratched at the shadow of stubble on his jaw, then he quickly changed the subject. 'Fancy another glass of that wine we opened last night?'

'Why not?' Wine might help to steady her nerves.

While he collected the bottle and glasses, Holly set her book aside and stood quickly, taking a surreptitious peek at her reflection in the long mirror on the opposite wall. It was silly. Really, she knew the neatness of her hair, the fit of her jeans or the flounces on her cream silk blouse were of no interest to Gray. But the conversation she was about to launch was almost a job interview. Checking her appearance was an automatic reflex.

'You look great,' Gray said, coming back into the room more quickly than she expected.

Flustered, she fought off a blush and sat quickly, wishing she could think of a witty retort.

'No, honestly, that new hairstyle suits you,' he said, handing her a glass of the rich Australian red.

A trip to the hairdresser had been part of Holly's post-Brandon recovery plan, but she was amazed that Gray had noticed.

'Thanks.' She raised her glass. 'Here's to settling the twins happily in Australia. May it all go super-smoothly.'

'Amen to that.' Gray settled into an armchair and stretched his long legs in front of him, crossing them at the ankles.

Holly tried not to stare, but Gray had a way of catching her eye. His jeans were soft and worn and faded, hugging his strong thighs. His elastic-sided boots were tan and clean and made of finely cut leather. Lamplight caught the dark sheen of his hair and accented the ruggedly masculine planes and angles of his face and the shadow on his jaw.

There was no denying the man was bone-deep sexy. At Chelsea's wedding, even Holly's grandmother had been all girlish and coy in Gray's presence.

Perhaps she shouldn't say anything about Australia after all. She didn't want to spend the next couple of months stealing sneak peeks at Chelsea's ex just because she was currently without a boyfriend. She was supposed to be getting on with her exciting new single life, making plans for her brilliant career.

She drank some wine, buying time to compose herself, but her brain refused to let go of one particular thought and suddenly the words just tumbled out. 'I've been thinking that you might need help with the children when you first arrive in Australia.'

Gray nodded calmly. 'I've been thinking the same thing. I wondered if I should phone ahead to an employment agency.'

'An agency in Australia?'

'Yes.'

Holly felt a surge of emotion, almost panic. 'I'm at a loose end.'

Oh, cringe. How annoying that she could say something in her head all day and it sounded fine, but now, as soon as she said it out loud, it sounded utterly dumb.

It didn't help that Gray's head snapped back as if he'd been punched in the jaw. He was staring at her as if she'd announced she was planning to fly into outer space. On a broomstick.

'How do you mean—a loose end?' he asked quietly.

'I'm free—for a month or so.'

'I thought you were starting work in a school.'

Holly's mouth was suddenly parched. She took a sip from her glass and to her dismay her hand was shaking. 'The schools here are about to close for the summer.' She wished her voice wasn't shaking as well. She cleared her throat. 'I wouldn't be expected to start in a new job until August, or possibly September.'

His eyes widened. 'So you're free through the rest of June and July?'

'As long as I'm still in phone or Internet contact. For interviews.' Seeing the surprise in Gray's eyes, Holly's nervousness accelerated. 'It's just a thought. A possible option.'

'But it's a fantastic option.' His eyes were gleaming, and his face broke into a fully fledged smile. 'You'd be perfect.'

For God's sake, stay cool.

'Do you have a passport?' Gray asked, clearly thinking more calmly than she was.

Holly nodded. She'd studied Italian at school and her parents had scraped and saved to send her on a fabulous school excursion to Tuscany. Her passport was still valid.

Gray's smile was replaced by a quick frown. 'Are you sure you wouldn't mind giving up so much time?'

'I'd be happy to come. I'm really interested in this School of the Air. I'd love to see how it works and, of course, I'd really like to help Anna and Josh to settle in.'

Gray was frowning again and he launched to his feet, pacing the room as if something troubled him. 'I promise you'd have nothing to worry about—' He swallowed and looked awkward. 'I mean—accompanying me and the kids—no one out there will jump to conclusions about us. I...I mean no one will assume we're a couple.'

Looking distinctly embarrassed, he gave a forced laugh, as if he was trying to make a joke but knew it wasn't funny.

To Holly's dismay, she felt her face flame. 'Well, that's good,' she hurried to assure him. 'And you certainly don't need to worry from my end. Romance is totally off my agenda. I've just broken up a long-term relationship, and it was harrowing to say the least, so it'll be a very long time before I start looking for any kind of—' She couldn't quite finish the sentence.

Gray nodded thoughtfully, his eyes sending a message of sympathy, and Holly felt a clear wave of relief to know that they had the ground rules sorted.

Just the same, she couldn't help also feeling the teensiest sting over Gray's mega-eagerness to make it clear that he wasn't romantically interested in her.

How crazy was that? She dropped her gaze to her wine

and reminded herself exactly why she'd made this offer. Gray needed help, Anna and Josh needed a nanny, and she needed to feel she'd done everything she could for Chelsea's children.

She was the perfect person to help Anna and Josh to adjust to their new life in Australia.

'So that's definite, then?' Gray was serious again. Businesslike. 'You'll come?'

Suddenly it felt inevitable. Predestined. As if this question was always going to be asked. And the answer was always going to be...

'Yes.'

CHAPTER FIVE

GRAY was surprised by how over-the-top pleased and light-hearted he felt now that he knew Holly would be accompanying them on the return journey.

Now, the challenge of becoming a single father no longer loomed as forbidding as Mount Everest and, over the following days as they finalised the packing, even Anna came to look on the move as a huge adventure.

By the time the foursome reached JFK Airport, they were all keyed up and looking forward to the flight.

It was while they were waiting to get through Security, with the line shuffling ever closer to the X-ray machines, that Holly received a call on her cellphone.

Gray assumed it was yet another of her many friends ringing to wish her well and he watched with a ready smile as she answered the phone. He saw the sudden tension in her eyes.

She turned away, her dark hair swinging with the movement. She pressed her fingers to one ear to block out the airport noise as she frowned and gave her caller her full attention.

Gray realised he was watching her more closely than was polite, but he couldn't help it. Holly might not have Chelsea's beauty, but she had something else—something, he suspected, more lasting than prettiness. At times like now, when her face was animated and her dark eyes were sparkling with excitement, she looked utterly enchanting.

Snatches of her conversation drifted his way.

'Yes…yes…that's wonderful…yes. Oh, wow, thank you.' And then, 'Australia…a family commitment…just away for the summer…' She was nodding and smiling, looking flushed and pleased.

The phone call ended just as it was their turn to go through Security, so it wasn't till they'd reached the other side and had collected their watches, wallets, passports and backpacks that Holly turned to Gray with a wide and happy smile.

'So it was good news after all?' he asked.

'Yes. At first I thought it might have been Brand—might have been someone ringing to say goodbye. But it's even better than that. It looks like I've landed a job.'

To Gray's surprise, he felt a snaking of alarm. How would this affect their plans? Was Holly still free to help? 'When do you start?'

'Not till August.' Holly's smile widened into a beaming grin, then she gave a little skip and punched the air. 'I can't believe it. This is my dream job! My first choice. The school I've always wanted to teach at.'

Gray nodded, willing himself to be pleased for Holly. Judging by her excitement, this was very important. She must have been the pick of the applicants. Good for her!

It hit him then that he knew very little about her. It seemed she was very smart—an ace teacher—and his kids were lucky to have her even for a short time.

He was pleased for her. In fact, he was pleased for all of them. Everything was working out perfectly. By August his children would be settled into their new home and school and, with Holly's help and approval, he'd have hired a new nanny. Then Holly would head for home to start this new flash job.

It made absolutely no sense that he couldn't dredge up more enthusiasm. It was sheer selfishness not to be happy for Holly.

'Fantastic,' he said and he held out his hand. 'Congratulations.'

At last, he cracked a smile.

Landing in Sydney was a total surprise for Holly.

Throughout the journey, she'd been mentally preparing herself for the Australian Outback. It was, she knew, a challenging place of wide red plains, isolation, dust and heat.

She hadn't given much thought to Sydney, hadn't expected to fly in over gorgeous golden beaches to a big and modern city heart crowded with skyscrapers. She also hadn't expected to find Gray's mother waiting to greet them at Sydney Airport.

Holly had vague memories of Sasha Carlisle from the wedding. She was tall and silver-haired, strikingly attractive and well dressed. Today she was wearing a white linen trouser suit, with sparkling jewellery at her wrist and a long black and white silk scarf draped with unfussy elegance. There was no doubt about it; she'd nailed casual chic for the older woman.

Beside her, Holly, in jeans and a crumpled T-shirt, with her hair hanging limp after more than twenty hours in a pressurised cabin, felt decidedly drab. But she soon forgot about that as she watched the greeting between mother and son.

No warm hugs. Just a cool—

'Hello, dear.'

'Hello, Mother.'

And an expertly made-up cheek held at an angle for Gray to kiss.

The tension was so thick Holly would have needed a very sharp knife to cut through it. It evaporated quickly, however, when Gray's mother turned her attention to her grandchildren.

'Sweethearts,' she cried, opening her arms to Anna and Josh. 'You remember your Australian granny, don't you?'

Fortunately, the children obliged her with warm smiles, and they submitted to hugs and kisses without complaint.

'Your granny's missed you so much.'

Brightly wrapped packages were produced from a voluminous designer handbag, and Holly was pleased to see that Anna and Josh looked quite thrilled and remembered to say thank you.

Gray placed a hand on Holly's shoulder, almost making her jump out of her skin. 'You might not remember my mother, Sasha Carlisle.'

With her shoulder still tingling from the warmth of his touch, Holly held out her hand. 'I do remember you, Mrs Carlisle. How do you do?'

Gray's mother shook hands super-carefully, as if she were afraid Holly might be grubby.

'Holly was one of Chelsea's bridesmaids,' Gray reminded her.

'Ah, yes, and now she's the nanny.'

'Holly's going to help us with School of the Air,' Josh explained importantly.

'Is she now?' Sasha's eyebrows lifted high and she shot a chilling but meaningful glance to Gray. 'Is she properly trained?'

Bristling at being discussed as if she wasn't even there,

Holly decided to speak up for herself. 'I'm a fully qualified English teacher.'

The older woman smiled faintly. 'Thank heavens for small mercies.'

What was going on here?

The chilling tension was broken by Anna, who urgently wanted to find a bathroom. Grateful to escape, Holly accompanied her and, by the time they returned, Sasha had left.

'My mother had a function she needed to attend,' Gray said smoothly. The expression in his eyes lightened and he smiled at Holly. 'Come on, let's find a taxi.'

Their evening in Sydney was fun. The four of them dined out at a fabulous Thai restaurant and then they walked back to their hotel, enjoying the mild winter night and the brightly lit streets. The children were drooping by this stage, however, and Gray had to carry Anna for the last block. She and Josh were so tired they fell straight into bed and were asleep before anyone could think of finding a story to read.

Gray stayed behind to share a nightcap with Holly in the cosy sitting room that was part of the luxurious suite he'd booked for her and the children.

They found ice and glasses and little bottles in the minibar and then they sat in deep comfy armchairs. Holly wasn't sure how relaxed she'd be, or what she and Gray would talk about, so she was totally thrown when he steered the conversation to her break-up with Brandon.

'What went wrong?' he asked, watching her through slightly narrowed eyes.

'Oh, the usual.' Holly had only talked about her break-up with her mom and one or two girlfriends, and it felt weird to try to explain it to a man she hardly knew. 'He was more interested in another woman.'

'So he was a fool,' Gray said sympathetically.

'Yes, he was a total idiot.' She forced a smile. 'But it was partly my fault, I guess. I moved away to New York and, in this case, absence did not make his heart grow fonder.'

Gray nodded and took a thoughtful sip of his drink. 'Don't know if it helps...but after Chelsea took off with the kids...I thought I'd never get over it, and yet, after a time, the worst feelings began to fade.'

Holly wanted to ask him what had gone wrong in his marriage, but it felt too intrusive to ask Gray when Chelsea had been so close-lipped about it.

Instead, she said, 'I guess Chelsea must have loved it here in Sydney.'

Gray's smile vanished as if someone had flicked a switch. 'I'm sure Chelsea must have told you how she felt about Sydney.'

'No.' Holly blinked. 'If she did, I don't remember. She would never say much at all about her time in Australia.'

He downed a hefty slug of Scotch and scowled into his glass, and Holly felt compelled to explain her comment. 'It's just that I was surprised to see how busy and cosmopolitan it is here. Bright lights. Masses of skyscrapers. Lots of people. So many theatres and restaurants. It's everything Chelsea loved.'

She watched Gray's mouth thin into a downward curve.

He sighed. 'Yeah, Chelsea loved Sydney all right. She used to fly down here for two or three days and stay for two or three weeks.'

'Oh.' Sensing that she'd awoken bad memories, Holly tried to make amends. 'I suppose she dropped in to chat to the dance companies here and—'

Suddenly, she wasn't sure how to finish what she'd started. She was trying to defend her cousin when she had no idea really...

'This place had *everything* Chelsea needed,' Gray said bleakly.

Holly wondered if this had been the heart of the problem with their marriage. 'Did you ever—' she began hesitantly. 'I mean, I don't suppose you...um...considered moving here? Or...or living closer...'

'No.'

There was quiet vehemence in that single syllable. Gray's face was a grim stony mask as he stared down at his almost empty glass.

'I guess it would have been difficult to move.'

She was trying to be diplomatic, but she knew she was on shaky ground. Just the same, she couldn't help thinking that if Gray had really loved Chelsea he might have been prepared to make sacrifices. Couldn't he have given up cattle farming and tried something more suited to his wife's temperament and talents?

If he'd wanted to save his marriage...

'Moving was out of the question,' he said with a marked air of finality.

Right.

It was time to drop this line of conversation. Holly wondered if stubborn inflexibility was Gray Kidman's Achilles heel.

Or was that a bit harsh? After all, her cousin had been adamant when she married him that she was happy to give up her career to live with him in his Outback.

Whatever. It's none of my business.

To change the subject, Holly said, 'I'm looking forward to tomorrow and finally getting to see your place.'

She saw Gray's shoulders relax then, and he looked

directly into her eyes and smiled slowly in a way that started her tummy fluttering. 'So am I,' he said. 'I'm always glad to get home.'

The warmth in his eyes suggested that he wasn't just voicing a cliché. He really meant it. He felt nostalgic about his home in the vast empty Outback. Holly understood this. She always felt a catch in her throat whenever she drove back to her family's farm and saw the green pastures and red barns of Vermont.

Tomorrow Anna and Josh would reach their new home. Holly hoped, for their sakes, but more especially for Gray's sake, that they liked it. Actually, it was her job to make sure that they did.

Gray couldn't sleep.

Leaving his bed, he prowled the length of his hotel room, trying to shrug off the tension that kept him awake. He'd lied to Holly tonight. He'd told her that feelings and memories faded with time but, after his mother's cool reception at the airport today, and his conversation with Holly about Chelsea, he was once again battling with the feelings of inadequacy and failure that had dogged him all his life.

As a child he'd never lived up to his mother's expectations. Hell, he hadn't even come close. He could still hear the way she'd yelled at his father.

The boy's hopeless. Unteachable. A disgrace.

Even now, the memory brought his clenched fist slamming into his palm.

Was he never going to shake off these patterns of failure? First his mother had left Jabiru, never to return, and then his wife had left, and both times he'd known he was a major cause of their problems.

If he'd been able to, he would have taken Chelsea to live in Sydney, as Holly had so innocently suggested. He would have taken her to New York or wherever she wanted to live.

But, thanks to his lack of schooling, he was unemployable in the city, and even if he'd sold his property and invested in stocks and shares to eke out a living, he would have gone mad in the claustrophobic city. After twenty-four hours, he was always chafing at the bit to get away to the bush.

He'd tried his best to love and support Chelsea at Jabiru. When the twins arrived, he'd done everything he could to hold his little family together. He'd been a hands-on father, taking his turn at bathing and changing and walking the floors with the crying infants.

But the timing had been lousy. The babies' arrival had coincided with a downturn in the cattle industry. Overseas markets had collapsed. Money had been tight and, before the babies were six months old, he'd been forced to lay off the fencing contractors and the mechanics he'd hired, and he'd taken on these jobs himself.

When these tasks were added to the usual demands of running a vast cattle property, his available time to help at the homestead had been minimal. He'd kept on his housekeeper, who'd also helped with the twins, but the toll on Chelsea had been visible.

Gray had been shocked to see her growing thin and drawn and faded, so he'd sent her to Sydney for short breaks. And, as he'd admitted to Holly, the times she'd spent away had become longer and longer.

When his wife had told him she needed to go home to New York, he'd let her go, taking the children with her, even though he hadn't been free to accompany them. By then he'd known that to try to hold her was too cruel.

When she'd rung from New York to tell him she wasn't coming back, Gray had been heartsick but not surprised.

He'd agreed to the divorce, accepting that he'd had no other option.

He'd tried his hardest and failed, and he had no idea what else he could do. He would rather admit defeat than watch his wife become trapped and embittered the way his mother had been.

But his sense of failure was overwhelming, even worse now that Chelsea had passed away. He hated to think that his love had made any part of her short life unhappy and he was determined that he wouldn't fail her children as well. He couldn't, he mustn't.

These next two months were critical. He would be guided by Holly and he wouldn't be too proud to accept her advice. Sure, there were bound to be humiliating moments when his inadequacies were exposed once more, and Holly would probably be as disdainful of his home as Chelsea had been.

But he could face another woman's scorn—as long as his kids still looked up to him—and as long as he didn't let them down.

By the following afternoon, they were finally in Far North Queensland, barrelling over flat, pale grasslands in a big four-wheel drive which threw up a continuous plume of dust. The vehicle had a luggage rack on top, and bull bars protecting the engine—from kangaroos, Gray told them—and there were water tanks on board as well. To Holly it felt like an expedition.

Wide open plains sprinkled with straggly gum trees and silvery grey Brahman cattle stretched in every direction. Flocks of white birds wheeled in the blue sky like fluttering pieces of paper.

In the back seat, the children watched the panorama excitedly, waiting for their first kangaroo sighting.

'This is my country,' Gray told Holly and his emphasis on the word *country* seemed to instil it with special meaning.

Holly had to agree there was something primitive but almost spiritual about the vast stretch of empty space. She could feel an awareness of something greater than herself and, strangely, it wasn't unlike the way she'd also felt the first time she'd walked into the huge book-lined silence of the New York City Library.

Every so often their vehicle would climb over a rocky ridge, giving a view of grasslands stretching for ever. At other times the road would dip downwards to cross a single lane wooden bridge over a stream. Some creeks only had a concrete ford disappearing beneath brown muddy water.

'There's no water here at all in the dry season,' Gray told her.

They came to a wider river, so deep that when Gray pushed the vehicle through, the water threatened to seep under the doors.

He grinned at Holly. 'This is where I did my ankle in, but the creek was flowing a lot faster then, of course.'

The tops of the banks were still covered in flattened grass and the small twisted trees were all leaning in one direction, clear evidence of how high and savage the floodwaters had been.

Holly hated to think what it must have been like to try to drive through it.

'I thought you had an airstrip at Jabiru,' she said. 'Couldn't you have flown instead of driving?'

Gray shook his head. 'The ground was too boggy for a normal plane to land—and all the choppers were needed for emergency rescues. I waited for the water to go down a little, then took my chances.'

How scary. Holly shuddered, as she tried to imagine pushing a vehicle through a raging flood.

'And that was when you broke your ankle?' she asked.

'I was testing the bottom before I drove across. Foot went down into a crevice.'

'You weren't on your own, were you?'

'Sure.'

'You mean you had to rescue yourself?'

'It was either that or—' He flicked a glance over his shoulder and dropped his voice. 'Or this pair would have been orphans.'

Holly shivered, chastened to remember how she'd rolled her eyes and complained loudly when Gray had telephoned to say he was held up in Australia by floods and a broken ankle. Now that she was here, and could see where the accident had happened, she was appalled.

No wonder Gray gave off an aura of hidden toughness and competence.

As they cleared the creek and continued over flat land again, squawks from the back seat reminded Holly of her duties. Anna and Josh were pinching each other and poking out tongues. Clear signs of boredom. Very soon they'd start, *Are we there yet?*

She rummaged in her bag and produced a CD. 'This might keep them entertained,' she said, waving it at Gray.

'Good idea. What is it?'

'Winnie-the-Pooh.'

His brow wrinkled. 'Never heard of them. Are they a new band?'

She laughed. 'Oh, that's a good one.'

He turned, sending her a puzzled grin. 'Seriously, who are they?'

Her mouth dropped open. How could he ask? 'You know Winnie-the-Pooh—the children's story. You must have read it when you were little. The bear who loves honey.'

He pulled a face and shrugged. 'Whatever. We've got about three-quarters of an hour to go, so if you think it will keep the kids happy, bung it on.'

Bemused, she slipped the CD into the player and soon the cabin was filled with the storyteller's beautifully modulated English voice. The children stopped squabbling and listened. Gray seemed to listen attentively, too, and he actually chuckled at the antics of the famous characters as if the funny bits were a brand new experience for him.

How curious.

The CD hadn't finished when they turned in at big metal gates beneath an overhead sign with *Jabiru Creek* painted in white.

'We're here!' Anna cried enthusiastically. 'This is your place, isn't it, Daddy?'

'That's right, pumpkin, but we're not at the homestead yet. It's about another fifteen minutes.'

Resigned, the children slumped back in their seats.

'I'll get the gates,' Holly announced, opening her passenger door.

Gray's eyebrows shot high. 'You don't have to.'

'It's fine,' she called over her shoulder as she jumped down from the vehicle. 'I'm a farm girl.'

She turned, saw the surprise in his blue eyes.

'When were you on a farm?'

'I grew up on a farm in Vermont.'

Through the dusty windscreen she saw his smile and a new light in his eyes—keen interest, extra warmth. She blushed and felt flustered. *Idiot.* Abruptly, she turned and paid studious attention to the gates.

By the time the gates were shut once more and she'd

climbed back in the cabin, Gray was closing his satellite phone. 'I let them know at the homestead that we're nearly home. Almost time to put the kettle on.'

Anna leaned forward as far as her seatbelt would allow. 'Will we see the puppies? Are they borned yet, Daddy?'

'Sorry, I forgot to ask.' Gray grinned back at his daughter. 'You'll soon find out.'

They drove on and the CD resumed, preventing conversation or questions about Holly's life on the farm. But Holly couldn't stop thinking about the surprised delight in Gray's eyes. Why should it matter where she'd grown up?

The bush was thicker now, and the gum trees threw shadows across the narrow wheel ruts that formed the rough track. Several times, Gray had to brake suddenly as a kangaroo appeared on the edge of the road, bounding unannounced from a shadowy clump of trees.

Each kangaroo sighting was a source of huge excitement for Holly and the children, but Holly could tell that the animals' sudden arrival on the track was dangerous. In the fading light they were hard to see. She switched off the CD so Gray could concentrate.

'That wasn't a bad story,' he said. Then he called over his shoulder, 'Hey, kids, what do you reckon? Is that Pooh bear almost as good as Hector Owl and Timothy Mouse?'

'Nah. Winnie-the-Pooh's for babies,' Josh replied, even though he'd spent the best part of an hour listening to the CD quite happily. 'Hector Owl's much better. Hector Owl's awesome. He killed the Bad Bush Rat.'

Holly smiled. How could poor Winnie compete with a murderous owl?

But it still puzzled her that Gray spoke as if he'd never heard of Winnie-the-Pooh. How could that be? Surely almost every child in the US and Australia was familiar with the honey-loving bear.

Should she be dreading what lay ahead? Would Gray's house be as stark and unappealing as that lonely homestead on the back of the playing cards he'd bought?

She was about to find out.

Ahead of them, the track rounded a corner and they emerged into open country once more. Holly saw tall corrals and stockyards, home paddocks fenced with timber instead of the barbed wire she'd seen everywhere else. Then, ahead, more buildings began to appear—machinery sheds, silos, bunk houses, barns, even an aircraft hangar—it was almost a small village.

Clearly Jabiru Creek Station was a much bigger concern than the farms she was used to.

'Which one is your house, Daddy?' Anna wanted to know.

'That place straight ahead with the silver roof.' Gray pointed to a long, low, white timber building surrounded by surprisingly green lawns.

To Holly's relief, Gray's home looked inviting. It was a simple homestead, but it was large and rimmed by verandas. Across the front of the house a deep shady veranda was fringed with hanging baskets filled with ferns, while the verandas on either side were enclosed from floor to ceiling with white timber louvres.

The lawns in front of the house were divided by a gravel path and on either side stood massive shade trees with deep glossy foliage.

'I can see a swing,' Anna shouted, pointing to a rubber tyre hanging by thick ropes from the branch of one of the trees.

'It's waiting for you,' Holly told her, and already she was picturing Anna and Josh playing on this smooth sweep of lawn, swinging in the tyre, riding bikes, throwing balls, chasing puppies...

The front door opened and a woman came out with a beaming smile, wiping her hands on an apron. She was aged somewhere beyond sixty and was dressed in a floral cotton dress, with wisps of grey hair escaping from a haphazard knot on top of her head.

'My housekeeper, Janet,' Gray said as he turned off the engine. 'She helped us to look after the twins when they were babies and she can't wait to see them again.'

Janet looked perfect, Holly thought, watching the woman's happy face glow pink with excitement as she waved to the children.

'Come inside where it's warm,' Janet said when they'd clambered from the car and she'd given them all, including Holly, huge hugs. 'The chill starts early on these winter afternoons, and I've got a heater on in the kitchen.'

As they followed her into the house, which was warm and fragrant with baking smells, Holly thought everything about Gray's home seemed comfortable and welcoming. Her fears, it seemed, were unwarranted.

Of course, first impressions could be deceiving. No doubt Jabiru Creek Station would soon reveal its downside. There had to be a downside. Right now Holly couldn't imagine what it might be, but something had driven Chelsea away from here.

CHAPTER SIX

THAT evening the sky put on a show, as only Outback skies could. A mass of brilliant crystal stars blazed in the vast black dome that arced from one distant horizon to the other. Gray stood on the front steps, drinking in the silence and the grandeur.

After the non-stop pace of New York, the crowds in the busy airports and the bustle of Sydney, it was good to let the tranquillity of his home seep into his veins. Since Chelsea's passing he'd been on a constant roller coaster of worry and despair, but tonight he felt calmer than he had in a long time.

Behind him, in the house, Janet was pottering about in the kitchen and he could hear the clink of cutlery and china as she stowed things away in the big pine dresser. Holly was in the bedroom down the hall, putting his children to bed, calming them after the excitement of their arrival, and the discovery of a basket of tiny three-day-old puppies in the kitchen by the stove.

Gray chuckled, remembering the shining adoration in Anna and Josh's eyes as they'd knelt by the basket, begging permission to pat the little pups that wriggled and squirmed against their mother.

Of course the children had begged to be allowed one puppy each to keep as a pet, and of course Gray had said yes, they could choose their pups as soon as their eyes were open. But no, they couldn't *both* have the all black one, and if there was any fighting neither child would have a puppy.

Holly had been a major help, backing him on this ruling and then diverting the children by offering to read them one of their favourite stories about a runaway cocker spaniel.

Already, he owed a great deal to Holly.

She'd been fabulous while they were travelling, keeping Anna and Josh entertained and comfortable, and remembering to tell them what to expect on each leg of the journey. Gray couldn't help noticing that she wasn't just capable—she was genuinely fond of his children—and he was beginning to suspect that it would be a real wrench for her to finally be parted from them.

She was quite a surprise package, actually. He'd assumed she was like Chelsea, a city girl born and bred.

Today, however, in her simple T-shirt and jeans, she'd deftly unhooked the notoriously tricky rural gate, and she'd looked every inch the country girl she'd claimed to be.

He recalled the cheeky smile she'd tossed over her shoulder when she'd told him that she'd grown up on a farm. Her dark eyes had sparkled and her lips had curled and—

'Gray.'

Holly's voice brought him swinging round.

She was standing in the doorway and she smiled shyly. 'Two little people are waiting for their goodnight kiss.'

'Right.' He spoke a little too gruffly because she'd caught him out. 'Thanks.'

He crossed the veranda to where she stood, backlit by the light spilling down the hall. Her dark eyes were shining and her pretty lips were pink and soft and wonderfully inviting...

It would be so easy, so tempting to ask his children's

nanny if she'd like a goodnight kiss, too. She was kissing close and she smelled of flowers and—

And the last thing Gray wanted was to start flirting with Chelsea's young cousin when she'd come to his home as an especially kind favour to his kids.

I must be one post short of a fence.

Relieved that he'd come to his senses in time, he strode on past Holly, down the passage to the room where Anna and Josh were waiting.

Holly lay snuggled beneath a soft, warm duvet in a pretty room that had one doorway leading to a hallway and another onto a veranda. She listened to the night sounds of the Outback, which amounted to silence mostly, punctuated by the occasional owl hoot or the soft, distant lowing of cattle. She thought how amazing it was that she could be so far from Vermont and still hear the same sounds she'd grown up with.

After the long journey she was dog-tired and tonight she'd broken the habit of a lifetime and left the book she was currently reading unopened on her nightstand. Right now, she simply wanted to take a moment, before sleep claimed her, to relive her first evening at Jabiru.

Already, to her surprise, she'd found much to like—this pleasant bedroom, for example, and its old-fashioned double bed with gorgeous brass ends, and the big homey kitchen filled with timber dressers and tempting aromas. The children's room was similar to hers, but was cheery with matching multi-coloured duvets, and Holly really liked the inviting verandas scattered with cane loungers, not to mention the cuter than cute puppies that had so enchanted the children.

She even liked the scents of grass and animals and dust that filtered in from the outdoors. She felt amazingly at home here and, despite the flight inland to Normanton and the long car journey, she found it difficult to remember she was miles and miles from anywhere. She'd expected to feel lonely and isolated, but she only had to look out of her window to see the lights of the stockmen's cottages twinkling in the darkness like friendly stars.

She thought about Chelsea and wondered how she'd felt on her first night in Gray Kidman's home. As a born and bred New Yorker, she might have found it all very strange. The children seemed to have settled in happily enough, however, although Gray wasn't as relaxed as she'd expected. Actually, there was something about him that puzzled her.

Most of the time, he had an air of quiet confidence and competence that was very reassuring. But every so often she caught a hint of his vulnerability, lying surprisingly close beneath his strong exterior. She'd glimpsed it at times when she'd least expected it—like tonight when she'd called him in to say goodnight to Anna and Josh.

Was he more worried about his new responsibilities than she'd realised? Was he scared that his children would soon grow tired of this place and want to hightail it back to New York?

Somehow, Holly didn't think that was likely and she would do her best to make sure Anna and Josh settled in smoothly but, after Chelsea's reaction to Jabiru, she could understand Gray's concern.

As she nestled more snugly under the duvet, she remembered there was one other thing about Gray that had bothered her—

His books.

Or, rather, the lack of his books.

Where were they?

As a lifelong lover of the written word, Holly had always

found herself sneaking peeks at other people's bookshelves. It wasn't so much that she was looking for books to read—this time she'd brought a good supply and she could easily order more over the Internet—but she'd always been fascinated by what books revealed about their owners—their hobbies and interests and tastes in fiction.

For her, books had always been a kind of getting-to-know-you shortcut. So far, in Gray's house, she'd seen a few recipe books and women's magazines in the kitchen, but they were obviously Janet's. Where were Gray's books?

Perhaps he was a very orderly man who liked to keep all his reading material in one place—in his study, possibly.

Yes, his study was sure to have floor-to-ceiling bookshelves. Content with that thought, she fell promptly asleep.

Holly was in the depths of sleep when the screams started, so deeply asleep, in fact, that she almost ignored them. One part of her brain urged her to respond, but she felt drugged, glued to the mattress.

But then she remembered it was Anna who was screaming.

Fighting desperate weariness, she opened one eye and saw moonlight streaming through an unfamiliar window. For a frantic moment she panicked. Where was she?

It came in a flash and she sat up, her heart thudding as she threw back the bedclothes. Shivering in the sudden cold—it was winter here, after all—she switched on her bedside lamp, shivered again when her feet met icy floorboards. Regrettably, Outback homes did not have central heating.

But there was no time to hunt for a warm dressing gown. Anna's screams had risen several decibels and she'd wake everybody in the outlying cottages. Holly dashed from her room and down the passage to the children's room.

Gray was already there. In the dark, Holly could see him sitting on the edge of Anna's bed, trying to calm her.

'Shh, Anna,' he was murmuring as he drew the little girl into his arms. 'You're okay, baby. Shh.'

Anna continued to scream.

Holly stepped closer and, although she couldn't see Gray's face, she sensed how helpless he felt. Poor man. She knew he was horrified by his daughter's terror, and tonight he was probably also worried that the screams would alarm everyone within hearing range.

Gently, Holly leaned closer and stroked Anna's hair and her soft cheek. 'Hey, Anna,' she said in her most soothing voice. 'It's okay, honey. You've had another nasty nightmare, but it's all over now. You're okay. I'm here with you, and Daddy's here, too.'

To her relief, the screams began to subside, reducing in time to shuddering sobs.

Beside her, Holly heard Gray's heavy sigh.

'It might be best if I take her back to my bed,' she offered, knowing the strange environment would make it harder for Anna to settle back to sleep this time.

Gray didn't hesitate. 'Okay. Thanks. Let me carry her for you.'

Holly nodded, then went over to Josh's bed. 'Are you okay, champ?'

'Yeah,' the boy murmured sleepily.

'I'm taking Anna through to my room, okay?'

'Okay.'

Holly gave him a reassuring hug, loving the scent of baby powder on his skin. She tucked the duvet more closely around him, then went with Gray, down the cold passage to her room. She was shivering as she climbed into bed again—was too cold, in fact, to worry about the intimacy of having Gray Kidman in a T-shirt and striped pyjama bottoms in her bedroom.

At least Anna was calmer now. She blinked in the lamplight as Gray lowered her into bed beside her.

His arms brushed Holly's arms, electrifying her, leaving her nerve endings jangling as he straightened once more and stood beside the bed.

When Holly looked up, she saw tortured darkness in his eyes.

'Anna's all right now,' she told him.

'But is she?' he whispered, unable to hide his anxiety. 'Are you sure?'

'Yes, Gray. She'll be fine. I'm sure.'

The mattress dipped as he sank onto the side of Holly's bed and she could see his hand shaking as he stroked Anna's hair. 'I'm so sorry, baby.'

He spoke in a tight voice, as if he was somehow responsible for Anna's distress. Holly had read somewhere that parenting was mostly about guilt. Looking at Gray, she could believe it.

She wanted to reassure him that he was doing a great job with his kids, but she couldn't talk about it now in front of Anna.

'You're going to sleep now, aren't you, Anna?' she said instead as the child snuggled close.

Eyes closed, Anna nodded against Holly's shoulder.

Even though the little girl was calm again, Gray continued to sit there, watching her. Holly realised she was holding her breath. He was so close she could almost feel his body heat, and he looked so impossibly gorgeous in the lamplight, so dark and manly and—

Holly caught the tropical scents of his cologne as he leaned forward and kissed his daughter.

'Goodnight, poppet.'

His blue eyes gleamed as he smiled sadly at Holly. 'Thank you,' he whispered. 'You're wonderful, Holly. Thank you so much.'

And then, before she recognised quite what was happening, he kissed her cheek.

Her entire body flared like a freshly struck match.

Gray's kiss was no more than a friendly glancing brush, but it was positioned very close to the corner of her mouth, and her libido seemed to have developed a mind of its own, creating all kinds of pleasurable expectations.

Gray straightened and stood. 'Is there anything else I can do for you? Anything you want?'

Oh, man. Holly might have laughed if she wasn't so stunned. She might have answered if she wasn't too breathless to speak. Thank heavens Anna was there, preventing her from saying anything reckless.

'I...I'm fine,' she managed, eventually. 'Anna and I will...um...both be fine now. Thank you.'

Gray stood again, looking down at them, his eyes dark once again and serious. 'Goodnight, then.' He cracked a tiny, crooked, utterly gorgeous smile. 'I hope you both sleep well.'

Holly couldn't reply, could merely nod as she watched him leave her room—watched his shiny dark hair, his broad shoulders, his perfect butt and his long legs disappear through her doorway.

'Josh?' Gray whispered into the darkness.

He heard the rustle of bedclothes and a sleepy voice.

'Is that you, Dad?'

'Yeah. I came back to make sure you're okay.'

Light spilling through the doorway from the hall showed his small son curled on his side, with the bedclothes tucked up to his chin, his longish dark hair framing his soft, fresh cheeks.

The boy was only six—so little—and yet there were times when Gray thought he caught glimpses of the man his son would one day become.

Cautiously, he sat on the edge of the bed, and the small mound beneath the bedclothes wriggled to make room for him. 'It's pretty scary when Anna screams like that, isn't it?'

Josh nodded solemnly. 'But she's getting better.' He sounded surprisingly grown-up. 'Holly says it'll stop eventually.'

'I'm sure Holly's right.' Gray was thinking of a conversation in New York when Holly had talked about his children and their grief. Ever since then, he'd felt guilty that he'd shied away from raising the subject of Chelsea's death with them.

If he took Holly's advice and talked about it more, he might be able to save Anna from her nightmares. Holly was in there now with Anna, soothing her, doing everything she could to help his daughter to feel safe…to heal.

But in a few weeks Holly would be gone, and it would be up to him. And for all he knew, Josh might need his help, too. At the moment the boy seemed to be coping just fine, but how much pain had he kept bottled up?

'Josh, I've never thanked you,' Gray began unsteadily, and already, just thinking about what he wanted to say made his eyes sting and his throat choke up. 'I've never thanked you for ringing the ambulance for your mom—'

He stopped, took a breath to clear the shake out of his voice. 'That was such smart thinking. I'm so proud of you, son.'

At first there was no sound from the bed. And then, 'But

I didn't save her.' In the darkness, Josh's voice sounded extra-tiny and quivery. 'Mommy died.'

A sob brimmed in Gray's throat and he gulped it down. 'Sometimes we can't save people, Josh.' He took a breath. 'But the big thing is, you did your best and that's so fantastic. That's why I'm so proud of you. Your mom would have been proud, too.'

Tears threatened again and the next breath Gray drew shuddered in his chest. To his surprise, he felt two wiry arms winding around his neck, and then Josh was clinging to him, his bony head pressed hard under Gray's jaw.

'Thanks, Dad.'

Gray smelled the warm just-bathed scent of his son, mingled with a faint whiff of puppy, and he was flooded with love. Then he felt hot tears wetting his T-shirt. A beat later, Josh was crying noisily, weeping as if his heart would break.

Fighting his own tears, Gray gathered the boy in and held him close, felt his small body shaking as the grief poured out of him.

Poor little kid. Gray could remember how he'd looked when he was born—tiny, red, fists curled ready to take on the world. He pictured again the fine man the boy would grow up to be.

'I'm here for you, Josh,' Gray whispered. 'I promise. I'll be the best dad ever. No matter what it takes.'

It was some time before Josh was calm again. Worn out from crying, he finally sank back onto the pillow and looked up at Gray with tear-washed eyes.

'Dad, do you think if we'd stayed here with you that Mommy wouldn't have died?'

Gray stifled a groan of dismay. His throat closed over and he couldn't speak.

'No,' he finally managed in a tight voice. 'I'm afraid it wouldn't have made any difference, mate.'

'Why didn't we stay here?'

'Didn't—' This was so hard. 'Didn't your mom explain?'

'She just said she needed to work at the ballet.'

'That's right. Your mom's work was very important to her. She was very talented and she needed to live in New York.'

Josh nodded and sighed, then rolled sleepily onto his side. To Gray's surprise, the boy was very soon asleep, his breath falling evenly and softly.

But when he went back to his own room, he lay staring at the ceiling, thinking once again about his marriage, about Chelsea, and his wonderful kids...

His old fear returned. How he could pull off being the 'best dad ever'? He wanted to be everything Anna and Josh needed, but they needed an educated father, someone who had the right connections, someone who'd learned so much more than running a cattle station.

He thought of Chelsea again, of her growing disappointment and unhappiness. He thought of his own mother, who still to this day managed to make him feel unbearably deficient.

How long would it be—years or only months—before Anna and Josh saw through his bluff and discovered the failings he'd worked so hard and so long to hide?

'Your dinner's keeping warm in the oven,' Janet told Gray two nights later, when he arrived home after a long day of shifting cattle on his western boundary. 'I've left Holly's dinner in the oven, too. Right now, she's putting the children to bed.'

'Already?' Gray glanced at the clock on the wall in surprise. It was only ten past seven. 'The kids aren't sick, are they?'

Janet laughed. 'Heavens, no. If that pair were any fitter they'd be dangerous.'

He sent Janet a cautious glance. 'How was their first day of school?'

'I'll let them tell you.'

Her enigmatic answer caused a twinge of fear—the old fear that had haunted him as long as he could remember—but Janet was smiling, so he decided he was overreacting. He set off down the hall.

Even before he reached the children's room, he heard their laughter, but then he realised the sounds were coming from Holly's room.

His pace slowed, then stopped altogether. For the past two days and nights, he'd been dealing with images of Holly in bed—which only proved he wasn't the brightest young bull in the paddock. In the midst of his poor little daughter's distress, he'd been distracted by an overpowering urge to kiss her nanny—despite the nanny's sensible flannelette pyjamas.

It was an unforeseen problem—this tendency to find his thoughts flashing to Holly. It was the last thing he'd expected, the last thing he wanted. He had no intention of setting himself up for another romantic disaster.

A burst of laughter from the bedroom was accompanied by Holly's voice, high-pitched and squeaking. Actually, the sound was more like quacking, as if Holly was acting out a story. Gray drew a bracing breath and continued on to the doorway of her room.

To his surprise, the room was in darkness. In the dim light he could see that Holly's bed had been transformed into a tent made from sheets draped from the tall brass bedposts and joined in the middle by large safety pins. The silhouettes of his giggling children and their nanny were illuminated by torchlight inside the tent.

It looked like incredible fun.

Gray stood in the darkened doorway, watching them, hands sunk in the pockets of his jeans…moved beyond reason…flooded by memories of his own lonely childhood in this house and his parents' constant bickering and battles.

Never once had he experienced anything close to this level of fun or fellowship. Later, he'd enjoyed yarns around campfires and he'd discovered the camaraderie of the stockmen in the mustering team, but his early home life had been constantly marred by his parents' tension and deep unhappiness.

By contrast, Holly was going out of her way to keep his children entertained and happy and secure. Her generosity was a revelation to him. Damn it, he was fighting tears.

Taking a deep, steadying breath, he knocked on the bedroom door.

'Who's there?' called Josh, sounding important.

'Hector Owl,' Gray responded in his most booming voice.

'Daddy!' squealed his children, and two little faces appeared from beneath the side wall of the tent.

'Hey, there. Looks like you're having fun.'

'We're putting on a puppet show.' Grinning widely, Josh lifted the sheet to reveal Holly caught in a beam of torchlight and sitting cross-legged at the bottom of the bed. Her hand was encased in a glove puppet that vaguely resembled a duck.

She blushed when she saw Gray.

'I don't want to interrupt,' he said.

Holly shook her head. 'You're not interrupting. We were only filling in time until you got home.'

'But don't let me stop your fun. Keep going.'

She smiled shyly. 'Um...well...'

'Just tell me something first,' he said, quickly. 'How was school?'

'Awesome!' his children shouted in unison.

'Really?'

Anna's eyes were almost popping with excitement. 'It's a rocket ship school, Daddy. Me and Josh and Holly are in one rocket ship and we talk on our radio to all the kids in the other rocket ships.'

'A rocket ship?' Gray shook his head in bemusement. 'Sounds exciting.'

'It is exciting. And we've already learned all kinds of math and about wombats.'

Gray smiled at Holly—seemed he wanted to smile more and more lately. 'I'll get all the details from you later.' Already he was looking forward to their conversation.

'But you'll play with us now, won't you?' demanded Josh.

'Ah...' Gray hesitated. They were probably acting out another story he'd never heard of. An excuse—an urgent need to see a man about a dog—was ready on the tip of his tongue.

'Here, Daddy,' cried Anna bossily. 'You can have a puppet.' She held up something made of bright pink fabric. 'You can be the pig.'

'The pig,' he repeated, feeling instantly inadequate, just as he had on the night Holly had pushed him to read a bedtime story.

But, despite his misgivings, he knew he *needed* to learn how to do this stuff. For his kids' sake, he had to make the most of these next few weeks while Holly was still here to show him the ropes.

'Sure,' he said, bravely walking closer to the bed and holding out his hand for the pig. 'What do I have to do?'

CHAPTER SEVEN

'So, TELL me,' said Gray after he'd heard Holly's full report on his kids' first day in their new school, 'is our Outback as bad as you expected?' He was smiling but Holly thought she detected tension in his eyes, as if her answer really mattered.

'I wasn't expecting it to be bad,' she said.

'Not even after Chelsea's warnings?'

She shook her head. 'I'm not like Chelsea,' she told him bluntly. 'Chelsea was a city girl through and through—city girl lifestyle, city girl career, city girl clothes. Not that I need to tell you that.'

They were sitting at one end of the kitchen table eating their heated-up meals. The puppet play had been a great success and Gray had joined in with gusto. Now, Janet had retired to her cottage and the children were in bed, so Holly and Gray were alone in the big silent house.

Gray had showered and changed into a fresh white shirt that made the tanned skin at his throat even darker. His hair was damp and he'd shaved, and Holly could see a small scar on his jaw she'd never noticed before. She told herself this was an everyday, average evening meal and it made no sense that she felt all fluttery every time their gazes met across the table.

'Don't you think of yourself as a city girl?' Gray asked her.

She shook her head. 'You know what they say. You can take the girl out of the farm, but you can't take the farm out of the girl.'

He smiled. 'So what kind of farm did you grow up on?'

'A dairy.'

'Really?' His eyebrows lifted with surprise. 'Dairies are hard work.'

Holly laughed. 'And your kind of farming is easy?'

'Piece of cake,' he said with a sparkle in his blue eyes that sent her hormones rattling. 'Except for when I'm driving a truck through floodwaters.'

'Or wrestling with crocodiles.'

'Yeah, or wrangling wild bulls.'

They shared another smile. Holly, trying to ignore another flutter, asked quickly, 'So how big is Jabiru Creek Station?'

'Close on a million acres.'

'Wow.' She stared at him. 'I'm sure there are countries in Europe that are smaller than that.'

Gray shrugged. 'A few, I believe.'

'But Janet told me you run this place all by yourself. She said you've been in charge here for almost ten years.'

'I have, more or less, but I couldn't have done it without the help of Ted. He's my manager and he keeps the books and looks after the paperwork. I couldn't have managed without Janet, either. She and Ted are a great backup team.'

'But you don't have any other family here?'

'No.' Gray concentrated on spearing a bean with his fork. 'As you know, my mother's in Sydney. She and my dad split up when I was a nipper. Later, my dad's health went downhill, so he moved to Cairns to be closer to doctors. But he's okay, as long as he has regular check-ups.'

Gray lifted his gaze. 'Tell me about your farm. Do your parents still run it?'

'Sure—with my eldest brother's help. He and his family live with my parents.'

'Your *eldest* brother?' Now Gray looked amused. 'So how many brothers do you have?'

'Three. All of them are older.'

Smiling, he pushed his empty plate aside and leaned back in his chair in a way that somehow made his shoulders look huge. 'So you're the only girl and the baby of the family.'

'Yes.' Holly couldn't help returning his smile. 'I know, I know. I must be a spoiled princess.'

'I can't see any signs of spoiling,' he said, letting his gaze run over her.

To her surprise, a happy kind of buzz started inside her, something she hadn't felt in a very long time. 'You haven't mentioned any brothers or sisters,' she prompted. 'Are you an only child?'

'Yeah. But I can't claim to have been spoiled.'

'No,' she agreed quietly, remembering his mother's cool reception at the airport.

Setting her knife and fork neatly together, she said, 'Actually, my brothers are my stepbrothers.'

'Really?' Gray was too well mannered to ply her with awkward questions, but she could tell he was curious. She decided she wanted to tell him.

'I've never met my real father, you see. He took off when I was a baby, so my mom was a single mom, a hairdresser, and until I was five we lived in town. Just the two of us in a little flat above her hairdressing salon. Then one day this nice guy came into her salon with three young sons who needed haircuts.'

She smiled. 'Turned out he was a lonely widower, a dairy farmer. He and my mom hit it off and, when they married, we became a family.'

To Holly's surprise, Gray frowned. 'And you've all lived happily ever after?'

'We have indeed.' Sending him a deliberately light-hearted smile, she added, 'So you know the moral of that story, don't you?'

'Do I?'

'Sure. Next time you're in town, you have to keep an eye out for a friendly but lonely hairdresser.'

It was supposed to be a joke, but she could see it had fallen flatter than Kansas.

'I'm not looking for a second wife,' Gray said grimly.

Okay. Point noted.

Holly had been thinking of her stepdad and how happy he was with her mom, how happy they both were—but perhaps she'd been insensitive. She hoped she hadn't sounded as if she was pushing Gray to find a replacement mother for his kids.

It was clear she'd upset him. Gathering up their plates, she carried them to the sink, mad with herself for spoiling a perfectly pleasant conversation. For a moment there, Gray had looked as if he wanted to pack her bags and put her on the next mail plane out of Jabiru.

Knowing a change of subject was needed, she asked, 'While I'm up, would you like a cuppa?'

'Thank you.' Already, he was sounding more conciliatory. 'I'll stack the dishwasher.'

She tried to ignore the view of him from behind as he bent over to load their plates. How could ordinary old blue jeans be so attention-grabbing?

'By the way,' she said casually as her gaze flickered to his low-slung jeans, then away. Then back again. 'I meant to thank you for letting us use your study as a schoolroom.'

'No worries.' Gray finished with the dishwasher and leaned casually against the kitchen counter, arms crossed, his eyes friendly once more. 'You're welcome to use the study.'

'It doubles really well as a school room, but I've told Anna and Josh they have to keep it tidy for you.'

He pulled a face. 'Doesn't really matter if they mess that room up. I'm not in there a lot.'

'I must admit I was surprised to find it so tidy. I thought it would be full of your books.'

Gray frowned and his eyes narrowed. 'Why?'

'Well, there are hardly any books anywhere else in the house. I thought they'd be in the study, but you obviously keep them somewhere else. I must admit I kept all mine in my bedroom in Chelsea's flat. I had them double stacked on floor-to-ceiling shelves, piled on the nightstand, on the floor—'

As Holly said this, she realised that Gray's expression had changed.

Again.

This time, however, she saw a flash of pain in his eyes. *Real* pain.

What was the matter now? What had she said wrong?

Behind her the kettle came to the boil and she whirled around quickly. Confused, embarrassed, she concentrated very carefully on pouring hot water into mugs.

When she looked back at Gray again, a cool mask had slipped over his face and his blue eyes were almost icy. 'I never have time for reading,' he said.

Okay. So here was another subject that was a conversation stopper for this man. First, she'd upset him by asking about his former wife's preference for Sydney. Then she'd made a light-hearted comment about his marital future and hit a brick wall. Now his taste in books was a taboo topic...

Aware that the evening's lovely relaxed mood would almost certainly not revive, Holly suggested that she might take her tea through to her room and Gray looked relieved. They exchanged very polite goodnights and parted.

In bed, however, nursing her mug of hot tea, Holly couldn't help conducting a post-mortem of their conversation. She thought how much she'd enjoyed Gray's company up until the point when she'd apparently put her foot in it. Gray wasn't just a sexy dude. She'd seen glimpses of a really nice, friendly guy.

Then she'd spoiled everything. For heaven's sake, who was she to judge his reading habits? What did she know about the responsibilities involved in caring for a million acre property? Gray couldn't have been much more than twenty when he'd shouldered that responsibility, and it wasn't so remarkable that he hadn't had time to laze about with his nose in a book.

Just the same, it was clear there was more to Gray than met the eye. He might seem to be a straightforward Australian cattleman with a down-to-earth manner but, beneath the simple and sexy blue-jeans-and-riding-boots exterior, he was a complicated puzzle.

Working him out wasn't part of Holly's job description. But, if she was to leave Anna and Josh in his care, shouldn't she try to understand him?

After Holly left, Gray stayed behind in the kitchen, brooding as he stared out through the window at the dark, starless sky.

He'd been steeling himself for Holly's nosy questions.

She was, after all, a teacher but, truth to tell, her question about his books hadn't bothered him nearly as much as her suggestion about his plans for the future.

Whenever he thought about the rest of his life stretching ahead into his forties, fifties and beyond, his heart felt rimmed with ice. But was he really going to close down his emotions and never look at another woman again? Was it okay if his children never had a stepmother? Weren't Janet and a nanny enough?

He'd always looked on Chelsea's arrival in the Outback as a gift from the gods, but he'd wrecked that chance.

Had it been his only chance?

What was he planning for the rest of his life? Would he simply take advantage of casual opportunities? Or would he put himself in the marketplace—like those crazy TV shows—*Cattleman wants a Wife*.

He hadn't come to terms with any of these questions yet—and he sure as hell wished Holly hadn't raised them.

By Friday afternoon, the children were well settled into their new home. The school week had gone really well and now Anna and Josh were out of the school room and playing on the swing. It was a favourite afternoon pastime that came a close second to admiring their growing puppies, which now resembled fat little sausages with lovely seal-smooth coats.

Selections had been made and Josh was the proud pre-owner of the all black male, while Anna had settled on a sweet little blue-speckled female.

From the kitchen Holly could hear the children's voices drifting through the window, squealing with delight as they pushed the swing higher.

Janet, in the kitchen, was browning chicken pieces at the stove.

'Let me help you,' Holly said. 'Maybe I can chop something?'

Janet tried to shoo her away. 'Your job's in the school room, lovey. I don't expect you to help in here.'

'But I'd like to.' Holly was thinking of all the times she'd chopped ingredients for her mom in the pretty blue and yellow farmhouse kitchen at home. For some reason she couldn't quite explain, this afternoon she was feeling homesick.

She told herself it had nothing to do with the fact that Gray had made himself scarce all week, ever since Monday night's conversation.

'Well…' Janet took a good long look at Holly and apparently made up her mind about something. 'You could chop carrots and celery if you like. I'm making chicken cacciatore.' Then she sent Holly an unsettling wink. 'It's one of Gray's favourites.'

Hmm…Gray again…

It was surprising the number of times Janet mentioned her boss to Holly. She'd even tried to suggest that Gray was happier now that Holly had come to Jabiru Creek.

But if Gray was happier, Holly knew it was because his children were here now, and it had nothing to do with her presence. Quite the opposite. Whenever she'd talked to Gray she'd pressed the wrong buttons and upset him. Ever since Monday night he'd been avoiding her and that bothered her more than it should.

Admittedly, a cattleman needed to rise early and to be away from the house, working on his vast property from dawn until dusk. But each night, after Gray indulged in a quick after-dinner romp with his children, he took off for one of the machinery sheds, claiming he had a problem with a broken tractor.

Holly told herself that mending tractors was what men of the Outback did in the evenings instead of reading the paper, or watching TV like their city counterparts. Her father loved to tinker in his sheds, and she mightn't have minded Gray's absence so much if she hadn't been almost certain that he was dodging conversation with her.

Was he worried that she was waiting to pounce on him with more questions?

Now, at the end of a week of tractor-mending, she wished she knew if she'd said something that had really upset him, or if she was making a mountain out of a molehill. Surely her mind could be put to rest after a simple quick chat?

As she chopped carrots, she decided she would head out to that machinery shed this evening and offer Gray some kind of olive branch…

There was no helpful moonlight when Holly cautiously descended the homestead steps at half past eight, after the children were safely tucked in bed. She made her way across the paddock to the shed by the feeble glow of her flashlight.

A shadow rose from the grass beside her and large wings flapped, making her jump. With a hand pressed to her thumping chest, she thought about turning back, then told herself it was probably an owl and that crossing a paddock at Jabiru Creek was no different from playing hide-and-seek in the barns back home with her brothers.

Just the same, it felt like ages before she reached the yellow light shining through the doorway of the tall corrugated iron shed.

The sound of hammering came from inside. Or was that her heart?

A few more steps brought her through the doorway and inside the shed. She saw rubber tyres of all sizes stacked against a wall. Bits and pieces of rusty machinery. An intact tractor.

Gray—not in the expected overalls, but in his usual faded jeans and an old navy-blue woollen sweater with the sleeves pushed back and a hole at one elbow—was working at a long wooden bench. He'd stopped hammering now and was planing timber, smoothing down the edges of a very large box-shaped object.

Intent on his task, Gray turned slightly and Holly saw the strength in his hands and forearms. She could even sense the movement of his shoulder muscles beneath the thick wool of his sweater.

She turned off her flashlight and put it in her coat pocket. Her palms were sweaty, so she jammed them in her pockets too. Then, feeling like an intruder, she took a deep breath and went three steps deeper into the shed.

She felt ridiculously nervous. Any minute now Gray would look up and she would have to explain why she was here.

She tried to remember the opening she'd rehearsed. *Something about his tractor.* But he wasn't working on the tractor…

With her gaze firmly fixed on Gray, she took another step forward—and tripped on a metal pipe, sending it rolling and clattering across the concrete floor.

Gray's head snapped up and his blue eyes widened with surprise. 'Holly.'

'I'm sorry,' she cried, bending down to rub her smarting ankle.

'Are you okay?'

'Yes, I'm fine.'

He came hurrying over to her, wiping his dusty hands on an old rag. 'Are you sure you're all right?'

'The pipe's probably worse off than I am. It's okay. Really. Just a bump.'

'I hope you don't end up with a bruise.' A beat later, he said, 'What are you doing out here?' His smile was quickly replaced by a frown. 'Is something wrong? Is it Anna?'

'No, no. Nothing wrong. A-Anna's fine.' Holly's mouth was suddenly as dry as the sawdust on the floor. She tried to swallow, then remembered that she'd planned to smile to set the right mood. 'There's no problem, Gray. The children are sound asleep.'

'That's good to hear.' With hands on his hips, he studied her, a puzzled gleam lurking in his bright blue eyes. 'So, what brings you out here at this time of night? I thought you'd be curled up with your nose in a book.'

Yes...well...

Now that he was waiting for her answer, Holly felt more foolish than ever. Gray seemed totally relaxed and not at all put out by her sudden appearance, so how could she suggest there was a problem that needed sorting?

'Have...have you finished the tractor?' she asked.

'The tractor?'

'I...um...thought you were working on one.'

'Oh, yes. You've blown my cover.' Gray's eyes twinkled, and then he turned to the bench where he'd been working. 'I've been making something for Anna and Josh, actually. It's almost done.'

'Oh,' she said in a very small voice.

'Would you like to take a look? I still have to paint it.'

Without waiting for her answer, Gray went back to the bench and picked up the large boxlike frame he'd been working on. Not quite hiding his pride in his workmanship, he set it on the floor.

'Oh,' Holly said again when she saw it properly. 'It's… it's a puppet theatre.'

He was grinning. 'I made the stage high enough for Anna and Josh to stand behind.'

'It's perfect.' Holly meant it. She was amazed and she felt so silly for thinking he'd been avoiding her. She wasn't even on his radar.

'They'll love it,' she said. 'Wow. You've even made a pointy roof and a little wooden flag to go on top.'

'And Janet's making red velvet curtains.'

'Fantastic!'

So Janet was in on this, too? Holly felt as if the rug had been pulled from beneath her. Here she'd been, all week, stewing about Gray's sensitive reaction to their conversation, while he'd been busy creating a wonderful surprise for his children.

'It's a fabulous idea,' she said, running her hand over the smooth silky wall of the stage and admiring the fine craftsmanship. 'Did you say you're going to paint this?'

'I thought the kids would like something bright.' He scratched at the side of his neck. 'But don't ask me about colour schemes. Apart from painting the roof red, I'm a bit stumped.'

'You can't just nip down to a hardware store, so I suppose it depends on what paint you already have.'

'Practically every colour under the sun, actually.' He went over to a cupboard against the wall and flipped it open to reveal several shelves lined with spray cans. 'Last year there was a ringer working here who moonlighted as a rodeo clown and I helped him to make his props.'

Holly laughed. 'So you have enough colours to make a rainbow.'

'I guess I do.'

'Rainbow walls would be fiddly, but they'd look fabulous.'

Gray considered this, a smile pulling at a corner of his mouth. 'I'm no Vincent Van Gogh.' He shot her an amused glance. 'What about you? Are you handy with a spray can?'

Holly had wielded many a spray can while making children's library displays, and she'd discovered a creative streak she hadn't previously known she possessed.

'We—I mean *you*—would need to work from the top down,' she said. 'And you'd have to use something like cardboard as a shield.'

'You'd help me, wouldn't you?'

She knew she shouldn't feel so flattered. 'I'd be prepared to give it a go.'

'Terrific,' he said, matching her enthusiasm.

And then, looking straight into her eyes, he smiled. *Oh, man*. His smile packed a wallop.

Not that she should be noticing.

It shouldn't have been so much fun—working hard and staying up till nearly midnight to get the last rainbow stripe in place. Holly enjoyed every second of the project.

Early in the evening, while the undercoat was drying, Gray boiled a billy on a small gas ring and made tea. He had milk and sugar in a battered old cooler and even a packet of cookies.

They sat on rickety camping stools in the middle of the messy shed, drinking sweet hot tea from chipped enamel mugs and eating cookies.

'Yum,' Holly said as she helped herself to a second one.

'Good to see a girl with an appetite.' Gray took a second

cookie as well. 'Chelsea was always so careful about what she ate.'

'All dancers seem to diet. They're very strong-willed,' she suggested.

'Obsessed,' Gray said tightly.

Holly now knew better than to pursue this sensitive topic. After all, she'd come here to hold out an olive branch.

Smiling, she said brightly, 'So tell me, Gray, does your hat still fit?'

He looked at her with puzzled amusement. 'Last time I tried it. Why?'

'Janet and Ted have both been praising you to the skies this week and I thought you might have a swelled head.'

Looking down at the curls of shaved wood on the floor, he shrugged. 'That pair are biased.'

'Maybe, but they're not easily hoodwinked. They told me you're a brilliant cattleman, highly respected and looked up to by others in your industry. Ted said that when you took over the reins here ten years ago, you dramatically improved the carrying capacity and diversified the cattle breeds. And you placed yourself at the cutting edge of land management and water conservation.'

Gray was staring hard at his mug. 'Sounds a bit grand when you put it like that, but when I'm out, driving around, I listen to a lot of agricultural radio programmes. It's a good way to learn things.'

'According to Ted, you hoard all that info in your brilliant memory and then put it into practice.' Holly smiled. 'He also said you're fantastic with figures. He called you a human calculator.'

Gray shrugged again. 'That man has far too much to say. I'm not paying him to gasbag.' His eyes flashed a cheeky challenge. 'And why are you trying to flatter me?'

'I'm not flattering you. I'm giving you positive feedback. You can blame my teacher training.'

'Yeah, right.' He gave a smiling shake of his head. 'But shouldn't we be working out how we're going to paint these rainbow walls?'

They decided on a plan. They would start at the top with orange just beneath the red roof, then progress downwards through blue and purple to finish with green at the base.

With the plan settled and the undercoat dry, they got back to work. After a short trial run, Gray admitted that Holly could produce the most even spray paint finish, so they agreed that he should hold up the cardboard shield for her.

As they worked, she engaged him in safe topics—mostly about the twins and their first week of school. She told him that Josh was very clever at arithmetic and had developed a passion for Natural Science—particularly frogs.

'I hope you don't mind. This afternoon we converted a pickle jar into a tadpole aquarium,' she told him.

Gray laughed. 'I was mad about spiders when I was a kid. Tried to start a redback spider farm in an ice cream container.'

'Eeeeww.' Holly gave an elaborate shudder, then told him that Anna was the twin who was curious about spiders. 'She also has beautiful handwriting and a musical ear and an exceptionally vivid imagination.'

Holly enjoyed herself immensely, which surprised her, considering that once upon a time she'd looked forward to sharing this sort of task with Brandon. She'd even been silly enough to imagine that she and Brandon would paint a nursery for their first baby, and she'd actually picked out a colour scheme of white and sunshiny yellow with a brightly coloured rainbow frieze.

How strange that this puppet theatre inspired her now almost as much as her old dream had.

On Sunday morning, Gray rose just as the screeching corellas took off from the trees along the creek bank, and he crossed the frosty grass to the shed where the puppet theatre stood in all its rainbow-walled, red-curtained glory.

He grinned when he saw it. It looked so bright and cheerful and, even if he did say so himself, very professional. Almost as good as the puppet theatre he and Holly had taken the children to see in New York.

His kids were going to love it.

All thanks to Holly, of course...

Without her, he wouldn't have known such things existed. And without Holly he wouldn't have enjoyed the final decorating tasks nearly as much. She was so easy-going and comfortable to be with.

Gray totally understood why his kids loved school when Holly was around to help make it fun.

How would they cope when she left?

Soon, he would have to seek her help in posting an ad for a replacement nanny, and then he'd also need her input when he vetted the applicants.

Right now, Gray couldn't think of a more unpalatable task, couldn't imagine another woman filling Holly O'Mara's shoes.

A movie director couldn't have created a more pleasing scene than Anna and Josh's discovery of the puppet theatre. They bounced into the kitchen for breakfast, spied the theatre positioned just outside the flyscreen door, and reacted just as Holly had hoped they would—with dancing and squealing and their eyes almost popping out of their heads with excitement.

'And it isn't even our birthday,' Josh exclaimed in grinning disbelief as he and Anna took turns to pull the cord that drew the splendid red curtains open and shut.

Anna was beaming, too. 'I can't believe we have a theatre *and* our puppies. Wow, Daddy, this is so cool.'

Together, the children squeezed inside the 'back door' and examined the stage. When they plied Gray and Holly with questions, they were stunned to learn that their dad had actually made this glorious construction with his own hands.

Holly smiled at Gray, taking in the quiet satisfaction in his eyes.

'They'll remember this day for the rest of their lives,' she told him quietly.

He merely nodded, but this time when he smiled back at her, she had to look down. The crackling *something* in the air was suddenly too much.

After breakfast, the children jumped straight into presenting their premiere puppet show on the veranda, and of course Holly, Gray and Janet were the audience, very happy to sit on a row of chairs, with the basket of puppies at their feet.

'The puppies have to watch, too,' Anna had insisted.

Naturally, the show was received with thunderous applause, and afterwards the children rushed straight off to plan their next performance.

'We'll soon be calling them Shake and Speare,' Janet muttered good-humouredly, before she returned to the kitchen to make a batch of scones for morning tea.

Holly might have followed Janet if Gray hadn't detained her with his hand on her arm. She jumped at his touch as if he'd burned her, and then she felt seriously foolish.

'Would you like to come for a drive with me?' he asked.

'A drive?' She needed a moment to catch her breath. 'I'm sure we won't be able to prise Anna and Josh away from their puppets.'

The tanned skin around his blue eyes crinkled. 'I wasn't planning to invite the children. I'm sure they'd rather stay here, and they'll be fine with Janet.'

'But—' Holly's heart gave a strange thump. 'Are you sure Janet doesn't have other plans?'

'I'm certain of it, Holly. I've already spoken to her, and she'd love to spend a day with the twins. In fact, she's already started on a picnic lunch for us.'

'Oh? I...I see.'

'You've earned a day off, and I thought you might like to see the gorge.'

It was kind of Gray to take the trouble to entertain her. 'Thank you.' Holly's voice was a shade too proper and polite. 'I'd love to see the gorge. I'll explain to Anna and Josh—'

He held up a hand. 'I can do the explaining while you get ready. You'll need sunscreen and a hat and sturdy shoes.'

She was being bulldozed—steamrollered—but for once she didn't mind.

In her room, as she grabbed her shady hat from its hook on the back of her dresser, she caught sight of her reflection in the mirror. She was, as usual, in a boring old T-shirt and jeans, with her hair tied back and a new crop of freckles on her nose.

If she was in New York, she was quite sure that if a new man invited her out for the day she would go to a great deal of trouble, hunting through her wardrobe for the perfect outfit, ringing her friends for fashion advice, going for a manicure, a pedicure, a leg wax.

It was strange to think that she was now going to spend an entire day alone with a man who was *not* Brandon, and yet she didn't feel an overwhelming urge to worry about how she looked. It was rather comforting to know she didn't have to try too hard with Gray Kidman.

After teaming with him on the puppet theatre, they'd reached a comfortable working relationship and she could save her dating charms for the new man she was bound to meet once she was back home again in the fall. The sizzle she felt around Gray Kidman was nothing more than hormones—and she supposed she should be grateful to know they were still in working order.

CHAPTER EIGHT

As GRAY drove away from the homestead with a cloud of dust pluming behind his vehicle, Holly was reacquainted with how very isolated Jabiru Creek Station really was.

They'd only just passed the last outbuilding before they were once again following a faint dirt track across endless plains that stretched and stretched to the distant horizon. She saw nothing but cloudless blue skies, red dirt and dusty faded grass, with occasional mobs of silvery hump-backed cattle sheltering in the scant shade of straggly white-trunked trees.

'It must be fabulous to tear across this country on horse-back,' she said, partly because she meant it, and partly because she wanted to say something positive about the monotonous scenery.

Gray turned to her, clearly surprised. 'Do you ride?'

'I haven't for ages.'

'But you know how to.'

'Sure. There was a time when horse-riding was my favourite sport.'

His eyebrows shot high. 'Why didn't you tell me?'

'I came here to be your children's nanny. Not to prance around on horseback.'

Still watching the track ahead, Gray shook his head.

'But I'm sure you could squeeze in a little riding time while you're here.'

'That would be wonderful—although I'm sure I'd be sorry when I was stiff and sore.'

His eyes sparkled as he turned to her. 'You'll soon loosen up.' A little later he said, 'I'm planning to teach Anna and Josh how to ride.'

'Oh, good. They'll love it.'

'Even Anna?'

'Especially Anna,' Holly assured him. 'She's getting more into life in the Outback every day.'

Gray smiled. 'I'll have to measure them up for riding helmets.'

After that, he seemed to lapse back into thoughtful silence, and Holly sensed his focus shift from conversation to the ancient landscape all around him.

Eventually, a red range of hills appeared, rising out of the flat land ahead of them. Holly was reminded of the backdrops of the old western movies her dad used to watch on Sunday afternoons, and she almost expected to see smoke signals puffing from the jagged ridges.

When they crested a hill, Gray braked and in front of them the land dropped away, plunging, without warning, down sheer red cliffs.

'Oh, my gosh!' Holly was glad of her seatbelt. Leaning as far forward as the belt would permit, she peered through the dusty windscreen. 'I guess this must be the gorge?'

'It's not quite the Grand Canyon.'

'But it's spectacular.' She glanced back over her shoulder to the rear window and the view of the empty plains they'd just crossed. 'Are we still on your land?'

'Sure.' Already Gray was opening the driver's door. 'Come and take a look. I love it out here.'

Outside, the sun was scorching hot. Holly jammed her

hat firmly on her head, but she wasn't keen to step any closer to the edge of the gorge. It was an awfully long way down to the glinting water of the rock pools at the bottom. After just a hasty glance down there she felt dizzy.

'Here, come with me.' Gray had retrieved their backpacks from the rear of the truck and he handed the smaller one to Holly. 'I'll show you the best way to see the view.'

She almost declined. She had quite a nice view from where she was standing, and she had a safe hold on the truck's sturdy metal bull bar, thank you very much. But Gray was holding out his hand to her, and his air of confidence was very convincing.

Summoning her courage, she managed to loosen her grip on the bull bar and his hand holding hers felt wonderfully strong and trustworthy, but she clung to him so tightly she was afraid she'd leave bruises.

To her relief, he led her away from the cliff's edge to what at first seemed like a hole in the ground, but turned out to be a man-made staircase cleverly hewn out of the rock.

'This leads down through the roof of a cave,' he said.

'Wow. Did you make these stairs?'

Gray laughed. 'No way. They've been here for over a hundred years, but my grandfather helped to carve them out.'

Intrigued, Holly allowed him to guide her down the rocky staircase. Already she could see that the cave below them wasn't gloomy or dark, but filled with sunlight. And it had a wide sandy floor, so she began to feel calmer.

By the time they reached the bottom of the steps, she looked around with amazed delight. The cave was set into the side of the escarpment and it formed a safe shelf, a fabulous, cosy viewing platform offering a spectacular view all the way down the gorge.

'Gray, it…it's fabulous.'

His blue eyes met hers, watching her closely, as if he was intensely interested in her reaction. Apparently satisfied, he smiled. 'Not bad, is it?'

'It's amazing. I think I'll sit down though, so I can take it all in.'

By this time, she'd become super-aware of their linked hands—of the heat of Gray's palm against hers, of the pressure of his fingers as he gripped her firmly and safely. To her surprise, she was incredibly reluctant to release his hand before she lowered herself to the sandy floor.

Once she was seated, Gray edged forward, closer to the mouth of the cave, and he hunkered down, taking in the view. He loved this place with its rock pools that reflected the sky and the spectacular sandstone escarpments carved out of the ancient landscape. He never failed to be moved by its grandeur.

But today he was trying to imagine how the gorge might look through Holly's eyes. He wasn't sure why it mattered so much, but he found himself hoping that she might some-how understand what it meant to him.

At least she wasn't talking non-stop. She seemed happy enough to drink in the atmosphere, or to quietly take pho-tographs with her small digital camera.

In the languid silence Gray let his shoulders relax against a warm wall of sandstone. He heard the warbling notes of a pied butcherbird and a flock of galahs calling in the distance. Below, on the water, a pair of grebes floated.

After a while, he asked quietly, 'So, what do you reckon?'

'This is so beautiful,' Holly said softly. 'It feels almost… spiritual.'

A good answer. 'It *is* spiritual,' he said. 'At least it is for the Aborigines.'

And for me, he added silently, thinking of the many times when his life had hit rock bottom and he'd come to this place to search for some kind of peace.

Moving carefully on her hands and knees, Holly crawled a little closer, then sat cross-legged, looking out. 'It's awesome. Unforgettable.' She spoke in a hushed undertone, the way people talked in church.

She took a few more photos, then lowered her camera. 'I'm sure this gorge has been here for ever. A dinosaur could come lumbering out from behind a rock and it wouldn't look out of place.'

Her face was soft, her dark eyes luminous with wonder. And Gray had to look away, concentrating his attention on a lizard as it disappeared down a crack in a rust-stained rock.

He'd hoped Holly would like this place, but he hadn't expected her to so totally *get* its timeless mystery.

'Is it weird to feel that there's someone here?' she asked. 'A gentle spirit, looking after us?'

He had to swallow the hard lump in his throat before he could speak. 'Not weird at all. That's why I love it. Sitting here quietly, taking in the silence, always makes me feel stronger. Uplifted. The Aborigines call it "listening to country".'

He turned and saw Holly nodding slowly, a pretty smile lighting her eyes.

'Listening to country,' she repeated softly. 'I like that. I used to do a lot of that when I was growing up in Vermont. On my way to school I used to love walking over the covered bridge on Staple's Brook and along the banks beneath sugar maples and birches. *Listening to country.* I am so on that page.'

Launching to his feet, Gray moved to the very mouth of the cave, appalled to realise he'd been on the brink of tears. He'd never expected to meet a woman like Holly, someone lovely and sweet and in tune with his world. For a heady moment there, he'd almost pulled her close and kissed her, tasted her smile, her laughter.

Not a bright idea. She was here to help his children, and she was going home to America to start a fancy new job. Besides, she'd just had her heart broken by some fool of a boyfriend. Last thing she needed was her cousin's Australian ex making a move on her. Especially as that ex was absolutely useless at making women happy—or keeping them happy, at any rate.

For all kinds of reasons, he'd be a fool to start anything with Holly. Even if she did claim to love his Outback, he couldn't expect her to want to stay here. Not with him. She'd soon realise her mistake, just as his wife had.

Hell. He should wear a danger sign, warning women to keep their distance.

'This country must inspire musicians and artists,' Holly was saying. 'Or writers. I've never read any literature about your Outback, but there must be novels and poetry. Do you have any—?'

She stopped in mid-sentence and her face turned bright red, as if she realised she'd made a dreadful gaffe. 'Sorry. I know reading's not your thing.'

Gray's entire body tensed, as if the cliff had suddenly crumbled away beneath his feet. Fear knifed through him—the fear of ridicule that he'd never managed to shake off.

His only hope was to change the subject...

'I could give you a few lines of bush poetry,' he said quickly.

Anything, even the embarrassment of a recitation, was better than risking exposure of his incompetence.

'Poetry?' Holly sounded shocked, and already he was feeling foolish.

She was leaning forward now, hands wrapped around bent knees. 'Gray, I'd love to hear some bush poetry.'

Of course he was already regretting the offer. He wasn't a performer and he wished he could come up with an excuse—he'd forgotten the lines—anything. 'It's pretty basic stuff. Hardly Wordsworth or Shakespeare.'

'But the simplest things are often the truest.'

Damn. Gray knew he'd talked himself into a corner. He'd look even more foolish if he backed out now. He made a show of clearing his throat and then, keeping his gaze fixed on the gorge, he began to recite.

'I've crossed harsh country parched and red,
With ghost gums shining white,
Where sand dunes choke the river bed,
And all day I prayed for night.
I've heard that country sing to me
In the stillness of my mind,
A Dreamtime chant from rock and tree—'

Gray paused and he realised that Holly was staring at him, her eyes full of questions.

'Sorry.' He could feel his face burning. Why the hell had he grabbed onto the poem to get him off the hook?

'Don't apologise. I loved it, Gray.'

He shrugged elaborately and looked away again, down the gorge to where a mob of black-tailed rock wallabies were feeding quietly on the moist vegetation at the edge of a waterhole.

'When did you learn that poem?' she asked, with the nosiness he should have expected from a teacher.

Gray shrugged. 'Can't remember.'

'Who wrote it?'

The heat in his face deepened and he answered

brusquely, without looking at her. 'It's nothing. Just something I made up.'

He heard her shocked gasp. 'You made it up?'

'Yeah. No big deal.'

'But...when did you write it?'

He gave another big-shouldered shrug. 'Years ago. I can't really remember. Beside a campfire. Sitting here. Alone.' Sure that his face was crimson now, he got to his feet and scooped up his backpack, eager to be done with this conversation.

'Gray, please don't be embarrassed, but it *is* a big deal that you've made up such a lovely poem. I'm seriously impressed.'

'Thanks.'

'Did Chelsea love it?'

Chelsea? He sighed, then stared out at the deep blue of the sky and the deeper red walls.

'I shared my poetry with her once, but she saw it as yet another excuse to plead with me to give up my cattle and head for the city. She wanted us to be artists together—she could be a choreographer in Sydney and I could perform my poetry.'

'That doesn't sound very...practical.'

'She was convinced I'd be a great hit. She was always looking for something else for me to do besides raising cattle.'

Holly made no comment, but she was frowning and then, as if she'd been struck by a bright idea, she flipped open her backpack and pulled out a notebook. 'I'd like to write your poem down.'

'Why?' Still thinking about Chelsea, Gray growled the word suspiciously.

'Because it's great. I really like it. I want to be able to read it again later, when I'm back in America.'

Already, she was sitting with her small spiral notebook in her lap, open at a blank page, her pen poised, ready to write.

Gray forced himself to relax. There was no threat in Holly's request. He actually liked the idea of her taking out her notebook when she was back in busy, bustling Manhattan, turning to his poem...reading it... Maybe she'd recall this moment. This peace.

Where was the harm in that?

Feeling self-conscious but no longer uncomfortable, he began to recite again: 'I've crossed harsh country parched and red...'

Holly's pen flew across the page leaving a neat curving script in its wake.

'With ghost gums shining white...'

She nodded enthusiastically as he continued on to the end of the first verse, then added a second stanza.

'Wow, that's fabulous,' she said when he'd finished. 'Thank you.' She spoke warmly, and her cheeks were flushed and her dark eyes were suspiciously shiny as she slipped the notebook back into the pack and closed the flap.

'You're welcome.'

'Having a copy of your poem makes this trip to the gorge even more perfect.'

He was more pleased than he should have been, but he was determined not to show it. Poker-faced, he said, 'So... would you like to keep going all the way to the bottom of the gorge?'

'Sure.' Holly scrambled to her feet and accepted his hand with almost childlike trust. 'Lead the way.'

Gripping Gray's hand once more as they made their way carefully down the rough, steep track to the bottom of the gorge, Holly discovered she was in deep, oh-my-God trouble.

She'd learned two important things about Gray just now—his soul-deep love of his land, and a strong reason for the breakdown of his marriage.

And then she'd learned something about herself.

While she'd sat in the cave in the middle of Gray's shatteringly beautiful wilderness, listening to him shyly recite his poetry, something huge had happened, something totally unexpected, something guaranteed to break her heart.

The noonday sun reached deep into the gorge, warming the wide ledge of rocks where they ate their simple picnic of egg and lettuce sandwiches on homemade bread, along with doorstop slices of rich fruity cake, and oranges.

Holly leaned down, dipping her fingers into water so clear she could see tiny silvery fish feeding on the sandy bottom.

Gray was busy lighting a fire for their billy tea and he called to her, 'Is the water cold?'

'Cool, but not freezing.'

'We could go for a swim if you weren't afraid of crocodiles.'

'Well, of course I'm afraid of crocodiles. Who wouldn't be?'

Catching his grin, she knew he'd only been teasing.

She sat up to watch him work, to watch the smooth tanned skin on the back of his neck and the damp line of sweat on his collar, the stretch of his cotton shirt over his wide shoulders, his long fingers deftly snapping twigs and poking them into the flames.

She imagined changing into bathers and swimming with him—if there were no crocodiles—and sweet shivers ran through her.

'The billy will take a few minutes to boil.' Gray's voice broke into her musings. 'We may as well make a start on our tucker.'

Holly discovered, to her surprise that she was ravenous and the sandwiches were surprisingly fresh with just the right balance of mayonnaise and pepper.

The gorge was completely silent now. Earlier there'd been bird calls but, in the midday stillness, the birds had retreated. Gray, looking very relaxed, sat with his back against a warm rock wall, his long jeans-clad legs stretched in front of him, his face shaded by his broad-brimmed hat.

Holly was quite prepared to eat her lunch in silence, lazing like a lizard in the sun and growing drowsy. And she was sure that was what Gray wanted, too, so she was surprised when he spoke suddenly.

'So…what made you decide to become a teacher?'

'Oh, that's easy,' she said. 'I was inspired by my fourth grade teacher, Miss Porter. She was lovely and brilliant and kind. And she turned our whole class onto books and reading.'

Gray nodded slowly, watching her from beneath his shady brim.

'I started out as a regular classroom teacher in Vermont,' Holly explained. 'That was fine for a few years, but all the time I was in the classroom I could feel the library calling to me, so I decided to get extra qualifications to run school libraries. That's when I moved to New York.'

'And you left your boyfriend behind.'

'Yes.' Holly waited for the slug of pain that always hit her when she thought about Brandon. It eventually came, like a delayed reaction, and it still hurt but, to her surprise, it was no longer crippling.

She realised that Gray was watching her, but he swiftly

switched his gaze to the fire and the boiling billy and he lifted it from the fire, then added tea leaves and gave them a stir.

'Are you ready for your tea?' he asked after a few minutes.

'Thank you.' Gratefully, Holly accepted an enamel mug of tea that was black and sweet and hot. Sipping it helped to calm the strange new tension inside her—a tension that had nothing to do with talking about Brandon and everything to do with her present company.

'Gray—'

'Hmm?' He leaned comfortably back against the rock and sipped his tea.

'Did you have School of the Air when you were a child?'

'Do you *have* to start talking about school right now?'

'I don't suppose it's essential, but I just told you about my favourite teacher. And I was thinking about your lovely poem, and I wondered where you learned about poetry.'

'It certainly wasn't on School of the Air.'

'Did you go away to boarding school?'

This was greeted by a deep sigh. 'Can we give this a miss, Holly?'

'I'm a teacher. I can't help wanting to know these things.'

'School is not everyone's favourite subject.'

'Is this another conversation stopper?'

He frowned. 'What do you mean?'

'It seems to me that every time I have a conversation with you I run into trouble. There's always something you don't want to talk about. Chelsea, I can understand. But what's wrong with talking about school?'

'The school a person went to doesn't matter out here in the bush. We're not snobs about that sort of thing.'

'I'm not asking you to show off. I was just curious—
anything about your school would do. Best teacher, worst
teacher. Favourite subject, favourite sport—'

There was a movement on the rock beside her. A beat
later, Gray was close beside her, leaning in to her, and Holly
realised with a shock that he was planning to kiss her.

Small explosions detonated all over her body.

She was sure she should say something to stop him, but
her brain refused to cooperate.

When Gray touched his lips to hers, her surprise melted
like sugar in hot tea and—*oh, man*—she responded like a
person in a dream.

His mouth was like the sun burning across the sky,
moving over her mouth, inch by fiery inch, cautious at first,
and testing. Holly remained perfectly still, afraid that at
any moment she might wake up and feel obliged to behave
responsibly.

She didn't want to behave responsibly. She was too curious initially and then she was bewitched by his totally
masculine enchantment.

Already, she was melting, softening and, when her lips
drifted apart, Gray accepted her invitation without hesitation. His hands cradled her head and his kiss, tasting faintly
of orange and tea, became clever and darkly seductive.

She could smell the sunlight on his skin, could feel its
warmth on her closed eyelids, and she was sinking beneath
it. Melting beneath his persuasive lips. Melting and needy.
So needy. She could no longer resist him even if she'd
wanted to.

A sweet, compelling ache started low inside her, urging
her to lean into him, to link her hands behind his neck
and to return his kiss, to communicate with her body the
shocking, thrilling impatience that had taken possession.

Oh, heavens, she might die if he stopped.

A sound broke the noonday silence—half a whimper, half a moan. Amazingly, it had come from her, but she couldn't stop to worry about decorum now.

But, to her dismay, Gray pulled away from her.

'Holly.'

Noooo. She kept her eyes tightly closed.

In the stillness she could hear the hammering of her heartbeats and the reckless pace of Gray's breathing.

He dropped a soft kiss on the bridge of her nose, then moved further away.

'What—?' she began, then had to pause to catch her breath.

His sexy blue eyes were apologetic. 'I'm sorry,' he said.

Sorry?

Oh, God. How could he share the hottest kiss of her life, possibly the most fabulous kiss since the beginning of time, and then apologise as if it were a mistake?

Distraught, Holly stared at him. 'Why are you sorry?'

'I shouldn't have done that.' His throat rippled as he swallowed. 'Please don't read too much into it.'

'But why did you do it? Why did you kiss me?'

He offered her a rueful smile. 'It seemed like a good idea at the time.'

'You kissed me to shut me up?'

Gray merely shook his head and Holly sank back against the rock in dismay.

What a klutz she was.

She'd gone into swoon mode, allowing herself to be completely carried away, while Gray had merely found a new technique to stop her from asking nosy questions.

'I'm an idiot,' she said out loud.

'No, Holly.'

'What am I, then?'

His answer was a smiling shake of his head. 'Another question? I should've known it's dangerous to kiss a teacher.'

'Yes, you might learn something,' she snapped, but her response was even testier than she'd intended. She'd never been any good at jokes, and light-heartedness was doubly impossible when she was so upset.

Damn Gray. She could still feel the warm pressure of his lips on hers. She could still smell him and taste him, could still feel the ripples of pleasure pooling low and deep inside her, like aftershocks.

But for Gray the kiss had been a game, a purely practical ploy to stop yet another annoying conversation.

Not daring to look at him, Holly jumped up quickly and, in a bid to cover up her embarrassment, she began to tidy away their picnic things.

As they took the climb back to the top in easy stages, Gray was uncomfortably aware that he'd spoiled a perfect day. He'd let Holly think that he'd kissed her to distract her and, yes, it was true. More or less. She'd pushed their conversation in a direction he had no wish to follow. She'd been holding his feet to the fire of a secret shame and he'd had to stop her.

It was a bad habit that had started during his marriage. Whenever his wife had come up with one of her grand schemes for getting them away from Jabiru Creek, he'd found it easier to seduce her than to tell her the truth—that he had no employable skills beyond running this cattle property.

But, although his initial impulse to kiss Holly had been self-preservation, everything had changed the instant their lips had touched.

A kind of spell had come over him. Admittedly, it was way too long since he'd kissed a woman, so that might explain why he'd been so totally fired up. But abstinence couldn't explain why he'd felt emotionally connected to Holly, or why there was so much that felt *right* about kissing her, so much that felt right about just being with her.

In spite of her nosy questions, she was amazingly easy company, and she was surprisingly at home here in his Outback. He found himself wanting a deeper connection with her, and his body still throbbed with a need to lose himself in her sweet, willing embrace.

It was a lucky thing that her soft needy cry had brought him to his senses. Without that warning, he might never have found the willpower to stop. But now he'd hurt Holly by once again going into defensive mode. He'd protected himself, but he'd spoiled something special.

Damn it, he should have known better.

Hadn't his marriage taught him that he was no match for a clever, educated woman, no matter how strong her appeal? Hadn't his life lessons proved that he was better on his own?

He was fine on his own.

Or at least he would be until his kids' education caught up with him.

The journey back to the homestead was wrapped in uncomfortable silence, which meant Holly had plenty of time to brood as they rumbled across the trackless plains.

She thought about the moment, while she and Gray were looking down at the gorge, when she'd experienced a feeling of true connection with him. In the same moment, she'd realised something else—she hadn't wanted to fall for Gray but it had happened, almost against her will.

Which meant he had the power to hurt her, just as Brandon had.

She shouldn't have allowed him to kiss her. Why hadn't

she shown more sense? Here she was—still suffering from shell shock after Brandon's dumping—and the last thing she wanted was another romantic entanglement—especially with Chelsea's ex.

She wanted freedom, not complications. Why would she put her heart at risk when she had a fabulous job lined up to go home to?

Please don't read too much into it he'd said.

How could Gray kiss her into oblivion simply to shut her up? What was his problem? Where was the crime in asking him about his school? Or about his lack of books, for that matter.

He knew schools and books were her thing, and just because—

Oh, my God.

A sudden chill skittered down Holly's spine as all sorts of puzzling things about Gray suddenly started to fall into place.

The lack of books in the Jabiru homestead. The fact that he'd never heard of Winnie-the-Pooh. His reaction in New York when she'd suggested he should read to his children. The way he'd waved away menus, and brushed aside the Central Park pamphlet—

Could he have literacy problems?

She stole a glance at him now…at the snug stretch of denim over his thighs to his strong, sun-weathered profile.

Gray Kidman…expert cattleman, gorgeous, take charge of anything…

Surely he couldn't be illiterate?

It was hard to take in.

But if he'd grown up out here, miles away from schools and possibly without a tutor, it wasn't too much of a stretch to believe that he might never have learned to read. He

probably knew a few words that enabled him to function—
Departures and Arrivals in airports, for example—but
beyond that—

Holly remembered his mother's lack of warmth. What
had her role been in her son's early years? Had the tension between them started decades ago? Holly knew from
her teacher training that literacy problems often stemmed
from emotional issues connected to early schooling
experiences.

She also knew that illiterate people could still be incredibly astute and competent—and Gray was clearly intelligent
and gifted. He made up poetry in his head. How many
people did that? With Ted's bookkeeping help, he managed
his business very successfully.

Her soft heart ached to think that a proud and capable
man like Gray could have a problem he'd felt compelled
to hide, managing superbly in spite of it.

Then again, she might be overreacting—jumping to
totally incorrect conclusions.

The last of the daylight was turning the paddocks to
pink and mauve as they pulled up outside the homestead.
Crickets and katydids were already singing their dusk
chorus in the trees by the creek.

Anna and Josh, freshly bathed and in their dressing
gowns and slippers, came running down the front steps to
greet Holly and Gray, while Janet hurried after them like
a fussy mother hen.

'They've been no trouble,' Janet assured Gray. 'They've
been busy in the school room for most of the day.'

'I thought they'd be playing with their puppets,' he
said.

'The puppets have had a good airing, but mostly they've
been doing their homework.'

'Homework?' Holly frowned. 'But I didn't set any homework.'

'Well, they've been beavering away on some kind of writing project for the puppet house.' Janet laughed. 'I'm definitely renaming them Shake and Speare.'

'We're going to have a puppet show after dinner,' Anna explained with great excitement. 'And there's a part for everyone.'

Out of the deep pockets of her cherry-red dressing gown, she pulled folded sheets of paper and, glowing with pride, the little girl separated three pages for Holly, three for Janet and three for Gray.

Each sheet was covered in photocopies of her best printing.

'You're Hector Owl, Daddy, and I'm Timothy Mouse and Josh—'

Holly didn't hear the rest. She was too busy watching Gray and the dawning horror in his eyes.

Her heart galloped as she looked down at the paper in her hand. Clever little Anna had written a rudimentary play script with a list of characters and lines of dialogue beside the characters' names.

It was the sort of creative writing exercise the twins had been encouraged to try at their progressive school in Manhattan, and Holly wanted to be thrilled for them. She *was* thrilled, actually, but she was also very worried about Gray.

Were her suspicions about his literacy correct? Was this his personal D-Day?

Judging by the sudden paleness of his complexion and the unhappy twist of his mouth as he stared at the paper, the answer was...

Yes.

Her heart broke for him as she watched him force a crooked smile.

'Wow,' he said. 'A play. Aren't you two clever?'

'You have to put on your growliest voice,' Josh informed him.

'I see.' Gray tapped the paper and blew out his cheeks thoughtfully. 'So have you changed much of my original story?'

'We've changed lots!' exclaimed Anna. 'See!' She pointed importantly to her script. 'You can read it all here. We've made up a whole new story, so we can have the owl and the mouse, as well as a frog and a wombat and a pig. There are parts for everyone.'

Gray looked decidedly ill.

CHAPTER NINE

GRAY looked down at the script in his hand, fighting hot panic. It was covered in Anna's childish, clever printing and, as always, he could catch a word here or there, but then the letters of all the other words blurred. He couldn't breathe. His heartbeats hammered in his ears.

I've got to get a grip. I can't lose it now.

As casually as he could manage, he said, 'But you can't have a puppet play without puppets and you don't have an owl puppet, do you? I'll have to make one before you put on the show.'

'No need, Dad,' said Josh. 'Janet's already made us an owl. She's made it out of a tea cosy.'

Gray was very familiar with the brown and yellow knitted cosy that Janet used to keep the breakfast teapot warm, and he could imagine how easily it would have converted into a perfect owl puppet.

'Your play sounds very exciting,' Holly told the children in her best kind-but-firm nanny voice. 'But, right now, your father and I need to collect our picnic things from the truck and put them away, and then we have to get cleaned up for dinner.'

Grateful for her intervention, Gray turned back to the vehicle to fetch their backpacks. To his surprise, Holly came with him.

'Organise a phone call,' she said cryptically out of the corner of her mouth.

'A phone call?'

'Yes.' Her gaze was very steady, her dark eyes huge and shining with determination. 'If one of your friends calls you straight after dinner—an important business call that you have to take in your study—you'll miss the puppet play, but the twins will get over their disappointment.'

Gray stared at her, stunned.

Holly smiled gently and placed her hand on his wrist. 'Janet and I will play puppets with Anna and Josh. We'll send them to bed happy.'

Oh, God, Holly *knew*.

She knew everything.

Gray's throat tightened on a razor-sharp knot of shame.

Holly knew. She'd guessed the weakness that hurt him so deeply he couldn't even bring himself to name it in his private thoughts.

Today he'd kissed her in a desperate bid to stop her from talking about it. Now he was in danger of being exposed in front of his children and he didn't deserve Holly's help, but she was offering him a lifeline.

'You're right,' he said, resisting an urge to sweep her into his arms. 'A phone call's a good option. Thank you.'

He spoke more gruffly than he'd meant to. Then he slammed the door on the back of the vehicle and swung his pack over one shoulder.

He couldn't look at Holly as they walked back into the homestead together. It was hard to accept that the shame he'd successfully covered up for more than twenty years was finally out in the open. Right now, he couldn't bear to see Holly's lovely eyes brimming with sympathy.

He felt like such a fraud. This evening Holly was saving

his bacon, but what would happen tomorrow and the day after that? He couldn't keep hiding the truth from his children. The fate he'd always feared had now arrived, and he had no choice but to brace himself for humiliation.

Around eight-thirty, Holly tapped on the door to Gray's study.

'Who is it?' he called cautiously.

'It's Holly.'

'Come on in. The door's not locked.'

When she pushed the door open she found him sitting at his desk in a pool of lamplight. He rose stiffly from the chair, giving the surprising impression that he'd aged in the hour and a half since dinner. He had a sad and caved-in air, as if he'd received a terrible blow.

'Are the children in bed?' he asked.

'Yes, all tucked in.'

'Are they happy?'

'As pigs in mud.' Deliberately, Holly smiled as if nothing was wrong. 'They were disappointed you couldn't join them in the fun, but they understood about the phone call.'

'Thank you.' He spoke with almost formal politeness.

She felt compelled to warn him. 'Anna and Josh are treating this evening's performance as a dress rehearsal.'

'Right.' Gray's mouth twisted in a wry attempt at a smile. 'So they still plan to have a grand performance?'

'I'm afraid so. With a full cast, including the hero, Hector Owl.'

His mouth tilted again, faintly. 'When? Tomorrow night?'

'That's what they're hoping.'

He nodded glumly and looked so unhappy Holly was moved to the edge of tears.

'Don't worry, Gray,' she said quickly. 'I can help you with this. I'm actually quite good at this sort of problem.'

He shook his head. 'I'm quite sure you're a brilliant teacher, but—'

'Before you say *but,* take a look at this.' She pulled a folded sheet of paper from the pocket of her jeans and, as she handed the sheet to him, she drew a deep breath, hoping it would calm her. She was almost as nervous as he was.

Gray unfolded the sheet and swept a brief glance down the page. His mouth tightened. 'What is this?' His blue gaze flicked to her, flinty with anger and despair.

'It's your poem, Gray. I've printed it out for you.'

'My poem?' His eyes flashed disbelief, but then he looked down at the page again.

Holly held her breath as she watched him—the formidable, proud cattleman standing in the middle of his study, with photographs of prize bulls on the wall behind him and a shelf full of silver trophies that he'd won for campdrafting.

Now, with his shoulders braced, boots planted firmly on the Oriental rug, he was frowning at the sheet of paper with deep concentration…

And then…she saw his lips begin to move as he followed the words across the page, sounding out each familiar syllable beneath his breath.

I've…crossed…harsh…country…parched…and… red…

Her throat stung to see this big, capable man reduced to small boy vulnerability. She swallowed and blinked madly, not daring to shed tears in front of him.

He continued on until he reached the bottom of the page. When he finished, he looked up, a dazed kind of hope shining in his eyes.

His throat worked and deep colour stained his cheekbones. 'I'm sorry. I should have offered you a seat.' He indicated the sofa against the wall, deep and inviting with plump vermillion and green striped cushions. 'Please, sit down, Holly.'

As she obeyed him, he returned to the chair at his desk and, almost immediately, as if he couldn't resist it, he began to read his poem again.

When he finished he looked up. 'So...how does this work? Is it like a code? If I become familiar with these words, do you think I can use them to decipher all the others?'

'That's one of the tools you can use,' Holly said. 'As for the puppets, I can easily go through the play with you, and we can rehearse your lines the way actors do. It's not exactly a three-act Shakespearean drama. Anna and Josh probably won't even notice if you ad-lib the odd line here and there.'

Gray nodded slowly, then pulled out the sheets of the play script from a drawer in his desk. A tiny spark shone in his eyes and he sent her a playful wink.

'Okay, teacher. I'm game if you're game.'

He came and sat on the sofa beside her.

It was fun—way too much fun, really. Holly loved every minute of sitting with Gray, trying to ignore the tingles his proximity caused as she read through the script with him.

It didn't take long for him to get the gist of the simple little story and his character's role, and only a little longer to learn his lines. He had an excellent, well exercised memory.

Afterwards, they sat in the late night silence, basking in a warm sense of accomplishment.

'Anna's so clever, isn't she?' Gray said, looking down at the script with bemusement.

'She's your daughter, Gray.'

'She's her mother's daughter. Chelsea was clever and creative.'

'And so are you.'

As she said this, she saw the shutters come down on his face.

'It's true,' Holly insisted. 'You're every bit as clever as Chelsea, or your children. You're missing one skill set—that's all—and I think I can help you with that.'

With a groan, he launched to his feet. Holly jumped up beside him. 'I'd be sorry to see you run away from this again.'

He sent her a sharp glance, piercing, almost venomous.

Holly stood her ground. 'You've learned your lines tonight and you'll get through the play tomorrow with flying colours. But what about all the times after that? You know there'll be more challenges.'

'I'll manage.'

'Yes, you will. You've managed very well for a long time, but you'd manage so much better if you could read and write.'

There. She'd brought the harsh truth out into the open.

A terrible sound broke from Gray as if something inside him had fractured. His face contorted with pain and Holly felt her heart stand still. The tears she'd been holding back spilled down her cheeks.

This was *so* hard for him. She had said out loud the words he couldn't bear—that he couldn't read or write.

Had she been too cruel?

She'd only spoken up because she was sure she could help him. If she was strong enough—if they were both strong enough—she could get him through this. And then he'd be free...

Savagely swiping away her tears, she reached out and touched Gray's arm.

'Why don't we just talk about it?' she said gently.

He answered with a groaning sigh.

But Holly wasn't prepared to give up. 'I'm guessing that something happened when you were little. Can you tell me?'

He shook his head. 'What's the point?'

'It could be important. I know you're intelligent and exceedingly capable, which means there's probably an emotional reason why you didn't learn to read. Have you ever talked to anyone about this?'

'No.'

'Not even with Chelsea?'

He shook his head.

Holly wasn't surprised. She'd often suspected that her cousin had fallen in love with Gray's gorgeous looks, but had been unable to meet his deeper needs. Which meant he'd carried this burden alone for too long.

'I'm no shrink,' she admitted. 'But I think talking about it might be the first step.'

'Talking? You want me to lie down on the couch and talk about my childhood?' He stared at her, jaw stubbornly jutting forward.

Holly held her breath, and waited. Then, to her relief, she saw a glimmer of a smile.

'All right, Dr O'Mara. I may as well give it a shot.'

Gray didn't actually *lie* on the couch, but they both made themselves comfortable. He poured them both a Scotch, which Holly wasn't used to drinking but, to be companionable, she sat nursing her glass.

Gray took a gulp from his glass. 'Okay—where do you think I should start?'

'Did anyone ever begin to teach you to read?'

Gray sighed. 'My mother tried.'

Holly remembered the woman she'd met at Sydney Airport and the obvious tension she'd sensed between mother and son. 'Was she living here with you at Jabiru?'

'Yes. We had the lessons—if you could call them lessons—right here in this room. I hated it,' Gray said. 'I loved my mother, of course, but I used to dread our reading sessions.'

'Why?'

'I knew they were a chore for her, and she was always impatient. I used to panic, trying too hard to please her, but then I'd be slow and she'd get frustrated, and she'd end up in tears.'

Oh, Gray. Holly hated to think of that poor little boy trying to please his difficult mother and failing dismally.

Gray downed the second half of his Scotch and set the glass aside. 'It didn't help that my mother hated living out here. She and my dad had terrible rows almost all the time. They were heading for divorce, although I didn't realise it. Then my reading—or rather my lack of it—became a huge issue during their pre-divorce wrangling. My mother blamed my father. He blamed her.'

'They argued about your reading in front of you?'

'Sometimes,' he said bleakly. 'But even when they were behind closed doors, I could still hear their raised voices. I felt so guilty. I was the cause of all their unhappiness. I knew if I could read they'd love each other again and everything would be okay. But my mother had already washed her hands of me.'

He stood and went to pour another drink, then changed his mind and came and sat beside her again. 'No point in getting sloshed over something that happened years ago.'

'You can have mine if you like.' Holly held up her

glass. 'I've only had a few sips. I'm not much of a Scotch drinker.'

He took it with a watery smile. 'Thanks.' After a sip, he said, 'You're right. I think it does help to talk about this. I've never really allowed myself to think about it.'

'I can see how the reading broke down,' she told him. 'You developed an emotional block about it.'

'My writing was just as bad. The crunch came just before my mother left Jabiru. I wanted to beg her to stay and I thought if I wrote her a letter and told her how much I loved her that of course she'd stay. No question.'

He forced a bitter laugh, but Holly could hear the terrible pain in it. She wanted to pull that hurt little boy into her arms, to hold him and comfort him.

'The letter was going to be a wonderful surprise for her,' Gray went on. 'I slipped it under her bedroom door. Worst mistake of my life. My parents had the ugliest fight over my spelling.'

Slumping back against the cushions, he closed his eyes. 'They were yelling and I heard every word. She said my letter was illegible. I was hopeless. Unteachable. A disgrace.'

Holly shuddered, but she could so easily imagine the note full of spelling mistakes. Shaky printing. Almost no punctuation. And yet it would have been a message straight from the heart of a distraught little boy. How could Gray's parents have ignored that?

'It sounds as if your mother couldn't cope,' she said. 'But surely your dad stood up for you?'

Gray shook his head. 'That was the other side of the problem. My old man never had much faith in book learnin'. That's what he called it. He hadn't had much schooling and most of his mates hadn't, either, and he reckoned they were okay. Who needed Will-bloody-Shakespeare and encyclopaedias? Books couldn't help a man to catch a wild bull, or strain fencing wire.'

Holly nodded, imagining the situation—the stubborn, uneducated cattleman married to the tense, unhappy city woman. In the next generation, history had repeated itself in Gray's marriage to Chelsea.

'Did your mother leave?' she asked.

Gray let out another hefty sigh. 'It happened a few days later. She left us and went to live in Sydney, and it wasn't long before she found a new husband. A property developer. Their son went to the best schools, and now he's a bright young investment banker.'

'And you stayed here with your father?'

He nodded. 'My education was purely practical from then on.' From beneath lowered lids, Gray sent her a lazy, lopsided smile.

Holly shivered as a wave of longing washed through her. When he looked at her like that, she could only think about snuggling up to him and running her fingers over his skin. She clenched her hands tightly to stop herself from reaching out to touch him.

'So,' she said primly, 'you didn't have a nanny, but what about School of the Air?'

Gray shook his head.

'You mean you had no schooling?'

'That's…the story, I'm afraid.'

'But how could your father get away with that? Surely there must have been someone in the Education Department asking questions about you?'

'Probably.' His shoulders shifted in a shrug. 'I think my dad made sure I was away with the mustering team whenever anyone official came snooping around asking nosy questions. He prided himself on teaching me practical skills and keeping me clear of books and schools. When

I look back, I can't help thinking he kept me away from books as a reaction to Mom leaving us.'

But that's a crime! Holly wanted to shout, but she bit down on the words. Criticising Gray's father was not going to help him now.

'By the time I was old enough to understand what a handicap I had, it was more or less too late, and by then I was also too proud and stubborn.' He gave another shrug. 'As I said, I've managed.'

'You've managed brilliantly.'

'I made sure I knew how to write my name and my address, and how to fill in basic forms. If I'd really wanted to, I might have found a way to teach myself more. But I never really needed reading in my line of work. And now—' He paused and frowned at the glass in his hands.

'I'm guessing that you'd rather Anna and Josh didn't have to know too much about your lack of schooling.'

He stared at the glass. He hadn't finished drinking it, but he set it aside. Very quietly, he said, 'I can't go on hiding it from them. And I'm sure it's too late for me to start learning now.'

'I don't think so.' Holly spoke just as softly as he had. Then, because she couldn't help herself, she leaned closer and kissed his cheek. 'In fact…I'm quite sure it's not too late.'

Their faces were only inches apart. She could see his individual eyelashes and the tiny flecks of grey floating in the blue of his irises. She felt her skin grow hot.

Her words *I'm quite sure it's not too late…* seemed to hang in the air. It was almost as if she was no longer talking about reading. Gray was looking at her with a burning intensity that stole her breath.

It would be so easy to lean closer still, to fall into his

arms and invite a repeat of their kiss. She wanted nothing more.

But somehow she found the strength to move away. She had to think clearly. She had to remember that the kiss at the gorge had not been prompted by Gray's desire for her. He'd made that quite clear. The important thing now was to remember that she only had a few weeks left in Australia and she had to at least make a start in teaching him to read.

She would never forgive herself if she didn't try.

'Actually, it's probably too late to start reading lessons tonight,' she said, keeping her eyes lowered. 'But we could certainly try for tomorrow night—once the children are in bed.'

Then she looked up, she saw the shimmering emotion in Gray's eyes. He lifted a hand, as if he was going to touch her hair. She felt a hot flame rush over her skin, then he seemed to think better of it and he let his hand fall.

'Thank you,' he said simply.

'You're welcome.'

'I mean it, Holly. Thank you so much. You're an amazing girl. You have no idea—'

'But I do,' she said. 'I have a very good idea.' She forced a small smile. 'That's why I'd really like to help you.'

He grinned, looking suddenly younger, lighter, freer. 'You've done so much for me. What can I do for you in return?'

Kiss me again? Good grief, where was her common sense? 'Maybe you could organise some riding practice?' she said quickly, grasping at straws. 'Not just for me, for the kids as well.'

'I will. First thing in the morning.'

Gray sat for ages after Holly left, looking around at the four walls of his study and replaying the memories he'd bared to her. To his surprise, the unhappy recollections were already losing their power to hurt him. It was as if talking about his memories, setting them before Holly—Exhibit A, Exhibit B—had made them real, no longer private nightmares, but clues in a crime.

At some deep level, he'd always believed that the not-reading business was his fault. He'd let Chelsea walk away from him because he'd always known that he wasn't really worthy of her. But the reality was: his mother had stuffed up teaching him to read. His father had held him back from a decent education.

Okay, his dad had taught him almost everything he knew about cattle and engines and carpentry, but the world was a big and complicated place and homespun knowledge only took a man so far.

For the first time Gray felt entitled to accept that he wasn't totally to blame for his inadequacies. Then again, it *was* his fault that he'd done nothing about the problem he'd been left with. Hell, if he'd had a physical handicap, he would have sought medical help; he certainly wouldn't have tried to cover it up.

Then again, it was true that practical skills were highly valued in the Outback. In a way his dad was right. You didn't need book-learning to ride a fleet-footed horse or to clear heavy bullocks out of the scrub, or to sell and buy cattle at an auction.

But, in the scheme of things, the Outback was a limited world and he wanted his kids to have choices he'd never had. Choices meant education.

Holly would never know how much it had cost him to admit to her that he couldn't read or write. Hell, he still flinched just saying the words 'read and write' in his head. But, thanks to her, the words no longer made him feel sick and hopeless. With her help, he was finally going to do something about it.

He felt like a man who'd been let out of jail.

He should tell Holly that some time. It would probably make her smile, and he really liked—no, he downright *loved*—to see her smile.

'Now it's Holly's turn,' Gray told his children. 'She's going to show us how a farm girl from Vermont mounts a horse.'

He'd woken them all early, declaring it was time to start riding lessons before school, and he'd brought four of his gentlest horses into the home paddock. Already, Anna and Josh were smugly sitting astride small, quiet ponies, while Gray held their reins.

Holly had hoped to get in a little riding practice without an audience, but now three pairs of eyes were watching her first attempt.

She shot them a warning frown. 'I told you it's a long time since I've been on a horse.'

'But you won't have forgotten how,' Gray assured her.

'My muscles might have forgotten.'

He grinned. 'That's defeatist talk.'

Holly knew he was probably right, and perhaps it was her attitude that brought about her problems for, no matter how hard she tried, she could *not* swing her right leg up over the saddle. After the umpteenth embarrassing try, she felt like a ninety-year-old former ballet dancer who'd insisted she could still do an arabesque.

'Here, let me help you,' Gray said, handing the reins to his children and instructing them not to move till he returned.

'I'm sure I'll get the hang of it—' Holly insisted as she began to lift her leg one more time.

Then she felt Gray's hands on her bottom. With a firm shove, he hefted her high and suddenly she was up in the air and she swung easily into the saddle.

Anna and Josh cheered.

'Thank you,' she said, but when she looked down into the smile in Gray's eyes, her breath caught. His eyes were shimmering with a special light.

Just for her.

Small fires flared in the pit of her stomach. She could still feel the warm imprint of his hands on her behind and now she was remembering the way he'd kissed her at the gorge. She was almost certain that he was remembering it, too. She'd always thought that he'd kissed her to shut her up. Now she wasn't so sure…

The atmosphere in the study that evening was different right from the start.

Gray was in high spirits after the puppet play. Anna and Josh had been thrilled with his Hector Owl rendition, which wasn't surprising considering how heartily he'd thrown himself into the role.

The children had been overexcited, actually, and they'd taken a while to settle to sleep, but all was quiet now. Janet had retired to her cottage for the night, and Holly had joined Gray in his study.

He could hardly wait to get started on the reading lessons and his eyes were shining. 'Take a look at this.'

From a drawer in his desk he produced a manila folder, letting small squares of paper flutter from it onto the desk's surface.

Holly picked up a square and turned it over to find the word 'red'.

'I recognise that printing. It's mine. Did you cut it out of your poem?'

Gray grinned. 'I photocopied the poem, then cut out all the words.' He looked incredibly proud of himself, exactly the way Anna had looked when she'd produced her play script. 'Choose any word,' he said. 'Test me to see how many I know.'

Holly hesitated. She wanted to ask if he'd had enough time to learn all these words. There were rather a lot of them, after all, but if she showed any sign of doubt, she would undermine his confidence.

'It's okay,' he said, sensing her hesitation. 'I've been practising out in the shed all afternoon.'

'Wow. That's conscientious.' She picked up a piece of paper and handed it to him.

'Dreamtime,' he said, smiling broadly. She tried another word and another and he knew them, too.

Holly grinned at him, thrilled for him, knowing how pleased he was. 'I knew you were brilliant.'

And suddenly his arms were around her and she was being squeezed against his big broad chest, and then they were dancing a crazy jig, bumping into the desk and knocking over a chair and not caring two hoots.

Breathless with laughter, they finally collapsed onto the sofa, panting and grinning stupidly. Holly was quite sure she'd never felt happier, or more uplifted and exultant.

Or more in lust.

Then Gray went very still and everything changed as the air became electrified with tension.

His tension and hers.

'Holly,' he whispered, trailing his fingers down the side of her neck to her collarbone.

She tried to reply but no sound came out. She was too aware of his body pressing against her, too aware of his arousal, and of her own desire coiling and tugging low inside her.

Heat flooded her. She struggled to ignore it. This shouldn't be happening. Wasn't she supposed to be still in love with Brandon, still pining after Brandon…?

She was super-aware of how different Gray was from her ex-boyfriend—he was a bigger, more muscular man, darker, more intense. Everything was different…the feel of his skin beneath her fingers…his breath on her neck…

And ever since he'd kissed her yesterday she'd been aching for more…

Even though he'd tried to dismiss the kiss as a mistake, she'd been yearning for the heady closeness of his lips locked with hers, of his arms about her, of his strength binding her…

She longed for his touch…couldn't bear it if he turned her away now.

'Please don't tell me this is wrong,' she whispered.

'Holly, I wouldn't dare.'

It was all the permission either of them needed. His lips grazed her cheek, then he kissed his way to her mouth… first taking her lower lip and drawing the soft flesh between his teeth in wonderfully intimate possession.

He was an expert, she realised gratefully, and already she was kissing him back. Indeed, she couldn't stop kissing him.

As she wriggled beneath him, positioning herself against his hardness, she heard his groan and, when he touched his tongue to hers, their kiss turned wild.

Moments later, they were helping each other out of their clothing.

CHAPTER TEN

THE next morning there was school and Holly was grateful for the routine of breakfast, bed-making and setting up the school room. Gray had already breakfasted and left before she and the children woke, so she didn't have to worry about catching his eye across the kitchen table.

That was a good thing. If he'd been there, she might have found herself blushing—and who could blame her after the sexy moves they'd made on each other last night?

Now she had a whole day to compose herself, and to convince herself that last night had been a celebration, but nothing more. They had both been thrilled about Gray's breakthrough, and then they'd experienced a kind of romantic movie moment, when they'd been a little carried away.

Well, okay, more than a little carried away.

Nevertheless, it was time to remind herself that Gray wasn't looking for a serious relationship. Last night had probably only happened because she was the only young woman within a hundred kilometre radius.

For her part, she'd decided that making love with Gray had been a necessary step in her post-Brandon recovery plan. A healing tonic.

At least, that was what she tried to tell herself, but as soon as she'd woken this morning she'd wanted to dwell on every amorous and blissful detail of Gray's lovemaking, wanted to savour his sweet tenderness and his breathtaking passion.

But now she had to put a lid on those memories. It was time to put these last few weeks with Gray and his children into perspective.

In a month's time—maybe less than that—a new and permanent Australian nanny would arrive, and that woman would occupy the teacher's seat in Gray's study. That woman would join in the puppet plays and that woman would, no doubt, be taken to admire the beautiful gorge. She might even go horse-riding with Gray and the children.

Holly's future lay in America—in a new city and a new school. All kinds of opportunities were bound to open up for her there. Maybe even a new man.

Why couldn't she feel happier?

'I think we should agree that last night was a one-off, don't you?'

Holly had been practising this suggestion all day and, now that she and Gray were alone in his study for another reading session, she was relieved to get it out in the open—especially as the sizzle between them was even more obvious than it had been last night.

'I mean,' she said now, feeling obliged to explain her point, 'we both know we could never have anything more than a fling, and flings are—'

'Fun?' Gray suggested with a smile that was hard to read.

'I was going to say dangerous.' Holly sat primly away from him on the sofa with her arms and her legs crossed. 'I'm your children's nanny, after all.'

'That's true,' he said, in a tone that suggested this wasn't a convincing argument.

'We have to think of Anna and Josh,' she added quickly before she tossed prudence out of the window. 'It could be disastrous if they cottoned onto any...um...liaison between us.'

'I guess you're right.' This time Gray sighed, then reached for her hand and gave it a gentle squeeze. 'Damn it. I suppose teachers are always sensible and right.'

Feeling the warm pressure of his fingers, Holly was overwhelmed by a need to throw herself into his arms. One more time.

Heavens, she was a hypocrite. Now that Gray was agreeing with her, she felt disappointed. Truth was, she'd never experienced such exciting, heart-thumping sex, hadn't known she had it in her to be so passionate.

Now, she had to forget her newly enhanced libido and she had to remember why she'd started this conversation.

'Children can't be expected to understand casual relationships. It's not healthy for them—and after everything Anna and Josh have been through—'

Gray nodded and then he frowned. 'I wish I knew what to say. Thank you sounds crass. But I have so much to thank you for, Holly.'

His smile was both sad and cute as he lifted a strand of her hair and tucked it behind her ear. 'Last night was amazing and special and unforgettable. We shouldn't look on it as a mistake.' His eyes shimmered and his throat rippled. 'We need to be friends for a long, long time.'

'Yes.' It was little more than a whisper.

'But what you're doing for my kids is more important than anything.'

Determined not to cry, she spoke without looking at

him. 'My job now is to prepare Anna and Josh for their
new nanny.'

She was relieved that Gray agreed. Really, she was, or
at least she would be once she was back home and safely
embarked on her new career.

The question of the replacement nanny came to a head
two weeks later.

The day started on a high note when the mail plane
landed on the dirt airstrip with its load of newspapers,
letters, catalogues and packages.

Like everyone else at Jabiru Creek, Holly looked forward to the weekly mail delivery. It was a major social
event and Gray, Holly and the children piled into the truck
to go down to the airstrip to chat with George, the mailman,
and any passengers he might have brought with him 'for
the ride'.

Sometimes George had time to come back to the homestead for a cuppa and a gossipy chat, but this week he
was in a hurry, with engine parts needed urgently by their
neighbours at Half Moon Station.

Holly grabbed a moment for a quick word with George
about an idea she'd had for a book exchange between the
women she'd met via School of the Air. He thought this
was a great idea and promised to spread the word.

Back in the homestead kitchen, they opened their mail.
There were the usual bills and letters to be handed over to
Ted, as well as books Holly had ordered over the Internet—
for herself, for the children, and now, discreetly, adult literacy books for Gray as well. He was making fantastic
progress.

This week there was also an unexpected package.

'What's this?' Anna cried. 'It's got your name on

it, Holly.' She gave the parcel a squeeze. 'It feels like clothes.'

'Clothes?' Holly looked up with a frown. 'I haven't ordered any clothes.'

She saw a hasty, almost smug look flash between Gray and Janet.

What was going on?

With a little shove, Anna sent the parcel sliding over the table to Holly. 'Open it,' the little girl urged with a giggle of excitement.

'I don't know if I should. It might be a mistake.' Holly gave the package a tentative squeeze. It certainly felt like clothing. She double-checked the address. It was definitely addressed to her. 'This is weird.' She checked the postmark. 'It's from Melbourne.'

'They have lovely dress shops in Melbourne,' Janet remarked, staring rather fixedly at the teapot.

'I'm sure there are very nice dress stores in Melbourne, but I didn't—'

'Oh, go on and open the thing.' Gray was almost scowling at her. At least he was trying to scowl, but his eyes betrayed an ambiguous, half-amused glint. 'It's obviously for you.'

It seemed silly to hesitate any longer. 'Can someone pass me the scissors?'

Josh was closest to the old ginger jar on the kitchen dresser, where scissors, wooden spoons and other utensils were kept. Like most boys, he wasn't interested in clothing but, after he'd delivered the scissors, he hung around Holly's chair to watch her cut through the thick tape.

Everyone in the room was watching Holly, especially Gray. Her heartbeats picked up speed.

'It's wrapped in beautiful tissue paper and looks like

it must be terribly expensive,' she said as she opened the padded envelope.

She shot a shocked look Janet's way. About ten days ago, right here in this kitchen, she and Janet had been poring over catalogues together. They'd decided to order riding gear for the twins and, once that was organised, they'd idly thumbed through the women's fashion pages and Holly had gone into a swoon over the most beautiful cocktail dress.

It had just been a bit of fun. Holly had never spent exorbitant amounts of money on her clothes. Chelsea was the one who'd been fashion mad, while Holly had lashed out on books.

'Hurry up and open it.' Josh gave Holly's elbow a nudge and she opened the tissue-wrapped parcel carefully, trying not to tear the fine pearl-grey paper.

All eyes were on her.

And, suddenly, the last layer was lifted and there it was— the beautiful red wool crepe dress from the catalogue.

Holly couldn't speak. She was stunned. She shot a questioning glance to Janet, who lifted her hands in a don't-ask-me gesture and nodded her head towards Gray.

'Do you like it?' Gray asked, frowning.

'It's gorgeous,' she could only whisper.

'Hold it up,' Anna demanded. 'We want to see it properly.'

Holly pushed her chair back so she had room to stand, then displayed the dress by holding it against her. It was divine. The wool crepe was so soft and refined, the finishing was superb and the colour was strong but not gaudy.

'That red is perfect with your dark hair,' Janet confirmed.

'It looks like it should fit you.' Gray spoke casually enough, but he was watching Holly with a breath-robbing intensity.

'It does seem to be my size,' Holly agreed, checking the label. 'But…but I don't understand.'

'It's a thank you present.' From across the table, Gray's eyes gleamed. 'From all of us.'

'Oh.'

Her spirits soared for a beat and then, just as quickly, the wind dropped out of her sails. It was silly to be suddenly upset, but it occurred to her that a thank you present was more or less the same as a farewell present. Everyone here was quite calmly preparing to wave her goodbye.

Holly, on the other hand, was finding it harder and harder to think about leaving here. She loved these people. More than ever now, Anna and Josh felt like her own children, Janet was fast becoming a close friend, and Gray—well, her feelings for him were in a league of their own. But everyone at Jabiru Creek was very dear to her.

To her horror, she was struggling not to cry. How silly. They weren't about to give her marching orders.

'Thank you,' she finally managed to say. 'Thank you so much. I've never had such a lovely dress.'

'You should try it on,' Anna urged.

'Now?'

'Wear it for us tonight,' Janet suggested. 'I'll cook something special for dinner and we'll eat it in the dining room.'

'And I'll put on a tie,' Gray added with a smiling wink.

'Wow! A party!' Anna clapped her hands. 'A new dress party.'

'I guess that's better than a farewell party.' Holly couldn't help it. The comment just slipped out.

It was met by a circle of such puzzled glances that she wondered if she was reading too much into this.

She went back to her room and hung the dress on a padded hanger in her wardrobe and decided that yes, she'd probably been jumping to conclusions about the significance of this gift. It was just a kind thought. Not a clear goodbye.

After all, there was still almost a month before she was due back in the United States.

One thing was certain: she was not wearing this elegant dress to dinner without first spending time on her grooming. She would have loved to rush out to the nearest beauty spa to be professionally made over from head to toe but, as that wasn't an option, she retired to the bathroom as soon as the children were released from the school room.

A shampoo and blow-dry, a manicure, a pedicure and a DIY leg wax—*ouch*—were all on the agenda. Holly spent ages over each task, wanting to be as close to perfect as the beautiful dress deserved.

She chose her best uplift bra and her barely-there panties and, when at last she was ready, she tried the dress on in front of the long oval mirror on her wardrobe door and she…was…

Gobsmacked.

Wow. Was the vision in the mirror really her?

She turned left and right, spun around to check out the back view. The dress was divinely cut with a deep V neckline and had no sleeves and an elegant side tie. The colour made her complexion glow and the fitted bodice and slim skirt gave her more noticeable curves and a glamour she'd never dreamed of. Even her hair looked more glamorous than usual—extra glossy and dark and bouncy.

Thrills of excitement tingled all over her. What would Gray think of his lovely gift now?

When Gray came home that evening he sensed a general air of excitement in the homestead. Delicious aromas wafted from the kitchen and from the dining room there came the tinkle of silver and glassware as Janet set the table with the best dinnerware. From the children's bathroom came the sound of taps running.

In his bedroom, he was surprised to discover that his housekeeper had taken the trouble to lay out clothes for him—well pressed moleskin trousers, a crisp pale blue shirt and his best navy-blue and silver tie.

It was clear Janet wanted this evening to be a big success. She was very fond of Holly and she'd taken a great delight in helping him to think of the right gift for her.

'That dress is perfect,' Janet had said. 'It's something Holly would never think to buy for herself.'

Gray had been worried that Holly wouldn't like something so...so dressy. He'd only ever seen her in the simplest of T-shirts and jeans. Her taste in clothes was almost the opposite of Chelsea's. His former wife had always wanted her clothing to be that little bit different from everyone else's, with one shoulder bared, or keyholes cut in the back, or frills where you least expected them.

Holly's simple styles suited her calm, warm spirit—the spirit and sense for which he was so increasingly grateful. Of course she'd been right to stop their affair before it had barely started.

It nearly drove him crazy to spend each evening working with her on his reading instead of making slow, languorous love to her. But he was grateful—or, rather, he was *amazed* at the progress he'd made. With Holly, reading had become an exciting challenge instead of a black art to be feared.

He'd wanted to thank her and Janet had convinced him that the dress was the answer.

'Holly spent ages looking at it in the catalogue,' Janet had assured him. 'And it's not frilly or fancy. It's a classic look. She'll knock your eyes out when you see her in it. Just you wait and see.'

At the time he'd almost imagined that his housekeeper was trying to matchmake, but why would she bother? She knew as well as he did that Holly would be gone in a matter of weeks. Besides, Janet had witnessed the disaster he'd made of his marriage.

He was also surprised that Janet had pushed for this dinner party. When he'd ordered the knockout dress, he'd never expected that Holly would actually parade around in it here at Jabiru Creek. He'd only ever imagined her wearing it when she was back in America.

He could easily picture her at a cocktail party—somewhere flash with marble floors and fountains and a string quartet playing beneath potted palms. She'd sip a Martini and converse with some handsome Ivy League guy about Tolstoy and Beethoven and quantum physics.

But, if Gray was honest, he should admit that deep down he also hoped that wearing the dress would prompt Holly to remember him. And his kids, of course. And the time she'd spent here.

Would she miss them as much as they were going to miss her?

Hell. Alarmed by how suddenly downbeat he felt, Gray hurried through to his bathroom to shave with extra care.

'Wow, you look awesome, Daddy!'

Anna was the first to greet Gray when he arrived in the kitchen, dressed and ready for dinner.

'You look pretty swish, too,' he said, as his daughter performed a pirouette in her green plaid party dress. 'And so do you, Josh.'

Josh, in jeans and a button-down shirt, was more interested in playing with the puppies.

Janet was busy at the stove and she was wearing an apron over her best black dress and turquoise beads, and

Ted was there, too, standing in the corner, looking scrubbed and smart with his damp hair carefully combed over his bald patch.

'Don't you get paw marks on your shirt,' Janet told Josh, then she let her eyes run over Gray and gave him a nod of approval.

'Thanks for ironing these,' he said.

'I didn't want you slinging a tie on over a crumpled old work shirt and jeans.'

He grinned. 'You know me too well.' Taking a step towards the stove, he sniffed. 'Dinner smells great. What is it? Roast beef?'

'Roast rib of beef with Yorkshire pudding.'

'And your special gravy and horseradish sauce?'

'Of course.'

'Fantastic. I could eat a horse and chase the rider.'

'Daddy!' cried Anna, shocked.

Gray laughed and tickled her tummy. 'Where's Holly?'

'Still getting ready.' His daughter pulled a face. 'She's been getting ready for hours an' hours.'

'Maybe she wants to make a grand entry,' suggested Janet.

Gray shook his head. 'That's not Holly's style.'

Janet turned from the stove. 'Well...everything's more or less ready here. Why don't you pop along to Holly's room to let her know?'

Something like a bolt of lightning ripped through Gray. Going to Holly's bedroom was not a great idea, not with all the fantasies he fought off on a daily basis. He almost suggested that Anna should go to fetch Holly, but then...

His curiosity overpowered him. He was dead anxious to see her all dressed up.

Ridiculously, his throat was dry and his palms clammy

as he walked down the hallway and tapped on her door. 'Dinner's almost ready,' he called.

The door opened and Holly peeped out, and the top half of her, which was all Gray could see, looked amazingly beautiful. Holly was always pretty, but tonight she'd done something special with her hair, and with her make-up.

He'd never dreamed that eye shadow and mascara and lipstick could make such a dramatic difference. Combined with the dress, the whole effect was breathtaking.

'Wow,' he whispered.

Holly rolled her eyes. 'But, Houston, we have a problem.'

'A problem?' What on earth could it be?

Of course, he'd still only seen the top half of her, but she looked sensational. 'Is there something wrong with the dress?'

Holly shook her head. 'The dress is perfect. *However*—' She gave a sheepish smile as she opened the door fully. 'Ta-da!'

The dress *was* perfect. Holly was perfect. She looked like a princess, a movie star, a fashion model. Except...

Gray's eyes travelled down to her feet.

'Not a good look, is it?' she said with an embarrassed smile.

She was wearing sneakers.

'I didn't bring anything with heels, Gray. I was coming to the Outback, you know, so I brought sneakers and walking boots.'

He felt an urge to laugh, but Holly looked as if she might tip either way—into hysterical laughter or into tears.

'It's my fault,' he said quickly. 'I should have thought to order glass slippers.'

And then, because it was the most natural thing in the world to do, he opened his arms to her.

Her hair was silky and fragrant, her skin deliciously scented, and her body felt sensational beneath the soft fabric of the dress. In a New York second, Gray was overwhelmed with the need he'd been battling since their night together.

Unfortunately, what he had in mind would almost certainly mess up Holly's perfect make-up. Her lipstick and mascara would end up all over his shirt. And then...for sure, his shirt and her dress would have to go...and...

And he dropped his hands before he weakened.

'I think these shoes are perfect for tonight,' he murmured against her ear. 'Everyone's going to love how you look.'

Perhaps it was best that Holly wasn't wearing high heels. Gray's lovely embrace had thrown her completely off balance and her legs were dangerously wobbly as they went down the hallway to the kitchen.

He'd awoken every memory of their one night together—the scent of his skin, the hardness of his body, the daring intimacy of his touch and the incredible fireworks.

Fortunately, by the time they joined the others, she'd taken enough deep, slow breaths that she was calmer. More or less.

And the sneakers provided a welcome distraction. They were greeted by smiles of sympathy, and everyone was gratifyingly complimentary about the dress. Holly was truly made to feel like the guest of honour.

The meal was superb. Holly had never eaten golden, sumptuous Yorkshire pudding with roast beef. It was delicious, and it was such fun for everyone to be all dressed up and to eat in the dining room. They were in high spirits and, even though the conversation was mostly about puppies, or the horse-riding lessons the children were about to begin, no one minded. Best of all, Holly's feet were hidden under the table for most of the evening.

Throughout the meal she was super-aware of Gray. Their glances kept colliding and, each time, tingles broke out on her skin. The warmth in his eyes seemed to suggest that he was remembering all the things they were supposed to be forgetting.

Every time she caught him looking at her, her body would flash and she'd remember the thrill of his arms wrapped around her and the seductive scent of his after-shave, his powerful body burning against hers.

It was something of a relief, at the end of the meal, to jump up and help Janet to clear the table.

Of course, Janet tried to protest. 'You don't have to help, Holly.'

'I do. You've been slaving all day, and I'm very grateful. But now I'm going to wash up while Gray tells the children a bedtime story. No arguments, please, Janet. You go off and put your feet up and read your new magazine.'

Holly didn't check to see how Gray felt about this arrangement. This evening, she didn't want to be involved in helping him with the children. She was happy to stay in the kitchen. Really. It was a matter of self-preservation.

'You're a living treasure,' Janet told her fondly. 'I must admit my bunions are killing me. But at least put an apron on.' She unhooked a long white wraparound apron from the back of the kitchen door.

Holly was still wearing this when Gray came back into the kitchen half an hour later, just as she finished scouring the last baking dish.

Of course she looked totally unglamorous now, wrapped in the voluminous apron, with her hands in rubber gloves, her bare ankles showing and her feet in sneakers. But perhaps it was just as well, she thought. She'd had a lovely evening, and the dress had been fabulously exciting, but it was time to come back to earth.

Gray had taken off his tie and loosened his shirt collar, but nothing could dim his gorgeousness.

'You really are Cinderella tonight,' he said. 'Home from the ball and straight into the kitchen.'

Holly snapped off the rubber gloves and smiled. 'I don't mind. It's the least I could do after Janet cooked such a fabulous meal. That roast was so tasty and the lemon syllabub was divine.'

Reaching behind her, she untied the apron strings, but she felt strangely self-conscious. With the red dress about to be revealed once more, and Gray's intense gaze fixed on her, removing the apron felt as risqué as a striptease.

She concentrated on *not* blushing as she hung the apron on its hook behind the door.

'I think that dress might be the wisest purchase I've ever made,' Gray said, watching her from behind.

Holly concentrated harder on remaining calm. 'It really was very kind of you to buy me something so beautiful.' Slowly she turned around, only to find his blue eyes watching her with heartbreaking attention.

She dropped her gaze to her sneakers. Surely they would sober her.

Gray said, 'You're the one who's been kind, Holly. You've given up your summer holiday to help the children, and now you're helping me as well—'

'It hasn't felt like I've given up anything. I love Anna and Josh and—' Holly bit down on her lower lip before she said anything dangerous that she'd regret. 'And I've had so many wonderful new experiences.'

She looked down at her hands. It had been a stroke of luck that she'd brought red nail varnish with her, especially as the colour matched the dress perfectly. But now, in the homestead kitchen, the bright nails looked citified and out of place.

Forcing a laugh, she said, 'Listen to us. We're talking as if I'm leaving already, when I still have weeks to go.'

'Yes,' Gray said, but he made an uncomfortable throat clearing sound. 'That's something I wanted to speak to you about.'

Holly felt suddenly ill. Reaching behind her, she grabbed the edge of the sink for support. 'Do you want me to leave earlier?'

'No, no. No way. You're welcome to stay as long as you like.' He let out a heavy sigh. 'But it's time I sent off the ads for the new nanny, and I was hoping you could help me with the wording.'

'Oh, yes, of course.'

It was ridiculous to feel so abruptly miserable. She knew that Gray wasn't going to take one look at her in the red dress and suddenly change his mind about never wanting another wife.

Fortunately, he'd never know that, despite her protests that they mustn't get too close and that she had an all-important job to return to, she'd still foolishly fallen in love with him.

'Of course,' she said quickly. 'I'd be happy to help you work up an ad.'

She had to keep busy—busy and businesslike.

'When do you want to start? Now? Why don't we do it here in the kitchen? There's pen and paper right here in the dresser.'

Holly was gabbling, talking to fill in gaps. Gaps were dangerous—they left room for tears.

Without waiting to gauge Gray's reaction, she retrieved the pen and paper and sat down at the kitchen table.

Gray moved more slowly, taking his time to stroll around

the table and sit opposite her, leaning back in his chair, long legs stretched beneath the table.

Not wanting to see the expression in his eyes, Holly kept her gaze on the page and, when he was seated, she spoke in her most businesslike voice. 'Right. Let's see what you'll need. I imagine you'll want someone over eighteen years of age?'

When he didn't answer immediately, she shot him a sharp look. 'You want an adult to look after your children, don't you, Gray?'

'Yes,' he said, frowning and looking uncomfortable. 'Yes, sure.'

Holly began to make a list. 'And someone who enjoys and values working with children?'

Gray nodded.

She made another note. 'With a first aid certificate?'

'I…I guess that would be handy. Mostly, I want a good teacher.'

'You'd be unlikely to attract a person with teaching qualifications, but you should aim for someone who can provide stimulating activities for the children.'

'That's right.'

Oh, God. This was killing her. 'I'm sure you'd prefer someone who can produce a variety of age appropriate activities that encourage the development of life skills.'

Gray blinked. 'That sounds good.'

'And you'd want to be able to check this person's references.'

He nodded unhappily.

'What about public liability insurance?'

'We'd need to sort out something. I already have employee insurance.' Letting out a sigh, Gray reached for the salt and pepper shakers that had been left in the middle of the table and began to move them about like chess pieces.

Under the table, Holly squeezed her left fist tightly, letting her fingernails dig into her palm. The more it hurt, the better—anything to distract her from getting too emotional. 'I think this list covers the most important requirements,' she said. 'Can you think of anything else?'

'No.'

'If you tell me which newspapers you'd like to advertise in—'

'I'll get Ted to give you a list of them in the morning. And...er...I think there are sites on the Internet as well.'

'Yes, there are bound to be.'

'Ted will know.'

'Great.' Holly noted: *Internet—ask Ted*. And she pressed so hard she made a hole in the paper. She set the pen down and rubbed her arms. Now that this discussion was over, she felt a chill, as if she was coming down with something.

'I guess we won't bother with the reading tonight,' Gray said.

'That might be best.' Again, she kept her eyes on the page. 'It's been a big day. You could always read one of your new books in—' her cheeks burned '—in...bed.'

'Now that's a novel idea.'

Keep busy...

Holly rubbed at her eyes as if she were sleepy, but mostly she wanted to make sure there were no tears. Then she tore the page with her list from the notepad and got up to put the pad and pen away in the drawer. Behind her, she heard the scrape of Gray's chair on the timber floorboards.

She realised she was shaking from the effort of holding herself together. What an idiot she was. She couldn't fall apart now just because they'd drawn up an ad for her replacement. She'd always known this was going to happen. It was what she'd planned right from the start when Gray first asked her to help him out. How crazy to feel so upset. Anyone would think she'd just signed her own death warrant.

Turning back to the table, she reached for the list, but she still couldn't bring herself to look at Gray, even though he was now standing quite close to her.

She heard his heavy sigh, felt it reverberate all the way through her. What did he have to sigh about?

'I wish it could be you,' he said softly.

Holly froze.

'I know it's selfish,' he said, still in that same soft, low voice. 'But I wish we didn't have to find a new nanny.'

She allowed herself to look at him then. His eyes were extra-shiny and his mouth tight as if he, too, were holding his emotions in. He sent her a quarter smile and his shoulders lifted in a shrug. 'Where are we going to find another Holly?'

Her heartbeats thundered in her ears. Wild, extravagant hope lifted her like a high wind. She struggled to ignore it. 'I'm replaceable.'

'No, you're not.'

She gasped, had to grip the back of the chair. 'Are you saying that you want me to stay?'

'I know you can't stay. You're lined up for a fabulous new career.'

'But if you really needed me—'

His eyes widened. 'You'd stay?'

'I...I might.'

Had she really said that? Had she deliberately put herself out on a limb? Was she out of her mind?

Gray's throat worked. 'It would be perfect, wouldn't it? The kids love you. You're so good for them, Holly.' His words flowed freely enough, but he was standing to attention as if he were facing a court martial.

Holly waited for him to go on, waited for him to tell her that it wasn't only his children who needed her.

Please, please let him need me, too.

Perhaps now was the time to admit that she'd been falling steadily in love with him since she'd arrived at Jabiru. They could both admit that their night together and the closeness they'd shared on so many levels had grown into something deeper—something lasting and wonderful.

As they stood in the middle of the kitchen, Holly felt the Outback night close in around them. The only sound was the ticking of the old-fashioned clock on the wall beside the dresser. She could see the baking dishes on the drainer, shiny and silver after her conscientious scouring.

She saw Gray's hands clench and unclench. Remembered the way those strong hands had held her this evening, remembered the burning need she'd sensed in him.

Say something, Gray. I won't stay unless you want me, so just tell me the truth about how you feel. Let me off the hook, or reel me in, but don't leave me dangling.

When he didn't speak up, Holly knew she had to say something or scream.

'What about you?' Her voice sounded impossibly loud, bouncing off the walls. Then, in a more moderate tone, she asked, 'Do you want me to stay?'

CHAPTER ELEVEN

Do you want me to stay?

Gray bit back a groan of frustration. Of course he wanted Holly to stay, but how could he ask that of her?

It meant asking her to give up *everything*—her job, her home, her country. It meant asking her to commit to *his* lifestyle, *his* family, *his* country. And it meant taking their relationship to a whole new level, a committed level.

He'd vowed he'd never take that risk again.

Chelsea had quickly come to resent this place, just as his mother had. They'd been miserable here. He couldn't bear to make Holly unhappy.

Okay, it was true that she seemed to like the Outback. And if he'd been looking for a wife and had made a wish list of qualities he needed, Holly would score a tick in every box.

She was fun to be with. She fitted into Jabiru as if she'd been raised in the Outback. His kids adored her. Janet and Ted adored her.

And he owed her so much. She'd lifted such a burden from him, and she'd shown him that his future was not restricted by his past. But beyond all that she was so sweet and sexy and she was—*Holly*.

She'd wound her way around his heart. He wanted her—wanted her kisses, her warm sexy body. Tonight, seeing her in the red dress and keeping his distance had been torture.

His imagination kept playing scenes in his head of peeling the lovely red dress from her, slowly, slowly… And, as each inch of her soft, silky skin was revealed, he'd shower her with kisses until they were both almost blind with wanting, and then he would make love to her. Tenderly or passionately.

Her wish would be his command.

But he couldn't indulge his selfish fantasies. He had to be practical and clear-headed, had to remember that where women were concerned he'd fooled himself too many times. Holly was an educated city woman—like his mother and Chelsea. Eventually, her enjoyment of his isolated lifestyle would begin to pall and she'd long for her old life.

He had to be strong, and his task was painfully clear. He had no right to keep Holly here. He had to set her free. Now. Tonight. He had to send her back to the brilliant career and the secure future that awaited her in America.

Hands plunged in his pockets to stop himself from weakening and touching her, he gave her the only possible answer. 'I can't ask you to stay, Holly.'

Her head jerked up and she opened her mouth as if she was about to speak, but he held up his hand.

Now that he'd started, he had to get this out.

'I know my children are very important to you, and I know you'll miss them and they'll sure as anything miss you. But I'll do my best for them, Holly. You've shown us the way.'

He had to pause to swallow the brick that had wedged in his throat. 'I…I think we'll be okay from now on. We'll always be incredibly grateful to you.'

Holly's lips trembled and Gray felt his courage failing. 'You have a wonderful job to go back to,' he said quickly, before he changed his mind. 'A great life in America. You know I couldn't possibly ask you to give that up.'

She stood very still, not meeting his gaze, with her arms wrapped over her stomach as if she were nursing an ache.

'You have your wonderful family there, too,' he added. 'And I know how important your new job is. I've never seen anyone as excited as you were when you got that phone call at JFK. Your face lit up and you punched the air like you'd won a gold medal.'

Her eyes widened with surprise, as if he'd reminded her of something she'd forgotten.

'You need to go home, Holly.'

'You want me to go.' It was a statement rather than a question.

'I don't want you to be trapped here.'

Her intelligent gaze narrowed and for a moment he thought she was going to debate this final point, but then her mouth twisted into a grotesque attempt at a smile. She snatched up the piece of paper with the list she'd made for the ad, turned and almost ran from the room.

Gray watched her red dress and sneakers disappear and his heart was as heavy as a stone.

Holly reached her room without crying, but she was trembling all over. In all her life, she'd never felt so filled with despair. Worse, she wasn't even sure how she'd reached this point.

Until this evening, she hadn't realised how very badly she wanted to stay at Jabiru. Now she knew she wanted it so desperately she felt as if her happiness depended on staying here. But she could only stay if Gray felt as strongly about her as she felt about him. Tonight, he'd only talked about his children's needs.

Couldn't he guess she needed him?

She loved him.

Oh, help. That was the truth of it, although she had no idea when it had happened. Was it tonight when Gray had held her? Or at the point when she'd picked up the pen and paper to make the fateful list? Or had it started at the gorge?

Perhaps she'd been changing from the moment Gray had walked into the apartment in New York?

Oh, God, why hadn't she been more careful? She'd known all along that Gray would never risk a second marriage—especially to another American—and if he'd asked her to stay he would have felt obliged to marry her.

How could she let this happen to her again—this cruel, unbearable pain? This cold ache in her heart was so much worse than after the break-up with Brandon. When she left Jabiru she would leave part of her soul behind.

It was ages before she rose from the bed and super, super-carefully took off the lovely red dress and hung it back on its hanger. Then she changed into her pyjamas and went through to the bathroom to take off her make-up, telling herself that the routine would help.

It didn't.

When she climbed into bed and opened the book on her nightstand, she knew she had no hope of reading herself to sleep. She lay there, replaying every painful word of the night's terrible conversation.

When she finally turned out the lamp, she buried her face in her pillow and let her tears fall...

'You're so comfortable and capable with your children now,' Holly told Gray several evenings later. 'Those riding lessons have made such a difference. They're proper little

Outback kids now and you're going to manage just fine on your own.'

'I don't think I'm ready to fly solo yet.'

'Of course you are,' she said with necessary briskness. 'You've made great strides with the reading, and it's just a matter of practice now. You should read to Anna and Josh. They'll love it.'

The suggestion seemed to please him and he grinned, looking unbearably cute, like Josh. 'I have to admit I feel as if a huge burden has rolled off my shoulders.'

'I'm glad.' Ignoring the sudden nervous tumble in her stomach, she said, 'Actually, as things have turned out, you'll have to manage on your own quite soon.'

Gray frowned. 'How have things turned out? What do you mean?'

'I've had an email from the principal at my new school and she'd like me to start work earlier than we'd originally planned.'

He stared at her, shocked. Then his blue eyes narrowed suspiciously, as if he sensed something wasn't quite right about her claim.

The tumbling in Holly's stomach intensified. Could Gray guess that she'd engineered this new development?

She'd felt so despairing and heartbroken that she'd had to do something. Staying at Jabiru Creek had become the worst form of self-torture. Each bird call, each sunset, each family meal, each evening session alone with Gray reminded her of everything she was losing. In desperation, she'd written to the principal, advising that she was available to start sooner, if it suited them.

'What's the rush?' Gray asked, so quietly Holly could only just hear him.

'A benefactor has died and left a large sum of money to the school library, so they'd like me to start early, buying in new books for the new school year.' She flashed a falsely bright smile. 'A spending spree. Lucky me.'

He sank back in his chair, his expression gratifyingly sombre, but Holly no longer fooled herself that his gloominess was of any special significance. Her early departure would be an inconvenience, but Gray would manage. Anna and Josh would manage, too. They had a father who loved them, who would do anything for them.

The advertisement for the new nanny had been sent to several newspapers and Internet sites, so that ball was rolling. Until the nanny arrived, Janet could be taught how to set up the School of the Air each morning and the teacher would take it from there. Meanwhile, for Holly, leaving early had become an increasing necessity, a sanity saver.

'When do you have to leave here?'

'I thought I'd get a lift on the next mail plane.'

Shock flared in Gray's eyes. 'But that's only three days away.'

'Yes.'

He launched to his feet, ploughed a frantic hand through his hair. 'What about the children? They'll get such a shock.'

'Not really. They've known all along that I was eventually leaving and I've already been preparing them for their new nanny.'

He came to an abrupt halt with his hands sunk in his pockets, his cheeks leached of colour. 'They'll still be shocked. When will you tell them?'

'I was hoping we could both tell them together, tomorrow morning.'

This was met by stormy silence.

'You'll do that, won't you, Gray? You'll back me up?'

It was ages before he answered. But, to her relief, he finally nodded, said very quietly, 'Yes, of course.'

* * *

The only good thing about the next three days was that they were incredibly busy. Suddenly there was so much for Holly to organise—flights home, a hotel booking in Sydney, detailed notes for the new nanny and farewell emails to all the Outback mothers, teachers and governesses she'd met via School of the Air.

She spent as much time as she could with Anna and Josh, and of course there were weepy moments and lots of questions and reassuring hugs.

'You'll come back to us, won't you?'

Holly couldn't answer this. 'I'll see you when your daddy brings you to America to your grandma and grandpa,' she said instead.

She set them up with email accounts, so they could write to her when she was back in the US.

There were no more reading lessons with Gray. The evenings were taken up with farewell activities. Janet insisted on a party and she invited everyone on the property, including the ringers. Holly really liked these easy-going, laconic men and partying with them reminded her of how much she was going to miss their dry jokes and colourful stories about mustering and droving.

On the last night Gray made a campfire down on the riverbank and he roasted freshwater crayfish that he'd caught in the river that afternoon. They ate out under the stars and the food was delicious, the evening magical. The children danced their own version of an Aboriginal corroboree around the fire and Gray told another Hector Owl story. Holly had no idea how she held back the tears.

The actual farewell the next morning was the worst moment, of course. No one—not even Gray—could pretend to be cheerful, and down at the airstrip, the children clung to Holly, tears flowing.

'I love you, Holly,' Josh whispered.

'I love you, too, darling.'

Anna cried. 'I don't want you to go.'

'I know, but you have Daddy now, honey. And you remember what we said? You're going to be brave, aren't
you?'

Holly was sure she could actually feel her heart breaking. These gorgeous children had lost their mother and
now they were losing her. She wasn't going to be like her
own mom who'd married a lonely widower to become his
cherished wife and his children's dearly loved stepmom.

She was flying out of their lives.

Janet was too grim-lipped to speak. She gave Holly a
fierce, silent hug.

But it was the bleak look in Gray's eyes that almost burst
Holly's floodgates.

'All the best with the new job,' he said gruffly, hugging her close so that she felt his heart thundering before
he stepped quickly away. 'I hope that school knows how
lucky they are to have you.'

By a minor miracle Holly managed not to cry, but the
worst was yet to come—climbing into the tiny plane and
taking off, watching the homestead and the outhouses
and the tiny figures beside the airstrip growing smaller and
smaller until they were no more than dots...

The pilot sent her a sympathetic smile. 'You'll be back,'
he said.

Holly shook her head. She would write emails and letters
and make phone calls to Anna and Josh, and she would see
them whenever they came to the States, but she wouldn't
come back to Jabiru Creek.

She couldn't bear to be received as a visitor, an outsider,
in the place where she'd left a huge chunk of her heart.

* * *

They were asleep at last.

Gray held his breath as he closed the story book and backed out of the children's room.

Contrary to Holly's predictions, Anna and Josh had reacted rather badly to her departure and he expected them to wake again at any moment. For now, thank heavens, they were sleeping like baby angels.

He tiptoed down the hall to his study, steeling himself for the empty space on the sofa. Even so, Holly's absence hit him like an icepick in the chest.

He'd done the right thing by letting her go, but he couldn't believe that doing the right thing could feel so bottom-of-the-pit bad.

How amazing that one girl had made such a difference in the lives of all of them here. Everyone at Jabiru loved Holly. They'd all been cheered by her sunshiny personality. They'd respected her knowledge and skills, and they'd appreciated her genuine interest and desire to help. With her latest book-swapping scheme, she'd even begun spreading the goodwill further to women in outlying properties.

Gray didn't dare—or, rather, couldn't bear to list his private reasons for missing Holly.

He *might* have felt better about waving her off if he'd been confident that she was happy to go. But that was the killer, the worry eating away at him now like a worm in an apple—Holly had been a different girl these past few days.

She'd put on a brave face, smiling her way through all the farewell activities but, although she'd laughed and said how wonderful it all was to have so many great memories to take home, Gray had been watching her closely and he'd seen her frightening fragility. He'd seen the tremble in her smile and the new cautiousness, as if she was scared she might crack like an eggshell unless she was very, very careful.

He'd been so sure he was doing the right thing in sending her away, but now he felt sick and uncertain. And bloody lonely.

'You're a sight for sore eyes,' Janet remarked the next morning when Gray came into the kitchen, yawning.

'Anna had a nightmare last night,' he said, rubbing a hand over his unshaven jaw. 'I took her in to sleep with me, and then I couldn't get back to sleep.'

Janet paused in the process of stirring scrambled eggs. 'That's the first nightmare Anna's had for ages, isn't it?'

He nodded as he poured himself a mug of tea.

'Gray, you know what's caused it, don't you?'

'I guess she might be missing Holly.'

His housekeeper shot him a look that made it clear she considered him one sandwich short of a picnic. 'Of course the poor little lamb is missing Holly.' Turning the gas beneath the saucepan down, Janet came over to him and lowered her voice. 'Where are the children now?'

'They're still getting dressed. They slept in. Why?'

'I've got something to say to you. Unfortunately, I had to wait till Holly was gone before I thought you'd be ready to listen.'

His housekeeper studied him, and then she nodded smugly. 'You're in a bad way, aren't you? Can't sleep, face like a dropped meat pie.'

He began to make excuses. 'But Holly was—'

'You've realised you made a big mistake, letting Holly go.'

Gray almost denied this, but what was the point? 'I had to.'

'Forgive me for saying this, Gray, but that's rubbish.

That wonderful girl loved living here, and she was perfect for Jabiru in every way. If you think she's cut from the same cloth as your former wife, then you're thicker than two short planks.' Janet leaned closer. 'And the really terrible thing is Holly *loves* you, Gray. You must know she's mad about you. She loves all of us, bless her tender heart. She loves this place. But even a blind man could see how she feels about you.'

The kitchen swam before Gray. His throat stung. 'But her job—'

'Do you really think Holly would care two hoots for that job if she thought she could be here with you?'

He had to set his mug of tea down before it slipped from his shaking fingers.

'Have I been a coward, Janet?'

'Lord love you, no. You're just a man, after all.' Picking up a corner of her apron, Janet dabbed at her eyes. 'And I understand you're scared you'll be hurt again.'

'I'm not, actually. Not with Holly. It's *her* happiness I'm worried about.'

'Then you should stop worrying right now and do something about it. If you let Holly get all the way back to America, I might never forgive you.'

'But she's already on her way home.'

Janet shook her head. 'She has a two-night stopover in Sydney. Thought she might as well see a little more of Australia before she leaves.'

'Two nights.' Gray's heart swooped high, then took a dive. 'But she only has one night left. How the hell can I get to Sydney by tonight?'

Janet smiled and patted his cheek. 'Where there's a will there's nearly always a way.'

* * *

Sydney was a beautiful city. Holly woke to a sunny and dazzling winter's day—and where better to spend it than out on the Harbour?

She walked to Circular Quay and took a ferry ride, cruising beneath the famous coat-hanger bridge and past the dramatic sails of the Opera House, stopping at a five star seafood restaurant right on the sparkling waterfront.

She tried to enjoy herself. Honestly. But it wasn't easy to have fun when her senses were completely numb.

This stopover in Sydney was so different from last time, when she'd first arrived here with Gray and the children, all excited about their new adventure. It felt like a lifetime ago. Was it really only a month?

In the evening, she forced herself to go out again. She'd bought a pair of snappy high heels to wear with the red dress. Why waste it?

After a toss-up between a musical, a play or a movie, she opted for the play because one of her favourite actresses was in the leading role. It was rather embarrassing, though. She cried rather noisy buckets in the third act—which was all very tragic—and people around her stared.

She managed a little make-up repair in the Ladies room and then treated herself to coffee and dessert at a trendy little wine bar. Normally, a chocolate soufflé would lift her spirits, no matter how low they'd been.

Not tonight.

Gray paced the hallway outside Holly's hotel room, his stomach bunching with nerves. It was past eleven and she still wasn't back. How much longer could he wait before he was accused by a hotel employee of stalking?

Everything had been going his way until now. It was quite amazing the way fate had smiled on him this morning when he'd rung an old mate, a charter pilot, on the off chance. Luckily, Jack had been willing to juggle schedules just to get Gray to Sydney on time, and Janet had been able to tell him where Holly was staying.

The only spanner in the works was Holly, who was clearly spending a night on the town.

Gray patted his jacket pocket and felt for the small rectangular envelope, and the knots in his stomach pulled tighter than fencing wire. A hard lump filled his throat. Could he do this?

He'd left messages on Holly's phone, but if she got back very late there was every chance that she wouldn't bother to check them.

Could he follow through with his alternative? Could he risk the pain that had haunted him all his life and leave this note under her door?

Memories crowded in—awful, sickening memories of the one other time he'd tried such a desperate measure—his plea to his mother to stop her from leaving Jabiru.

The stress of repeating history brought him out in a cold sweat. This time he had everything to lose.

And everything to gain.

His hand was shaking as he took the envelope from his pocket. It was such a small piece of paper, so few words. Such a simple task to slide the note through the narrow crack below the door. Such a small window of opportunity in which to convince Holly.

As he knelt in the empty hallway, his mind flashed an image of a heartbroken boy, trembling with hope as he slipped a note beneath his mother's door.

Was he mad to try this again?

After her coffee and dessert, Holly wandered back to her hotel but she felt lonelier than ever. The streets were *full* of couples—couples holding hands and laughing, couples with their arms around each other, couples kissing in shadowy doorways.

It was a relief to reach her hotel. The girl at the front desk sent her a smile when she came in, but Holly thought she saw sympathy in the girl's eyes, as if she was sorry for her—all dressed up and on her own. She hurried into the elevator and whizzed up to the nineteenth floor.

As the elevator doors opened and she stepped out into the carpeted hallway, she saw her reflection in a gilt-edged mirror hanging above an elaborate flower arrangement.

Her red dress looked as gorgeous as ever. In fact it looked even better now—she'd lost weight in the last week and she'd acquired cheekbones and a tragic air. Like a heroine in a sad love story.

Ha, ha. Not funny.

She continued down the hall to her room, slotted the key in the lock, heard its click and the door swung silently open. So much for her last night in Australia.

CHAPTER TWELVE

THERE was a white envelope lying on the carpet just inside the door. Holly saw it, but she knew it would be her bill and she was too weary and despondent to worry about it now. Stepping over it, she told herself she would deal with it first thing in the morning when she checked out.

She went through to the luxurious bathroom with its gorgeous plunge bath and gold taps and rows of pretty little bottles. A warm bath with fragrant oils might help her to sleep.

Sitting on the edge of the bath, she started the water running and unscrewed the lid on one of the bottles. She poured the liquid, inhaling the scents of jasmine and rose but, as she watched it swirl then foam and turn into bubbles, something tugged at a corner of her mind.

Something about that white envelope—

Perhaps she should take another look at it.

Leaving the bath running, she went back to the little entrance hallway. Her name was on the front of the envelope and it was handwritten, or rather printed in an unskilled hand. Picking it up, she felt a nervous flurry in her chest. Then shivers ran down her arms.

Her heart began to race.

Stop it. Calm down.

It wasn't a hotel bill. It was the last thing Holly had

expected—something she'd never thought she'd see in this lifetime—a note handwritten in familiar shaky printing. Her legs were so weak she had to lean against the wall as she read it.

The message was perfectly simple.

Please stay. I love you. G xxxxxxxxx.

A sob broke from her and her hand flew to her mouth. Her vision blurred and her heart pounded like a marching band.

She could scarcely see the note for her tears. Her mind was a whirlpool of disconnected thoughts. How had the note got here? Where was Gray?

But, before she could begin to think about answers to these questions, she heard an ominous trickling sound. *Oh, God.* The bathwater was overflowing.

As she dashed into the bathroom to turn off the taps, the phone beside her bed began to ring.

'I'm sorry, sir. There's still no answer from Room 1910.'

Gray muttered his curt thanks and prowled back to his post on the far side of the hotel lobby. It was close to midnight now and he wasn't sure how much longer he should pace the hotel's marble floors.

Once or twice he had ducked outside to stroll along Castlereagh Street for a breath of fresh air, but he'd always checked back with the concierge desk on his return. He was sure he hadn't missed Holly, and this last call to her room had still brought no answer.

Where was she? He was fast losing hope.

Tired of pacing, he sank into the leather armchair and thought about ordering another coffee. But he'd consumed so much caffeine tonight, his eyes would soon be out on stalks.

'Sir?'

A voice at Gray's elbow brought him leaping to his feet.

The uniformed concierge, a man of around fifty with a florid face, smiled. 'Mr Kidman?'

Gray's heart thudded. 'Yes.'

'Miss O'Mara has returned. She telephoned the desk and left a message for you.' He handed Gray a folded piece of paper.

Gray opened it, and died a thousand deaths.

It was a handwritten note, not printed, but written in a spiky script with curls and flourishes disfiguring the familiar shape of the letters. He hadn't a hope of deciphering it.

Already the concierge was returning to his desk. Gray hurried after him.

'Excuse me.'

The man turned, eyebrows raised. 'Can I help, sir?'

Gray's face burned crimson. His throat closed over and he wanted to turn and run for the hills. In the past he would have found any excuse to avoid this embarrassment. He would have given up and walked away rather than expose his shame.

Now, his hand shook as he held out the note. 'Would you—' he began, but his voice was hoarse and choked. He tried again. 'Would you mind telling me what this note says?'

The concierge covered his surprise quite creditably once he got over his initial jaw-drop.

'Of course, sir,' he said super-politely. 'Perhaps I should

apologise for my handwriting.' He cleared his throat. 'The note says: *Sorry I missed your calls. I'm in my room now. Please come up.*'

Holly was waiting by the door, and she opened it at the first knock.

Gray was dressed in a dark jacket and tie, and he looked more heartbreakingly handsome than ever. She wanted to hurl herself into his arms; she'd been bursting with excitement since she'd read his note.

But she didn't move. She was worried that she might have somehow misread his message—although how could you misinterpret *I love you?* There was always the chance that it didn't mean quite what she'd instantly hoped. Tonight she couldn't risk taking anything for granted.

'I know it's late,' Gray said. 'But I had to see you.'

Despite her wildly thumping heart, she tried to speak calmly. 'I've been out. I went to a play.'

'How was it?' He looked and sounded as nervous as she felt, probably because he could see how red and swollen her eyes and nose were.

'The play was fabulous.' She waggled her fingers at her puffy face. 'Sorry about this damp look. I'm okay, really. Just being a girl, as my brothers would say.'

He looked worried. 'It must have been a sad play.'

'Yes, it was a tragedy.'

'Can I come in, Holly?'

'Oh, yes, of course. Sorry.'

Dizzy with excitement and fear, she led him down the little hallway that opened into her room which was dominated by a very large king-size bed.

There was only one chair, a pretty pink upholstered armchair in the corner beside a standard lamp.

'You take that,' she said, pointing to it and feeling

uncomfortably like a movie director trying to direct a scene without having first read the script. 'I can sit on the bed.'

'I'd rather not sit.' Gray's wide shoulders and height seemed to take up a great deal of space in the middle of the room. His blue eyes shimmered. 'You got my note, didn't you?'

'Yes, it was such a surprise.' *Understatement of the century.*

'I kept it brief. Less risk of getting the spelling wrong.'

'I thought it was very brave of you,' she said, knowing what it must have cost Gray to repeat an action that held so many sad memories.

He shook his head. 'I shouldn't have left it so late.'

'Well, no, you shouldn't. It's after midnight.'

He reached for her hands and her whole body flamed at his touch. 'I should have spoken up before you left. I should have thrown myself in front of the plane.'

'Maybe I should have been brave enough to tell you I didn't want to go.'

He smiled. 'Really?'

'Of course. Leaving Jabiru was the hardest thing I've ever done.'

'I was so worried that I'd trap you if I asked you to stay.'

'I know. You're worried because of Chelsea.'

'I always felt as if I failed her. Our feelings for each other weren't enough to bridge the huge gaps between us. I didn't want to fail you, too, Holly.' He gave her hands a gentle squeeze. 'But you've taught me something important—to stop dwelling on the failures of my past.'

Looking down at her hands, he rubbed the backs of her knuckles with his thumbs. 'I was fooling myself when I said the kids and I could manage without you.' He smiled crookedly. 'We tried. We tried playing with the puppets, we tried reading stories and lighting a campfire down by the river. But none of it was any fun without you, Holly.'

She was starting to feel giddy with relief.

'There's so much about you that I've missed,' he murmured, reaching out and tracing her cheek with his thumb.

A tremor of happiness ran over her skin.

Gray smiled, then he let his hand drop and he was looking serious once more. 'But we need to talk about this job of yours. I know how much your career means to you and—'

Holly silenced him with a shake of her head. 'The job is just—a job, Gray. When I applied for it, there were at least sixty other people after it.'

'Which means?'

'Which means that one of those sixty can have it.' She smiled into his eyes. In the lamplight they were as blue and bright as the skies above his home. 'I'm a farm girl from Vermont, remember. I love your Outback and, better still—I grew up in a patchwork family.'

'So you did. I'd forgotten that.'

'The only job I really want is the one I left behind at Jabiru.'

Gray laughed, then he gathered her in for the most tender and gorgeous and earth-shattering kiss of her life. She never wanted it to end.

When he finally released her, he said, 'There's still one really important thing that I haven't told you.'

'What's that?'

As if he couldn't bear to not be touching her, Gray picked up her hands again and began playing with her fingers. 'The thing is that now, thanks to you, I know how to study and get new skills and a different job.'

'Why would you want a different job?'

'I would if you wanted me to.' He lifted her hands to his lips and began, very gently, to kiss her fingers. 'If it made you happier, I'd study, take a course. If you wanted to live in New York I'd learn how to be a fireman—whatever.'

'Wow. A New York fireman. Now, that's a tempting option.' To Holly's surprise, Gray didn't show the slightest double take, and that was when she knew for sure that they were going to be all right. His willingness to walk away from the security of Jabiru Creek Station was a bigger gesture than any avowal of love, written or spoken.

'I happen to be in love with you exactly the way you are,' she assured him. 'But I'm very honoured that you'd be willing to change your life for me.'

'I want us to be together for a very long time.'

'That happens to be my personal fantasy.'

She smiled again, letting the brilliance of her happiness show. Then, lifting her face, she brushed her lips over his. 'I'm a girl with simple needs. Truth be told, *this* is what makes me happy.'

With another brush of her lips, their kiss became even more spectacular and glorious than the last one.

Then, with one arm around Holly's shoulders and another beneath her knees, Gray scooped her into his arms.

'Wow,' he breathed.

'I know. I'm heavy. Sorry.'

He laughed. 'Not that. I've just noticed your fabulous new shoes.'

'Oh, yes.' Floating with happiness, Holly lifted her legs high, in a move that might have impressed dancers at the Moulin Rouge. Now they could both admire her slender black patent shoes with pointy toes and follow-me-home heels.

'I'm glad you like them,' she said. 'I think they go really

well with this lovely dress, and they're a definite improvement on the sneakers.'

'They're very elegant,' he murmured sexily in her ear. 'But I love you in sneakers. I might have to ask you to wear them for our wedding. What do you reckon?'

She grinned at him, more gloriously happy than she'd ever thought possible. 'If we're married out at your beautiful gorge, I might need sneakers.'

Gray smiled into her eyes. 'That sounds like a plan.'

'An absolutely perfect plan,' Holly agreed.

SAVED BY THE SINGLE DAD

ANNIE CLAYDON

For the real Cassandra

CHAPTER ONE

JACK PUT HIS head down, trying to shield his face from the stinging rain. Behind him, his ambulance was parked on the road, unable to make it across the narrow bridge that was now the only way into the small village of Holme. Ahead of him, a heavily pregnant woman who should be transported to hospital before the late summer floods in this area of Somerset got any worse.

He and Mimi had been in worse situations before. They'd crewed an ambulance together for the last seven years, Mimi in the driver's seat and Jack taking the lead in treating their patients. They were a good team.

But, however good they were, they couldn't stop it from raining. The main road to the hilltop village was under three feet of water and this back road led across a narrow bridge that was slick with mud. Rather than risk the ambulance getting stuck halfway across, they'd decided to make the rest of the journey on foot.

There were still plenty of options. The patient wasn't in labour yet, and maybe a four-by-four could bring her down the hill to the waiting ambulance. Maybe the storm would clear and the HEMS team could airlift her out. Maybe the support doctor Jack had requested would arrive soon, and maybe not. If all else failed, he and Mimi had delivered babies together before now.

His feet slid on a patch of mud and he gripped the heavy medical bag slung over his shoulder, lurching wildly for a moment before he regained his balance. 'Careful…' He muttered the word as an instruction to himself. Slipping and breaking his leg wasn't one of the options he had been considering.

'One, two, three…' In a grim version of the stepping game he played with Ellie, his four-year-old daughter, he traversed the bridge, trying to ignore the grumbling roar of thunder in the hills. He'd wait for Mimi on the far bank of the river. She'd walked back up the road a little to get reception on her phone and check in with the Disaster Control Team, but they shouldn't lose sight of each other.

He thought he heard someone scream his name but it was probably just the screech of the wind. Then, as the roar got louder, he realised that it wasn't thunder.

Jack turned. A wall of water, tumbling down from the hills, was travelling along the path of the riverbed straight towards him.

His first instinct was to trust the power and speed of his body and run, but in a moment of sudden clarity he knew he wouldn't make it up the steep muddy path in front of him in time. A sturdy-looking tree stood just yards away, its four twisting trunks offering some hope of protection, and Jack dropped his bag and ran towards it.

He barely had a chance to lock his hands around one of the trunks and suck in one desperate breath before the water slammed against his back, expelling all of the precious oxygen from his lungs in one gasp as it flattened him against the bark. A great roar deafened him and he kept his eyes tight shut against the water and grit hitting his face. *Hang on.* The one and only thing he could do was hang on.

Then it stopped. Not daring to let go of the tree trunk,

Jack opened his eyes, trying to blink away the sting of the dirty water. Another sickening roar was coming from upstream.

The next wave was bigger, tearing at his body. He tried to hold on but his fingers slipped apart and he was thrown against the other three trunks, one of them catching the side of his head with a dizzying blow. There was no point in trying to hold his breath and a harsh bellow escaped his lips as his arms flailed desperately, finding something to hold on to and clinging tight.

Then, suddenly, it stopped again. Too dazed to move, Jack lay twisted in the shelter of the branches, his limbs trembling with shock and effort. He was so cold...

Mimi... He tried to call for her, hoping against all hope that she hadn't been on the bridge when the water had hit, but all he could do was cough and retch, dirty water streaming out of his nose and mouth.

He gasped in a lungful of air. 'Mimi...'

'Stay down. Just for a moment.'

A woman's voice, husky and sweet. Someone was wiping his face, clearing his eyes and mouth.

'Mimi... My partner.'

'She's okay. I can see her on the other side of the river.' That voice again. He reached out towards it and felt a warm hand grip his.

He opened his eyes, blinking against the light, and saw her face. Pale skin, with strands of short red hair escaping from the hood of her jacket. Strong cheekbones, a sweet mouth and the most extraordinary pale blue eyes. It was the kind of face you'd expect to find on some warrior goddess...

He shook his head. He must be in shock. Jack knew better than most the kind of nonsense that people babbled in situations like this. Unless she had a golden sword tucked away under her dark blue waterproof jacket, she was just an ordinary mortal, her face rendered ethereal because it was the first thing he'd seen when he opened his eyes.

'Are you sure? Mimi's okay?'

The woman glanced up only briefly, her gaze returning to him. 'She's wearing an ambulance service jacket. Blonde hair, I think…'

'Yes, that's her.' Jack tried to move and found that his limbs had some strength in them now.

'Are you hurt?'

'No…' No one part of him hurt any more than the rest and Jack decided that was a good sign. 'Thanks…um…'

'I'm Cass… Cassandra Clarke.'

'Jack Halliday.'

She gave a small nod in acknowledgement. 'We'd better not hang around here for too long. Can you stand?'

'Yeah.'

'Okay, take it slowly.' She reached over, disentangling his foot from a branch, and then scrambled around next to him, squeezing her body in between him and one of the tree trunks. With almost no effort on his part at all, he found himself sitting up as she levered her weight against his, her arms supporting him. Then she helped him carefully to his feet.

He turned, looking back over the bridge to find Mimi. Only the bridge wasn't there any more. A couple of chunks of masonry were all that was left of it, rolling downstream under the pressure of the boiling water. He could see Mimi standing on the other side, staring fixedly at him, and beside her stood a man who he thought he recognised. Behind them, the lights still on and the driver's door open, was a black SUV.

'All right?' Now that he was on his feet, he could see that Cass was tall, just a couple of inches shorter than him.

'Yeah. Thanks.' Jack felt for his phone and found that

he had nothing in his pocket apart from a couple of stones and a handful of sludge. 'I need to get to a phone...'

'Okay. The village is only ten minutes away; we'll get you up there first.' She spoke with a quiet, irresistible authority.

Jack waved to Mimi, feeling a sharp ache in his shoulder as he raised his arm. She waved back, both hands reaching out towards him as if she was trying to retrieve him. Moving his hand in a circular motion as a sign that he'd call her, he saw the man bend to pick something up. Mimi snatched her phone from him and looked at it for a moment and then turned her attention back on to Jack, sending him a thumbs-up sign.

'Did you mean to park the ambulance like that?' There was a note of dry humour in Cass's husky tones.

Jack looked over the water and saw that the ambulance had been washed off the road and was leaning at a precarious angle against a tree. He muttered a curse under his breath.

'I'll take that as a no.'

Jack chuckled, despite the pain in his ribs. 'What are you?'

She flushed red as if this was the one question she didn't know how to answer. In someone so capable, the delicate shade of pink on her cheeks stirred his shaking limbs into sudden warmth.

'What do you mean?'

'None of this fazes you very much, does it? And you've been trained in how to lift...' Jack recognised the techniques she'd used as very similar to his own. A little more leverage and a little less strength, maybe. And, although Cass didn't give any orders, the men around her seemed to recognise her as their leader.

'I'm a firefighter. I work at the fire station in town, but I'm off duty at the moment. On duty as a concerned family member, though—my sister Lynette's the patient you're coming to see.'

'Then we'd better get going.' Jack looked around for his bag and saw that one of the men was holding it, and that water was dripping out of it. He really was on his own here—no Mimi and no medical bag. He turned, accepting a supportive arm from one of the men, and began to walk slowly up the steep path with the group.

This wasn't what Cass had planned. She'd hoped to be able to get Lynette safely to hospital well in advance but, stubborn as ever, her sister had pointed out that it was another two weeks before her due date and flatly refused to go.

The hospital was now out of reach, but a paramedic was the next best thing. And the floods had finally given her a break and quite literally washed Jack up, on to her doorstep.

Despite the layers of clothing, she'd still felt the strength of his body when she'd helped him up. Hard muscle, still pumped and quivering with the effort of holding on. It had taken nerve to stay put and hang on instead of trying to run from the water, but that decision had probably saved his life.

He was tall as well, a couple of inches taller than her own six feet. And despite, or maybe because of, all that raw power he had the gentlest eyes. The kind of deep brown that a girl could just fall into.

Enough. He might be easy on the eye, but that was nothing to do with her primary objective. Jack was walking ahead of her and Cass lengthened her stride to catch up with him.

'Lynette's actually been having mild contractions. She's not due for another two weeks, but it seems as if the baby might come sooner.' It was better to think of him as an asset, someone who could help her accomplish the task ahead. Bravery had got him here in one piece and those tender eyes might yet come in useful, for comforting Lynette.

'Her first child?'

'Yes.' And one that Cass would protect at all costs.

'Hopefully it'll decide not to get its feet wet just yet. The weather's too bad for the HEMS team to be able to operate safely tonight, but we may be able to airlift her out in the morning.'

'Thanks. You'll contact them?'

'Yeah. Can I borrow your phone? I need to get hold of Mimi as well.'

'Of course, but we'll get you inside first. Who's the guy with her?'

'If it's who I think it is, that's her ex.' A brief grin. Brief but very nice. 'Mimi's not going to like *him* turning up out of the blue.'

'Complicated?'

'Isn't it always?'

He had a point. In any given situation, the complications always seemed to far outweigh the things that went right. Which meant that someone as gorgeous as Jack was probably dizzyingly complicated.

'She'll be okay, though? Your partner.'

'Oh, yeah. No problems with Rafe; he won't leave her stranded. He might have to tie her to a tree to stop her from killing him, but she'll be okay.' Despite the fact that Jack was visibly shivering, the warmth in his eyes was palpable.

Maybe Cass should have done that with *her* ex, Paul. Tied him to a tree and killed him when she'd had the chance. But he was a father now, and probably a half decent one at that. He had a new wife, and a child who depended on him.

'I don't suppose there's any way we can get some more medical supplies over here?' Jack's voice broke her reverie. 'Rafe's a doctor and, knowing him, he'll have come prepared for anything. I could do with a few things, just in case.'

Cass nodded. 'Leave it with me; I'll work something out. You need to get cleaned up and into some dry clothes before you do anything else.'

'Yeah.' The tremble of his limbs was making it through into Jack's voice now. 'I could do with a hot shower.'

'That's exactly where we're headed. Church hall.'

'That's where we're staying tonight?' He looked towards the spire, which reached up into the sky ahead of them like a beacon at the top of the hill.

'Afraid so. The water's already pretty deep all around the village. In this storm, and with the flash floods, there's no safe place to cross.'

She could count on the water keeping him here for the next twenty-four hours at least, perhaps more if she was lucky. He might not want to stay, but there was no choice.

'I'm not thinking of trying to get across. Not while I have a patient to tend to.'

'Thank you. I really appreciate that.' Cass felt suddenly ashamed of herself. This guy wasn't an asset, a cog in a piece of machinery. He was a living, breathing man and his dedication to his job wasn't taken out of a rule book.

She reminded herself, yet again, that this kind of thinking would only get her into trouble. Paul had left her because she'd been unable to get pregnant. Then told her that the problem was all hers, proving his point by becoming a father seven months later. In the agony of knowing that she might never have the baby she so wanted, the indignity of the timing was almost an afterthought.

That was all behind her. The tearing disappointment each month. The wedding, which Paul had postponed time and time again and had ended up cancelled. Lynette's baby was the one she had to concentrate on now, and she was going to fight tooth and nail to get everything that her sister needed.

* * *

Jack was taking one thing at a time. He fixed his eyes on the church steeple, telling himself that this was the goal for the time being and that he just had to cajole his aching limbs into getting there.

Slowly it rose on the horizon, towering dizzily above his head as they got closer. The church had evidently been here for many hundreds of years but, when Cass led him around the perimeter of the grey, weatherworn stones, the building behind it was relatively new. She walked through a pair of swing doors into a large lobby filled with racks of coats. At the far end, shadows passed to and fro behind a pair of obscure glass doors, which obviously led to the main hall.

'The showers are through here.' Cass indicated a door at the side of the lobby.

'Wait.' There was one thing he needed to do, and then he'd leave the rest to Cass and hope that the water was hot. 'Give me your phone.'

She hesitated. 'The medical bags can wait. You need to get warm.'

'Won't take a minute.' He held out his hand, trying not to wince as pain shot through his shoulders and Cass nodded, producing her phone from her pocket.

'Thank you. Tell her that we're going back down to fetch the medical supplies. I think I know how we can get them across.'

It didn't come as any particular surprise that she had a plan. Jack imagined that Cass was the kind of person who always had a plan. She was tall and strong, and moved with the controlled grace of someone who knew how to focus on the task in hand. Now that she'd pulled her hood back her thick red hair, cut in a layered style that was both practical and feminine, made her seem even more gorgeously formidable.

His text to Mimi was answered immediately and confirmed that it was Rafe that he'd seen. Jack texted again, asking Mimi to pack whatever spare medical supplies they had into a bag.

'Here.' He passed the phone back to Cass. 'She's waiting for your call.'

'Thanks.' She slipped the phone into her pocket. 'Now you get warm.'

She led the way through to a large kitchen, bustling with activity, which suddenly quieted as they tramped through in their muddy boots and wet clothes. Beyond that, a corridor led to a bathroom, with a sign saying 'Women Only' hung on the door. Cass popped her head inside and then flipped the sign over, to display the words 'Men Only'.

It looked as if he had the place to himself. There was a long row of handbasins, neat and shining, with toilet cubicles lined up opposite and bath and shower cubicles at the far end. The place smelled of bleach and air freshener.

'Put your clothes there.' She indicated a well-scrubbed plastic chair next to the handbasins. 'I'll send someone to collect them and leave some fresh towels and we'll find some dry clothes. What size are you…?'

The question was accompanied by a quick up and down glance that made Jack shiver, and a slight flush spread over Cass's cheeks. 'Large will have to do, I think.' She made the words sound like a compliment.

'Thanks. That would be great.'

'Do you need any help?' She looked at him steadily. 'I'm relying on you, as a medical professional, to tell me if there's anything the matter with you.'

If he'd thought for one moment that Cass would stay and help him off with his clothes, instead of sending someone else in to do it, Jack might just have said yes. 'No. I'll be fine.'

'Good.' She turned quickly, but Jack caught sight of a half-smile on her lips. Maybe she would have stayed.

Working in an environment that was still predominantly male, Jack doubted that she was much fazed by the sight of a man's body.

He waited for the door to close behind her before he painfully took off his jacket and sweater. Unbuttoning his shirt, he stood in front of the mirror to inspect some of the damage. It was impossible to tell what was what at the moment. A little blood, mixed with a great deal of mud from the dirty water. He'd shower first and then worry about any bumps and scratches.

A knock at the door and a woman's voice, asking if she could come in, disturbed the best shower Jack could remember taking in a long time. Hurried footsteps outside the cubicle and then he was alone again, luxuriating in the hot water.

After soaping his body twice, he felt almost clean again. Opening the cubicle door a crack, he peered out and found the bathroom empty; two fluffy towels hung over one of the handbasins. One was large enough to wind around his waist and he rubbed the other one over his head to dry his hair.

He looked a mess. He could feel a bump forming on the side of his head and, although his jacket had largely protected the rest of him, he had friction burns on his arms, which stung like crazy, and a graze on his chest from where the zip on his jacket had been driven against the skin.

'Coming in...' A rap on the door and a man's voice. A slim, sandy-haired man of about forty entered, carrying a pile of clothes and a pair of canvas shoes. 'Hi, Jack. I'm Martin.'

He was wearing a light windcheater, white letters on a dark blue background on the right hand side, in the same place that Jack's paramedic insignia appeared on his uniform. When he turned, the word was repeated in larger letters across his back.

'You're the vicar, then.' Jack grinned.

'Yeah. My wife seems to think this is a good idea, just in case anyone mistakes me for someone useful.'

'I'd always be glad to see you coming.' Hope and comfort were often just as important as medical treatment.

'Likewise. We're grateful for all you did to get here.' Martin propped the clothes on the ledge behind the washbasins. 'They look nasty.' His gaze was on the friction burns on Jack's arms.

'Superficial. They'll be okay.' Jack riffled through the clothes. A T-shirt, a grey hooded sweatshirt and a pair of jeans that looked about his size. He picked the T-shirt up and pulled it over his head so that he didn't have to think about the marks on his arms and chest any more. 'How's my patient?'

'Lynette's fine. She's over at the vicarage, drinking tea with my wife and complaining about all the fuss. She seems to have got it into her head that she's got some say about when the baby arrives.'

'You were right to call. At the very least she needs to be checked over.'

Martin nodded. 'Thanks. Cass has gone to get your medical supplies. Goodness only knows how she's going to manage it, but knowing Cass…'

Even the mention of her name made Jack's heart beat a little faster. 'She seems very resourceful.'

Martin nodded. 'Yeah. Bit too resourceful sometimes. Now, important question. Tea or coffee? I don't think I can keep the Monday Club under control for much longer.'

Jack chuckled. 'Tea. Milk, no sugar, thanks.'

'Good. And I hope you like flapjacks or I'm going to have a riot on my hands.'

'You seem very organised here.'

Martin nodded. 'This church has been taking people in for the last eight hundred years. Wars, famine, fires… Now floods. I've never seen anything like this, though, and I've been here fifteen years. Half the village is flooded out.'

'How many people do you have here?'

'Just a couple of families staying overnight. We've found everyone else billets in people's homes. But everyone eats here, and we have an action committee...' Martin shrugged, grinning. 'That's Cass's baby. I confine myself to tea and sympathy.'

Jack reckoned that Martin was downplaying his own considerable role. 'And hospitality.'

'We've never turned anyone away before, and that's not going to start on my watch.' A trace of determination broke through Martin's affable smile and was quickly hidden. 'Anything else you need?'

'A phone? I'd like to call home.'

'Yes, of course. The landline at the vicarage is still working; you can use that.' Martin turned, making for the door. 'Come to the kitchen when you're ready and I'll take you over there.'

CHAPTER TWO

MARTIN OPENED A side door that led out of the kitchen and they walked along a paved path, sheltered by makeshift awnings that boasted a few scraps of soggy coloured bunting hanging from the corners. Then through a gate and into the vicarage kitchen, which oozed warmth and boasted a table large enough to seat a dozen people.

Lynette was red-haired like her sister, her features prettier and yet somehow far less attractive. She was heavily pregnant and Jack's first impressions were that she was in the best of health. Although she'd been having minor contractions, she seemed stubbornly positive that the baby wasn't coming yet. Jack begged to differ, but kept that thought to himself.

He left Lynette on the sofa by the kitchen range and sat down at the table, where a cup of tea was waiting for him. 'I'll be able to examine you a little more thoroughly when your sister gets back with my medical bag.'

'Thanks. But there's really no need to worry. First babies are always late, aren't they?'

Sue, the vicar's wife, frowned. 'Not necessarily. My Josh was early.' She pushed a large plate of flapjacks across the table towards Jack. 'If I eat another one of those I'll be sorry when I get on the scales. I wish the Monday Club would stop cooking...'

Lynette laughed. 'Not much chance of that. Mrs Hawes doesn't like to see anyone going hungry.'

Sue sighed, looking up as someone rapped on the glass pane of the back door. 'It's open...'

The door swung inwards and two bags were placed inside. Then Cass appeared, her hair wet and slicked back from her face, holding her muddy boots in one hand and her wet jacket and overtrousers in the other. Sue relieved her of them and disappeared to put them in the front porch.

'You got two across?' Jack bent to inspect the contents of the bags.

'Yeah, we got a line over about quarter of a mile down from the bridge. Mimi's okay and she's going back to the hospital with what's-his-name.' The corners of her mouth quirked into an expression that would have been unfathomable if Jack hadn't been able to guess the situation. 'She sends you her love.'

Jack nodded, drawing a stethoscope and blood pressure monitor from the bag. 'Right, ladies. If you're comfortable here, Lynette, I'll get on and do a more thorough examination.'

He'd given Lynette one last flash of those tender eyes and smiled at her, pronouncing that everything was fine. Lynette hadn't even noticed what he hadn't said, but Cass had.

'She's in the early stages of labour, isn't she?' Cass had shown him through to the small room behind the church hall, which had been earmarked as his sleeping quarters and already boasted a hastily erected camp bed in the corner, with sheets and blankets folded on top of it.

'Yes. Although this could be a false alarm...'

Another thing he wasn't saying. 'And it might not be.'

'Yes.' He scrubbed his hand back across his scalp, his short dark hair spiking untidily. 'I have everything I need, and I've delivered babies plenty of times before.'

'Really?' Jack was saying everything she wanted to hear, and Cass wondered how much of it was just reassurance.

'It's not ideal, but we'll get her to the hospital as soon as the weather lifts. In the meantime, you've done your job and you can rely on me to do mine.'

A small curl of warmth quieted some of the fear. 'Thanks. This baby is...' Important. All babies were important, but this one was important to her.

'I know. And he's going to be fine.' His eyes made her believe it. 'Is the father on the scene?'

'Very much so. He's not here, though; Lynette's husband is in the Royal Navy and he's away at the moment. My father works abroad too; Mum was going to come home next week to help out.'

'So it's just you and me then.' He contrived to make that sound like a good thing. 'You're her birth partner?'

'Yep.' Cass pressed her lips together. Going to classes with Lynette had seemed like the most natural thing in the world. The most beautiful form of sharing between sisters. Now it was all terrifying.

'Good.' His gaze chipped away at yet another piece of the fear that had been laying heavy on her chest for days, and suddenly Cass wondered if she might not make a half decent job of it after all.

'I'd rather be...' Anything. 'I'd rather be doing something practical.'

He laughed. 'This is the most practical thing in the world, Cass. The one thing that never changes, and hopefully never will. You'll both be fine.'

She knew that he was trying to reassure her, and that his *You'll both be fine* wasn't a certainty, but somehow it seemed to be working. She walked over to the coil of ropes and pulleys that had been dumped here while she'd taken the bags through to the vicarage.

'I'll get these out of your way.'

'Let me help you.' Before she could stop him, he'd picked up the rope, leaving Cass to collect the remaining pulleys and carabiners up and put them into a rucksack. 'You used this to get the bags across?'

'Yeah.' Hopefully he was too busy thinking about child-birth to take much notice of what he was carrying. The cut end was clearly visible, hanging from the coil of rope. 'I borrowed the gear from one of the guys in the village who goes mountaineering.' She slung the rucksack over her shoulder and led the way through to the storeroom, in-dicating an empty patch of floor, but Jack shook his head.

'Not there; it's too close to the radiator and rope degrades if it dries out too fast. Help me move these boxes and we'll lay it flat over here.'

Cass dumped the rucksack and started to lift the boxes out of the way. 'You know something about rope?'

'Enough to know that this one's been cut recently, while it was under stress. Mountaineering ropes don't just break.' He bent to finger the cut end and then turned his gaze on to her.

The security services had missed a trick in not recruit-ing Jack and putting him to work as an interrogator. Those quiet eyes made it impossible not to admit to her greatest follies. 'I…cut the rope.'

Somehow that wasn't enough. He didn't even need to ask; Cass found herself needing to tell him the rest.

'Mimi shouted across, asking if we had a harness. They both seemed determined to try and get across, and medical bags are one thing…'

'But lives are another?' he prompted her gently.

'Yeah. I was worried that they'd just go ahead and do it, and as soon as one of them put their weight on the ropes I wouldn't be able to stop them. So, when we got hold of the second bag, I cut the rope.'

He grinned. 'I couldn't see Mimi letting you haul a bag over and staying put herself on the other side. Nice job.'

Cass supposed she might as well tell him everything; he'd hear it soon enough. 'Not such a nice job. I miscalculated and the rope snapped back in their direction. Another few feet and it would have taken Mimi's head off.'

'It was…what, thirty feet across the river?'

'About that.'

'Weight of the bags…' He was obviously doing some kind of calculation in his head. 'Wouldn't have taken her head off. Maybe given her a bit of a sting.'

'Well, it frightened the life out of me. And what's-his-name…'

'Rafe…'

'Yeah, Rafe tackled her to the ground.'

Jack snorted with laughter. 'Oh, I'll bet she just loved that. Rafe always was a bit on the protective side where Mimi's concerned.'

'She didn't seem too pleased about it. What is it with those two? Light the blue touchpaper?'

'Yeah and stand a long way back.' Jack was still chuckling. 'Shame, really. They're both good people, but put them within fifty feet of each other and they're a disaster. Always will be.'

'I know the feeling…' All too well. Only Cass would be a disaster with any man. She'd never quite been able to move on from what Paul had said and done, never been able to shake the belief that he was right. She'd felt her heart close, retreating wounded from a world that had been too painful to bear.

He didn't reply. As Jack bent to finish arranging the ropes so they'd dry out properly, Cass couldn't help noticing the strong lines of his body, the ripple of muscle. That didn't just happen; it must have taken some hard work and training.

'So you're a mountaineer?'

He shook his head, not looking at her. 'No. My father. It's not something I'd ever consider doing.'

That sounded far too definite not to be a thought-out decision. 'Too risky?' Somehow Cass doubted that; Jack had just braved a flood to get here.

'There's risk and risk. My father died when I was twelve, free climbing. Anyone with an ounce of sanity would have used ropes for that particular climb, but he went for the adrenaline high. He always did.' The sudden bitter anger in Jack's voice left Cass in no doubt about his feelings for his father.

'I'm really sorry...'

He straightened up. 'Long time ago. It was one of the things that made me want to go into frontline medicine. Going out on a limb to save a life has always seemed to me to be a much finer thing than doing it for kicks.'

'And of course we both calculate the risks we take pretty carefully.' Cass wondered whether Jack knew that the current calculation was all about him. She wanted to know more about the man who was responsible for Lynette's safety, to gauge his weaknesses.

He nodded. 'Yeah. Needs a cool head, not a hot one.'

Good answer. Cass turned to the door. 'Shall we go and see whether there's any more tea going?'

They collected their tea from an apparently unending supply in the kitchen, and Jack followed Cass as she dodged the few steps into the back of the church building. She led him along a maze of silent corridors and through a doorway, so small that they both had to duck to get through it.

They were in a closed porch. Arched wooden doors led through to the church on one side and on the other a second door was secured by heavy metal bolts. Tall, stone-framed windows, glazed in a diamond pattern of small pieces of glass, so old that they were almost opaque. A gargoyle, perched up in a corner, grinned down at them.

'I reckoned you might like to drink your tea in peace.' She reached up to switch on a battery-operated lantern, which hung from one of the stone scrolls which flanked the doorway. 'Martin's lent me this place for the duration. I come here to think.'

It looked more like somewhere to hide than think. Jack wondered why she should need such a place when she was clearly surrounded by family and friends here. She seemed so involved with her community, so trusted, and yet somehow she held herself apart from it.

All the same, for some reason she'd let him in and it felt like too much of a privilege to question it. Jack took his jacket off and sat down on one of the stone benches that ran the length of the porch. She proffered a cushion, from a pile hidden away in an alcove in the corner, and he took it gratefully.

'You've made yourself at home here. It's warm as well. And oddly peaceful.' Jack looked around. Listening to the storm outside, rather than struggling against it, made the old walls seem like a safe cocoon.

'I like it. These stones are so thick it's always the same temperature, winter or summer.' She laid her coat out on the bench and smoothed her half-dried hair behind her ears.

'Makes a good refuge.' He smiled, in an indication that she could either take the observation seriously or pass it off as a joke if she chose.

'Yeah. You should ask Martin about that; he's a bit of a history buff. Apparently there was an incident during the English Civil War when Cavaliers claimed refuge here. They camped out in this porch for weeks.'

Fair enough. So she didn't want to talk about it.

'I'd like you to stay with Lynette tonight, at the vicarage. Keep an eye on her.'

She nodded. 'I don't have much choice. My house is a little way downriver from the bridge. It was partially flooded even before this afternoon.'

'I'm sorry to hear that.'

Cass leaned back, stretching her legs out in front of her. 'I've been expecting it for days and at least I had a chance to get everything upstairs, which is a lot more than some people have had. It's my own stupid fault, anyway.'

'So you're the one, are you? That's been making it rain.'

She really was stunningly beautiful when she smiled. Warm and beautiful, actually, with a touch of vulnerability that belied her matter-of-fact attitude and her capable do-anything frame. But she seemed far too ready to blame herself when things went wrong.

'I wish. Then I could make it stop. The house has been in my family for generations and it's always been safe from flooding.'

'But not on your watch?' Jack realised he'd hit a nerve from the slight downward quirk of her lips.

'There used to be a drystone wall, banked up on the inside, which acted as a barrier between the house and the river. My grandparents levelled a stretch of it to give easy access to build an extension at the back. When they died they left the house to Lynette and me and, as she and Steven already had a place up in the village, I bought her out. I was pretty stretched for cash and thought I couldn't afford to reinstate the wall for a few years. Turns out I couldn't afford not to.'

'You're being a bit hard on yourself, aren't you? I'd be devastated if my place were flooded.'

Cass shrugged. 'I'm concentrating on Lynette and the baby. Bricks and mortar can wait.'

Jack nodded, sipping his tea.

'So how about you?' She seemed intent on changing the subject now. 'You have children?'

'A little girl. Ellie's four.'

She smiled. 'That's nice. I'm sorry we're keeping you away from her.'

If he was honest, he was sorry about that too. Jack knew exactly what it was like to have to come to terms with the idea that his father was never coming back, and he'd promised Ellie that he would always come back for her. Right now the storm and the floods made that impossible, and the feeling that he was letting Ellie down was eating at him.

Cass didn't need to know that. 'I'm concentrating on Lynette and the baby too.' He received a bright grin in acknowledgement of the sentiment. 'I'd really like to call my daughter to say goodnight, though. Would you mind if I borrowed your phone?'

'Yes, of course.' She stood up, handing her phone over. 'I'll leave you to it.'

'That's okay. Say hello to her.'

She hesitated and then sat back down with a bump. Awkwardly, she pointed to one of the icons on the small screen.

'You could try a video call. She might like to see you.'

'Yeah, she would. Thanks.'

Jack couldn't remember his sister's mobile number so he called the landline, repeating Cass's mobile number over to Sarah. 'My sister's going to get back to us.'

'Your wife works too?'

'I'm a single father. Sarah has a boy of Ellie's age and she looks after her when I'm working.'

'Sounds like a good arrangement.' She seemed to be getting more uncomfortable by the minute. If he hadn't already come to the conclusion that Cass could deal with almost anything, he would have said she was flustered.

He didn't have time to question why because the phone rang. Cass leaned over, jabbing an icon on the screen to switch on the camera and answer the call.

* * *

He was so in love with Ellie. Cass had reckoned that a wife and family would put Jack firmly out of bounds, which was the best place for him as far as she was concerned. But he was handsome, caring, funny…*and single.* She was going to have to work a little harder now, because allowing herself to be tempted by Jack was just an exercise in loss.

'Daddeee!' An excited squeal came from the phone and Cass averted her gaze. Jack held the phone out in front of him, his features softening into a grin that made her want to run away screaming.

'Ellie! What are you up to, darling?'

'We're having tea. Then Ethan and me are going to watch our film.'

'Again, sweetie? Doesn't Auntie Sarah want to watch something else on TV?' He chuckled as a woman's voice sounded, saying that if it kept the kids quiet, she was happy.

'Listen, Ellie…' He waited until the commotion on the other end of the line subsided. 'Ellie, Daddy's got to work, so you'll be staying with Auntie Sarah for tonight.'

Silence. Then a little voice sounded. 'I know. Miss you, Daddy.'

Cass almost choked with emotion. When she looked at Jack, he seemed to have something in his eye. 'I miss you too, sweetie. You know you're always my number one girl. And I'll be back soon to give you big hugs.'

'How big?'

'As big as a bear. No, bigger than that. As big as our house.'

A little squeal of delight from Ellie. Cass imagined that Jack's hugs were something to look forward to.

'As big as our house…'

'Yeah.' Jack was grinning broadly now. 'Be good for Auntie Sarah, won't you.'

'I'm always good.' Ellie's voice carried a note of reproof.

'Sure you are. Would you like to meet my new friend?' He winked at Cass and her heart jolted so hard she almost fainted. 'She's a firefighter.'

'She has a fire engine?' Ellie was obviously quite taken with the idea.

'Why don't you ask her?' Jack chuckled and handed the phone over to Cass.

A little girl was staring at her. Light brown curls and luminous brown eyes. She was the image of Jack.

'Hi, Ellie. I'm Cassandra.' She wondered whether Ellie was a bit young to get her tongue around the name. Child development wasn't her forte. 'All my friends call me Cass.'

'You're a fire lady? With a fire engine?' Ellie was wriggling excitedly.

'Yes, that's right.'

'Do you have a ladder?'

'Yes, more than one. And we have a hose, for putting out all the fires.'

'Auntie Sarah...!' Ellie clearly wanted to share this exciting news.

'Yes, I heard. Tell Cassandra that you've seen a fire engine.' The woman's voice again, laughing.

'I've seen a fire engine.' Ellie turned the edges of her mouth down theatrically. 'It was a long, long, long way away...'

Suddenly Cass knew exactly what to say to Ellie. 'Tell you what. We're having an Open Day at our fire station soon. We're showing all the children around...' She was about to add that Ellie would have to ask her father if she might come, but that seemed to be a foregone conclusion.

'Yesss! Daddeee!'

Jack shot Cass a wry smile. 'Do I get to come along too, Ellie?'

Cass thought she could almost see the little girl roll her eyes.

'You have to take me, Daddy. I can't drive...'

'Ah, yes, of course. Looks like it's the two of us, then. Say thank you to Cassandra.'

Jack leaned in, speaking over her shoulder, and Cass swallowed a gasp, suddenly aware that his body was very close.

'Thank you, Cassandra.'

Ellie managed the name without even blinking, and Jack chuckled.

'Time to say bye-bye now, sweetheart.' Ellie responded by waving and blowing a kiss, then Jack took the phone from her to say his own goodnight to his daughter.

Cass stood up, her limbs suddenly trembling. It was impossible to fall in love in so short a time and over the phone. And, if she was honest with herself, she hadn't fallen in love with Ellie's brown eyes but with Jack's. But he was a grown man. It was much easier to admit that his child was all she could see.

'She's gorgeous.' Cass had let him finish the call, looking away when he blew kisses to Ellie.

'Yeah.' His fingers lingered lovingly over the blank screen for a moment, as if he couldn't quite let go of the memory of his daughter's face, and then he handed the phone back. 'I didn't think she'd manage to pronounce *Cassandra.*'

The second time he said her name was just as disturbing as the first. Awakening thoughts of what it might feel like to have him whisper it.

'She must be growing up fast.'

'Seems too fast, sometimes.' He shrugged. 'She loves fire engines…'

'Yeah, me too. You didn't mind me asking her to the Open Day?'

'Mind…?' He laughed. 'Sounds like fun. Do I get to sit in the driver's seat?'

'No. Children only. Dads get to watch.'

CHAPTER THREE

THEY'D EATEN IN the church hall, the dreaded Monday Club turning out to be a group of perfectly nice women who cooked good food in large quantities and didn't mind a laugh. The evening was spent at the vicarage with Lynette and Cass, who persuaded Martin to make up a fourth for board games. Then Jack made his apologies and retired to his sleeping quarters, shutting the door and lying down fully dressed on the camp bed.

Suddenly he felt very alone. Ellie would be tucked up in bed by now and although he knew that Sarah would have given her bedtime kisses on his behalf, he hadn't been there to give them himself. Mimi was probably exhausted and looking forward to a good night's sleep. Cass was…

He wasn't going to think about where Cass was. He had a child, and he had to protect her. Jack had made up his mind a long time ago that the best thing for Ellie was that he remained single.

He must have drifted off to sleep because the next thing he knew was a tingle behind his ear, and his eyes shot open involuntarily as he realised that someone was rubbing their finger gently on his skin. He blinked in the light that was flooding in through the doorway and saw Cass.

For one moment all he could think was that this was a delicious way to wake up, coaxed out of unconsciousness by a red-haired goddess. Then the urgency on her face snapped him back to reality.

'Her waters have broken. Jack…'

'Okay. I hear you.' Jack swung his legs from the bed and shook his head to bring himself to. He'd been hoping that this wouldn't happen. He had the training and the experience for it, and this certainly wasn't the most outlandish place that he and Mimi had delivered a baby before now. But without the possibility of any backup, and only the medical supplies that Rafe had sent, it was a heavy responsibility, which he had to bear alone.

This was no time to panic. Contrary to all his expectations, Cass was panicking enough for both of them at the moment.

Keeping his pace brisk but unhurried in an effort to slow Cass down a bit, he picked up his medical bags and made for the vicarage. As they reached the back door they passed Martin, who was hurrying in the other direction, a sleeping child in his arms.

'Go through, Jack. Just getting the kids out of the way.'

Jack nodded. Following Cass through the kitchen and up the stairs, he found Sue and another woman on either side of Lynette, supporting her as she paced slowly up and down.

'We'll take her into my bedroom.' Sue looked up at him. 'There's an en suite bathroom, and the mattress in here is wet.'

'Thanks.' First things first. Jack smiled at Lynette, wiping a tear from her face. 'How are you doing?'

'Um… Okay. I think.'

'Good. You want to walk a bit more?'

Lynette nodded.

'All right. I'm going to get the other room ready for you, and then we'll take it from there. Tonight's your night, eh?'

'Yes… Thanks.'

Cass took Sue's place at Lynette's side, and Sue led him

through to her own bedroom. Jack pulled the plastic under-sheet from his bag, silently thanking Rafe for thinking to pack it, and Sue set about stripping the bed.

When Cass supported Lynette through to the main bed-room, it seemed that everything was ready. She helped her sister sit down on the bed. 'Do you want your scented candles?'

'No!' Lynette's flailing hand found Jack's sweatshirt and held on tight. 'I want to keep a close eye on the guy with the pain relief…'

'I'm here.' Jack was calm and smiling. 'I'm going to wash my hands and I'll be right back, okay.'

'Yeah. Whatever.' Lynette frowned and closed her eyes.

Get the candles anyway… Jack mouthed the words to Cass and she hurried through to the other room to fetch Lynette's hospital bag.

When she got back, Sue waved her towards the bathroom door and Cass tapped on it tentatively. Jack was standing in front of the basin, his T-shirt and sweatshirt hung over the side of the bath, soaping his hands and arms. 'There's a clean T-shirt and some dressings in my medical bag. Will you get them, please?'

'Dressings? What's the matter?'

'Nothing. They're for me.' He grinned, turning round, and she saw the new bruises on his chest, the bright red gashes that ran across his sternum and upper arms.

Her sister was in labour. Now was a fine time to notice that his muscle definition was superb. Or to feel a tingle at the warmth of his smile. Cass swallowed hard.

'How did you do that…?' She pointed to the spot on her own arm to indicate the patch of red, broken skin on his. That had to hurt.

'It's just a friction burn. It's bleeding a little so best I cover it up.'

She nodded and went to fetch what he'd asked for. The dressings, along with a roll of tape and some scissors, were right at the top of the bag. Jack must have been thinking ahead.

'Okay, will you tape these on for me, please? Right around the edge so that there are no openings anywhere.'

Couldn't Sue do it? The temptation to run away and hide from his body almost made her ask. But her sister was out there having a baby, and Cass had already decided she'd do whatever it took.

He held the gauze in place and she taped around it for him. Trying not to notice the fresh smell of soap on skin. Trying not to think about how close he was, or how perfect.

'Thanks. That's great.' He nodded his approval and Cass stepped back, almost colliding with the linen basket. Then, thankfully, he pulled the T-shirt over his head.

'Ready?' His smile held all of the warmth that she could want for Lynette. Which happened to be a great deal more than Cass could deal with.

'Yes. I'm ready.' Cass had told herself that this was going to be the best night of her life. Being with Lynette all the way, seeing her nephew being born. Now, all she could feel was fear, for everything that could go wrong.

He was calm and quiet, soothing Lynette when the contractions eased and helping her concentrate and breathe when they came again. When Lynette became frightened and overwhelmed, he was there with reassurance and encouragement. When she wanted to change position, he let her lean on him. When she needed pain relief, he was there with the Entonox.

Lynette seemed almost serene when she wasn't crying in pain, switching from one to the other with astonishing rapidity.

'Is this right?' Cass mouthed the words to Jack.

Jack's gaze flipped to the portable monitors at Lynette's side. 'Yeah, we're okay.'

'It's so fast...' Cass had been preparing for a long haul, but it had barely been an hour since she'd woken him up and already he was telling Lynette that they were nearly there.

'That's a good thing. Lynette's fine and so is the baby.'

Ten minutes later, her nephew was born. Jack cleared his mouth, rubbing his chest gently. Everyone held their breath and then the little man began to cry. Lynette squeezed Cass's hand so tight that she thought she was going to break her fingers.

'Say hello to your mum...' Jack laid the baby on Lynette's chest and covered him over with a towel. The two women lay on the bed together, cradling the baby, in a daze of happiness.

Suddenly, it was all perfect. Martin had welcomed the newest member of the village to the world, and Sue went to make tea and toast. Jack managed everything perfectly, melting into the background, clearing up and making the medical checks that were needed, without intruding into their bubble.

Then the call came from Lynette's husband, saying he'd received the photo that Cass had sent and was ready and waiting for a video call. Lynette was left alone for a few minutes to talk to him and show him their new son.

Cass waited outside the door, a sudden heaviness settling on her. However close she and Lynette were, however much her sister had needed her, it wasn't her baby. It was Lynette and Steven's. Their joy. One that she would only ever feel second-hand.

This wasn't the time. There were too many special moments ahead for her to spoil with her own selfishness. And they came soon enough. The moment when Jack helped Lynette to encourage her son to feed, and he finally got the hang of what he was supposed to do. The moment when his eyelids flickered open and Cass stared for the first time into his pale blue eyes.

'Do you have a name for him yet?' Jack was busy re-packing his medical bag.

'We did have. But we've decided on something different.' Lynette smiled. 'We reckon Noah.'

'Very appropriate.' Jack chuckled.

'Is Jack a nickname for John?' She was beginning to tire now, and had lost the thread of what she was saying a couple of times already.

'Yep. Named after my grandfather. They used to call him Jack as well.'

'Noah John has a nice ring to it, don't you think?'

Jack turned. 'What does your husband think?'

'Steven suggested it. What you did tonight meant everything, to both of us, and we'd really like to have your name as his middle name. If you don't mind, that is.'

A broad grin spread over Jack's face. 'I'd be very honoured. Thank you.' He walked over to the bed, bending down to stroke the side of little Noah's face with his finger. The tiny baby opened his eyes, seeming to focus on Jack, although Cass knew that he couldn't really focus on anything just yet.

'Hey there, Noah.' Jack's voice was little more than a whisper. 'We guys have to stick together, you know. Especially since we share a name now. What do you say we let your mum get a bit of rest?'

'Will you and Cass look after him for me? I just want to close my eyes; I don't think I can sleep.'

'Of course.' Sue had prepared the Moses basket that she'd used for her children and Jack took Noah, setting him down in the cradle. But he immediately began to fret and Jack picked him up again, soothing him.

'Now what do we do?' Cass whispered the words at Jack.

Sue and Martin had quietly left at the first suggestion of sleep, and Lynette's eyes had already drooped closed. It seemed that they were quite literally left holding the baby.

Jack chuckled quietly, nodding towards the easy chair in the corner of the room. 'Sit down. Over there.'

'Me?' She was suddenly gripped with panic. 'You want *me* to hold him?'

'I've got things to do. And it's about time he got acquainted with his aunt.'

It was almost a bitter thought. Holding her sister's baby and not her own. But in the peace and quiet of the room, candles guttering in their holders and a bedside lamp casting a soft glow, it was easy to forget that. Cass plumped herself down in the chair, wondering what Jack was going to do next.

'Suppose I drop him?'

'You won't.' Jack seemed to be able to manage the baby in one arm while he picked up a pillow from the bed in the other hand, dropping it on to her lap. 'Here you are. That's right.'

The sudden closeness felt so good she wanted to cry out. Jack's scent, mingling with that of a baby. Instinctively her arms curled around Noah and she rocked him gently, holding him against her chest. He fretted for a moment and then fell into a deep sleep.

'I just want to wake him up. See his eyes again...' She looked up at Jack and, when he smiled, Cass realised that all the wonder she felt must be written clearly on her face.

'Yeah, I know. Let him sleep for a while; being born is a tiring business.'

Jack fetched a straight-backed chair from the kitchen and sat in the pool of light from the lamp, writing notes and keeping an eye on everyone. When Cass could tear her gaze from Noah, she watched Jack. Relaxed, smiling and unbearably handsome. She envied the shadows, which seemed to caress his face in recognition of a job well done.

When Noah woke and began to fuss a little, Lynette was immediately alert, reaching for her child. Jack delivered him to her and this time there were fewer grimaces and less messing around to get him to feed. Cass watched from the other side of the bed and, when he'd had enough and fallen back into sleep, she curled up with her sister on the bed, holding her hand until they both followed Noah's example and slept.

The morning dawned bright and clear. Jack had managed to sleep a little, in the chair in the corner of the room, and now he had heard from the HEMS team. They were flying, and would take advantage of the break in the weather to take Lynette and Noah to hospital.

Despite the early hour, a few people had gathered around the village green. An excited chatter accompanied the landing of the helicopter and a ragged cheer went up when its crew followed Jack towards the vicarage.

He said his goodbyes to Lynette and Noah inside, keeping his distance as the HEMS team took them outside with Cass. Jack wondered if this would be the last he ever saw of her and, despite all his resolutions, he found himself staring at her, as if to burn her image into his mind. But she waited for Lynette and the baby to be safely installed in the helicopter and then jogged back to stand at his side.

'There goes your last chance of getting out of the village today. The roads are still blocked.' Cass's eyes seemed to be fixed on the disappearing speck in the sky.

Jack nodded. 'Yours too.'

'What does that make us?' She turned her querying gaze on to his face.

Jack shrugged. 'It makes us people who know our families are safe, and that the village might still need us.'

'It's not easy…'

'I don't think it's meant to be.' Jack's decision to stay had been made in the small hours of last night and it had torn him in two. Doing his job and being a good dad was a complex and sometimes heartbreaking juggling act.

'Well, it's done now. The only thing I can do to justify it is to make today count.' She smiled suddenly. 'Hungry?'

'Famished.' He looked at his watch. 'What time's breakfast?'

'Not for a couple of hours. We'll raid the kitchen.'

The kitchen was empty and she made toast while Jack made the tea. She rummaged in the cupboard, finding a couple of jars, and picked up two bananas from a crate in the corner. Then she led the way through to her private hidey-hole in the church porch.

'What is that?' It appeared that instead of choosing what she wanted on her toast, Cass was going for everything.

'Chocolate spread, then peanut butter and mashed banana. Try it; it's really nice.'

'Maybe another time. When I'm planning on not eating for the next two days.'

'A good breakfast sets you up for the day. You should know that; you're a medic.'

'Yeah. Perhaps I'd better not mention the sugar in that.' She shrugged. 'I'll work it off.'

They ate in silence. His first slice of toast with peanut butter and his second with chocolate spread. Jack supposed that since he was going to eat the banana afterwards, he couldn't really poke too much fun at Cass's choice of breakfast.

It was still early and the glow of a new day, diffusing gently through the thick ancient glass, seemed to impose a relaxed camaraderie. Grabbing meals at odd hours after working most of the night. Talking, saying whatever came to mind without the usual filter of good manners and expediency. It felt as if anything could be asked, and answered.

'Is there someone waiting for you when we get out of here?'

She shrugged. 'Lots of people, I imagine.'

'I meant a partner...' It was becoming important to Jack to find out about all the subjects that Cass seemed to skirt around.

'Oh, that.' Jack wondered whether she really hadn't known what he was talking about. 'Big red truck. Makes a noise...'

'You're married to your job, then?'

She nodded, taking a bite from her toast. 'You?'

'I never married. And I don't get much time for socialising any more; when Ellie came along I had to make quite a few changes.'

She turned her querying eyes on to him and Jack wondered whether she wanted to know about him as much as he wanted to know about her. It was strangely gratifying.

'Then you have a *past*? How exciting.' The curve of her lip promoted an answering throb in his chest which made it hard to deny how much he liked it when Cass teased him.

'It's not that exciting.' Looking back, it seemed more desperate than anything. Desperate to find the warmth that was missing from his broken home, and yet afraid to commit to anyone in case they let him down, the way his father had let his mother down.

She gave him that cool once-over with her gaze which always left his nerve endings tingling. 'Bet you were good at it, though.'

That was undeniably a compliment, and Jack chuckled. 'I kept my head above water.'

Her eyes were full of questions, and suddenly Jack wanted to answer them all. 'Ellie's mother was the daughter of one of my dad's climbing partners; we practically grew up together. I went off to university and when I got back Sal was away climbing. It wasn't until years later that we found ourselves in the same place at the same time, for the weekend…'

'Okay. I've got your drift.' Cass held up her hand, clearly happy to forgo those particular details. 'So what about Ellie?'

'Fifteen months later, Sal turned up on my doorstep with her.'

'And you didn't know…?'

'Sal never said a word. She only got in touch then because she needed someone to take Ellie while she went climbing in Nepal.'

Cass choked on her toast. 'That must…I can't imagine what that must have been like.'

'It was love at first sight. And a wake-up call.'

'I can imagine. Bachelor about town one minute, in charge of a baby the next. However did you cope?'

'Badly at first. Sarah took me in hand, though; she got me organised and offered to take Ellie while I was at work.' Despite all of the sleepless nights, the worry, it had felt so right, as if he'd been looking for something in all the wrong places and finally found it on his own doorstep. He'd had no choice but to change his lifestyle, but Jack had done so gladly.

'And Ellie's mother?'

'She never came back. Sal died.'

Cass's shoulders shook as she was seized with another choking fit. Maybe he should wait with the story until she'd finished eating.

She put the toast down on to her plate and left it there. 'Jack…I'm so sorry. She was killed climbing?'

'No, she was trying to get in with an expedition to Everest. Of course no one would take her; there's a waiting list to get on to most of the peaks around there and you can't just turn up and climb. She wouldn't give up, though, and ended up sleeping rough. She was killed in a mugging that went wrong.'

'Poor Ellie...'

Her immediate concern for his child touched Jack. 'She's too young for it to really register yet. I just have to hope that I can be there for her when it does.'

Cass took a sip of her tea. 'I have a feeling you'll do a great job of helping Ellie to understand about her mother, when the time comes.'

'What makes you say that?'

She flushed pink. 'Because you're very reassuring. You were great with Lynette last night. In between all the grimaces, that was her *I'm very reassured* face.'

'Well, that's good to know. And what was yours?' He pulled a face, parodying wide-eyed panic.

Cass giggled. 'That was my *I hope no one notices I'm completely terrified* face.'

'Thought so.' He leaned towards her. 'I don't think anyone did.'

'That's okay, then.' The sudden glimpse behind the barriers that Cass put up between her and the world was electrifying. Her smiles, her laughter were bewitching. If things had been different...

But things weren't different. Ellie had already lost her mother. No one should feel that loss twice, and if it meant that Jack remained steadfastly single it was a small price to pay for knowing that no one would ever have the chance to leave Ellie again.

He took a gulp of tea. Maybe it was better to just stop thinking about any of this and focus on the here and now. 'So what are your plans for the day?'

Crisis bonding. That was what it was. Jack wouldn't seem half as handsome or a quarter as desirable if it hadn't been for the floods and a long night, filled with every kind of emotion imaginable. A little sleep and a lot of coffee would fix everything.

Somehow Cass doubted that. But she had to tell herself something before she started to fall for Jack. Because, when it came down to it, his expectations were most probably the same as any other man's.

And she would never really know what his expectations were until she was in too deep. When Paul had first proposed to her he'd never mentioned children, but the pressure had started to grow as soon as it became apparent to both of them that there might be a problem. She couldn't risk the pain of trying again and being rejected when she failed. No man, not even Jack, could guarantee that he wouldn't leave her if she couldn't give him children.

It was better to accept being alone. And to concentrate on today.

'Martin and I were going to go and visit Miss Palmer. She's eighty-two and won't leave her house. She's pretty feisty.'

He chuckled. 'What is it about this village? It's like a nineteen-fifties horror film—some poor hapless paramedic washed up to find himself in a remote place where all the women are terrifying...'

He wasn't terrified at all; he was man enough to enjoy it. Cass grinned. 'We *are* all terrifying. There's something in the water.'

Jack leaned back, his shoulders shaking with laughter. 'I'll stick to bottled, then. And I don't much like the sound of an eighty-two-year-old on her own in these conditions. Want me to come along?'

'Yes. Thanks. Maybe we can grab a couple of hours sleep first, though. And some coffee.'

CHAPTER FOUR

'I WONDER IF she's got any cake.' Sleep seemed to have made Cass hungry again.

'Almost certainly.' Martin opened the front gate of one of a small, neat row of houses. 'I gather that the Monday Club came round here yesterday, after your visit.'

'That's all right then. What we can't eat, we can use to shore up the flood defences.' Cass stopped at the end of the path and Jack decided to wait with her, leaving Martin to approach the cottage alone.

The door was opened by a small, neatly dressed woman who might or might not be Miss Palmer. She didn't look eighty-two.

'Vicar. Lovely to see you.' She craned around to look at Cass and Jack. 'You've brought reinforcements, I see.'

Martin's shoulders drooped. Clearly, reinforcements were exactly what he needed.

'That her?' Jack murmured the words to Cass and she nodded, turning her back on the front door.

'Yep. She's…'

'Cassandra!' Cass jumped and swivelled back to face Miss Palmer. 'Do turn around, dear; you know I can't hear you.'

'Sorry. I forgot…'

Miss Palmer pursed her lips in disbelief. 'Well, come

in and have a cup of tea. And you can tell me all about last night.'

'News travels fast.' Cass strode up the front path. 'They're calling him Noah. Eight pounds, give or take.'

'Good.' Miss Palmer beamed her approval, leaning round to examine Jack. 'Is this your captive paramedic, dear?'

Jack was beginning to feel as if he was. Captivated by Cass's smile, longing to hear her laugh. Wanting to touch her.

'Yes. We found him washed up by the side of the river and we've decided to keep him. We've had him locked in the church hall.'

Miss Palmer nodded, enigmatic humour in her face. 'Leave your boots in the porch.'

The sitting room was bright and frighteningly clean, with the kind of orderliness that Jack remembered from before he'd had a child. One wall was entirely given over to glass-fronted bookcases and another was filled with framed photographs.

'My travels.' Miss Palmer caught Jack looking at them and came to stand by his side. 'Papua New Guinea... South Africa...'

Jack studied the black and white photographs. Some were the kind a tourist might take, posed with landmarks and things of interest, and others told a different story. Groups of children, ramshackle schools, a young woman whose air of determination couldn't be disguised by time and who had to be Miss Palmer.

'You worked abroad?'

'Yes. I'm a teacher. I came home when my mother became ill and looked after her for some years. Then I taught in the school, here.'

'And this one?' A colour photograph of Miss Palmer, done up in waterproofs and walking boots, standing on high ground. Next to her, Cass had her arms held aloft in an unmistakable salute to some victory or other.

'Ah, yes.' Miss Palmer shot Cass a smile. 'We climbed Snowdon.'

'Miss Palmer raised a whole chunk of money...' Cass added and Miss Palmer straightened a little with quiet pride.

'Surprising how much people will sponsor you for when you're in your seventies.' A slight inclination of the head, as if Miss Palmer was sharing a secret. 'They think you're not going to make it to the top.'

'We showed them, though.' Cass broke in again.

'Yes, dear. We did.' Jack found himself on the end of one of Miss Palmer's quizzical looks. She was probably checking that he understood the point that she'd just made. If she could do all this, then a flood wasn't driving her from her home.

'I'll go and make the tea. Make yourselves comfortable.' Martin sat down suddenly, as if responding to an order. Jack reckoned that any prolonged exposure to Miss Palmer would have that effect on someone.

'I'll come and give you a hand.' Jack ignored Cass's raised eyebrows, motioning for her to stay put. He wanted to speak with Miss Palmer on her own.

She bustled, tight lipped, around the small modern kitchen. Jack gave her some space, leaning in the doorway his arms folded.

'So. What are we going to do, then?'

Miss Palmer faced him with a look of controlled ferocity. Jack imagined that she was used to a whole class quailing into silence at that.

'I had assumed you might be off duty.' She glared at his T-shirt and sweater.

'I'm never off duty. I dare say you can understand that.' Miss Palmer didn't stop being a teacher as soon as she was out of the classroom. And Jack didn't stop being a paramedic just because his ambulance had been wrecked and his uniform soaked through.

'Yes, I do.' She laid cups and saucers carefully on a tray.

'Your friends are concerned about you. My job is to find out whether that concern is justified. To check whether you're okay, and if you are to leave you alone.'

Miss Palmer's set expression seemed to soften a little. 'This house is well above the flood line, and I'm lucky enough to have electricity and my phone still. Is it so much to ask, that I stay in my own home?'

'No. And I'll do my best to make sure that happens, but you've got to help me. If we can address any potential problems now, then that's a good first step.'

'Is this the way you deal with all the old ladies?'

'Yes, of course. Is this the way you deal with all your pupils?'

Miss Palmer smiled suddenly, her blue eyes twinkling with amusement. 'A hundred lines, young man. *I will not answer back.*'

Jack chuckled. He could see why Cass liked her so much; they were birds of a feather. Both as feisty as hell, with a sense of humour. 'Are you on any medication?'

Miss Palmer walked to the refrigerator and drew out a cardboard packet, which Jack recognised. 'Warfarin. What's that for—you have a blood clot?'

'A very small one. The doctors picked it up on a routine screening six months ago. I had an appointment for an X-ray a couple of days ago, to see whether the clot had dissolved yet, but I couldn't make it.'

'Okay. When was your last INR test?'

'Two weeks. I can't get to the hospital.'

'I'll get a test sent over; I can do one here.'

Miss Palmer nodded. 'Thank you. My INR is usually quite steady but...'

'Best to check.' The Warfarin would be thinning her

blood to dissolve the clot. The INR test made sure that the dose was correct. 'Do you have some way of calling someone? In an emergency?'

Miss Palmer opened a cupboard and reached inside, producing a panic alarm.

'Is that working?' First things first. Then he'd tell her that there wasn't much point in keeping it in the cupboard.

'Yes, I try it out once a week.'

'I want you to check it every evening. And I want you to wear it.'

He was expecting some kind of argument but Miss Palmer nodded, putting the red lanyard around her neck and tucking the alarm inside her cardigan.

'I want it within reach at all times. Particularly when you're in bed or in the bathroom.'

'You're very bossy, aren't you?' Miss Palmer seemed to respect that.

'Yeah, very. But I'll make you a deal. You wear the alarm and let me give you a basic medical check, and I'll get everyone off your back.'

Miss Palmer held out her hand and Jack smiled, stepping forward. Her handshake was unsurprisingly firm. 'All right. Deal.'

Jack had obviously been carrying out some negotiation in the kitchen. When he reappeared with Miss Palmer, carrying the full tray of tea things for her, it was apparent that they'd struck up some understanding. At least he'd got her to wear her alarm.

Tea was drunk and Martin excused himself, leaving to make a call on another family in the street. Cass concentrated on her second slice of cake while Jack busied himself, taking Miss Palmer's blood pressure, asking questions about her general health and checking on her heart and breathing.

Finally he seemed satisfied. 'Congratulations. I can find absolutely nothing wrong with you.'

'Not for want of looking.' Miss Palmer gave a small nod as Jack slipped the blood pressure cuff from her arm and she rolled down her sleeve. She liked people who were thorough in what they did, and clearly she approved of Jack.

'I'll be back with the INR test, and I expect to see you wearing your alarm.' Jack grinned at her. 'I might try and catch you by surprise.'

Miss Palmer beamed at him. 'Off with you, then.' She hardly gave him time to pack his bag before she was shooing him towards the door. Cass followed, hugging Miss Palmer and giving her a kiss on the cheek.

'Go carefully, Cassandra.'

'I will. You too, Izzy.' She whispered the name. It was something of an honour to call Isobel Palmer by her first name, reserved for just a few dear friends, and Cass didn't take it lightly.

She followed Jack down the front path and walked silently beside him until she was sure that Miss Palmer could no longer see them from her front window. 'All right, then. Give.'

He turned to her, raising an eyebrow. 'I've done a deal with her. She gets to stay as long as I'm allowed to satisfy myself that she's well and taking sensible precautions.'

'I don't like it.' Cass would much rather have her friend looked after for the time being. Martin had offered a place at the vicarage and, now that Lynette was gone, there was more than enough room.

'I know you don't. Look at it this way. What's important to her?'

'Her independence. I know that. But this wouldn't be for long.'

'That doesn't make any difference. Her community has

still told her, loud and clear, that she can't cope. How do you suppose that's going to affect her in the long term?'

He had a point. 'But... Look, I really care about her.'

'Yes, that's obvious. And if there were any medical reason for her to leave her home, I'd be the first to tell you. But I'm not going to provide you with an excuse to make her leave, because taking away an elderly person's independence isn't something that anyone should do lightly.'

Cass pressed her lips together. Izzy had helped her be independent when no one else could. Maybe it was fate that Jack was asking her to do the same for Izzy.

'Okay. You're right.' She pulled her phone out of her pocket and stuffed the earbuds into her ears. Before she got a chance to turn the music on, one of them flipped back out again as Jack nudged the cable with one finger.

'So what's the story with you and her? She was your teacher?'

'Yeah.'

'And you stayed in touch with her when she retired?'

He seemed to see almost everything. Which was obviously a good thing when it came to his patients, but Cass reckoned it could get annoying for everyone else.

'She was my teacher for twenty years. Still is, in some ways. I have dyslexia, and she took me on. I used to go to hers to do my homework after school every day and she used to help me.'

'And she let you struggle a bit with things?'

A grudging laugh of assent escaped her lips. 'She let me struggle all the time. She was always there to catch me, though.'

He nodded. 'Then perhaps that's your answer.' He picked up the earbud, which dangled on its lead against the front of her jacket, and gently put it back into her ear. Cass pretended not to notice the intimacy of it, but shivered just the same.

It appeared that even though the crisis was over, the bonding part wasn't. And wanting him, wanting Jack's strength and his warmth, would only end badly. She and Paul had tried for two years to have children, and by the end of it she'd been a wreck. Sex had become a chore instead of a pleasure and Cass had felt herself dying inside, unable to respond to a touch.

Worst of all, she'd become fearful. Afraid of a future that seemed to depend on her being able to have a child, and hardly daring to get out of bed on the mornings when her period was due. Fearful of the heartbreak that had come anyway, when Paul had left her.

That fear had paralysed her whenever she'd even thought about starting a new relationship, because any man would be sure to react in the same way as Paul had. So Cass had turned to the parts of her life where she'd already proved she could succeed. Her job. Taking care of her family and friends. Overcoming her dyslexia. If wanting Jack brought her loneliness into sharp focus then he would be gone soon, and the feeling would pass.

Cass had withdrawn into silence as they'd trudged back to the church hall. The weather was getting worse, rain drumming against the windows, and when Cass didn't show up for lunch Jack wondered if there was something wrong. It seemed almost as if the violence of the storm might be some response to the unspoken emotions of a goddess.

Nonsense. She might look like an ethereal being but she was all woman. Tough and proud on the outside but with a kernel of soft warmth that showed itself just briefly, from time to time. Each time he saw it, the urge to see it again became greater.

And that was nonsense too. His own childhood had been marred by loss and he wanted no more of it, not for himself or for Ellie. The uncertain reward didn't justify the risk, even if he did crave the sunshine of Cass's smile.

Cups and saucers were filled and the lines of diners started to break up into small groups, talking over their coffee. At the other end of the hall, Martin was on his feet, talking intently to a man who had hurried in, a small group forming around them. Someone walked out of the hall and Jack heard Cass's name being called.

Ripples of concern were spreading through the community, people looking up from their conversations and falling quiet. Jack stood up, walking across to Martin.

'What's going on?'

'Ah, Jack.' Martin's face was creased with anxiety. 'We've got a lost child...'

Activity from outside the hall caught Jack's attention. The shine of red hair through the obscure glass of the doors and then Cass was there, the man who had gone to fetch her still talking quickly to her, obviously apprising her of the situation.

'What do you want me to do?' Without noticing it, Jack seemed to have gravitated automatically to her side.

She looked up at him. The defeated droop of her shoulders that he'd seen earlier was gone; now Cass was back from whatever crisis she'd been facing. Full of energy and with a vengeance.

'We have a ten-year-old who's gone missing. We'll split up and search for him in teams. You're with me?'

Jack nodded. Of course he was with her.

CHAPTER FIVE

JACK FOUND HIS jacket amongst the others, hung up on the rack in the lobby, and pulled his boots on. People were spilling out of the church hall, finding coats and forming into groups. Everyone seemed to know what they were doing and Cass was at the centre of it all.

Suddenly, she broke away from the people around her, walking over to a young woman in a wet jacket.

'We're going to find Ben now, Laura.' Cass put an arm around the woman's shoulders. 'Can you think of anywhere he might have gone?'

'He might be looking for Scruffy. He ran off and we couldn't find him. Pete went out this morning, but there was no sign of him back at the house.'

Cass nodded. 'Okay. And where might Ben be looking?'

'I don't know...' Laura shook her head and Cass took her gently by the shoulders.

'It's okay. Take your time.' She was calm and quite unmistakably in charge of the situation. Just what Laura needed at the moment.

Laura took a deep breath. 'Maybe... Oh, Cass. Maybe he's gone down to the river. We take Scruffy for walks along there.'

'Whereabouts? Down by my place?'

'Yes... Yes, that's right.'

'Okay, I'll check that out.'

'I'm coming...' Laura grabbed hold of Cass's jacket.

'I need you to stay here so that we can bring him straight back to you when we find him. Join the group that's searching the church buildings and keep your phone with you so I can call you. All right?'

Laura nodded. Jack knew that Cass was keeping her away from the river, and the reason didn't bear thinking about.

'Let go of me, then...' Cass gently loosened Laura's fingers from her jacket and turned, leaving her with Martin. Her face set suddenly in a mask of determination as she faced Jack.

'I'll get my bag...' The heavy bag would slow him up but he might need it.

'Thanks. If you give it to Chris, he'll stay here with the car. He can get whatever we need down to us quickly.'

'Okay. Makes sense.'

Jack fetched his bag and handed it over to a man standing by an SUV which was parked outside the church hall. Then he joined Cass's group and they set off, moving quickly through the village and down the hill.

They passed the spot where the bridge had been washed away yesterday, and Cass stopped to scan the water. 'I can't see anything...' She stiffened suddenly and pointed to a flash of blue and red in the branches of a partially submerged tree. The wind caught it and it flapped. Just a torn piece of plastic.

'Where *is* he?'

The exclamation was all she allowed herself in the way of emotion. After surveying the river carefully, she started to walk again. They scaled a rocky outcrop which afforded a view across the land beyond it.

Nothing. Jack strained his eyes to see some sign of the boy. The house ahead of them must be Cass's, stone-built and solid-looking, the extension at the back blending so well with the stonework at the front that it would be difficult to say for sure that it was modern if he didn't already know. He hoped that Ben hadn't got in there; the river had broken its banks and the place was surrounded by water.

'Ben...' Cass filled her lungs and shouted again. 'Ben!'

She stilled suddenly, holding her hand out for quiet. Nothing. Just the relentless sound of the rain. Then she suddenly grabbed Jack's arm. 'Can you see something? Down there?'

Jack squinted into the rain but all he could see was the swollen river, flanked on this side by twenty feet of muddy land. The river must have flooded up across it in the night and receded slightly this morning because he recognised part of the bridge sticking out of the quagmire.

She pulled a pair of binoculars from inside her coat and trained them down on to the mud. Then her breath caught. 'Got him. He's down by that bit of bridge. He's covered in mud and it looks as if he's up to his waist in it.' She lowered the binoculars, feeling in her pocket. Jack squinted at the place she'd indicated and thought he saw movement.

Cass handed a set of keys to one of the other men in the group. 'Joe, I've got a ladder in my garage and a couple of tarps. Can you guys go and find them, please?'

'Okay. Anything else?'

'Yeah, just pump out the water and clear up a bit while you're there.' A small twist of her lips and that wry joke was all she allowed herself in the way of regret.

She was off before Jack could say anything to her, scrambling down the other side of the ridge. The four men with them headed towards the house and Jack followed Cass, getting to the bottom before she did and catching her arm when she slipped in the mud.

'Careful...'

'Yeah, thanks.' One moment. There was no time to tell

her that he was sorry to see her house flooded, and no time for Cass to respond. But her brief smile told him that she knew and she'd deal with it later. Jack resolved to be there when she got around to doing that.

They set off, jogging towards Ben. Jack could see him now, covered in mud, sunk up to his waist, right next to the remains of the bridge. And, huddled next to him, wet through and perched on one of the stones, was a small black and white dog.

'He must have seen the dog and tried to get out there to fetch him.' Jack supposed that Scruffy was light enough to scamper across the mud, but the boy had sunk when he'd tried to follow him.

'Yeah. Wonder how close we can get.'

Jack had been wondering that himself. It was likely that the ground all around Ben was completely waterlogged.

'Ben… Ben…' Cass called over to the boy and Jack saw his head turn. 'Ben, stay still for me. I'm coming to get you.'

'Cass…' The boy's voice was full of the excitement of seeing the cavalry ride over the hill. Full of the panic that he must have felt when he'd started to sink into the mud and found he couldn't get out.

'Ben—' Cass came to a halt at the edge of the mud. 'Ben, I want you to look at me. No…don't try to move. Stay still.'

The boy was crying but he did what she told him. 'I… can't…'

'I know. Just hang on in there and I'll be out to get you in a minute. Then your mum gets the job of cleaning you up.'

Her grin said it all. She was trying to replace Ben's terror with the more mundane fear of a ticking off at getting himself so dirty. Cass was edging forward slowly, testing the ground in front of her before she put her weight on it. Jack followed, ready to grab her if she started to sink.

'You'll be able to tell your friends at school that you got rescued by the fire brigade.' She was grinning at Ben, talking to him as she tested the ground ahead of her and to either side, and the boy seemed to calm a bit.

Her foot sank into the mud in front of her, a good fifteen feet away from Ben, and he began to howl with terror. 'Okay. Okay, Ben. It's okay.'

She reached back and Jack clasped her arm. A brief smiling glance that seemed to sear through the urgency of the situation. 'Don't let me sink…'

'I've got you.'

Another tentative step in the clinging mud. Another and her boot sank as far as her ankle. Jack felt her fingers tighten around his and he reached forward, gripping her waist and pulling her back.

'I think that's as far as we'll get…' She looked around, pulling her phone from her pocket and dialling.

'Joe, I need the ladder now. And there's a toolbox in the garage—can you take a couple of doors off their hinges and bring them over…?'

She turned back to Ben. 'All right, Ben. Just waiting for my ladder. Then I'll be out to get you.' She was doing her best to turn this into an exciting adventure and, although it wasn't totally working, Ben was a lot calmer now.

Jack looked round and saw two men appear from Cass's garage, one on each end of an aluminium ladder. Wading through the water, they reached dry land and made for them as fast as the muddy terrain would allow.

'Here we go, Ben.' Cass was keeping up a stream of reassurance. 'They're on their way.'

As soon as the men reached them, she stretched the double length of the ladder across the muddy ground towards Ben. More than halfway. When it was extended fully, it would reach him easily.

'Thanks, Joe. Have you called the emergency services? She turned to one of the men who had brought the ladder.

'Yes. They'll do what they can. I called up to the church

and they're sending the medical bag down. Pete and Laura are coming too.'

'Great, thanks.'

Jack and the other two men helped Cass drag a couple of heavy branches over, putting them under the end of the ladder to try and stabilise it. Then she took a deep breath, turning her face up to him.

'Cover my back, eh?'

'You've got it.'

He tested the ground at their end of the ladder and put all his weight on it to steady it. Cass began to crawl along it, pushing the extension towards Ben.

'We're going back to help with the doors.' He heard Joe's voice behind him. 'The screws are all painted in, so they're not coming off that easily.'

'She's going to need some help out there. Use a crowbar if you have to.' Jack knew that Cass wouldn't hesitate to say the same.

'Right you are.' Joe turned, jogging back towards the house.

Ben gave a little cry of relief when the end of the ladder reached him, grabbing it and wrapping his arms around it. There was a click as Cass locked the extension in place, and then she began crawling along the extension.

Jack applied all his weight to his end of the ladder. The other end seemed to be sinking a little, but not so much that it stopped Cass from reaching Ben. He wondered whether the boy saw the same as he had, when he'd been tangled in that tree yesterday and he'd opened his eyes and seen her there.

From the way that Ben grabbed at her, he did. He heard Cass laugh and saw her wrap one arm around the boy, trying to loosen the mud around his waist with the other hand.

'I don't think…' She called back without turning her head, 'I'm going to need a hand with this.'

It was as Jack had expected. 'They're coming with the doors now. I'll be out in a minute.'

'That'll be lovely. Thanks.' Her tone was much the same as if she was accepting a cup of tea, and Jack smiled. She was unstoppable. And quite magnificent.

As soon as the ladder had reached Ben, Scruffy had bolted from his perch, running across her back and over the mud to get to dry land. Cass kept her attention equally divided between not falling off the ladder and keeping Ben quiet and stopping him from trying to move. She could hear signs of activity behind her, along with general instructions from Jack about tarps and doors. Then his voice, calling over to her.

'I'm moving off the ladder now. Watch out.'

She braced herself as the ladder moved slightly, sinking another inch into the mud. Then, as someone else applied their weight to the end of it, it steadied again. Above her head, she heard the beat of a helicopter.

'Are they going to pull us out?' Ben was shivering in her arms, his head nestled against her shoulder.

'No, they can't do that.' Trying to drop a line and pull Ben out might tear him in half. 'They're probably just flying over to see what the situation is and how they can help us.'

'And then the fire engine…?'

'Yeah. Then the fire engine.' If Ben hadn't realised that there wasn't a way for a fire engine to get to them, she wasn't going to disillusion him. 'But they won't have anything to do because we'll have you out before they get here.'

'Okay.' Ben sounded almost disappointed.

'Ben…?' Face down in the mud, Cass couldn't see what was happening behind her, but she recognised Laura's voice.

'Mum!' Ben's high-pitched shriek was directed straight into her ear.

'Ben, I want you to do exactly what Cass tells you. Do you hear me, darling?'

Good. Someone must be with Laura, calming her and telling her what to say. Jack, perhaps. Only she was rather hoping that Jack might be on his way towards her.

'Yes, Mum.'

'Tell your mum that you're all right. That you'll be out soon.' Cass grinned at Ben. It would do him good to say it, and do Laura good to hear it.

'Will I?'

''Course you will.'

Ben called out the words, this time managing to direct most of the volume away from Cass and towards his mother. Then someone tapped her ankle gently.

'Can I join you…?'

Jack's voice behind her.

'Feel free.' She squinted round as her kitchen door slid across the muddy ground towards her.

The door moved, and sank a little into the mud as it took his weight, and then he was there beside her. The relief was almost palpable.

'Hey, Ben.' He was lying on his stomach on the door, grinning broadly. 'How are you doing?'

'Okay, thanks.' Ben puffed out a breath. 'Are *you* going to pull me out?'

CHAPTER SIX

UNFORTUNATELY, PULLING BEN out wasn't an option. Mud rescue was difficult and physically demanding at the best of times, and this wasn't the best of times. The continuing rain meant that every time they moved some of the mud from around Ben's body, mud and water trickled back into the hole.

Working together, they found a solution. Jack reached down, scooping the mud up, while Cass shoved it as far from Ben as she could. As they worked, she became bolder, no longer shy of Jack's body. Using his strength to lever her own against, bracing her legs across his.

It was exhausting work. Ben was beginning to get really cold now and started to cry again, and Jack talked to him, encouraging him. Or was it Cass that he encouraged? She hardly knew, just that the sound of his voice kept her going, despite the growing ache in her arms.

'What do you reckon?' His eyes seemed almost brighter, warmer, now that the rest of him was almost entirely covered in mud.

'Yeah. Let's try it.'

'Okay. Be ready to take him.' Jack wrapped his arms around Ben. Gently, carefully, he began to lift him. Ben's feet came out of his wellingtons, leaving them stuck in the muddy pit, and Jack hoisted him clear.

A tremulous, excited babble of voices sounded behind them. Cass had almost forgotten that anyone else was here.

'Got him…?' Jack passed Ben over to her and the boy grabbed her, whimpering with cold and exhaustion.

'Yeah.'

'Okay, you shift over on to the door and I'll pull you both back.' Jack manoeuvred around her, working his way carefully back, and Cass felt him grip her ankles, pulling her back after him.

Her limbs were shaking with fatigue and Cass didn't know where Jack found the strength to drag her those few short feet. But he did, taking Ben out of her arms as soon as they were back on the grass and carrying him over to the SUV that was waiting to take them the short distance to the village. Laura and Pete followed, desperate to hold their son.

A hand gripped hers, hauling her to her feet. People clustered around her, patting her on the back and enquiring whether she was okay. Cass nodded shakily and, as she made for the car, a path opened up in front of her, everyone stumbling backwards to get out of the way.

Ben was in his mother's arms on the back seat of the car, Scruffy sitting close to him. The boy was wet, cold, very muddy, but seemingly otherwise unscathed. Jack gave Cass a nod in answer to her silent question. He was okay.

'We'll get him back now…' He signalled to the driver and got into the car next to Ben, Laura and the little dog. Pete pushed Cass into the front seat.

'Don't you want to go?'

'I'll see you up there…' Pete's eyes were glistening with tears. 'Go and get yourself dry.'

They drove to the vicarage and Martin ushered Jack upstairs, Ben in his arms. Laura followed and Sue propelled Cass into the kitchen.

'I'd hug you if you weren't so filthy…' Sue stripped off

her jacket and sweatshirt, nodding when she found that the T-shirt underneath was dry. 'Sit.'

Cass sat down, half in a dream. Sue's businesslike ministrations were just what she needed. She didn't need Jack to help her out of her overtrousers; he had other things to do. But a part of her wished that he didn't and that after the struggle that they'd shared so intimately they could have just a little time together.

'Feet wet...?' Sue loosened the laces of one of her boots, sliding two fingers inside as if she were a child. 'They feel all right. Drink this...'

Hot soup. Fabulous. 'Thanks, Sue.'

She sipped the soup, letting the warmth of the kitchen seep back into her bones. Then she laid her head on her hands. Just for a moment. She was so tired.

'Sorry about all the mess, Sue.' It seemed that Jack's voice alone, amongst all the other comings and goings in the kitchen, had the power to pull her back to consciousness. Cass looked up and saw him standing in the doorway. He'd taken off his muddy jacket and sweatshirt and his arms and face had been washed clean, presumably as a preliminary to examining Ben. His short hair glistened with a few stray drops of moisture.

'Nonsense.' Sue glared at him. 'How's Ben?'

'We've cleaned him up and I examined him. He's pretty tired now, and he had a nasty fright. But, physically, I can't find anything wrong with him.'

'Good. Anything I should do?'

'Plenty of liquids, something to eat. Keep him warm. Old-fashioned care.'

Sue smirked. 'I can do that. You two go and get cleaned up.'

Cass got to her feet and walked over to the sink. She'd

got mud on the table where she'd laid her head down. Sue whipped the wash cloth out of her hand.

'Leave that to me. Go.'

'No, it's okay…' Cass's protests were silenced by one slight incline of Jack's head. She was going with him.

He led her to the bathroom in the church hall, accepting towels from one of the Monday Club ladies who bustled in out of nowhere and left just as energetically. Putting them down on to the chair by the washbasins, he dumped a plastic bag he'd been carrying on top and then walked over to the door, flipping the lock.

'Boots.' His grin was warm, and far too tender to resist. Cass hung on to the washbasin while he unlaced her boots, pulling them off.

'What's this?' He'd tipped her face up to his, running his thumb across the sore spot in her hairline.

'Just a scrape. Is it bleeding?'

'Not all that much. I'll clean it up in a minute.' He searched in the plastic bag and produced a bottle of shampoo, which Cass recognised as her own, one of the toiletries that she must have left at Sue and Martin's. She reached for the bottle and he pulled it away.

'Let me do it.'

There was no desire in his face, no trace of wanting. Just the warmth of two comrades who finally had the opportunity to see to each other's needs instead of those of everyone else.

This would be okay. And she so wanted it. Someone to take care of her after a long night and an even longer day. There would be no complications, no threat of what might happen tomorrow, because Jack wouldn't be here tomorrow.

He pulled a chair over to the washbasin at the end of the row, which was equipped with a sprinkler tap. Testing the temperature of the water, he told her to close her eyes.

Cass felt herself start to relax. He was good at this, guiding the water away from her face, rubbing gently to get all of the mud out of her hair. Massaging the shampoo through, his firm touch sending tingles radiating across her scalp. His leg pressed against her side as he leaned over her.

Maybe there was just a bit of sensuality about this. Along with all the nurturing and the warmth—the things that she reckoned it was okay to take from Jack. Cass dismissed the thought. It was what it was and she was too tired, too much in need to question it.

Then the warm water running over her head and finally a rub with a towel. Cass opened her eyes, sitting up straight.

'Better now?'

'Much. Thank you.' She rubbed at her hair and he handed her a comb. She winced as the teeth passed over the abraded skin at her temple.

'Let's have a look at that.' He didn't wait for her to either agree or disagree, just did it. Gentle fingers probed and then he reached for the plastic bag again. 'I think you'll live. I'll put some antiseptic on it, though.'

The antiseptic stung for a moment but even that was refreshing. Jack had a lightness of touch that set her nerve endings quivering, but that would have to remain her little secret.

'Do something for me?' He raised one eyebrow and she smiled.

'What do you want?'

A slight twitch at the corner of his mouth. Then he sat down opposite her and carefully removed a haphazardly applied piece of plaster from his arm. Underneath, the skin was red raw, a fragment of wood protruding. Cass caught her breath. He must have ignored the injury, the splinter driving deeper into his skin as he'd worked, and it was going to hurt to get it out now.

'Do you have a pair of tweezers?'

He leaned over, producing a pair from the bag, but when

Cass reached for them he closed his hand over them, holding it against his chest. 'Gently does it, eh? I know you lot.'

'My lot?' Cass grinned. 'What's that supposed to mean? I'll have you know I'm medically trained.' All firefighters were.

'It's supposed to mean that you don't have to throw me over your shoulder and carry me out of here first. Then tip me in a heap on the ground and start pumping on my chest.'

'Think I couldn't? I have a technique, you know.' The truth was that she could just about manage it. He'd have much less trouble lifting her.

He was shaking his head, laughing. 'That's exactly what I'm worried about.'

He handed her the tweezers and pushed the bottle of antiseptic towards her. Cass positioned his arm on the vanity top and bent over it, looking carefully. He made no sound but the muscles in his arm twitched when she laid her finger close to the wound.

'You really should have a local anaesthetic for this.'

'Nah. Better to just get it over with. I've only got the strong stuff in the medical bag.'

And he was saving that in case someone else needed it. Cass gripped his wrist tight to steady his arm and drew out the first piece of the splinter. She was going to have to fish a little for the second piece, which had been driven deep into his arm.

She so hated hurting him but he was trusting her to have the nerve to do it. Trusting that her hand wouldn't shake and make things a whole lot worse. She steadied herself and pressed the tweezers into the raw skin, trying not to hear his sudden intake of breath.

'Sorry...' She had nothing to make the pain any better and Cass fought the urge to dip her head and kiss it away.

'That's okay. Got it all?'

Cass carefully examined the wound. 'Yes, I think so. Can't see anything else.'

'Antiseptic, then.'

She applied a generous measure, making sure that the wound was disinfected. 'Are your tetanus shots up to date?'

'Yes.'

'Then we're nearly done.' Cass leaned forward, stripping off his T-shirt, and Jack chuckled.

'What now? Is this all part of the technique too?'

'Just making sure there's nothing else you haven't told me about.'

She would have preferred to touch instead of just looking, but that would be a step too far. Cass found herself ignoring the scrapes and bruises and concentrating on the smooth contours of his shoulders and chest. Very nice. And, what was nicer still, he had the confidence to just sit there and meet her gaze without sucking in his stomach or trying to flex his shoulders. He was perfect, just as he was.

'Finished?' He raised an eyebrow.

'Yeah. I think you'll do. Do you want me to dress your arm?'

'We'll clean up first.' He gave her a bone-melting grin and stood up, picking his T-shirt up and throwing it over one shoulder. 'Stay there.'

He picked up the bag and disappeared around the corner, towards the showers. Then the sound of gushing water came from the only cubicle that contained a bath. He wouldn't. Would he? If he did, then she just might. Even thinking about it was sending shivers through her tired limbs.

'Come on.' He was back again, catching up two of the largest towels in one hand, and Cass followed him. When he opened the door of the cubicle a gorgeous smell hit her. Bath oil foamed in the steaming tub and there were candles propped on the window ledge and the vanity unit.

'You're not going to fall asleep in here, are you?'

She wondered what he'd say if she asked him to stick around and make sure. But he'd put one of the towels down on the rack and now he was halfway out of the door. It seemed he had no intention of staying.

'No. Just keep talking.'

'Right you are.' He closed the door behind him and Cass heard the sound of the shower in the next door enclosure.

She turned her back on the partition wall between her and Jack before pulling her sweater off and unbuttoning her shirt. As she slipped off her jeans, she caught herself instinctively glancing behind her as if his gaze, or perhaps her own fantasies, had the power to dissolve the partition while she wasn't looking.

When she stepped into the steaming water, sinking beneath the bubbles, she felt the warmth seep into her bones. Cass lay back, rubbing the ache out of her shoulders. Bliss. This was pure bliss.

Okay, so he'd been tempted. Jack would admit to that. But it was worth needing to apply a little self-control to have seen her face when she'd walked into the cubicle. When he'd found her slumped at the kitchen table, he'd known this was exactly what she needed.

'Still awake?' he called to her as the hot water drummed on to his shoulders, making the various scrapes he'd picked up over the last couple of days smart a little.

'Yes. You?' Cass's voice was clear, drifting through the gap between the top of the partition and the ceiling.

'Yeah, I'm awake.' Wide awake and trying not to think thoughts that he shouldn't. 'I'm sorry about your house.' He'd been meaning to say it for a while now, but Jack wasn't sure how to do it without hugging her. The partition between them rendered that now unlikely.

The sound of her moving in the water. 'It's okay. There are more important things.'

Yes, there were, and what had happened with Ben had underlined it. But that didn't mean that the loss of her house was nothing. Jack wondered when it was going to hit Cass, and renewed his promise to himself that he'd be there when it did.

'Thanks for the candles.' Her mind seemed to have drifted somewhere else. 'They're a nice touch.'

Jack couldn't stop himself from smiling. There was so little he could do for her. 'Wish I could have done more.'

'Cherubs? Or perhaps a few perfumed clouds hovering about...?' She laughed quietly.

'Both. Every cherub needs a cloud.'

'Ah. And a glass of champagne.'

'Why stop at a glass?' Jack smiled as he soaped himself, feeling the tension ebb from his shoulders. 'Want some caviar with it?'

'No. I'll take a burger. Home-made, with extra cheese. And chips. Plenty of salt and vinegar.'

'Of course you will. Anything else?' What would he do if she said the one thing he wanted to hear? It was a nice fantasy, but in reality he'd probably pretend he'd got soap in his ears and was temporarily deaf.

'Mmm. I'd normally say a mud mask, but actually I think I've had enough mud for one day. Someone to get the knots out of my shoulders.'

Jack didn't comment on that, for fear of sounding too interested in the position. 'And...?'

'A manicure. After I've had the burger, of course. What about you?'

Jack chuckled. 'Three or four handmaidens. One to hand me my towel and one to hold my champagne for me.'

'That's two spare. Send them in here, will you, I'll be needing some help with the after-bath beauty thing. And the swirling silken robes, of course.'

'Yeah. Naturally.' He stepped out of the shower and

switched off the water, dabbing at the abrasions on his chest and arms. 'What about the musicians?'

'Nah. Tell them to wait outside; it's getting a bit crowded in here.'

Jack pulled on the clean clothes that Martin had found for him and unlocked the cubicle door. The image of Cleopatra, rising from her bath and being dressed in silks and jewels, was doing nothing for him. Cass, wrapped in a towel, tired from the effort of saving a young boy's life, was far more entrancing.

When he heard her get out of the bath and pad over to the row of lockers by the showers, Jack kept his eyes, if not his mind, on the task of clearing away the shampoo and wiping the basin. A pause and then she appeared. Pink-cheeked and dressed in sweatpants and a sleeveless T-shirt, a hooded sweat top slung over her shoulder.

'I...thanks. For the bath.' It seemed that fantasy was only permissible when they weren't actually looking each other in the eye.

'My pleasure.'

She shrugged awkwardly. 'I might go and lie down now. Close my eyes.'

Her hand was on the door handle before he remembered what it was he'd been meaning to say to her. 'Hey, Cass. Wait.'

'Yes?'

'Do you think we made today count? Enough to justify staying behind?'

She smiled suddenly. 'Yes. We did.'

CHAPTER SEVEN

CASS HAD BEEN opening out her camp bed when Sue intercepted her. Jack had apparently just happened to walk over to the vicarage and mention that Cass was going for a lie down and Sue had a comfortable, warm nest all prepared for her on the sofa in her kitchen. Far nicer than a rickety camp bed in one of the chilly communal rooms behind the church hall.

Warm and relaxed from her bath, she fell asleep until Sue woke her for an evening meal. It seemed that Jack wasn't joining them and after waiting in the vicarage kitchen for two hours, not daring to betray her interest in him by asking Sue where he was, she went back to sleep on the sofa.

She woke early the following morning. Everyone in the house was still asleep and she donned her jacket and boots and crept out of the back door and to the kitchen in the church hall.

'Sleep well?' A voice behind her interrupted her thoughts and Cass jumped guiltily, sending a teacup rolling across the worktop. It seemed that even thinking about Jack could summon him up out of nowhere.

'Yes, thanks. What are you doing up?'

'One of the guys on weather watch last night… Andy, I think…he woke me up early. Apparently the water levels have gone down overnight, and you've got a couple of escape routes already planned. He said the one down by the motorway…'

So that was the reason for his early start, and the fact he was wearing his ambulance uniform. He couldn't wait to get home. The only thing that was unexpected about that was the feeling of disappointment which tore at Cass.

'Yeah. We reckoned that was most likely going to be the easiest. We've got a boat down there, and my car's parked on the other side, so I'll give you a lift. I need to go and get some supplies.'

'Actually, I was wondering if you'd do me a favour.'

'Of course.' Anything.

'Martin and I made a few visits last night. There are a couple of people running low on repeat prescriptions, and there's a man who is overdue for a pacemaker check. And there's the INR test for Miss Palmer. I'll speak to the hospital; they should be able to make the testing equipment available to me for the day, so I can do it here.'

'You're…' The only piece of information that her mind seemed to comprehend was that Jack was coming back.

'It'll take me most of the day to get across to the hospital and collect what I need, do the tests and then take everything back again. I was wondering if you might help with that, so I get a chance to see Ellie.' His eyes were clouded. Jack obviously didn't much like asking for favours. But he needed this one.

'Of course I will. You go straight home and I'll go to the hospital, collect what you need and get the prescriptions. I can pick you up again when I'm done.' She held out her hand. 'You have a list?'

He hesitated, his hand wandering to his pocket. 'That's really good of you. Are you sure it's okay?'

'Stop arguing and give me the list. Go see your daughter.'

* * *

They'd been piloted across the stretch of water which blocked the A389 by one of the men from the village, drowsy and complaining in the early morning light. Then the dinghy turned around, leaving them standing alone.

'What now?' Jack looked around for any clues as to what he was supposed to do next.

'We walk.' Cass shouldered her backpack and set off, not waiting for his reply. 'It's only a little way. I have my SUV parked in the driveway of that house up ahead.'

Jack followed her pointing finger. 'That's yours? The one camouflaged by mud?'

'Hey! I'll have you know that my car has the engine of a...' she flung her hands up, searching for a suitable description '...a cheetah.'

'A cheetah? What's that—likely to eat you if you get too close?' Jack teased her.

'No! The bodywork's a bit splashed, from when I drove it out of the village when the motorway started to flood.' She grinned up at him. 'You want to walk?'

'I'll take my chances.' Jack upped the pace a little and she matched his stride. The day ahead of them seemed suddenly full of promise.

She'd delivered Jack to a large, neatly groomed house on the edge of one of the villages, close to town. He'd left her with one of his delicious smiles to think about before jogging up the front path and ringing the doorbell. Cass thought about waiting to see whether Ellie would come to the door, and decided not to. She had other things to do and her own list, along with Jack's, would take a good few hours.

It took less than that, but she'd promised Jack that she'd pick him up at twelve and being early would only deprive him of precious time with his daughter. Cass stopped outside a coffee shop and found a seat at one of the smaller tables to drink her coffee alone.

At five past twelve she drew up outside the house again. Grabbing the bag on the front seat, she wondered for the fiftieth time whether this wasn't going to make her look an idiot.

'Sarah…?' A dark-haired young woman answered the front door. 'I'm Cass.'

'Come in.' Sarah shot her a broad smile that reminded her of Jack's. 'They're through here.'

She followed Sarah through to a large lounge. One end of it was strewn with toys and Jack was sitting at the other end in an armchair, a little girl on his lap, a child's picture book laid aside on the arm of the chair.

Two pairs of brown eyes. One shy and assessing, the other smiling.

'You got everything?'

'Yeah.'

Ellie's small fist was wound tight into her father's shirt and she was hiding her face now. Cass stood her ground, wondering what to do.

'Say hello to Cassandra, Ellie…' Jack nudged his daughter's arm, speaking quietly, and the little girl shot her a brief glance. 'She's a bit shy.'

'That's okay. I…er…I went for a coffee and happened to see this as I was walking back to the car. For Ellie…'

She proffered the package awkwardly. It was a mass of brown paper and sticky tape, probably not particularly attractive to a child. And Cass wasn't sure now whether the contents would be all that appealing either. Ellie looked like a very girly girl, in her little pink and blue dress and pink cardigan.

Jack rose from the chair, taking Ellie with him. The little girl clung to her father, hiding her face in his shoulder. 'Hey, Ellie. Cass has brought you something.'

Ellie turned, looking at her solemnly. Then suddenly she smiled.

'Hi, Ellie.' Cass smiled back.

'Hi, Cassandra.' Jack chuckled as Ellie once again managed to pronounce Cass's full name.

'Maybe Cassandra likes to be called Cass?' He raised one eyebrow and his daughter looked up at him.

'I like Cassandra,' the little girl corrected him firmly.

'Well, it's not a matter of what we like. We should call Cass whatever she likes to be called, shouldn't we?'

Ellie turned questioning eyes on to Cass.

'I like Cassandra too. It's just that most people call me Cass because it's shorter. But I'd like *you* to call me Cassandra.'

'See…' Ellie gave Jack an *I-told-you-so* look.

'Yeah, okay. Far be it from me to interfere…' He shot her a delicious grin. That hard, strong body, the tender eyes. The tough, unbending resolve that was all too easy for the little girl in his arms to conquer. It was like an arrow, straight to Cass's heart.

Ellie was reaching now for the parcel in her hand, and Cass handed it over. Jack peered at it. 'What d'you have there, Ellie?'

'I don't know…'

'Well, say thank you to Cassandra and then you can unwrap it.' Jack looked at the sticky tape. 'Maybe you can ask her to help you.'

He let Ellie down and she ran to the chair, putting the parcel on to the seat and pulling at the wrappings. Jack shrugged. 'Or she'll just try it herself…' He smiled at Cass. 'Thank you.'

'You're welcome. I just happened to see it and…'

'Cassandra!' Ellie had torn most of the brown paper off and scattered it on the floor, but the sticky tape was too much for her. Cass grinned, walking over to her and kneeling down next to her, tearing at some of the tape.

'Wow! Look at that, Ellie.' Jack's voice behind her. Ellie gifted her with a bright smile and suddenly everything was right with the world. 'Say thank you, and go and show Ethan and Auntie Sarah what you've got.'

'Thank you, Cassandra…' Ellie threw the words over her shoulder as she ran to the kitchen, where Sarah was making the tea.

'Every girl needs a fire engine?' When Jack turned, the curve of his lips was all for her. Not the indulgent smile that he had for Ellie, but something raw, male. The trace of a challenge, mixed with the promise of something heady and exciting, should she wish to take him up on it.

'I think so.' She was caught in his gaze, unable to back off.

'You're probably right.' He reached forward, brushing a strand of hair from her brow. 'Take your coat off. Sarah's making lunch and she won't let you go without something to eat.'

Sarah and Cass were a perfect foil for each other. Sarah loved to cook, and generally did so as if she were feeding an army, and Cass was perfectly capable of eating like one.

Ellie was allowed down from the table and disappeared off into a corner, clutching her fire engine and a red colouring crayon. Cass leaned back in her chair, her plate empty.

'Thank you. Your spaghetti sauce is really tasty.'

Sarah smiled brightly. 'Would you like the recipe?'

'If you don't mind. I'd like to have a go at this myself.'

Somehow Jack hadn't imagined Cass doing anything as mundane as exchanging recipes. Charging to the rescue seemed more her style. Or maybe testing her strength against his at midnight, under a starry sky. But, when he thought about it, the idea of coming home to find her cooking was equally intoxicating.

'You cook?' He smiled, as if the question were a mere pleasantry.

'I like to eat.' She grinned back. 'That generally involves cooking first.'

'I'll email it through to you. Text me your email address.' Sarah collected the plates and turned to the refrigerator. 'Anyone for cheesecake?'

Cass's grin indicated that she was more than a match for cheesecake.

Ellie had presented her with a picture. A large figure, which seemed to be her, from the amount of red crayon that had been applied around the head, towering over a red box on wheels. Cass hugged the little girl, genuinely delighted, and felt Ellie plant a kiss on her cheek.

Jack had pencilled in her name under the figure and Ellie had returned to her corner to laboriously trace out the letters, her tongue stuck out in concentration. Then it was time to leave. Cass bade Sarah and Ellie goodbye and waited in the car while Jack hugged his daughter.

He dodged out, rain spattering his jacket, and Cass whipped Ellie's picture off the front passenger seat before he sat on it.

'Not a bad likeness.' He smiled at her.

'She's even put a ladder in.' Cass indicated the miniature ladder that the giant figure was brandishing.

'Yep. She's got an eye for detail, even if she's a bit wobbly on scale still.' He regarded the picture thoughtfully. 'And your hair...'

'Yeah. Rub it in.' Sometimes Cass wondered whether her hair was all people saw about her. The phrase *'flame-haired firefighter'* had worn thin a while ago.

He gave her a reproachful look. 'I was going to say that

Ellie did her best with the colours she had. It would be a bit much to ask for her to do it justice.'

The look in his eye told Cass that this was a compliment. The thought that Jack liked her hair suddenly made all the jokes about it worthwhile.

'Would you mind if we stopped off at my place? I want to get a change of clothes...'

Cass caught her breath. Maybe the change of clothes was just for today. Maybe he wasn't thinking about staying. She didn't dare ask.

'Yes, if you want.'

'That's if I still have a bed for tonight, in the church hall.'

'Of course you do. Thanks.'

'And if we could stop at the phone shop as well—it's on our way, and hopefully I'll have a replacement phone waiting for me.' He grinned. 'I called them this morning and asked, told them it was an emergency and that I'm a paramedic. The woman on the other end was really helpful.'

The grey, clouded sky suddenly seemed warmer, less forbidding. Cass started the engine, craning around to see over the boxes stacked in the back of the SUV, and reversed out of Sarah's drive.

Jack's house was only ten minutes away. He motioned for her to follow him inside and left her in the sitting room while he disappeared upstairs.

The room had a nice feel to it. A little battered in places, which was clearly the result of a four-year-old's exuberance, and the toys in the corner were stacked anyhow, as if they'd been hurriedly cleared away before Jack left for a day's work. But it was comfortable. The way a home should be. A sudden vision of her own ruined home floated in front of her eyes and Cass blinked it away.

The open fireplace was obviously used, coal heaped in a scuttle beside it. The dark leather sofa was squashy and comfortable, piled with cushions, a couple of throws

across the back rest. Bookshelves, on either side of the
chimney piece, were stacked full, the bottom shelf clearly
reserved for Ellie, as it contained children's picture books.
The very top shelf boasted a set of leather-bound books and
Cass squinted up at the gold leaf titles on their spines. She
couldn't read all of them, the words that were faded and
cracked were a bit too much for her, but it was obviously a
set of Victorian classics.

Some framed photographs obscured the backs of the
books on the lower shelves. Pictures of Ellie, growing up.
Jack, with Ellie on his shoulders. A woman, sitting on an
elephant, her bright blonde hair obviously owing more to
a bottle of peroxide than nature. It was impossible to tell
whether Ellie's mother was like her at all; her face was
twisted into an open-mouthed expression of exhilaration.

Another shot, obviously taken at a beach bar, and next
to that one taken on the top of a snow-covered peak.

'The Matterhorn.' Jack came into the room.

'Looks fantastic.'

'Yeah. It's a popular peak.' When she turned, Jack's eyes
were fixed on the photograph and she felt a stab of jealousy
for Sal. Not because of all the places she'd been, the things
she'd done, but because she was the woman who'd made
love with Jack and borne his child. And that was wrong,
on so many levels, not least because Cass had decided that
she was not going to feel anything for Jack.

'You must miss her.'

Jack shrugged. 'These photos are here for Ellie, not me.
I cared about Sal as a friend, but there's a part of me that
can't forgive her.'

Cass could think of a number of unforgivable things
that Sal had done, but tact got the better of her. 'What for?'

'I'd hoped that when Sal got back from Nepal, we might
be able to come to some arrangement so that Ellie would

have a proper family. I was prepared to do anything to make that happen.'

'But…surely that wasn't her fault. She died…'

'Yeah. She never told me that she was going to Everest without the proper permits or a place on an expedition. It was just plain crazy and I would have stopped her if I'd known.'

Jack took a last look at the photograph. 'I didn't have the time with my father that I wanted, but at least I knew him. Ellie doesn't even have that; she doesn't remember Sal at all.'

'Ellie seems…' Cass tried to concentrate on something else '…very happy. Very secure.' She remembered seeing Jack hug Ellie when he'd left, and then, in a moment of stillness between the two, he'd put his hand on his heart. Ellie had mimicked him and then let him go without any tears.

'She knows I'll always come back for her.' He shrugged. 'But sometimes I wish…' He shook his head, as if wishes couldn't possibly come true.

Cass hardly dared ask. But she did, anyway. 'What do you wish?'

A sudden heat in his eyes, which turned from fierce intensity to something warmer. 'I miss being able to ask a woman out to dinner.' The tips of his fingers were almost touching her arm. Almost reaching for her, but not quite.

'And you can't do that?' There were plenty of single fathers that did.

'I reckon that the one thing that's worse for Ellie than not having a mother is having a succession of temporary ones. I can't let her lose any more than she already has. I wish it were different, but…'

'Yeah. I miss…' The warmth of having someone. The tingling sense of excitement every time Jack walked into a room had made her realise just how much she missed that.

'But aren't you married to your work?' He raised an eyebrow. 'You're not thinking of getting a divorce, are you?'

'No. That relationship's doing just fine, thank you.'

'Shame.'

The thought that maybe, just maybe, there was another option left her breathless. If they both knew that nothing could come of it, if no one ever knew, then there couldn't be any hurt. If neither of them expected anything, then surely neither of them could be disappointed.

Maybe it wasn't quite that simple. Jack had just the kind of body, just the kind of touch, which made sex for the sake of it seem like the best idea she'd had in years. But there was more to him than that, and his tenderness could make things very complicated.

She turned away from him, breaking the spell. 'We should get going if we want to get back to the village and then make another round trip this afternoon.'

Maybe her disappointment sounded in her voice. He smiled then caught up the bag that lay in the doorway, ushering her outside and then slinging his coat across his shoulders to run to the car.

CHAPTER EIGHT

As soon as they got back to the village they started on the round of visits that Jack had promised to make, Cass acting as his guide. The first on the list was Mr Hughes. He had refused to allow his wife to stay and watch while Jack checked on his pacemaker, and Mrs Hughes had refused to stay in the kitchen, so Cass waited outside the sitting room door with her.

'I really don't know why he didn't go to the hospital sooner. He missed his last appointment, and they said that he had to go in three months. He hasn't got much left on the battery...'

Cass nodded sympathetically, wondering when Mrs Hughes was going to stop with the barrage of complaints about her husband.

'Then, all of a sudden, it gets to be urgent and we can't go because of the floods.' Mrs Hughes gave a derisive sniff. 'Silly man. I wish he'd look after himself a bit better. I do my best.'

'I'm sure it'll all be okay.' Cass ventured some reassurance, based rather more on Jack's expertise than what she knew about Mr Hughes' lifestyle.

'He doesn't listen to me. I've told him more times...' Mrs Hughes broke off as Jack emerged from the sitting room. Behind him, Mr Hughes looked suitably chastened.

'I'm taking your husband's results to the hospital this afternoon.' He gave Mrs Hughes a smile and she brightened immediately.

'And...?'

'His consultant will review them and give you a call. There's nothing to worry about; his pacemaker is doing its job and there are no problems there, but I think that Mr Hughes may well benefit from taking a few measures to improve his general health.'

'Thank you, Doctor.' Mrs Hughes shot a look of triumph at her husband.

'I'm a paramedic.'

Mrs Hughes leaned towards Jack confidingly. 'I don't care who you are. Just as long as you told him...'

Jack nodded, clearly unwilling to commit himself about what he had or hadn't told Mr Hughes, and Mrs Hughes saw them to the front door. Cass followed him down the front path and fell in step with him.

'More exercise. Give up smoking and change his diet...'

Jack grinned. 'Very good. You want to take the next visit?'

Cass shook her head. 'Everyone in the village knows. I imagine the only person who *doesn't* know is the consultant at the hospital. When I asked Mrs Hughes if she'd spoken to him, she said she didn't like to.'

'Why not?'

Cass shrugged. 'Because he's far too important. And clearly far too busy to be worrying about his patients' health.'

Jack gave a resigned groan. 'Okay. He's actually a good man, and very approachable. I'll be making the situation clear in my notes and he'll follow up.'

'Thanks.' Cass swerved off the road and climbed over a stile, jumping down on the other side. 'Short cut.'

Jack had almost completely lost his bearings. Here, on

the other side of the village from the river, the land sloped more gently and houses were scattered between fields and copses of trees. The ring of water that surrounded the area spread out into the distance, encroaching wherever it could through gullies and streams and into homes. But Cass seemed to know every inch of the place, and so far they hadn't even got their feet wet.

'Any other bits of interesting gossip I should know about?' It sounded as if the villagers knew who needed medical help long before anyone else did.

'Don't think so. Joe Gardener pulled a muscle yesterday, carrying my kitchen door.'

'He mentioned that last night when I saw him. The tube of vapour rub from the chemist is for him. What about you?'

'Me? Nothing wrong with me.'

Jack had expected her to say that. But he'd heard a little village gossip too, last night. 'It's just that if there was someone who'd been up all night on more than one occasion in the past few weeks, who'd been holding down a physically demanding job, digging ditches and looking after a pregnant sister…'

She shot him a warning glare, compressing her lips into a hard line. Jack ignored it.

'…rescuing kids, and then going through the trauma of having her own house flooded, I'd be a bit concerned.'

'Would you, now?'

'Do you want to talk about it?'

She stopped short, almost tripping over a tree root when she turned to face him. 'What's all this about, Jack? I'm fine. I told you.'

'Okay. Just asking.' If she wasn't going to talk about it, then he couldn't make her. 'But if you do need anything.'

'So I'm needy now, am I?' She frowned at him.

'No. You might be human, though. And if it turns out that you are, and you need a friend…' He shrugged. Why should she turn to him? She was surrounded by friends here and she never seemed to want to take any help from anyone.

Suddenly she seemed to soften. 'Jack, I...' She shook her head and the moment was lost. 'Will you do something for me? As a friend.'

'Of course.'

'Will you just shut up?'

He'd obviously gone too far and Cass was withdrawn and quiet as they circled the low-lying areas of the village, dropping off prescriptions and visiting anyone who might need medical support. But, whatever sadness she concealed, and Jack was sure by now that she was hiding something, she never hung on to it for long. Cass was nothing if not resilient, and by the time they'd walked back up the hill to Miss Palmer's cottage, she was smiling again.

'I can't wait to see what Bathsheba's going to get up to next.' Cass grinned at Miss Palmer. While Jack had been checking her over and doing the INR test, Cass had produced an MP3 player from her pocket and plugged it into a laptop which lay on a side table.

'Oh, I think you'll be surprised.' Miss Palmer smiled enigmatically.

'Miss Palmer's reading Thomas Hardy. I can read it myself, but it's easier when she does it for me.'

'You can concentrate on what's happening, you mean?' Jack liked the idea, and it obviously gave both Cass and Miss Palmer a lot of pleasure.

'Yes. I get to enjoy the story.'

'It's our little secret.' Miss Palmer was looking at him speculatively, and Jack was learning never to ignore any of Miss Palmer's looks. 'Just between the two of us. Or the three of us, I suppose.'

Cass's cheeks flushed a little, but she didn't seem to mind. And Jack had the sudden feeling that the brick wall that Cass had built around herself had just crumbled a little. Not so much as to allow him to see over the top, but if he put his shoulder to it a few more times who knew what might happen?

They'd retraced their route back along the flooded motorway and to Cass's car. She'd waited in the hospital car park for him, plugging the MP3 player into the car's sound system while Jack returned the borrowed equipment and made sure that the results of the tests he'd taken would reach the right people.

'What time does Ellie go to bed?' When he climbed back into the SUV, she looked at her watch.

'In about half an hour. But if we go now, we'll get back across the water while it's still light.' Jack knew what she was thinking. He'd been thinking the same himself, but it was too late now.

She started the engine. 'Won't take long to kiss her goodnight, will it? And I've got a flashlight in the back of the car.'

'Anything you *don't* have in the back of your car?'

She chuckled. 'I like to come prepared.'

They were in time for Jack to put Ellie to bed. He walked back downstairs to find Cass alone in the sitting room, still listening to her MP3 player.

'Ready?'

'Yeah. Thanks.' He said a quick goodbye to Sarah, resisting the temptation to go and wake Ellie up, just to say goodnight to her again, and followed Cass to her car.

When they arrived at the motorway, she pulled a large flashlight from the car boot, switching it on. It illuminated the water in front of them as she swung it slowly.

'They must not be here yet.' There was no answering flash of light from the gloom on the other side. 'They won't be long.'

Suddenly, the men coming to fetch them could be as long as they liked. It could rain as much as it liked. Jack reached for her, wondering whether she would back away.

She didn't. Cass took a step towards him, the beam of the flashlight swaying suddenly upwards. They were touching now. Sweaters and coats between them, but still nothing to protect him from the intoxicating magic that she exuded.

'Switch it off.' His own voice sounded hoarse, almost abrupt.

An answering snap, and they were standing in semi-darkness. She pulled down her hood, rain splashing on to her face as she tipped it up towards him.

'Cassandra...' Jack had already lost sight of all the reasons why he shouldn't do this. All the things that stood between them seemed to have melted away.

'Jack...?' There were so many questions in the dark shadows of her eyes and he couldn't answer any of them.

'Yes?'

'...Nothing.' She whispered the word, her lips curving into a tantalising smile.

He was confused, torn apart by two equal forces pulling in opposite directions. Cass was the only thing that seemed real, the only thing he could take hold of and hang on to. He pulled her close, hearing the soft thud as the flashlight hit the grass at their feet.

CHAPTER NINE

HIS BODY WAS as strong, as delicious as she'd imagined it. When he held her there was no possibility of escape, unless he decided to free her. But Cass didn't want to be free of him.

Still he seemed to hesitate. Going slow, waiting for her to stop him. That wasn't going to happen. She pulled his hood back, laying her hands on either side of his face.

She could feel him breathe. Then he said her name again.

'Cassandra.'

'I'm right here, Jack.'

He touched his lips against hers, soft and gentle. That wasn't what she wanted and he knew it. When he came back for more, the sudden intensity made her legs wobble. Pinpricks of cool water on her face and the raging heat of his kiss. It was almost too much, but at the same time she didn't want it to end.

Layers of heavy-duty, high-performance waterproofing scraped together as he lifted her off her feet. Cass wrapped her legs around his waist and her arms around his shoulders, looking down into his eyes now. His hand on the back of her head brought her lips to his, their kiss annihilating her.

He could lay her on the grass… Suddenly the rain and layers of clothing meant nothing. The possibility that they might be discovered meant nothing. Nothing meant anything as long as he could find a way to touch her, in all the places that she wanted him to.

'Jack...' She moved against him so desperately that he almost lost his footing.

'Careful.' He nuzzled against her neck, the warmth of his lips against the cold rivulets of water that trickled from her wet hair. One hand cupped her bottom, supporting her, and the other seemed to be burrowing inside her jacket. Then she felt his fingers, cool on her spine, just above the waistband of her jeans.

His touch made her breath catch in her throat. Caressing, tantalising. If he could do that with one square inch of naked skin to work with, then goodness only knew what he might do with more.

Then, suddenly, he stopped. 'Cass... Cass, we have company...'

'Uh?' *No!*

'Feet on the ground, honey.' His voice was gentle, holding all the promise of what might have been if fantasy had any power to hold off reality. She slowly planted her boots back down on to the grass, feeling his body against hers, supporting her until she felt able to stand. When she turned, she saw lights tracing a path down towards where the dinghy was kept.

'Too bad...' She picked up the flashlight and switched it on, signalling to the group on the other side of the water.

His fingers found hers, curling around them. 'Yeah. I can't imagine...'

'Can't you?' She smiled up at him.

'Actually, I can. I'm imagining it right now.' He bent towards her slightly. 'What I'd do...'

'Don't. Jack...' Her skin suddenly seemed to have developed a mind of its own and was tingling, as if responding to his touch.

'What you'd do.'

'Jack, I'm warning you…'

'Yeah. I'll consider myself well and truly warned.' He squeezed her hand and then let it go, one last brush of his finger against her palm making her shiver. Lights shone across the dark water and the sound of the dinghy's motor reached her ears. And Jack's smile beside her, indicating that in his mind he was still touching her.

It was easy to tell himself that it had been a delicious one-off moment in time that wasn't going to happen again, when there was so little chance of he and Cass being left alone for long. They'd missed supper and ate in a corner of the kitchen, the bustle of clearing up after the evening meal going on around them. And afterwards there were people waiting to see Cass, to discuss plans for shoring up the makeshift dams which were keeping the water away from a number of houses in the village.

She didn't once mention her own house. A few times, Jack saw her press her lips together in an expression of regret over something she didn't want to talk about and he wondered whether he might get her alone, later. But by the time the meeting broke up, everyone was yawning, Cass included, and clearly they were all off to their own beds.

He hadn't kissed a woman since Ellie had come into his life. Maybe that was why he couldn't stop thinking about last night. Jack felt a quiver of guilt as he made his way to the church hall the following morning and deliberately slowed his pace. He shouldn't be so eager just to get a glimpse of Cass.

'Watch out!' A burly man in a red waterproof jacket cannoned straight into him as he walked through the lobby, and then shouted the warning in his face.

'Sorry, mate.' Jack stepped back as the man staggered a little. 'You all right?'

'Yeah. Sorry. Splitting headache this morning.' The man stopped and seemed to collect himself. 'Must be a stomach bug. The wife and kids have got it too; when I left, my youngest boy was throwing up.'

'Yeah? You need anything?'

'No, it's okay. The walk here seems to be clearing it.'

A slight prickling at the back of Jack's neck. It was probably nothing but he asked anyway, keeping his tone conversational. 'Any other families got it?'

'Not that I know of.' The man straightened. 'The power's off at my place and it gets cold at night, even though we keep the heater on in the hall. Probably just a stuffy head from too many blankets.' He took off his coat, hanging it with the others, and opened the hall door to let Jack through.

Cass was easy to pick out immediately, her red hair shining like a beacon that seemed to draw him in. Jack reminded himself that he had more important concerns at the moment, and that wanting to touch her could wait.

'Can I have a word?' He motioned her to one side. 'The guy in the brown sweater who's just arrived.'

Cass looked round. 'The one with the beard? That's Frank.'

'Where does he live?'

'Over on the other side of the village.' She shot him a questioning look. 'What's the matter?'

'Have you heard about anyone else with a stomach bug? Headaches, sickness?'

'No. We all know about the dangers of flood water, if that's what you're getting at. Everyone's drinking bottled.' She paused. 'The whole family usually comes up here for breakfast; the power's out down there.'

'He was on his own this morning. And he says that all of the family have had headaches and sickness, which clears in the open air.'

'You don't think...?' As a firefighter, Cass probably knew the symptoms of carbon monoxide poisoning better than he did.

'I don't know.'

'Best make sure.'

They found their coats, and Jack quickly packed a few things that he hoped he wouldn't need into a small rucksack. Cass led the way, turning away from the river, taking the path they'd taken yesterday. He wondered whether he should mention last night to her, perhaps even apologise, but Cass had already pulled her phone from her pocket and was scrolling through the contact list.

'No answer. Maybe they're on their way up to the church.' Even so, she quickened her pace, striding along the perimeter of a field of corn, the crop rotting where it stood. On the far side they slid down a steep incline and then back on to the road.

Cass had called again and there was still no answer. She and Jack almost ran the few feet along the road and then up the path of a large modern house. She banged on the door, bending down to look through the letter box.

'Someone's coming.'

The door was answered by a heavy-eyed lad of about eighteen. 'Cass?' He shielded his eyes against the light. 'What is it?'

'This is Jack; he's a paramedic. Can we come in, please, Harry?'

'Yeah. If you're looking for Mum, she's not very well. She and Alex have gone back to bed.'

'Are you okay?'

'Not too bad. I went out for a walk this morning and it cleared my head. But it's so stuffy in here...' The lad shrugged, standing back from the doorway and eyeing Jack. 'I heard all about you...'

It seemed that most of the village had heard all about

him, and at the moment that was a good thing because he could dispense with the usual formalities. Jack walked straight into the house and up the stairs.

Behind him, he could hear Cass telling Harry to wait in the hallway. There was a portable gas heater on the landing, which looked as if it had been hauled out of the garden shed and pressed into service when the power failed. Jack reached out, turning it off as he passed.

The first of the back bedrooms was in darkness, and from the mess of posters on the wall its occupant must be fifteen or sixteen. Jack opened the curtains and a drowsy protest came from the bed.

'Geroff. My head…'

'Alex, my name's Jack. I'm a paramedic. Get up.' Jack didn't bother with any niceties. He stripped the duvet off the bed and the dark-haired youth protested.

His speech was so slurred that Jack wasn't entirely sure what he was saying, but it sounded like a none-too-polite request to go away and leave him alone. He hauled the youth up on to his feet, pulling his arm around his neck. 'Walk. Come on.'

Jack supported the boy over to the bedroom door. He was showing all the signs of having flu—flushed cheeks, drowsiness and, from the way he was clutching one hand to his head, a headache. But flu didn't get better when you went out for a walk in the fresh air, and carbon monoxide poisoning did.

'Coming through…' Cass's voice on the landing. She was carrying a woman in the classic fireman's lift, her body coiled around her shoulders. She looked to be unresponsive.

'Harry, get out of the way!' Cass called to the lad, who was now halfway up the stairs, and he turned and ran back down again.

'Mum…? What's the matter?' He flattened himself

against the wall of the hallway, letting Cass past to the front door, and Jack followed.

'Harry... What's going on?' The boy at Jack's side grabbed at his brother.

'You'll be okay, but you need to get into the fresh air. Now.' Jack tried to reassure the panicking boys. He seized a couple of coats from the pegs in the hall and thrust them at Harry.

Harry transitioned suddenly from a boy to a man. 'Go on and help Mum. I'll see to Alex.'

Jack followed Cass out of the front door and she led the way round to the car port at the side of the house, where there was at least some protection from the rain. He tore off his coat, wrapping it around the woman as Cass lay her carefully down.

'Her name's Sylvie.'

'Thanks. Will you fetch my bag, please?' Sylvie's breathing was a little too shallow for Jack's liking, but at least she was breathing. Her eyelids were fluttering and she seemed lost somewhere between consciousness and unconsciousness. Cass nodded and a moment later the rucksack was laid down on the concrete next to him.

'Oxygen?' She anticipated his next instruction, opening the bag and taking out the small oxygen cylinder.

'Thanks. Can you see to the boys? And try and knock for a neighbour; this isn't ideal.'

'Right you are.' Cass disappeared and Jack held the oxygen mask to Sylvie's mouth. 'Sylvie... Sylvie, open your eyes.'

A figure knelt down on the concrete on the other side of the prone body. Harry picked up his mother's hand, his face set and calm. 'Mum...'

'That's right. Talk to her.' Jack knew that Sylvie would

respond to her son's voice better than his. He cradled her, holding the mask over her face.

'Mum… Come on now, wake up.' Jack allowed himself a grim smile. Harry's voice was firm and steady. 'Open your eyes, Mum. Come on.'

Sylvie's eyes opened and Jack felt her begin to retch. Quickly he bent her forward and she was sick all over the leg of her son's jeans. 'Nice one, Mum.' Harry didn't flinch. 'Better out than in…'

Jack grinned, clearing Sylvie's mouth and letting her lie back in his arms. She opened her eyes and her gaze found her son's face.

'Harry…I feel so ill…'

'I know, Mum. But Cass and the paramedic are here, and you're going to be okay.'

'Alex…'

'He's okay. He's gone with Cass.' Harry stroked his mother's brow.

'I'm going to put a mask over your face, Sylvie. Deep breaths.' Jack replaced the mask, and Sylvie's chest rose and fell as she breathed in the oxygen.

'That's right, Mum.' Harry's gaze flickered towards Jack and he nodded him on. 'Deep breaths, eh. Do as the man says.'

'Well done.' Jack didn't take his gaze from Sylvie but the words were for Harry. 'You just passed the first responder's initiation. Don't back off when someone's sick all over you.'

The young man gave a nervous laugh. 'What the hell's the matter with her…? With us?'

'I think it may be carbon monoxide poisoning. She seems to be coming out of it now.' Sylvie was quiet but her eyes were open and focused.

'What…like car exhaust fumes?'

'Something like that. One of those heaters may be faulty. Where did you get them?'

'Dad's mate lent them to us. He uses them in his green-house.'

Sylvie stirred in his arms and Jack smiled down at her. 'All right. You're doing just fine, Sylvie.'

Cass knelt down beside him. 'Next door. They're waiting for us.'

'Thanks. Help me lift her?' Jack gave the oxygen tank to Harry to carry, more as a badge of honour than anything else, and Cass helped settle Sylvie in his arms. A middle-aged woman was standing at the door of the next house, and Jack carried Sylvie carefully up her own front path and back down her neighbour's.

The house was neat and warm. He was waved through to a sitting room, two large sofas placed on opposite sides of the room. On one sat a man, his arm clamped tightly around Alex's shoulders.

'She's all right, Alex. She just needs fresh air and she'll be okay. We all will.' Harry seemed to have taken over Jack's role and he relinquished it gladly to him. When this was all over the young man could feel proud of the way he'd acted.

He laid Sylvie gently down on the sofa. A roll of kitchen towel was produced, to wipe Harry's jeans, and Jack asked him to sit with his mother. Cass appeared from the hallway, pocketing her phone.

'You'll be wanting her seen at the hospital?'

'Yeah. All of them need to have blood tests for carbon monoxide.'

'Okay, there are a couple of cars coming now, and we'll take them down to the motorway and get them across there. A lot quicker than calling an ambulance...' She stopped suddenly, reddening. 'What do you think?'

'I think we'd better get a couple of cars down here and take them across at the motorway. It'll be a lot quicker than calling an ambulance.' His eyes sparkled with amusement.

'Yeah. Right.' Cass wrinkled her nose at him and Jack tried not to laugh. She was irresistible when she second-guessed him, and that thing with the nose was the icing on the cake.

'How long?' He had to make a conscious effort to get his mind back on to the task in hand.

'Ten minutes. I'll go and get some clothes for them.'

'Just coats, from the hallway.' The front door must be still open and the air in the hallway would have cleared by now. 'I don't want to have to carry *you* out.' Though he'd carry her pretty much anywhere she liked if given half a chance.

'I'd like to see you try.' She turned her back on him and marched out of the room, leaving him to his patient.

CHAPTER TEN

SYLVIE'S HUSBAND WAS in one of the cars that arrived and the family was ferried down to the motorway together. Cass had disappeared, and Jack saw her waiting on the other side of the water with her SUV. She dropped the keys into Jack's hand and told him she'd meet him at the hospital and Jack helped Sylvie into the front seat, the rest of the family squeezing into the back.

He drove away, leaving her standing alone on the road. There wasn't any point in wondering exactly how she was going to get to the hospital. She'd said she'd be there, and Jack had little doubt that she would.

She arrived, pink-cheeked, nearly an hour later and sat down next to him on one of the waiting room chairs.

'Hey.'

'Hey yourself.' He wasn't going to ask.

'Everything all right?'

'Fine. They're being seen now.' Jack reached into his pocket and took out her car keys. 'Blue.'

'Blue?'

'When Sylvie was called in I nipped out and put your car through the car wash around the corner. Just in case you happened to be looking for it, it's blue.'

She gave him a sweet smile, refusing to rise to the bait. 'I'll bear that in mind. Thanks.'

They sat in silence for a few minutes. Cass took off her coat and dropped it on the chair next to her.

'You could at least ask.'

Jack smirked. He'd been determined that she would be the first to break. 'All right. How did you get here?'

'I walked for about a mile and then I hitched a lift. On the mobility bus.'

Jack snorted with laughter. 'The mobility bus? Didn't they want to see your pensioner's card before they let you on?'

'No, they did not. I showed the firefighter's ID card I have for home safety checks and cadged a lift.'

'And said you were on your way to a fire?' This was the first opportunity he'd had to sit and talk alone with Cass since they'd kissed. It felt almost as if he'd been holding his breath, waiting for this moment.

'Very funny. Next time *you* have a fire, don't expect me to put it out.' She turned her head away from him and Jack saw that she was blushing furiously at her own gaffe.

'I can put out my own fires, thank you.' Something about the delicate pink of her pale skin just wouldn't allow him to let this go. That, and the thought of letting her put out the delicious fire that her kiss had ignited.

She turned, grinning at him, and Jack suddenly wondered what he'd just got himself into. 'You're no fun, are you?'

That smile. Those dark eyes, full of all the things that might have been last night. She hadn't stopped thinking about it. It had been running at the back of her mind, like a piece of music playing over and over on the radio. Unnoticed for most of the time, but still there.

Maybe she should just get a grip. Put Jack away in a box, lined with tissue paper, ready to take back out again when she was old and grey and wanted to remind herself of what it was like to be young.

'That was a nice lift. Good technique.' He spoke quietly, almost daring her to rise to the challenge.

'Thanks. One of those things that firefighters do.' She shot him a smile, daring him back.

'Better than paramedics, you mean?'

'Much better.'

He was unashamedly sizing her up. Cass returned the compliment. Jack was a good deal heavier than her, but she'd lifted men before. It was all a matter of technique. And the stubborness to give it a go. Right now she'd do practically anything to avoid thinking about the responsibilities waiting for her back at the village.

He heaved a sigh, as if his next question had already been asked and answered. 'Car park?'

Cass nodded. 'Car park.'

Jack popped his head into the treatment area, checking that the family weren't ready to go yet, and they walked silently out of A and E.

'You're sure about this, now?' He was strolling next to her, his hands in his pockets.

No, she wasn't sure at all. Not about any of it. Cass stopped between two cars and stood in close, putting her right leg in between his, trying to imagine that he was a practice dummy. It wasn't working.

'Mind your back.' He chose this moment to grin at her and offer advice. Cass ignored it.

Grabbing his right arm, she positioned it over her left shoulder. Then, in one fluid movement, she bent her knees, wound her left arm around the back of his leg and lifted him off his feet.

'There. Easy.' She felt him put his free hand on the small of her back, balancing his weight and steadying her. It wasn't quite as easy as she was making out, but she could walk a dozen steps before she swung him back down on to his feet.

'Impressive.' He looked impressed as well. Some men would object to a woman being able to carry them, others might suffer it in silence, but she'd never imagined that it might be a cause for congratulation. But then Jack was different to most men.

Or perhaps he wasn't. His lips curled, and suddenly she was pressed hard up against him, his leg between hers. 'Hey…!'

'Sorry. That's not right, is it?' He eased back a bit, turning what felt a lot like an embrace into the exact position for a lift. Then she found herself swung up on to his shoulders with about as much effort as it would have taken to swat a fly.

His right arm was wound around the back of her knee, his hand holding her arm. Perfect form. Perfect balance.

'Not bad.'

He chuckled. 'What's wrong with it?'

What was wrong with it was that the primitive beat of her heart actually wanted him to carry her off to his lair and claim her as his. He'd lifted her with no apparent effort last night, and she'd always assumed that he was perfectly capable of slinging her over his shoulder, but having him do it was something different.

'You're not running.'

He settled her weight on his shoulders and started to stroll slowly back to A and E. 'Paramedics never run when they can walk. We don't go in for all that macho firefighter stuff.'

'Cheek!' She smacked at his back with her free hand. 'Are you calling me macho?'

'Never. Takes a real woman to do what you do.'

She tapped his shoulder. 'Thinking of letting me down any time soon?' She was getting to like this far too much.

His scent, the feel of his body. The sudden dizzy feeling that accompanied his compliments.

'Oh. Yeah, of course.' He didn't bend to set her back down on her feet, just shifted her around so that she slithered to the ground against his body.

'You lost marks there.' She stared up into his eyes.

'I know. Worth it, though.'

It was the most exquisite kind of letting go. Forgetting about the effort and the stress of the morning and taking something for themselves, even if it was just messing around in a car park, testing each other's strength. And if it meant any more than that, Cass was going to choose to ignore it.

'Suppose we should get back.' He nodded and they started back towards the hospital building. Back towards the cares of the day, the problems that still needed to be solved. And still neither of them had said anything about the one thing that she couldn't stop thinking about. That kiss.

The smell of a Sunday roast pervaded the church hall and people were busy smoothing tablecloths and positioning cutlery. Everything neat and tidy, as if the families of Holme were determined to show themselves, and each other, that despite everything which had been thrown at them in the last few weeks, life went on.

Jack popped his head around the kitchen door to ask what time lunch would be, fully expecting to be shooed away, but instead he was drawn in and questioned rigorously about Sylvie and her family. He imparted the news that they were all recovering well, that Sylvie was spending tonight under observation in the hospital and that the family would stay with her sister in town. In return, he was told that no one knew where Cass was, but that she'd gone out about half an hour ago, saying she wouldn't be long.

Armed with half a packet of biscuits, and the knowledge

that it would be another hour before lunch was served, he walked through the winding passageways at the back of the church, losing his way a couple of times, but finally managing to find the corridor that led to the porch. When he opened the door, no one was there.

He wondered whether he should sit down and wait for Cass. This was her private place and it seemed like an intrusion, but he needed to talk to her alone.

He had to make a choice. He could leave, and thank his lucky stars that the constant demands of other people had meant that one brief but sensational kiss was all they'd been able to share. Or he could live with that mistake and not let it stop him from doing the right thing.

He heard footsteps approaching the door. When she opened the door into the porch she was rubbing her face, as if supremely weary. In that moment, Jack knew that he cared about her far too much to leave her here, with such a heavy weight of responsibility on her shoulders.

'Jack!' As soon as she caught sight of him she seemed to rally herself. 'What's the matter?'

'Nothing.'

She shot him a puzzled look, then dropped the pair of waders she was holding and took off her coat.

'Where have you been?' She pressed her lips together in reply and Jack gave up trying to pretend that he didn't know. 'Your house?'

'Yeah.'

Jack swallowed the temptation to say that if she'd told him he would have gone with her. 'What's it like down there?'

She sat down, clearly trying not to look at him. 'Wet. Pretty dismal.'

'And how are you feeling?'

Cass gave a grim smile. 'Pretty dismal too.'

He leaned across, handing her the packet of biscuits. 'Chocolate digestive?' It was little enough, but at least she took them.

She unwrapped the packet, her fingers clumsy, as if she were numb. 'What are these for?'

'I want to talk to you. I reckoned that offering you food might keep you in one place for a minute.'

She pulled a biscuit out of the packet, the ghost of a smile playing around her lips. 'You have my undivided attention.' She waved the biscuit. 'Almost.'

Jack smiled at her. It wasn't much of a joke, but then she must be feeling pretty horrible right now. 'You're going back to work tomorrow? Your fire station's the one in town, isn't it?'

She nodded. 'Yeah. Early start. I'm trying not to think about it.'

She was going to *have* to think about it tomorrow. Trying to use the showers without waking everyone else up. Getting across the water, alone and in the chill darkness of an early morning. Arriving at work already exhausted. Jack tried one last gambit before he suggested the only other solution he could think of. 'You don't have anywhere you can stay in town? A friend?'

'Normally I would. But there are so many people flooded out that no one's got any room at the moment.'

'I live pretty close to town. You could stay with me and Ellie.' Including Ellie in the invitation might make it sound a little less as if he was trying to make a pass at her. 'I have a spare room so you'd have your own space.'

She stared at him blankly. 'My own space?'

'Yeah.' Saying that the kiss had meant nothing was far too big a lie to even contemplate. 'Last night is…then. And today is…'

'Now…?' Tension hovered in the air between them and

clearly Cass knew exactly what he was talking about. Perhaps she'd been thinking about it too.

'Yeah. Then and now. Concentrate on now.'

She shook her head slowly. 'I appreciate the offer. But I should stay here.'

'Cass, you know that's not going to work. Goodness only knows how long it'll take you to get to work from here. You'll do a demanding job, then come back here and find there are a load of other problems to deal with. It's too much and you know it.'

'I can manage.' Her voice was flat, measured. Jack knew that she was close to breaking point and if pushing her a little further was what it took to make her see sense...

'No, actually, you can't manage. This village owes you a great deal. But no one wants you here now. You need a break, and if you don't take it then you'll make a mistake. You and I can't afford to make mistakes, not in our jobs.'

Shock registered in her eyes and then she twisted her mouth in a parody of a grin. 'Kick a girl when she's down, why don't you.'

'If that's what it takes.' He'd resolved that he wouldn't touch her, that he'd demonstrate that he could keep his distance. But even a friend would offer comfort. Jack shifted over to sit next to her and wrapped one arm tightly around her shoulder. He might not have managed to persuade Cass, but he'd persuaded himself. Leaving her behind was totally out of the question.

He always seemed so warm. So solid. And she still felt as if the ground had been whipped out from under her feet, after the shock of wading through the dirty water that was almost a foot deep in the ground floor of her house.

'I suppose...' She shifted a little, wondering if he'd let her go, and gratifyingly he didn't take the hint. 'I suppose you're going to say that I don't have any other choice.'

'Nah.' He rested his chin lightly on the top of her head. 'I'm not going to waste my breath by telling you what you already know.'

Even now, he made her smile. If close proximity to Jack was hard, then continuing on here without him would be harder still. And since he seemed so intent on disregarding the kiss, then she could too. She could turn a blind eye to the clutter of Ellie's things around her and resist the temptation to pick the little girl up and hold her to her heart.

'Maybe just a couple of days. You won't know I'm there…'

'You can make as much noise and as much mess as you like. That's one of the rules of the house.'

Cass thought for a moment. 'I cook…'

'Great. Knock yourself out. We can take it in turns; I wouldn't mind a few evenings off.'

He had an answer for everything. And right now Cass couldn't see any further than a hot meal and a night's sleep, uninterrupted by worry. She straightened, disentangling herself from his arms, and Jack moved back quickly.

'Okay. Thanks.'

As soon as Jack made up his mind to do something, he just did it. No messing around, no fuss. Martin would keep an eye on her house while she was gone, and she was assured time and time again that she was doing the right thing. Jack had quietly overseen everything, and if the feeling that the whole village was handing her over to him was a little strange it wasn't a bad one.

Lunch had been eaten and Martin had stood up to make a brief speech, sending them on their way with the thanks and good wishes of the community. Hugs had been exchanged and they'd walked out into the sunshine.

'Not giving me a chance to change my mind?' Jack had propelled Cass firmly into the car that was waiting outside.

'May as well go now, while the rain holds off.' He shot her a sizzling grin. 'And I'm not giving you the chance to change your mind.'

By the time they reached his house, it was raining again. Jack showed her up to the spare room, told her to make herself at home and disappeared to collect Ellie, leaving Cass to sit on the bed and draw breath for the first time in what seemed like for ever.

She looked around. The room was clearly hardly used, meticulously tidy and a little chilly from having the door closed and the heating turned off. But it was bright and comfortable and, for the next few days, it was her space.

It was quiet too. After the bustle of the vicarage and the church hall, this seemed like heaven. She listened at the silence for a while. Maybe this hadn't been such a bad idea after all.

CHAPTER ELEVEN

THE EVENING HAD passed in a welter of good manners and keeping their distance. The next morning was rather less formal, on account of the rush to get Ellie up and both of them out of the house in time for work, but Jack reckoned that they were doing okay. Then he got the phone call.

He'd picked Ellie up from Sarah's in a daze of misery. Done his best to pretend that there was nothing wrong, until after he'd tucked Ellie in and kissed her goodnight. When he went back downstairs, the house was quiet.

'What's the matter?' Cass was sitting on the edge of one of the armchairs, looking at him thoughtfully.

'Nothing. Long day.' She'd come here for a break. He didn't want to burden her with his problems.

'Don't do that to me. I told you mine, and now you can tell me yours. That's the deal, Jack, and if you don't like it then I'm out.'

In that moment, Jack knew that this was all that he'd wanted. Someone to come home to. Someone he could share this with.

'It's Mimi. She's been hurt.'

'When?'

Jack slumped down onto the sofa. 'Yesterday afternoon. I heard about it this morning; Rafe called me when I was on my way to work. I went straight in to see how she was…'

He closed his eyes, the lump in his throat preventing him from saying any more.

The sofa cushions moved as Cass sat down beside him. 'And how is she?'

'She's in the ICU. None of her injuries are life-threatening, but she's in a bad way. I went up at lunchtime and they let me sit with her for half an hour.'

'Is she awake?'

He shook his head. 'It's better they keep her under sedation for a while.'

'Would you like to go back now? I'll stay here and look after Ellie.'

'There's no point. They won't let me in, and there's nothing I can do. Rafe's promised to phone if there's any change.'

He felt her fingers touch the back of his hand and he pulled away from her. That wasn't going to help. Nothing was going to help.

'What is it, Jack?'

'You think that this isn't enough?' He heard anger flare in his voice and it shocked him. When he glared at Cass, she flushed, pressing her lips together. Now wasn't the time for her to clam up on him.

'Just say it, Cass. You really can't make anything any worse.'

'Things could be a lot worse and you know it. Since when did you give up on anyone, Jack?'

'I am *not*...' The denial sprang to Jack's lips before he realised that Cass had seen a lot more than he had. Giving up on Mimi was exactly what he was doing.

All he wanted her to do was hold him. Maybe she saw that too because she reached across, taking his shaking hands between hers. Jack could never imagine that Cass's touch could be anything other than exciting, but now it was soothing.

'I'm afraid of losing her, Cass. She went into a building and it flooded…' He shook his head. 'Why did she have to go and do that?'

'Same reason you would, I imagine. This isn't really about Mimi, is it?'

Cass always seemed to see right through him, and right now it was the only thing that could bring him any comfort. 'I was so angry with my father when he died. I felt he cared more about getting off on the risk than he did about us. Sal too…'

Cass let go of his hands, curling her arms around his shoulders. Jack hung on to her as tightly as if he were drowning.

'I'd be angry too. But you have to forget that now because Mimi's your friend and she deserves your trust. You have to believe in her.'

She'd cut right to the heart of it. To his heart. The thought that once again he might lose someone who was important in his life had torn at him all day. He hadn't been able to see past his anger, hadn't even allowed himself to feel any hope for Mimi.

'I let her down, didn't I?'

'No. And you're not going to either, because you're going back to the ICU tomorrow and you're going to tell her how much you care about her, and that you know she's going to get better. Even if she can't hear you.'

'Perhaps she can. You always have to assume that even heavily sedated patients can hear what's going on.'

'Well, in that case you'd better make it convincing.' The flicker of a smile caressed her lips. 'Go on. Let's see your convincing face.'

She could make him laugh even when things were bad. She might not be able to make all the worry disappear, nor could she drive away all the simmering fear and anger, but she knew how to give him hope. Jack gave an approximation of his most earnest expression and she shook her head, laughing.

'I'd stick with the one you gave Lynette. I wouldn't buy a used car off you if you looked at me like that.'

She made him a drink, and got a smile in return, but she could still feel the pain leaking out of him. He wasn't just dealing with Mimi being hurt; he was dealing with all of the remembered pain of his father's death. All of the fears he had for Ellie.

The best she could do tonight was help him to switch off for a while. She knew his gaze was on her back as she ran her finger along the books on the shelf, spelling the titles out quietly to herself.

Reaching for the book that she and Izzy had shared, she turned to Jack. 'I don't suppose you'd like to read...'

He grinned. 'I'd be honoured. Will Miss Palmer mind?'

'She'll understand.' What he needed was to let it all go, just for a few hours. And Cass didn't know a better way than this. She handed him the book, settling down next to him on the sofa, and Jack opened it and started to read.

Slowly, they slipped into another world together. The space between them seemed to diminish as they travelled the same paths, thought the same thoughts. And Jack's voice lost the sharp edge of stress that she'd heard in it all evening.

He finished the chapter and they embarked greedily on the next. But it was too much. When they stopped for a while, to talk sleepily, the book slipped from Jack's fingers and Cass caught it before it fell to the floor.

He looked so peaceful. Waking him up would only bring him back to a present that he needed to forget for now if he was going to face it tomorrow. Carefully, Cass manoeuvred Jack round on the sofa, taking off his shoes, disentangling herself from his arms when he reached for her, and fetching the duvet and a pillow from his bed to keep him warm.

Maybe she should make some attempt to slip his jeans off; he'd be more comfortable. She reached under the duvet, finding the button on the waistband and undoing it. Jack stirred, and she snatched her hand away.

Enough. Go to bed. Cass left Jack sleeping soundly on the sofa and crept upstairs.

When Jack woke, the feeling of well-being tempered the knowledge that he wasn't where he was supposed to be. He was still in his clothes, but when he moved he realised that the waistband of his jeans had been loosened. He fastened the button again, a little tingle of excitement accompanying the thought that Cass must have undone it, and kicked the duvet off.

Exactly what clinical level of unconsciousness did a man need to attain before he didn't notice the touch of Cass's fingers? Jack dismissed the notion that she must have slipped something into his cocoa and sat up. A loud crash sounded from the kitchen, propelling him to his feet.

'Daddee…' Ellie was sitting at the kitchen table, holding her arms out for her morning kiss. Cass was on her knees, carefully scooping up the remains of a jar of peanut butter, and shot him an embarrassed look.

'Did we wake you?'

'No, he was awake.' Ellie settled the matter authoritatively. 'So we can make some noise if we like.'

Jack chuckled, lifting Ellie from her chair and kissing her. 'Yes, but you still can't make a mess. What do you say to Cass?'

'Sorry. My hand slipped.' Ellie repeated her current excuse for pretty much anything, and Cass got to her feet.

'That's okay, sweetie. There wasn't much left in there.'

'There's another jar in the cupboard.' It didn't look as if

Cass had started her own breakfast yet. 'Thanks for getting Ellie up.'

Cass grinned. 'Call it a joint effort. Ellie picked out what she wanted to wear and I helped with some of the buttons.'

He noticed that Ellie had odd socks on and decided not to mention it. He could rectify that easily enough when he got her into the car.

'I really appreciate it, Cass.' He tried to put everything that he felt into the words. 'Last night, as well…' Last night had helped him face everything a little better this morning.

For a moment her gaze rested on his face, asking all the questions that she couldn't voice with Ellie around. A sudden rush of warmth tugged at his heart, leaving Jack smiling, and she nodded.

'You're going in to see her today?'

'Yes. Shall I give you a call and let you know how she is?' That seemed important somehow. That Cass would be expecting his call.

'I'd really like that.'

Tuesday had brought no change in Mimi's condition, but Wednesday morning brought hopes that she might be woken later on in the day. Cass ate her lunch with her phone in front of her, on the table. When it buzzed, she snatched it up.

'Could I ask an enormous favour?' Jack asked a little awkwardly.

'Sure. Name it.'

'They're waking Mimi up today. Rafe and Charlie, her brother, are with her at the moment, but I'd really like to go in and see her after work.' A short pause. 'There are some things I'd like to tell her.'

'That's really good news. I'll get some shopping on the way home if you like.'

'No… We've got plenty of everything. I was wondering

if you could look after Ellie for a while. It's just that Sarah's going to her evening class tonight...'

Cass swallowed hard. Shopping would have been the easier option, but Jack needed time with Mimi. She could do this. 'Yes, of course. Take your time with Mimi; we'll be fine.' Her voice rang with a confidence she didn't feel.

'Thanks.' He sounded relieved. 'I really appreciate it. Sarah will drop her home on her way to her class...'

She took Sarah's mobile number just in case. Then Cass placed her phone back on the table, wondering what she'd just done.

'Guys...' The ready room was buzzing with activity, and most of her colleagues had children of their own. 'I need some help here. I'm looking after a four-year-old this evening. What am I going to do with her?'

Eamon turned, chuckling. 'Easy. First thing to do is feed her. No sweets or sugary stuff, or she'll be running around all night...'

Pete broke in. 'Find her something she likes on TV for an hour, and then ask her to show you her favourite story book. She'll tell you what it says; they know their favourites by heart.'

Cass laughed, spinning a screwed-up ball of paper at Pete's head. 'I can manage a kid's storybook. Big writing, spaced-out words.'

'There you go then. If in doubt, go for princesses; they're all the rage at the moment,' Eamon added with a laugh. 'Sorted.'

Cass wasn't so sure. A menu and a schedule of activities for the evening was the least of her worries. Looking after Jack's child, in Jack's house, was a mocking counterfeit of all the things she wanted so much but couldn't have. She was just going to have to rise above that and maintain some kind of mental distance.

Tea was accomplished, albeit with the maximum amount of mess. Jack had called, saying that after having slept for the whole afternoon, Mimi was now awake and relatively alert, and Cass told him to stay with her.

Ellie selected her favourite cartoon and Cass sat down on the sofa with her to watch it, while Ellie kept up a running commentary of what was going to happen next.

'The monster's coming...'

'Where?'

'They're going into the forest. He's hiding...' Ellie covered her eyes.

'Hey. It's okay.' Cass assumed that Ellie knew that too, but that didn't seem to erode the tension of the moment for her.

'Cassandra...' Ellie flung her arms around Cass's neck, seeming genuinely terrified, and every instinct demanded that Cass hug her back.

This moment should hurt, but Ellie was just a little girl and it was Cass's name she'd called. Cass felt herself relax, holding Ellie tight. It was just the two of them, and she and Ellie could protect each other from the monsters that lurked in both their heads.

When Jack got home the kitchen was empty, apart from the remains of a meal which looked big enough to feed a whole army of four-year-olds. Upstairs, Ellie was in bed and her room was uncharacteristically tidy. Cass was sitting by her bed, the closed book on her lap indicating that she'd resorted to improvisation for Ellie's bedtime story.

'Daddy...? I had a nice time...' Ellie's voice was sleepy and Jack leaned over, kissing his daughter's forehead.

Cass's face tipped towards him, tenderness shining from her eyes. He nodded in response to her mouthed question about Mimi, and she smiled.

'Do you want to take over?' She was halfway out of the

chair next to Ellie's bed and Jack shook his head. He'd worried about Ellie becoming too reliant on Cass, but in truth it was he who was beginning to feel he couldn't do without her. Ellie was clearly a lot more relaxed about things.

'What's the story about?'

Cass thought. 'Well, there's this princess. Beautiful, of course, and she's got her own castle.'

'Naturally.' Jack sat down on the end of Ellie's bed.

'And she wants her own fire engine…' Ellie woke up enough to show that she'd been following the plot.

'Right. And does she get it?' Jack found himself smiling. Not the tight, forced smile he'd been practising for the last couple of days, but one which came right from the heart.

'Only after she passes her exams and the fitness test.' Cass was clearly intent on making the thing believable.

'And she's going to rescue the prince.' Ellie chimed in.

Jack chuckled. 'Don't let me stop you, then. This I have to hear.'

The soft light from the bedside lamp had transformed Jack's features into that very prince. Handsome and brave. Someone who could fight dragons and somehow turn an impossible situation into a storybook ending. When the princess had finished rescuing him, he rescued her back and everyone lived happily ever after.

When Ellie finally drifted off into sleep neither she nor Jack moved. Holding on to the magic for just a little while longer, despite there being no excuse to do so.

But this was no fairy tale. Jack wasn't hers, any more than Noah or Ellie were. Cass rose quietly from her chair, putting the book back in its place, and walked out of the room, leaving Jack to draw the covers over his sleeping child.

The air in the kitchen was cool on her face. She stacked

the dishwasher and tidied up, then heard a noise at the doorway.

'Oh! You surprised me.' Despite all of her efforts to bring herself back to reality, Jack still looked like a handsome prince. 'How's Mimi?'

He nodded. 'Very drowsy, and a bit incoherent at times, but that's just to be expected. She's doing well. Thanks for looking after Ellie.'

'It's no trouble. How about you—are you okay?'

'I'm fine.' Cass sent him a querying look and he flashed her a smile. 'Really.'

Cass nodded, picking up a cloth and giving the worktop a second wipe. Jack didn't move and the silence weighed down on her, full of all the things they'd left unsaid.

'Would you like a pizza princess? There are some left over in the fridge. They don't actually look too much like princesses…' She was babbling and closed her mouth before anything too crazy escaped.

'I'd like to thank you—for what you said the other night.'

When she turned, the warmth in Jack's eyes seemed more like heat now. Delicious heat.

'I've been re-evaluating. Giving the believing thing a try.'

Something caught in her throat. 'H… How's that going?'

'It's…different.' His gaze dropped to the floor. 'Can I believe in you, Cass?'

She didn't know how to answer that. But it definitely needed an answer. She touched his hand and he gripped hers tight, pulling her towards him.

'I want you to know…' He shook his head as if trying to clear it. 'I didn't ask you here for this.'

'Anything can be re-evaluated.'

For a moment they were both still. As if the next move would be the deciding one, and neither quite trusted themselves to make it.

'I can't promise you anything, Cass. I'm not the man you want…'

He was exactly the man she wanted. No lies, no strings and none of the attendant heartbreak. He was saying all the right things, and making her feel all the right things too.

'Then we're even. I won't promise anything either.'

It was all either of them needed to know. There was no need to hide any more, and the air was electric with whispered kisses.

Then more. Much more, until the kitchen was no longer the place to be and the bedroom was the only place in the world.

They tiptoed up the stairs in an exaggerated game of having to be quiet. Jack looked in on Ellie, closing her bedroom door, and then turned to Cass.

'Asleep?' She allowed her lips to graze his ear.

'Fast asleep.' He led her to his own bedroom and as soon as he'd shut the door behind them, he pulled her close. 'Be quiet, now…'

That wasn't going to be easy. His kiss was just the start of it, and when his hand found her breast Cass swallowed a moan.

'Keep that up and I'll be screaming…' The thought of being in his arms, all the things that he might do, made her want to scream right now.

'No, you won't.' His body moved against hers, his arm around her waist crushing her tight so that she could feel every last bit of the friction. 'You're not going to have breath enough to scream.'

She could believe that. Cass fought to get her arms free of his embrace and pushed him backwards towards the bed. He resisted the momentum, imprisoning her against his strong body. 'Oh, no, you don't…'

Cass relaxed in his arms, letting herself float in his

kisses. Balancing her weight against him, curling her leg slowly around his.

'Oof…' He fell back on to the bed, caught off balance, and she landed on top of him, breaking her own fall with her arms. 'Nice move, princess…'

'I have more.' She pinned him down, running her hand across his chest, luxuriating in the feel of his body. He gasped as her hand found the button on his jeans, and she felt his body jolt as she slipped her fingers past the waistband.

'I just bet you do.' Suddenly she was on her back and Jack had the upper hand again. Holding her down, stretching her arms up over her head, dipping to whisper in her ear.

'I'm going to strip you naked… Then I'm going to find out just how many moves you've got…'

A shard of light from the hallway. Jack froze.

CHAPTER TWELVE

'DADDY! WHAT ARE you doing?'

The one question he'd never had to even consider an answer for. Jack closed his eyes in disbelief, feeling Cass wriggle out from under him.

'Don't hurt her, Daddy.' He heard Ellie pound into the room and he rolled over on to his back, feeling something soft smack against his legs. Ellie had obviously come armed with her teddy bear.

'It's okay, Ellie. It's all right…' How the hell was he going to explain this one?

'Ellie…' Cass's laughing voice. 'Ellie, it's okay. We were just playing. Daddy was tickling me.' Jack opened his eyes and saw Cass, on her feet and swinging Ellie up in her arms.

'Like this…' Ellie's fingers scrunched against Cass's shoulder in a tickling motion.

'Just like that.' She plumped down on to the bed, rolling Ellie on to her back and tickling her. Cass seemed to have a better handle on the situation than he did. Maybe because she didn't have to worry about surreptitiously refastening any buttons.

'What's the matter, Ellie?' He waited for their laughter to subside, wishing his wits would unscramble themselves.

'I had a bad dream.' Ellie remembered what she was here for and flung herself into his arms. 'Make it go away.'

'Okay.' He held her tight, flashing Cass an apologetic look, but she just grinned. 'Tell me all about it and we'll make it go away.'

It hadn't taken long to comfort Ellie and Jack had suggested that she might like to go back to bed, but she wouldn't budge. So Cass had put an end to the dilemma by getting Ellie to lie down on the bed next to her, with Jack on the other side.

'I'm sorry.' He mouthed the words quietly over the top of Ellie's head, a mix of uncertainty and regret on his face.

'That's okay.' This seemed so right, so natural. Lying on the bed with Jack, his child curled up against her.

'Really?' He stretched out his hand, brushing the side of her face.

'Not quite what I expected.' She whispered the words quietly so as not to disturb Ellie, and Jack dropped a kiss on to his finger and planted it on to her cheek. 'But it's really nice.'

'Could I hold your hand?' His eyes were so tender. When he folded his hand around hers, in the space above Ellie's head, it felt as if a circle of warmth had closed. One which included her. Cass had often wondered what this would feel like, and given up hope of ever knowing.

She had been so afraid of this, terrified of the hurt when she and Jack were torn apart again. But now that didn't seem to matter. It was complete, a thing of itself that couldn't be touched by anything. Tomorrow it would be gone—Jack wasn't hers to keep and neither was Ellie—but even that couldn't spoil tonight.

She stayed awake for as long as she could, knowing that when she slept it would be the beginning of the end. Ellie was sleeping soundly, and when Jack's eyes finally fluttered closed she watched him sleep. If tonight was going to have to last her for the rest of her life, and right now it felt that it could, she didn't want to miss any of it.

It had been almost forty-eight hours since he and Cass had lain down on his bed with Ellie. Thirty-six since he'd woken, stretching over to plant a parting kiss on Cass's fingers while she slept, before picking Ellie up and taking her into her own bedroom to get dressed. Jack had managed to spend one waking hour without thinking about it, largely due to a difficult call at work, although at night he wasn't doing so well. But he couldn't be expected to control his dreams.

He didn't speak about the shock of having Ellie walk in on them, or what had followed, which had somehow been so much more intimate than the night he'd been expecting. Cass said nothing either and their conspiracy of silence seemed to protect those few short hours from the indignity of careless words or doubts. Jack knew two things for sure. It had been perfect, and it mustn't happen again.

Then a girls' night out put all his resolve to the test. Cass had mentioned that she was going out on Friday night and so Jack and Ellie were on their own for supper. But when she came downstairs, fresh from the shower, her handbag slung over her shoulder and her car keys in her hand, what had seemed just difficult was suddenly practically impossible.

'Where are you off to?' He tried to keep the question casual but he heard a note of possessiveness in his voice. He was going to have to practise that and do better when Ellie was old enough to pick up *her* car keys and go out for the night.

'One of the wine bars in town. The one in Abbey Street.'

He knew the one. Quiet and comfortable, a good place to talk and a nice bar menu.

'Great. Well…' He suppressed the temptation to ask her what time she'd be home.

She glanced into the mirror in the hall, running her fingers through the burnished copper of her hair. The arrangement seemed somehow softer, brushed to lie heavy on her brow, and Jack could see sparkles of twisted silver hanging from her ears. Her lips were… Jack wasn't sure what shade of red that was. Delicious Red, maybe. Kissable Red.

'You look pretty.' Ellie supplied the words that he couldn't. She looked gorgeous. Boots, a black suede skirt and a sheer top with a sleeveless slip underneath, which allowed a tantalising glimpse of the curve of her shoulders and the shape of her arms.

'Thank you, sweetie.'

'I want a handbag like yours.'

'You like it?' Cass flushed a little at the compliment and Jack almost fainted. Was she actually trying to make him dizzy or did she really not know just how amazing she looked?

'I like the dangles…' Ellie ran up to her, tugging at the long fringe that hung from the sides of her bag. Jack imagined that when she walked it mimicked some of the graceful sway of her hips.

'Let Cass go, sweetie.' Ellie was about to throw her arms around Cass and the thought of rumpling such perfection was unbearable. 'She'll be late.'

'Bye, Ellie.' She bent down and gave the little girl a hug, somehow managing to keep her make-up intact and her hair just so. 'See you in the morning.'

'Yeah. Have a good evening.' Jack wondered whether he was going to wait up for her, and decided that if he did so it would be from the safety of his bedroom. Probably with most of the furniture piled up against the door, to at least provide some pause for thought before he marched out to ask her what kind of time she called this and then dragged her into his arms.

'Thanks.' She grabbed her coat, giving a little wave and a bright grin, and Ellie followed her to the front door, which gave Jack the chance to watch Cass walk down the front path and appreciate the fluid movement of her body.

Then she got into her car, a bright pearl shining in a sea of blue paint, mud and rust spots. Jack watched her draw away and turned, taking Ellie back inside. The house seemed suddenly very quiet.

He'd listened to the silence in the living room and then gone to bed early, just to see whether the silence in his bedroom might feel less grating. Finally, at eight minutes past one, Jack had heard the front door close quietly and then the pad of stockinged feet on the stairs.

The soft sound of her bedroom door closing allowed him to track her progress. Jack tried not to imagine her throwing her bag on the bed. Taking off her jewellery and slipping the sheer top from her shoulders. He turned over in bed and resolutely shut his eyes.

The silence seemed less a sign that something was missing and more an indication that all was well. Jack drifted off to sleep, but even then his unconscious mind was unable to filter Cass out of his dreams.

It seemed that Jack's unerring radar for detecting any signs of movement on Ellie's part had failed him once again. Cass, on the other hand, seemed to be picking up that instinct. Despite a late night, she woke early, to the sound of Ellie singing to herself in her bedroom.

She turned over in bed, trying to pretend she hadn't heard. Jack would be up soon and it was his job to look after his daughter. The singing continued, and she found herself out of bed, struggling into her dressing gown, before she had a chance to think about it any further.

'Go back to bed, sweetie…'

Ellie's answering smile indicated that she would do no such thing. She reached her arms up for a good-morning hug, and Cass gave in to the inevitable.

Toast and some juice were followed by coffee for herself and a glass of frothed milk for Ellie. The little girl sat at the kitchen table, carefully mimicking Cass's actions, sipping her milk slowly as if she too felt the caffeine bringing her round after a late night.

'Morning.' Jack was still bleary-eyed, his hair wet from the shower. Suddenly Cass was wide awake.

He looked good enough to eat. His washed-out jeans low on his hips, a dark shirt which seemed to have one of the buttons at the top missing, the extra inch or so of open neckline seeming to draw her gaze. Beautiful. From the top of his head to the tips of his sneakers.

Stop, it's not like that. I don't even fancy him. The lies she'd managed to half believe last night were coming back to slap her in the face this morning. And the questions from her friends about who she was staying with and what he was like had suggested possibilities that she'd been doing her best to ignore.

He bent to kiss Ellie and then turned his gaze on to her. 'Did you have a good evening?'

'Yes, thanks. Seems like an age since I've been out.'

He walked over to the kitchen sink, pouring himself a glass of water and downing it in one go. Cass got to her feet.

'I'd better get going. There's bunting to be hung.' She was trying not to notice what she fancied might be the remains of the look she'd seen in his eyes when she'd left the house last night.

'What time does it start, again?'

'Two o'clock.' Cass gave Jack a wide berth, making sure

she didn't accidentally brush against him as she walked out of the kitchen, heading for the shower.

The fire station was decorated with flags and bunting, standing to attention in the stiff breeze, and the two fire engines on the forecourt shone in the sun. Cass looked up at the sky.

'Think it'll rain?'

Mike, another of the firefighters, glanced at the clouds.

'If it does, then it'll add some authenticity to the demonstration.' He chuckled. 'After the last month, I'm not sure I'll be able to get a ladder up unless it's raining.'

'Me too.' Cass tipped her helmet on to the back of her head. 'Shame we don't have bigger puddles out back. We could have done rope and water rescue as part of the demonstration.'

'Don't push it, Cass. Have you seen the roof of the office?'

'No?' She looked across at the prefabricated office, on the far side of the yard.

'Enough water on that flat roof to bath a donkey. I'm surprised it hasn't leaked yet.'

'Suppose we could always take a shot at waterfall rescue.' Cass grinned.

'Is that in the manual? Come on, I bet you know what page.'

'Everything's in the manual. And I wouldn't tell you what page it was on even if I knew; you'd just call me a swot.'

'You're a swot. Everybody knows that.' Mike watched the stream of cars turning into the car park. 'Here they come. Prepare for terror like you've never known before.'

Cass looked for Jack in the sea of heads and saw him with Ellie, who was dressed in red wellingtons and a matching

waterproof coat. They were being guided across the yard
with the first of the visitors and into the garage, where Mike
was overseeing the most important part of the afternoon.
The demonstration and being able to see a fire engine up
close was the fun bit, but there was a serious message to
get across as well.

Everything was distilled down into easy steps that a
child might remember if faced with a fire or flood. Cass
leaned against the front of the tender, listening to the kids'
voices chanting along with Mike's. *Don't hide.* A child's
first instinct, to hide away in the face of danger, was every
firefighter's worst nightmare.

No nightmares today, though. Cass watched as the station commander's wife made a blood-curdling job of yelling
for help from the roof of the garage, and four firefighters
raced across the yard with a ladder. She was rescued with
the minimum of indignity, as befitted her status, and to general applause. Then some of the smaller kids were lifted up
on to a lower platform, where they were held safely by one
of the crew until a shorter ladder was run across the yard
to perform similar, if less hair-raising, rescues.

In between talking to the first of the groups which clustered around her and showing them around the fire engine,
Cass saw Ellie on the platform.

'Help! Fire!' she called across the yard at the top of her
voice. The firefighter squatting down next to her said a few
words and then grinned as she waved her arms energetically above her head. 'Help! Fire!'

Ellie was duly rescued, received a round of applause and
ran back to Jack. He hoisted her up on his shoulders and
started to walk towards Cass, coming to a halt behind the
family who had just approached her.

She bent towards the two little boys, seeing only Jack.
Tall and relaxed, smiling at her.

'What…' She cleared her throat, trying to dislodge the

lump that seemed to have formed. She'd already done this half a dozen times but she was suddenly acutely aware of being watched. And acutely mindful of the gentle dark eyes that were doing the watching.

'What have you learned today?' She waited for the boys' answers and then began to show them the fire engine, making a conscious effort not to rush them through. Finally they accepted the colouring sheets and badges that she handed them, along with the fire safety information for their parents, and walked away talking excitedly.

'Nice badges.' His lips were curved in a quiet smile. That smile of his should be X-rated.

'Sorry. Only for the under tens.' She dragged her gaze away from his and felt in her pocket. 'Which one would you like, Ellie? I've got a pink one here.'

Ellie nodded vigorously and Cass reached up, slipping the badge into her coat pocket. Her arm brushed against Jack's and she pulled it away.

'Would you like to come and see the fire engine, Ellie?'

'You missed a bit.' He lifted Ellie off his shoulders, setting her down on the ground, and leaned towards Cass, mouthing the words to her. *What about the message?*

'Ah. Yes.' This would be a great deal easier if he wasn't so distracting. Was it really legal to be so downright sexy, in public and in the presence of children?

'Ellie, what do you do if there's a fire?' She repeated the words numbly, wondering exactly why it was that suddenly all she could think about was Jack's touch. If she knew the answer, then that would at least be a first step to doing something about it.

'Don't hide.'

'Good. Well done.'

Jack nodded. 'And what else?' Cass frowned at him. He was pinching *her* lines now.

'You shout *Fire!* or *Help!*' Ellie decided to enlarge on

the instructions. 'As loud as you can. And you could wave if you liked.'

'Yes. Waving's good too. You have to make sure that someone sees you and knows you're there.'

'Would you like to see the fire engine, Ellie?' Jack smiled down at his daughter.

'Do you mind? This is all very carefully worked out; I can't have parents stealing my lines.' Cass glared at him and he shot back a mouthwatering look, half-humour, half-remorse, and wholly delicious.

'Sorry. Carry on, I'll just watch.'

'Thank you.' Cass caught Ellie's hand, walking her over to the vehicle.

Jack watched as Cass showed Ellie the fire engine. Then stepped forward when Cass climbed up into the driver's seat, to hand Ellie up to sit with her.

She seemed to light up around children. She was a little awkward with them, in the way that he'd been before he'd had his own child, but she obviously loved their company. Why she'd made the decision to concentrate solely on her career, a marriage to her job which couldn't give her what she so clearly wanted, was just another of the imponderables about Cass.

Jack waited, handing up his phone for a few pictures of Ellie at the driver's wheel and then taking it back for a couple of Ellie waving out of the window at him. Then one of Cass and Ellie, hugged up tight together.

Then Ellie got down, accepting the colouring sheets and running back to him, waving the fire safety instructions that Cass had given her. There was nothing in there he didn't know and practise already; Jack had seen too many burns victims to be anything other than rigorous about fire safety in his own home. But it would be a good exercise to read them through with Ellie, and for them to go round and double-check together.

The next group of children was heading towards them and it was time for him to move on now. He'd hoped that the feeling of tearing himself away from Cass each time they parted might lose its sting, but it never seemed to.

'We're…um…we're all going for a drink afterwards. Friends and families—we're going to a place just out of town with a kids' playroom. If you and Ellie…' She left the sentence unfinished.

'Thanks, but Ellie's been invited to tea with one of her friends. I'm going to take the opportunity to pop in and see Mimi.'

'Yes, of course.'

'Next time, maybe…' This was crazy. Even here, now, he couldn't quite let go. Not while there was still some glimmer in her eyes which told him that Cass had been thinking about how close they'd come to being lovers.

'Yeah. See you later, then.' One short moment of connection, in which Jack fancied that they both shared an understanding of how hard this was. Then he took Ellie's hand, listening to her excited chatter as he walked away.

CHAPTER THIRTEEN

CASS SAW JACK'S car ahead of hers on the main road and flashed her headlights as he turned into the road that led to his house. His hazard lights winked on and then off again, and his car came to a halt outside the driveway. Cass drew level with him, winding down the window as he leaned across.

'You're early...'

'Yeah.' Cass had nursed a glass of orange juice for half an hour, then decided to go home. And then she'd driven back here. She wasn't quite sure when she'd started thinking of Jack's house as home, but she supposed it must have something to do with looking forward to being there every evening.

She leaned round and saw that the child's seat in the back of Jack's car was empty. 'Where's Ellie?'

'Her friend's mum asked if she'd like to stay for a sleepover. And when I went in to see Mimi she just about managed a hello and then fell asleep.'

'Ah. So you've been deserted.'

He chuckled. 'Yeah. No one seems to want me tonight.'

Not true. And from the look on his face he knew it. She should go. Pretend she'd forgotten her purse and had just popped back from the pub to collect it. Then come back later, when Jack was asleep and the coast was clear.

'Ladies first...' He gestured towards the driveway.

'No, you go.' Probably best to leave a getaway option, just in case. Cass watched as he turned into the hardstanding in front of the house. When she followed suit, she took the turn a little too wide and a bit too fast and jammed her foot on the brake, feeling her front bumper touch something as she came to a halt.

She was shaking as she climbed out of the car, leaving the headlights on so that she could see whether there was any damage to the back of Jack's. A piece of mud had fallen from the front of hers and on to his back bumper and she brushed it away.

'It's okay... I hardly touched you.'

'Yeah? Too bad.' He was facing her, not even glancing at the back of his car. 'Do you want to give it another try?'

'I wouldn't want to dent your bodywork.' Suddenly this wasn't about cars. Cass turned away from him with an effort, reaching for the switch on the dashboard to kill her headlights. When she looked up again he was gone, the front door open and the light in the hall beckoning her.

He was standing in the hallway, leaning against the sturdy newel post at the bottom of the stairs. Waiting for her. Cass stepped inside, letting the door drift to behind her, and Jack smiled.

'So... You think you can put a dent in my bodywork, do you?'

The house was quiet. No need to keep their voices down either, because Ellie wasn't asleep upstairs. Jack seemed to fill the space completely.

'I can't say. Not without a more thorough examination.' She wanted to touch him so badly. Blind to anything else but Jack, because there *was* nothing else.

'You can be as thorough as you like. Since we have a little unexpected time on our hands...' His eyes held all the promise of everything they might just dare to do.

Jack walked towards her. Cass dropped her handbag, hearing her car keys spill out on to the floor as she pulled him close.

The kiss left them both breathless. No amount of air would be enough right now. No amount of that delicious feeling when his fingers brushed her face.

'Jack…' There was nothing left to say. They'd tried to keep their hands off each other and they'd failed. But at least they'd both failed together, and they both knew the terms of their failure.

'I can't do it, Cass… Can't pretend I don't want you.'

'Tonight you don't have to.'

He pulled the zip of her jacket open. No hesitation, but no rush either. She could feel his hunger as he kissed her.

His gaze never left hers as he reached behind her, pushing the front door fully closed. Cass heard the lock engage with a satisfying click and a little thrill of excitement ran through her veins. Locked in with Jack, and a whole house as their playground for the night.

He wrapped his arms around her shoulders, backing her into the sitting room and then settling her against him. 'Alone…'

Cass sighed. 'At last.'

Nothing short of an earthquake could stop them now. Cass could rescue him if the fire of their lovemaking got out of control, and he'd resuscitate her if she happened to pass out. They'd save each other from an impossibly long night spent alone.

Jack smothered the impulse to lead her straight upstairs and get them both out of their clothes as quickly as possible. The ultimate luxury had just dropped unexpectedly into their laps and they had time. Enough time to show her that it wasn't just sex he wanted, but a seduction.

'Light the fire.' Her lips curved. She knew just what he

wanted. The thought of their limbs entwined in the fire-light made him tremble but somehow the match sparked first time and he dropped it on to the kindling, which flared suddenly, licking around the coals stacked above it.

Each time he kissed her it felt new, different, like a first kiss. Jack helped her out of her coat and took his off, sling-ing them both on to an armchair.

'You are the most stunning woman I've ever seen. When I first opened my eyes and saw you, I thought that the heav-ens had opened up and you'd flown down to save me.'

She tapped her finger on his chest in laughing reproof. 'You should see someone about that. Want me to call an ambulance?'

'I think I'm beyond help.' He caressed the side of her face. 'My very own personal goddess…'

Cass giggled. '*Your* personal goddess? How possessive is that?'

He leaned in, whispering against her neck. 'Got a prob-lem with it?'

'No, I don't think so. But if I'm a goddess, then perhaps you should kneel.'

The way she bought into his fantasies was the ultimate thrill. 'I can do that.'

'Naked…'

'I can do that too.' He nipped at her ear and she shivered, her thrill of pleasure echoing in his own chest. 'Keep that thought for later, eh?'

'Why? Going anywhere?'

'No. But we need to talk about…to agree on…some means of contraception.' The words sounded unexpectedly hard and unromantic, but that couldn't be helped. The wild, reckless days when *It's all dealt with* was enough to reas-sure him were gone. He'd changed. Even though neither of them wanted a permanent relationship, he could still care about her and while she was with him he'd keep her safe.

She flushed. Something seemed to stop her in her tracks. 'We do?'

'We can't just leave things to chance, Cass. That's a stupid risk.'

'I wasn't suggesting that… But… Can't you just…do something?'

He wasn't exactly sure what she meant. But a prickle of alarm was working its way round the back of Jack's neck.

'It's a choice we need to make together, isn't it?'

'Yes, of course… It's just… But…' She seemed suddenly desperate. As if he'd just suggested something impossible. 'Whatever, Jack.'

He wasn't prepared for the sudden confusion which ate away at his desire and for the wounded look in Cass's eyes. She seemed determined not to talk about it and the thought occurred to Jack that she was hiding something. If she wanted him to trust her, that wasn't the way to do it.

'I don't understand, Cass. Help me out…' One last plea, in the hope that maybe she would open up. But she seemed to be shrinking away from him with every passing moment.

'Fine. Have it your way.' He turned suddenly, choked by the sour dregs of desire. Walking from the room, he heard the door slam behind him.

CHAPTER FOURTEEN

CASS DROPPED TO her knees, staring into the fire, hugging her arms across her stomach. She hadn't meant to react like that. Why hadn't she just smiled and forced herself to have that conversation. It wasn't as if Jack had suggested anything outrageous. Of course they needed protection.

But to her ears, speaking about it so bluntly had sounded like a contract, some kind of business proposal. And all of the agony of the past, all her feelings of failure, had come flooding back. Even talking about protection, or the lack of it, brought back memories of the bitterness that had pervaded her old relationship. Memories of the months that she hadn't fallen pregnant ever since they had decided to do away with contraception and try for a baby. Thinking about the possibilities and consequences of sex each and every time. Making it a transaction instead of something sweet.

There had been no interruptions, nothing else to blame, and still they'd fallen at the first hurdle. A kiss, a touch, and then they'd torn themselves apart. They couldn't even manage a one-night stand.

There was no way she could stay here now. She was going to have to suffer the humiliation of turning up on a friend's doorstep and begging a bed for the night. She'd heard Jack go upstairs and the house was silent now. Cass opened the door, tiptoeing up the stairs. If she could leave without having to face him again and see that coldness in his eyes, all the better.

She quickly stuffed her clothes into her bag. Her toiletries were in the bathroom but getting them seemed like too much of a risk, and she could replace them. Zipping her jacket up, she picked up her bag and opened the bedroom door.

All clear. Wherever Jack was, he wasn't going to stop her. It was almost a disappointment, but then what would she do if he did try? Neither of them had said anything too hurtful yet, and it was best she got out of here before they had that opportunity.

She walked quietly downstairs. The hall light had been switched off and she put her bag down, scanning the floor for her car keys.

'Looking for something?' She looked up and saw Jack in the sitting room doorway.

'Car keys.' Keep it short and relatively sweet. Maybe he wouldn't see that she had been crying.

He held something up and Cass saw her key fob dangling from his fingers. She stretched her hand towards it and he snatched his arm away, tucking the keys into his pocket.

Cass swallowed hard. The urge to charge at him, knock him off his feet and grab her keys wasn't productive. Anyway, it probably wouldn't work. 'Can I have my car keys? Please.'

'Yeah. In a minute.' He turned and walked into the sitting room. It seemed she had a choice. Either thumb a lift or break into her own car and hotwire it.

Or she could follow Jack. She'd have to be insane to do that now. It was no particular comfort to know that she could remind herself afterwards that she'd known this was a bad idea and she'd done it anyway.

He was sitting in one of the armchairs, his dark eyes following her every move. Jack waved her towards the sofa and like an automaton, programmed to respond to his every command, she sat down.

'I overreacted, Cass. I'm sorry.'

'That's okay. My car keys…'

'In a minute. Hear me out first.'

'It doesn't really matter, Jack.'

'It does to me. Look, it never much occurred to me to ask what went wrong with any of my relationships. It didn't matter—they were never going to last and it was better just to paper over the cracks and part friends. I made that mistake with Sal too, and now I'll never really know what was going on in her head when she left Ellie with me.'

'This has got nothing to do with you and Sal. You can't use me to put the past right.'

'No. But I can learn from my mistakes.'

Cass sighed. 'Look, the best thing we can do now is to forget about tonight and decide to go our separate ways. As friends…'

'And friends don't talk to each other?' He let the thought sink in for a moment. 'I know I was blunt, and I apologise for that. But I was just terrified of leaving anything to chance, giving history a chance to repeat itself. Surely you can understand that?'

'Yes, of course.'

'You want to say anything?'

'I… No.'

He got suddenly to his feet, frustration leaking from every gesture. Cass thought he was going to throw her keys at her and storm out again, but he grabbed her arms, pulling her to her feet.

'Damn, Cass.' He was clearly in the grip of some powerful emotion that he was struggling to control. 'We were going to sleep together. Is it so difficult to trust me?'

'That's just what I wanted to do, Jack. Trust you and sleep with you. Not have to go through some kind of soulless agreement. I've got enough memories of that to last a lifetime.'

'What do you mean?' Jack was clearly not about to give up.

'I tried for a baby with my ex. Didn't happen.' The coldness she heard in her voice was her only defence. 'He left me, and I don't much blame him. All the charts and the dates, working out when we were supposed to have sex... It turned into a chore and I just used to close my eyes and get it over with. And then, afterwards, when I didn't...' She paused. 'Well, when you stopped things and starting talking about...what we needed to do, it brought back bad memories. I couldn't do it. I didn't want it to be like that with you.'

For a moment Jack seemed paralysed, shock registering on his face. Then he pulled her into a tight hug. 'I'm so sorry, Cass.'

'Don't be.' She held herself stiff and unyielding in his arms.

'You want to argue about *that* as well?'

Suddenly all the fight went out of her. He must have felt it because he sat her back down on the sofa, his arms still around her.

'Can I ask you something?'

'Whatever you like.' It didn't much matter now.

'Did you go to the doctor?'

'Yes. He couldn't find anything wrong with either of us. But there was something—we tried for nearly two years, and it must have been my fault because Paul... He left me because he'd made another woman pregnant.'

He wiped his hand across his face, uttering a soft curse. 'Cass, I'm so sorry that happened to you. But there's no blame attached to this. And sometimes the cause is to do with both partners...'

'Don't try to make me feel better, Jack. Paul has a child. It must be me.'

'Not necessarily. It could have been a combination of factors, some to do with you and some with him. Didn't the doctor explain all this?'

'He gave me some leaflets but I was so stressed out about it all…' The words had seemed to mock her, performing a *danse macabre* on the paper.

'And you didn't ask for help, either?'

'No. I didn't want to admit it to anyone.' The secret had driven a wedge between Cass and the people she was closest to. 'You know what some people in the village say about Miss Palmer? They say *"Poor Miss Palmer"* because she never had children.'

'Really? I'm not sure that's something it would ever occur to me to say. Miss Palmer's a force to be reckoned with.'

'I think so too. I want to be like her…'

'The best at your job? Terrifying? I think you've got that taped…' Jack chuckled as she elbowed him in the ribs, and somehow Cass found herself smiling. The secret was out but it hadn't turned on her like some wild beast. Jack had kept her safe.

He *had* trusted her. He *had* believed in her. It had given him the strength to be sure that there must be a reason for Cass's attitude, and when she'd shared her fears with him he'd understood that reason. The suffocating weight of his own childhood and his concerns for Ellie had seemed to lift, as if naming their fears could somehow allow them to put them aside for a while.

'Do you think… That I could go back and start again?'

'Right to the beginning?' Jack had often wondered the same himself. What it would be like if he could rewind and do it all again, knowing what he knew now. 'I don't think that's possible.'

'Just a week or so.'

That was a bit more attainable. 'Can we leave the part where I'm almost drowned out?'

'Yeah. No getting wet.'

'And I doubt that Ben's all that ready for a repeat of the mud incident either.'

Cass laughed. 'No. I don't imagine he is.'

Jack pulled her close, and when she tipped her face up towards him he dropped a kiss on to her cheek. 'Here?'

'That would be a really good place to start.' He felt her lips move against his skin and suddenly he was right back in the place he'd been an hour ago. With a second chance.

'You keep your eyes open when you're with me, though. I promise you that I'll take care of you and keep us both safe, but you have to let me know that it's me you see. Nothing else.'

'I see you, Jack. Not enough of you at the moment...' She tugged at his sweater and he chuckled.

'Hold that thought. I'll be back in a minute. Less, if at all possible.'

'I'll be waiting.'

Jack fetched a quilt from the cupboard upstairs to spread out in front of the fire, concealing the condoms in its folds.

She sat, watching his every move, the flickering light playing across her smile. When she stood, reaching for him, Jack shook his head and pulled his sweater off.

'Not yet. There's something I want to do for you...'

Her gaze didn't leave his face as he pulled off his clothes. Then he fell to one knee in front of her.

He wasn't prepared for this. Jack had worked hard enough to be confident about his body, but the effect of kneeling before her, naked as the day he was born and offering himself to Cass, was extraordinary. When her smile told him that she liked what she saw, he felt his limbs begin to tremble. She ran one finger over his deltoid muscle and Jack felt his shoulders flex in response.

'Look carefully.' Her gaze was running across his skin like electricity and he didn't want this to end any time soon.

She shot him a smile, targeting his chest next, and then his abs. Then she moved behind him and Jack caught his breath as he felt her warm hands on his back. Cass leaned over, bending to brush her lips against his ear and he groaned.

'Very nice. Exceptional, in fact.'

His heart thumped in his chest as she circled him again, stopping to face him. He caught her hand, kissing her fingers. 'All at your service.'

'That I like. Very much.'

'I'll take good care of you, Cass.' He wanted her to know that. Wanted beyond anything for her to believe it.

'I know.' She pulled her sweater over her head and Jack instinctively dropped his gaze to the ground. He'd never much thought about the seductive quality of listening to a woman undress, but this was beyond anything he could have dreamed. The soft scrape of material against skin. When he heard her unzip her jeans, his head began to swim and he gasped for breath.

'Jack...' Her fingers stroked his jaw and he raised his head. The picture of Cass, standing in front of him, naked, proud and strong, her red hair gleaming in the firelight, burned itself into his consciousness like a brand. Jack knew he would never forget this moment.

He was beautiful. Shadows contoured the honed muscles of his shoulders, slipping downwards towards slim hips and strong thighs. Like a fine sculpture of a man, every inch of which had been fashioned by a master craftsman, in perfect form and proportion.

A man less confident about his body might have objected

to this. But Jack's strength allowed them to go places she'd never been before. Allowed them to act out the fantasy without the possibility of bruising his ego.

He wasn't just some abstract being, though. This gorgeous body would be nothing without Jack's warm eyes. The tenderness of his touch as he reached out, sliding his fingers along her curves.

'You are exquisite.' His hands moved to her waist and he drew her in, kissing her hip. Cass's legs began to shake and then gave way altogether, and his grip tightened, holding her as she fell to her knees. Then he pulled her against him in a movement of unashamed power.

Her gaze met his and he kissed her. The ache of wanting him so much was almost unbearable now and she clung to his neck as he picked her up, a tangle of trembling limbs, and laid her down in front of the fire.

Settling himself over her, one arm curled around her back, the other hand moving towards her breast. A bright shiver of anticipation and suddenly Jack stilled, his fingers just a moment away from her skin. Before he'd even touched her nipple it was tight and hard.

Just a breath, a brush of his lips, and then he turned his face up to her. 'Crazy for me?'

'You know I am, Jack.'

'Yeah. I'm crazy for you too, princess.' His hand trailed down, caressing, learning her body. Each time she caught her breath his fingers responded, lingering a little until he tore a cry from her lips. Caught in his gaze, she could hide nothing from him.

Jack didn't know how much more of this he could stand. He felt as if he was melting. So very hard, and so very soft, both at the same time.

She tightened the muscles which cradled him inside her and he gasped.

'You like that…?'

'Yes would be an understatement. Do it again.'

'Your wish…' She did it again, grinning as he cried out. 'Is my command.'

'And yours…' He cupped her breast, stroking the nipple with his thumb, and felt her jolt against him. 'Is mine.'

They'd tested each other and broken every limit that Jack thought he had. Balanced together on the edge of a precipice, one false move would send them over the edge. Jack staved off the inevitable for as long as he could.

His sweet Cassandra. The words echoed in his head for a moment as he saw her break, coming apart at the seams so completely that she took him with her. And, when he came, the sudden violence of each sensation robbed Jack of everything. He belonged to her now.

They rested a little, grinning breathlessly at the racing beat of each other's hearts. Jack folded her in his arms and they lay staring into each other's eyes.

It was still early, though, and they both knew that this wasn't even close to being over. A murmured conversation, stretching like cats in front of the fire. A bottle of chilled Prosecco from the kitchen, which popped satisfyingly, the cork hitting the ceiling. A book, chosen at random from the shelf, which turned out to be a collection of short mystery stories.

He propped the book on her hip, their limbs tangled together. He loved this simple pleasure. Reading to her in front of the fire, feeling her intent gaze.

'Had enough?' Jack got to the denouement of the first story and she moved, sending the book slithering to the floor.

'Not nearly enough.' She picked up his glass, holding it to his lips, and he took a sip. Then she ran the cool rim across the heated skin of his chest.

'Hey… Two can play at that game…' He grabbed the glass from her, touching it to her lips and then her nipple and she yelped, laughing. And then everything else was forgotten as he rolled on to his back, pulling her astride him.

'How many times…' She leaned down to kiss him and he cupped her breasts in his hands. 'How many times can you do it in one night?'

An hour ago, Jack would have said that he wasn't going to be able to move for at least another two days. But Cass had a way of confounding every expectation. 'I have no idea.'

She shook her head in smiling reproof. 'Everyone should know that.'

'Yeah. I guess everyone should.'

No one should have that kind of stamina. The man should come with a warning, stamped across his forehead. *Danger. You will be putty in my hands.* By the time Jack tipped them both out of bed and into the shower, late the following morning, he'd pushed her to her breaking point. Then past it, into a rose-tinted world that seemed to revolve entirely around his smile.

Cass started on Sunday lunch while Jack went to pick Ellie up. That afternoon he set about hanging wind chimes in the little girl's room, positioned so that they sounded every time the door opened. Ellie loved them, and Jack's grin made it quite clear that the loud jangling sound wasn't intended solely to amuse his daughter.

He didn't need to ask whether she would come to him that night, and Cass didn't need to answer. He was waiting, his eyes following her every move as she walked towards the bed. Jack's hand trembled as he pushed the silk wrap slowly from her shoulders.

During the day they never spoke of it, even when they were alone, and hardly even touched. Jack was a friend who had offered her a place to stay while her house was flooded. When darkness fell and the house was quiet, he was her lover. It was simple, intoxicating and they both knew that this relationship, with its split personality, couldn't last.

But for two weeks it did. A secret from everyone. Untouched by the past, because they both knew that there was to be no future to it.

CHAPTER FIFTEEN

'WAKE UP. WAKE UP…' Jack whispered into her ear, jerking the coffee out of Cass's way as she suddenly sat bolt upright in bed. That hadn't been quite the reaction he was looking for, but he'd watched her eyes flutter slowly open once already this morning.

'Uh… What's the time?'

'Eight-thirty.' She looked gorgeous when she woke. Particularly like this, the bedclothes slipping down to her waist, her hair in disarray.

'What?' Jack reared backwards as she shot out of the bed, affording him an even better view. Then she stilled. 'It's Saturday, isn't it.'

'Yeah.' He smiled. 'Coffee?'

She took the mug from his hand and took a sip. Then another thought occurred to her. 'Where's Ellie?'

'Downstairs. I heard her get up about an hour ago. I told her you were probably sleeping and not to come up here and disturb you.' Cass was up before Ellie during the week, and at weekends the wind chimes gave Jack a chance to head her off before she came into his bedroom. It had worked so far.

She took another gulp of coffee. 'I should be getting going.'

'Not without us, you're not.' Martin had called last night

to say that the flood water had receded from around Cass's house. He wasn't letting her go back there alone a second time.

'But I said—'

'Yeah. I said too.'

'Thought you might have forgotten that.' She pushed his legs a little further apart with her foot so she could perch on his knee. Jack took the cup from her hand, taking a sip.

'Post-coital memory loss isn't permanent. I'm coming to help. Whether you like it or not.'

'Too bad.' She took the cup back, raising it to her lips. 'It'll be cold and wet…'

'Are you even listening to me?'

She leaned forward, brushing a kiss on his brow. 'Yes, I'm listening. I'm just not sure how I'll feel about it all.'

'Then let me feel it with you. Whatever it is.' Jack stood up, tipping her off his knee and kissing her cheek. 'Get dressed.'

They were on the road by nine o'clock. The water had begun to drain away from the motorway and it was possible to take Cass's SUV across, Jack walking ahead to check the surface of the road for potholes while Ellie stared out of the window at the water swirling around the wheels. They drove up to the vicarage first to see Sue and Martin, and found Miss Palmer, drinking tea in the kitchen.

'I happened to pop in.' She addressed Cass, giving Jack a smile. 'Is this Ellie?'

Ellie clung to the bottom of Jack's jacket, trying to slide behind his legs. Miss Palmer smiled at her then bent to draw what looked like a large bundle of green felt out of a carrier bag at her feet. 'I can't get this quite right, you know. Oops.'

Something fell to the ground at her feet. Ellie peered at it then stepped forward to pick it up. 'Ah, thank you, dear.'

Miss Palmer took the plastic toy away from her and put it on the table.

'It's a dinosaur…'

'Yes, dear. I've got some more here somewhere.' Miss Palmer fiddled with the bundle of felt and another plastic dinosaur fell out. 'Ah, there it is.'

Ellie's shyness was no match for Miss Palmer and the little girl was hooked. She climbed up on to a chair next to Miss Palmer, craning across to see what she was doing. Sue went out into the hallway, calling up the stairs, 'Hey, you two. Dinosaur Park…'

Jack raised a questioning eyebrow in Cass's direction. 'Bit of a tradition around here. I used to love Dinosaur Park.'

By the time they'd drunk their tea, the felt had been rolled out on the table to display an impressive landscape—grass, rivers and desert—all sewn in a patchwork of colours. Ellie was wide-eyed, clutching a surprisingly life-like volcano made out of fabric, and Sue's children were carefully arranging a waterfall made out of sparkly thread, which came complete with a pool at the bottom. Miss Palmer was talking to them quietly, lining up plastic trees and a variety of prehistoric creatures on the table, ready to complete the scene.

'She can stay here if she wants.' Sue nodded towards Ellie. 'I doubt they'll be finished before lunchtime, and then there's the battle to do.'

'Battle?'

'Yeah.' Cass grinned. 'Don't you know anything about dinosaurs?'

Ellie had to be prompted to give him a hug and a kiss goodbye and turned back immediately to the task in hand. Jack followed Cass down the steep path that led to her house.

She was quiet, seeming to be preparing herself for what was ahead of them. Walking with her head down, across the mud which led to her house. Jack followed, wondering when she was going to stop and take a look around at the damage.

Clearly not until she got inside. The front door didn't move when she tried to push it open and Jack put his shoulder to it. It slowly opened, scraping across the carpet and making an arc in the sticky mud which covered the floor. A foul smell of damp and decay hit them.

This was worse than she'd thought. She'd expected the mud everywhere, the damp and the disgusting smell. Known that the plaster would be bulging and waterlogged, and that there would be brown watermarks on the walls.

And she'd known that it would be upsetting, but Cass hadn't prepared herself for feeling physically sick. She routinely saw a lot worse—homes that had been burned out or flooded. She hadn't lost her home and neither had she lost most of her possessions, as so many had. It was just a bit wet.

She produced a notepad from her pocket. 'Front door.' She wrote the words carefully, the first on a list that was undoubtedly going to get very long. But she was doing okay. She was getting a grip.

Jack followed her in silence as she walked through the hall, stopping to write things down as she went. In the kitchen it was the same story—mud, watermarks on all the floor cupboards and the same horrible smell. Cass had disconnected the cooker unit and propped it up on the worktop, but the unit which housed it was ruined, the particle board swollen and blown.

'Not so bad.' She tapped the floor tiles with the toe of her boot. 'I wonder if I can salvage these and re-lay them.'

'Cass...'

Not now. Not here. If he was too supportive, then she'd just want to cry. Then he'd hug her, and that wouldn't do because they'd agreed that the pleasures of the night shouldn't leak into the day.

She turned abruptly, marching back into the hall and through to the sitting room. Forming most of the large extension at the back of the house, it was usually a great place to sit and relax—large patio windows which looked out on to the river and the trees beyond it. Now it was ruined. The empty bookshelves and TV cabinet were practically falling apart and the same oozing mud disfigured the carpets and walls.

She tasted bile at the back of her throat. Retching and crying, Cass made a run for the kitchen, wrenching open the back door.

'Don't touch me!' She was bent over, the fresh air stinging her wet cheeks, and Cass felt Jack's hand on her shoulder. She heaved in a couple of breaths, beginning to feel a little better.

When she straightened up again, she saw him standing by the back door. 'Sorry about that. Must be the smell. Turned my stomach.'

'Yeah. Must be.' He was watching her intently.

'I'll...get some water from the car.' She walked past him into the kitchen, wondering what Jack was thinking of her.

'Cass.' His voice behind her. 'What we have. It's only nights, right?'

She froze. Cass had known it was a mistake to let him come here. Talking about it was sure to mess everything up. 'Yes...'

'I want one day too. Now... Today...' When she turned, his eyes were dark, with the same intensity she saw in them every night. Jack walked slowly towards her and wrapped her in a hug.

Without any warning at all, she started to cry. Big choking sobs, while she clung to his jacket. Jack soothed her,
kissing the top of her head, holding her tight.

She'd cried for a long time. Blown her nose and cried a bit
more. Jack had fetched water for her from the car, along
with the flask of hot tea, and they'd sat on the kitchen doorstep together, sharing a cup of tea. Despite the devastation
around them, Jack was beginning to feel that he could get
used to this daytime thing.

Someone banged on the door. 'Stay here. I'll get it.' Jack
hurried through to the front door, heaving it open.

Martin stood on the doorstep. On the road a small group,
mainly men but some women as well, all shod in wellington
boots. Jack recognised Ben's parents, his father carrying
a couple of shovels to help clear the mud from the floors.

'I know Cass doesn't want any help.' It seemed that Martin had been appointed to take the first crack at persuading her otherwise.

'She's taking any help she can get. Come in.' Jack stood
back from the door and Martin beckoned to the group behind him.

What's going on? She mouthed the words at him as he
entered the sitting room.

'Your friends have come to help you out.'

'They don't need…'

'Yes, actually, they do.' Jack put his arm around her,
bundling her through to the hallway, which was filling
up quickly.

'Martin…' Tears welled in her eyes again and she
clutched hold of Jack's sweater.

'Thanks for coming.' Jack voiced the words for her and
Martin gave a small nod.

'Where are we going to start, then?'

* * *

The amount that could be achieved by a dozen people in less than four hours was amazing. The house had been aired through, and mud shovelled into buckets to be carted out. Carpets had been taken up and some of the mud had been scraped from the floorboards. In the kitchen, the cupboards and floor were washed clean and the smell of disinfectant started to permeate the air.

The furniture left in the sitting room was beyond repair, and was dismantled and removed. At two o'clock Martin received a text, and called for everyone to down tools.

'Lunch in the church hall, ladies and gents. Half an hour.'

Cass had slipped from tearful and embarrassed, through red-cheeked and into beaming. Then back to tearful again as she stood at her front door, hugging everyone and thanking them as they filed out of the house.

'I don't know what to say...' She stood in the doorway waving as everyone made their way back along the track to the village.

'I think you said it, didn't you? Anyway, I think this morning was all about what the village wanted to say to you.'

'It was so good of them...'

'What goes around comes around, Cass.'

'Thank you. For today.'

He nodded. 'Do it again tomorrow?'

'No. You spend tomorrow with Ellie, and I'll come here. I feel better about things, seeing how much difference we've made today.'

'All right.' Jack would have a quiet word with Martin and make sure that Cass wasn't alone tomorrow. And maybe she was right. He'd asked for one day and she'd given it, and maybe that was enough for now.

CHAPTER SIXTEEN

THE WEEK HAD seen them slip back into their easy routine. Jack had been looking forward to the weekend, wondering if perhaps Cass might be persuaded to take some time off from her work at the house, for an outing with him and Ellie. And then, suddenly, nothing else existed. The phone call on Friday afternoon, from a parent of one of the kids from Ellie's class, drove everything else from his head. Just the need to drive, to be there.

He could hear sirens in the distance, and he willed them on. Jack knew they were probably going in the same direction as he was, and if he couldn't reach Ellie then someone had to. Anyone.

He took the turn into the small side road that led to the school and slammed on the brakes, narrowly avoiding a fire engine that was parked up ahead. Getting out of the car, he ran, not stopping to even close the driver's door, let alone lock it.

'Jack...Jack!' He heard a woman's voice and scanned the crowd. 'Jack!' The mother of a little boy in Ellie's reception class ran towards him.

'Hannah.' He caught her hand, then put his arm around her. 'What's happening?'

'All the other kids are out. But the annexe...' Hannah's chest started to heave and Jack willed her to stay calm.

'Sarah told me that part of the building had collapsed.' Ethan had stayed home today with a bad cold, but Jack had dropped Ellie off at school this morning.

'Yes. The ground's so wet… The kids' classroom looks okay from the outside, but they're still in there.'

'Okay. Hannah, they'll get to them. The firefighters are trained for this; they know exactly what to do…' Jack wasn't sure whether he was trying to reassure Hannah or himself.

Stop. Look around. Assess the situation, then act. His own training came to the fore and Jack swallowed down his panic, the overwhelming need to have Ellie safe in his arms.

A pattern emerged from the chaos. A line of older children were leaving the main entrance of the school, shepherded by their teachers towards the sports field, which was some way from the building. There, children were being counted and checked, while a small group of parents waited anxiously.

He took Hannah's hand, walking swiftly around the back of the building, trying to control the feeling that he just needed to sweep everything in front of him away and find Ellie. What had once been the school hall was now a pile of rubble and the two-storey annexe beyond it, which housed the reception classroom, was completely cut off.

'They got the class on the ground floor out through the windows.' Hannah was hiccuping the words out through her tears. 'But Jamie and Ellie were upstairs. I saw her in the window, Jack.'

Jack looked up at the window, his heart leaping as he saw a small figure, climbing up on to the low, wide sill. *Ellie.* She was waving her hands above her head and seemed to be shouting.

'Ellie…' He roared her name, but in the general activity she didn't hear. 'Ellie!'

Someone held him back and he struggled free. The firefighters already had ladders up at the windows, and one of them climbed up. Jack saw Ellie walk along the windowsill towards him, reaching through the safety bars to press her hands against the glass.

They seemed to be talking. The firefighter called for quiet and a hush fell on the people below.

'Good girl. We saw you. Get down from the window now, sweetie, and stand over there.' The firefighter pointed into the classroom and Ellie obeyed him.

'Good girl. That's my good girl.' Jack sent the whispered words up into the air, wondering if Ellie knew he was here for her. Praying that she did.

'Why don't they just break the windows?' Hannah had her eyes fixed on the huge picture windows, which looked out on to the rolling countryside beyond.

'Windows that size…if they break them they might hurt the kids.' Jack shivered as he thought of shards of glass raining down on Ellie's head.

'Where's the teacher…?'

Good question. The thought of fifteen four- and five-year-olds alone up there made his blood run cold.

He wrapped his arm around Hannah, hurrying to the cordon of police and teachers which surrounded the scene. 'Let me through. Paramedic.' At the sight of his uniform he was waved through and, taking Hannah with him, he made for the two ambulances, parked next to a fire engine.

'Josie—' he recognised the paramedic who was waiting by one of the ambulances '—what's happening?'

'There's a class of fifteen kids and a teacher, trapped in there. No sign of the teacher, but there's a little girl who keeps coming to the window. There's a fire crew gone in.' Josie pointed towards a pile of rubble which almost filled a gaping hole in the wall. Above it, clean plasterwork with a line of pictures still pinned to it in a parody of normality amongst the destruction.

As he watched, one of the pictures fluttered from the wall on to the ground. A groaning sound, and a chunk of plasterwork flattened it as it detached itself from the wall and crashed down. Hannah let out a little scream of terror.

'Okay, Hannah. It's just a piece of paper...' He tightened his arm around Hannah's shaking shoulders. The image of frailty, crushed and broken, had torn at his heart too.

Josie was shaking her head, her eyes fixed on the classroom windows. 'She didn't hesitate. That woman deserves a medal...'

'What?'

'The firefighter. She saw the little girl and she was the first in, even though there have been great chunks of stuff coming down. Three of the men followed her.'

'Red hair?' A trickle of hope found its way into Jack's heart.

'Dunno, she had a helmet on. I didn't know it was a woman but I heard her call out to someone.'

Cass. It must be Cass. 'I'm going in...' Jack let go of Hannah and started to walk, and Josie pulled him back.

'Don't be an idiot.'

'Ellie's in there.'

Josie paled suddenly. 'All the same, Jack. If you get hit on the head by a lump of concrete then that's just another thing they'll have to deal with.'

He didn't care. 'Stay here, Hannah. I'll find them.'

'Jack...' Both Hannah and Josie were pulling at him now, and Jack shook them off. Then he looked up. Two figures had appeared in the window, with dark jackets and yellow helmets. Firefighters.

Cass. She and the other firefighter were making short work of the safety bars across one of the windows, and they opened it wide. Jack wondered where the other two men who had gone in were, and hoped that their absence didn't mean that there were casualties to attend to.

'Jamie…' The children were being lifted out one by one, into the arms of the men on the two ladders which had been raised to the window, and passed down to the ground. Hannah sprinted forward, pushing a policeman who tried to block her path out of the way in a surprising show of strength. She reached her son and fell to her knees, hugging him close.

Ellie. Where was she? Why wasn't she the first? Jack looked up at the window and saw Cass, with Ellie in her arms. She was talking to her, waiting for the firefighter on the ladder to be ready to take her, and Ellie was nodding.

Then a kiss. Jack almost choked with emotion as he saw Ellie handed safely from the window and into the arms of the man on the ladder.

Cass's attention was now on the next child, lifting him up and talking to him. But all Jack could see was Ellie. He ran forward and heard her voice as she was carried down the ladder.

'I shouted for help…'

'That's right, sweetie. Well done.' The firefighter was smiling as he climbed down.

'Daddeee! Cassandra rescued me.' Ellie held out her arms to Jack and then he felt her small body against him. He stammered his thanks to the firefighter, who nodded, climbing back up the ladder to fetch the next child.

'Are you all right, honey?' His first instinct was just to hold her, but he forced himself to check Ellie's small body for any signs of blood or injury.

'Cassandra came to find me. I got rescued…' There was clearly nothing wrong with Ellie's lungs.

'That's right, darling.' He looked up and saw Cass pass the next child out of the window. When she'd done so, her gaze scanned the people below her and found Ellie, who waved at her excitedly. Cass's grin told Jack that she'd seen what she had been looking for, and that she knew Ellie was safe.

The children were being marshalled into a group around the ambulances by parents and teachers so that each could be checked over. Jack walked across, holding Ellie tightly against his heart.

He saw Sarah running towards them and Ellie waved to her.

'I was rescued!' Clearly Ellie wanted everyone to know. Sarah flung her arms around them both and Ellie struggled to get out from between their bodies so that she could see what was going on.

The last child was being brought down the ladder and Jack did a swift headcount. Fourteen. He made only fourteen. And where was their teacher? He heard Cass's shout behind him.

'Paramedic…'

Josie looked up and grabbed her bag, making for one of the ladders. Jack reluctantly passed Ellie into Sarah's arms.

'Will you take her?' The words tore at his heart but he knew what he had to do.

'Of course. As soon as she's been checked over, I'll take her back home. I left Ethan with my neighbour so I don't want to be any longer than I can help.' Sarah turned to Ellie. 'Daddy's got to go and help Cassandra. We'll wait for him at home, eh?'

Ellie nodded. 'Are you going to rescue Miss Elliott?'

'Yes, sweetie. I'll be back as soon as I can.' Jack turned and made for the ladders.

It was no surprise that after the first paramedic was helped through the window, Jack appeared right behind her. Both of them had been provided with helmets and jackets.

'Just couldn't stay away, could you?' Cass grimaced at him.

'Nope.' Jack looked around the empty classroom.

Cass nodded. 'Good. Keep the helmet on.'

She led the way across the empty classroom, holding her arm out in front of him to keep him back from the door as she opened it. She heard Jack let out a quiet curse as he looked along the corridor, at the gaping hole in the floor that separated the classroom door from the far end of the corridor. 'How did you get through here?'

'We made it.' It hadn't been easy, and they'd been showered with lumps of loose plaster falling from the ceiling. But when she'd seen Ellie up at the window, Cass had remembered the promise she'd made to the little girl. *'If you go to the window and call for help, the firefighters will rescue you.'* That wasn't the kind of promise you made lightly.

'What's the situation?'

'The teacher's at the bottom of the hole, with the boy. He's lying underneath her and we don't know how badly either of them are hurt yet. There's a team trying to get to her from the back, on ground floor level, but the doorways are blocked with rubble and at the moment the only way is through here. So a second team has been working to get a ladder down to her.'

'Can you get me down there?'

'It's not safe.' The roof was still intact but cables and lumps of ceiling plaster dangled precariously over the hole. The other paramedic had already backed away into the safety of the classroom, and if he was going to stick to protocol then Jack should as well.

'Tell me something I don't know. Get me down there, Cass.'

She nodded. 'Okay. It'll be a minute before we're ready to go down.'

'Is she conscious?'

'We think so. When we came along the corridor we heard her groaning, and when we called down she replied.

There was stuff coming down from the ceiling and she was covering the child with her body.'

'What happened?' Jack's face had formed into a mask of determination.

'I think the boy must have run out of the classroom and the teacher followed him. We found the door locked, and she must have thought to lock it behind her to keep the rest of the kids inside. Somehow, she and the boy both fell.'

He nodded. 'Can we get her up to this level?'

'We could, but it would be better to wait for the team coming in via the ground floor. We'll have to make a decision on that when you've assessed her injuries.' Cass looked up as someone called her name. 'They're ready.'

Jack followed her over to the mouth of the hole and Cass climbed carefully down, flattening herself against the ladder as a shower of dust and debris fell from the ceiling. Picking her way across the rubble, and what looked like the remains of a photocopier, she headed towards the woman.

'Annabel… Annabel, I'm Cass.'

Annabel's eyelids flickered and she moaned. 'Cass…'

'Lie still. Not too long now before we get you out of here.'

'Take him…' Annabel cried out in pain as she shifted slightly and a boy's dirty, frightened face peered out at Cass.

'Okay. Okay, we're going to take you both. Just hang in there.'

The boy started to crawl out from the crevice below Annabel's body. Somehow, even though she was clearly badly injured, she'd managed to get him into the safest place she could, protecting him in the only way that was available to her. Dust and plaster was floating down from above them and Cass crouched over Annabel, sheltering her and the child as best she could.

Jack was making his way towards her with the medical

bag, which had been lowered down after them. As soon as he reached them, Cass let go of the boy, who wriggled free of his hidey-hole and straight into Jack's arms.

The boy was handed back to the firefighter who had followed Jack down, ready to be carried back up to the classroom where the other paramedic was waiting. Cass held her position, sheltering Annabel, while Jack started to check her over, talking quietly to reassure her.

A piece of something hit the back of her helmet and Jack glanced upwards. 'Okay?'

'Yep. Keep going.' Annabel was injured and defenceless. And she'd already shown such bravery. Cass would keep shielding her with her own body for as long as it took.

Jack gave her the briefest of smiles and then turned his attention back to his patient.

'Sweetheart. Annabel… I'm giving you pain relief. It'll kick in pretty quickly.' He murmured the words and Cass saw Annabel nod.

'The children…' She opened her eyes, trying to focus on Jack. 'You're Ellie's dad…'

'Yes, that's right. The children are all safe, thanks to you. And Shaun is okay as well—the firefighters are taking him out of the building.'

'I picked him up and the ground just… My leg…'

'You did just great, Annabel. You protected them all.' Jack's sideways glance at Cass told her that he'd come to the same conclusion she had. Annabel and Shaun must have fallen together and she must have landed awkwardly, trying to protect him.

'So cold. Don't want to…die.' A tear dribbled from the corner of Annabel's eye and Cass shifted her position so that she could take her hand.

'You're not going to die.' Jack brushed the side of her face with his fingers to keep her attention. 'Hey… Annabel.'

'Yeah… Too much paperwork…' Annabel grimaced.

'Far too much. I know you're hurting, but you're going to mend. Just hold on to Cass and we'll be getting you out of here as soon as we can. Got it?' Cass knew exactly what the warmth in Jack's eyes could do. He could make her believe anything, and she hoped that Annabel would believe him now.

'Yes...'

News was passed through that the firefighters, working to get through at ground floor level, were almost there. Jack worked on Annabel quickly and carefully, preparing her to be moved. A neck brace and temporary splints for her legs. A thermal blanket, to try and warm her a little, and an oxygen mask.

Annabel's eyes followed him. Somehow, Jack had managed to become not just someone who could give her medical help but her lifeline. It was almost as if he was keeping her going, just by the sheer force of his personality, that warmth in his eyes. Staving off the shock which made Annabel's hand ice-cold in hers.

The noise of boots clambering over the rubble heralded the arrival of the stretcher. Jack slid a lifting board under her body and Cass helped him transfer her to the stretcher, quickly securing the straps and tucking the thermal blanket around her.

'Okay, sweetheart.' Jack smiled down at Annabel. 'We're on our way.'

CHAPTER SEVENTEEN

JACK WAITED UNTIL the ambulance had drawn away, carrying Annabel to the hospital. Cass came to stand beside him, watching the vehicle negotiate its way past the fire engines and down the lane.

'Brave woman,' she murmured.

'Yeah. Josie's going to find out how she is when she goes off shift, and call me.'

'Do you think…?' She shrugged. 'How did she seem, to you?'

'Shock. One leg broken, and the other is probably fractured. Cuts, bruises, and she's got a cracked rib and what looks like a broken wrist. I couldn't find anything else, but they'll be checking her over further at the hospital to make sure.'

Cass nodded. 'I hope she's all right. Are you going off shift now?'

'Yes, I want to take Ellie straight home.'

'Okay.' Cass turned towards the fire engine. 'See you later.'

He caught her arm. 'Cass. Thank you.' There was nothing more he could say. When he'd seen Ellie in Cass's arms his heart had almost burst with relief.

'Yeah. Any time.' She grinned up at him and he knew that she understood.

By the time Jack got Ellie home she was starting to ask questions, and to realise that her experience hadn't been just another game. Was her teacher hurt? Why did her school fall down—was their house going to fall down too? He tried to answer everything as honestly as he could without feeding his daughter's fears.

She wanted to hold on to him, and he settled down in front of the TV to watch her favourite film with her. Even that didn't seem to get her singing and dancing around the room, as it usually did.

Cass was a little later than usual and, when he heard the front door close, Ellie didn't get up and run to greet her. When she walked into the sitting room, she was smiling.

'Hey, Ellie.' She squatted down in front of her. 'How are you doing?'

'All right.' Ellie turned her solemn eyes on to Cass without letting go of Jack's shirt.

'I've got something for you.' Cass was holding one hand behind her back.

Ellie craned around, trying to see what it was. 'Sometimes we meet kids who are really, really brave. And we give them a special certificate.'

'Really?' Ellie's eyes widened, and Jack grinned. So that was what she'd been up to.

'Yes.' Cass produced a roll of paper from behind her back, tied with a red ribbon. 'So this is for you.'

Ellie took the paper and Jack pulled open the bow with his free hand and unrolled it on Ellie's lap. Her name was on it in large letters framed with curlicues. He ran his finger under the words.

'Junior Firefighter...' he read out loud. 'That's you, Ellie. And, look, everyone from the fire station has signed it.' He pointed to the group of signatures, strewn with kisses and hearts. Cass's name was there too, the writing careful and rounded.

He stopped to wonder for a moment how handwriting could possibly be sexy, and then turned his mind to the image at the bottom.

'And there's the fire engine.' The artwork was clearly downloaded from the Internet, but that wasn't the point. Cass had taken the time to print it off on thick paper, and to get it signed by everyone. And Ellie was proud of herself now, not fretful and worrying.

'Say thank you to Cass.' He turned his face up to her, mouthing the words for himself, wondering if she knew just how heartfelt they were. She smiled at him.

'What's for supper?'

Everything was clearly okay in Cass's world if she was hungry. Jack had come to recognise the signs. 'Pasta. Fifteen minutes. Why don't you take Ellie upstairs and you can find a place on her bedroom wall for the certificate. I'll get a frame for it, eh, Ellie?'

The bumps and bangs from upstairs, along with the sound of Ellie's chatter, indicated that there was rather more going on than just the choosing of a place on the wall. Jack laid the table in the kitchen and took the pasta bake from the oven, leaving it to cool. Curious to see what they were doing, he walked upstairs to fetch them instead of calling them down.

The curtains were drawn in Ellie's bedroom, and Jack's hand hovered over the light switch as he popped his head around the door. Then he saw the makeshift arrangement of sheets, held up with a couple of chairs and some twine, forming a tent at the end of Ellie's bed. The glow of torchlight and the mutter of voices came from inside.

For a moment he was transfixed. So this was what it was like. A family. He remembered playing in a tent in the garden with his dad before everything had been shattered and their home had become just a house where grief had pushed the laughter away.

Suddenly it hurt. That swell of pain, all the regret for things he'd never done with his father. For the first time, Jack wondered whether his father had really wanted to leave them like that. Whether, in those last moments, when death must have seemed inevitable, he had thought of his wife and children.

For a moment the feelings choked him. It had been so much easier to blame his father, to be angry at the choices he'd made. But perhaps he'd just been a dad, after all.

Quietly, he walked into the room. The sudden clatter of wind chimes startled him and Ellie came cannoning out of the makeshift tent, almost knocking it down. Jack hadn't noticed the trip wire at his feet.

'We got you, Daddy...' Ellie wrapped her arms around his leg, clinging on tight.

'Yeah, you got me.' He bent down to tickle her and she wriggled with laughter. Then he put one finger over his lips, assuming a stage whisper. 'Where's Cass?'

'In the tent,' Ellie whispered back, her hand shielding her mouth.

Jack dropped to his knees and followed Ellie. Inside the tent, a line of dolls greeted him, their faces impassive. And Cass, sitting cross-legged and a little nervous, as if she'd just been caught doing something she wasn't strictly meant to.

'Can I come in?' Jack grinned at her.

'Yes. Of course.' She shifted a bit to give him room to get inside the tent and Ellie clambered past him to her own spot, next to the dolls. 'Is dinner getting cold...? Ellie, we should go downstairs...'

'We could eat up here.'

'Yes!' Ellie gave him an imploring look and Cass reddened.

'Won't we make a mess?'

'Probably. That's what they make kitchen towel for.' He

met her gaze. Today had changed things. When he'd seen Cass and Ellie together in the classroom window, he'd realised that trying to protect Ellie from Cass's love was not only useless; it was counterproductive. When they'd worked together with Annabel, Jack had wondered just how much else they could achieve together, given the chance.

And Cass had changed too. She'd created a comforting world for Ellie, and it was one that all three of them could share. They hadn't been together like this since he and Cass had slept with Ellie, on his bed, weeks ago.

'I used to have a tent, when I was little.' He smiled at Ellie. 'Grandma used to make burgers and chips, and she'd bring them out to the tent for Grandad and Auntie Sarah and me.'

Two pairs of round eyes gazed at him, Ellie's filled with interest and Cass's with astonishment.

'Auntie Sarah says that my grandad is the same as Ethan's grandad.' Jack realised that Sarah must have talked to Ellie about their father but that he never had, and she was struggling with the concept. It was an omission that he should have rectified by now.

'Yes, that's right. Do you want to see a picture of him? With me and Auntie Sarah when we were little.'

Ellie nodded vigorously.

'Okay. We'll have supper first, though.'

'I'll come and give you a hand.' Cass moved in the cramped space, trying not to knock any of the dolls over.

'It's okay. Stay here.' They didn't need to talk about this. Tonight might be as terrifying in its own way as today had been, but it was long overdue.

They were having fun. The tent that Cass had intended as something to cheer Ellie up with, and would fit only two people and a line of dolls, had turned into a tent for three. Just like a proper family.

Jack had gone to fetch the photograph, disappearing for some time, and Cass supposed it was hidden away somewhere and he'd had to look for it. Ellie had drawn her own version, and Jack had watched thoughtfully.

'He looks like you, Daddy.'

'Yeah. He does, doesn't he?' There was no trace of the anger that surfaced whenever Jack talked about his father. He ran his fingers lightly over the photograph, as if he too were re-drawing it.

'Okay?' Ellie was busy with another picture and Cass ventured the question.

'Yeah. I think so.' Jack still seemed unsure about this, but he'd hidden the tremor in his hands from Ellie. 'You?'

It was nothing to do with her. It was Jack's father, his child, and his conflict...

But when she'd passed Ellie out of the window and seen Jack waiting at the bottom of the ladder, it had felt for a moment as if Ellie was her own child. As if all the pressure and fear were gone, swamped by their shared instincts to keep the little girl safe. Maybe...just maybe...there was some way forward for her and Jack.

'You?' He repeated the question, more pointedly this time.

'Yes. Fine.' Cass turned to the picture that Ellie was drawing, trying to avoid his gaze. 'That's beautiful...'

She'd spoken before she had even looked at the picture. And when she did look, it *was* beautiful. A house. A red crayoned figure who she'd come to recognise as herself, along with a tall figure who could only be Jack. Between them stood four small figures.

'That's me.' Ellie planted her finger on one of the smaller images. 'And Daddy and Cassandra, and my brothers. And that's my sister.'

'Sweetheart...' Jack's voice was strained and Cass couldn't look at him. Didn't dare let him see the tears as her own picture of her perfect family suddenly imploded, smashing itself into pieces.

'That's very nice, Ellie.' She cleared her throat. 'I'm...'

What? Living next door? Coming to rescue Jack and his family? For a moment she couldn't think of any other reason for her to be in the picture than the one that Ellie so obviously intended.

'Okay...' When Jack pulled the picture out from in front of her, she almost cried out with loss. His other arm curled around Ellie and he took her on to his lap for a hug. 'I think it's nearly bedtime, don't you, Ellie?'

'No.' Ellie's voice was indignant.

'I think it is...'

Suddenly Cass couldn't take it. The nightly debate, which Jack always managed to win one way or another. The kiss, before Ellie ran to her father to go up to bed. She squeezed past Jack, almost knocking the tent down in her haste to get out.

'Cass...?'

'I'm going to stack the dishwasher.' She didn't wait for Jack's reply but ran downstairs, turning on the kitchen tap to splash cool water on her face. She'd done the one thing that she'd promised herself she'd never do again. She'd fallen for Jack, and dared to dream about a happy ending. One that could never come true.

Jack tried to get Ellie into bed as fast as he could, but hurrying always seemed to have the same effect. The more he tried to rush, the slower Ellie went. He read Ellie's favourite story, hoping she wouldn't mind that he'd missed a few bits out, listening for any sign of movement downstairs. When he finally kissed Ellie goodnight, the house had been silent for a while.

She was sitting at the kitchen table, nursing a cup of

tea. Cass didn't need to look at him for Jack to know she'd been crying.

'I'm so sorry. She didn't mean it…' The words tumbled out. It was all his fault. If he hadn't talked about his own father, then Ellie would probably never have drawn the picture. Jack had broken his own rule, dared to include Cass in his and Ellie's tiny family unit. And he'd hurt her.

She shrugged. 'I know.'

'She draws whatever happens to be going on in her head at the time. It doesn't mean anything.' He was protesting far too much. Trying to deny the truth. It hadn't just been going on in Ellie's head; it had been going on in his. And, from the look in her eyes, it had been going on in Cass's too.

She shook her head. 'It's what she wants.'

Jack almost choked. 'Ellie has what she needs; this isn't about her.' On that level it wasn't. On another, deeper level, the thought of hurting her the way he'd been hurt, deliberately putting her at risk of losing a parent again, still terrified him.

'No? Then make it about you and me then. How would you feel, knowing that there was no possibility of having any more children?' The intensity in her quiet words made it very clear that they would have been shouted if there wasn't a sleeping child in the house.

'Honestly…?'

She looked up at him suddenly. Such pain in her eyes. 'That would be good. Honesty always is.'

'Honestly, I think it's you that needs to face that, not me.'

'My problem, you mean?' she flared angrily.

'No, I didn't mean that at all. I meant that you're the one who thinks it's a problem in our relationship, not me.'

'We weren't going to have this conversation, Jack. You said you'd keep me safe.'

The words stung because they were true. And wanting to change didn't mean that it was easy.

'It's been a hell of a day. Perhaps we should sleep on it.'

She nodded, her face impassive. 'Yes. I need to be up early tomorrow. I'm seeing the electrician at my house in the morning.'

Jack nodded. 'Are you coming to bed, then?'

He'd never had to ask before. Always known that Cass would go to her own room, to get ready for bed, and then come to his. The moments of waiting, which had seemed like hours in his impatience to hold her, were almost the best part of his day. Second only to when he actually did hold her.

'I don't want to disturb you in the morning. And I could do with some sleep tonight.'

Jack nodded. Saying it out loud had broken the spell. 'I'll see you for supper then. Tomorrow.'

'Yes.' She stood up, bending to kiss his cheek. That, somehow, seemed the most damning thing of all. That she still wanted him, maybe even loved him a little, but there was a gap between them which neither of them could bridge.

He didn't see her again until the following evening. She arrived home late, her face expressionless, and sat down with him in the lounge. Separate chairs, the way they always did, even if there would be no one to see if they curled up together on the sofa. It seemed almost normal, and strangely comforting after having brooded over the possibility that Cass might do what they'd agreed to do all along and take it into her head to call time on their relationship.

'How are things?'

'Fine. Good, actually. The electrician reckons it's safe to restore part of the power supply now, and that means I can get heaters in there to help dry the ground floor out a bit. The motorway's open again.'

One by one, the things that kept her here were disappearing. It was only a matter of time...

'I'm going to move back in.'

Jack swallowed. 'Already?'

'It's easier for me to be there. As long as I have somewhere to sleep, they're still doing lunches and an evening meal up at the church hall.' She pressed her lips together. Clearly she didn't want to talk about it.

'You have somewhere to sleep here.' His bed. In his arms.

'I know.' She sighed. 'But...'

Jack could feel it all slipping away. Protected by secrecy and the four walls of his bedroom, their love affair had blossomed, but as soon as they took it outside that, into the real world, it seemed unbearably fragile.

But maybe, with a little care, it could survive. 'Will you come out with me? One evening. A meal, perhaps.'

She blinked at him. 'You're asking me out on a date?'

'Yeah. I am. Sarah will look after Ellie...'

'I don't think that's a very good idea.'

'Why not?' Okay, so he knew the reasons. Had struggled with the reasons, and Jack still wasn't sure that they weren't valid ones. But surely Cass could give it a try?

'Because...' She stared at him for a moment, her gaze searching his face. 'Because there's no future in it, Jack. I know what it's like to want a child so badly that your whole life seems shattered every time your body tells you that you're not pregnant. I can't go through that again.'

'I'm not asking you to. All I'm asking is that we give it a little time. Find a way to work things out.'

She shook her head, her face suddenly impassive. 'No. That would be too cruel.'

She got to her feet, leaving the room without even looking at him and closing the door behind her in a clear sign that he wasn't to follow her. He heard her soft footsteps on the stairs and the sound of her bedroom door close. Then silence.

Jack stared into the gathering gloom, which had once been a thrilling first hint of the darkness ahead. Now all he could feel was anger. He'd risked everything for Cass, his own heart, and Ellie's. He'd trusted her enough to try to let her into his life but she was still too fearful to even make the effort, and now she was going to leave him.

Maybe she was right and it would never have worked out. And, if that was the case, then he needed to think of Ellie. He needed to protect her.

He sat for a long time, brooding into the darkness, then slumped round on the sofa, fatigue taking over from the what-ifs that were filling his mind. No point in going up to bed. He knew that Cass wouldn't be coming.

Cass was up and packed before there was any sound from Ellie's bedroom. By the time she heard the tinkle of wind chimes heralding the fact that the little girl was awake, she was sitting on the bed in the spare room, staring at the wall.

It was all for the best. This had never been anything other than something temporary, something that couldn't touch their real lives. It had been three weeks since their first night together. Just about the duration of a holiday romance.

The sounds of Jack and Ellie in the bathroom. The smell of breakfast. Everyday things, now tainted with sadness. She waited until she heard Ellie running around in the sitting room, ready to jump on the new day with her customary glee, and went downstairs.

Jack was drowsy and tight-lipped. He closed the kitchen door and turned to her, his face unreadable.

'You're going today?'

'Yeah.'

He nodded. 'Okay. I'm taking Ellie out to the petting

zoo this morning. They've just opened up again after the floods.' His eyes softened suddenly and a thrill of hope ran through her veins. 'Take your time packing.'

Even Jack couldn't fix this. Neither could she. All they could do was to act as if nothing had happened, and that was easy enough. They'd been acting as if nothing was happening practically since they'd first laid eyes on each other.

'I'm ready to go now.'

He nodded abruptly. 'We'll be going soon. Then you can go.'

He couldn't help it. However much he was trying to come to terms with the past, he couldn't do it yet. Jack was cutting her out of his life, another casualty of loss, just like his father and Sal.

'May I...' Cass almost choked on the words. Surely he couldn't be that cruel. 'May I say goodbye to her?'

'Of course.' A glimmer of warmth again in his eyes and then he turned, opening the kitchen door. 'Take whatever time you need.'

It was cold comfort. Cass explained to Ellie that she was going back home today and the little girl nodded, taking it in her stride.

'You're not going far.'

'No, sweetie, not far. You know where I live.'

'That's all right, then.'

Cass hugged her tight, squeezing her eyes closed to stop the tears. Jack called to her from the hallway, persuading her into her coat and wellingtons, and Ellie shouted a goodbye. When Cass went to the front door to wave them off, he didn't even look at her. If Ellie required a hug and a kiss goodbye, Jack obviously required neither.

CHAPTER EIGHTEEN

THE CLOCK RADIO blared into life and Cass cursed it, reaching out to shut it off. The sudden movement prompted a twinge in her shoulder.

Well it might. She'd been up until midnight last night, putting flat-pack kitchen units together, and they'd been heavier than she'd expected. Today, she might take some time to reflect on the considerable amount of work she'd done on the house in the last two months. Take a few 'work in progress' photographs to compare with the devastation of the 'before' photos and spur her on to the distant date when 'after' photos would be in order.

She took a long shower, still revelling in the fact that she had hot water again. Then padded back to her bedroom, sorting through her wardrobe and on a whim pulling out a skirt. Being able to wear something pretty in the house instead of muddying up her jeans yet again was novelty enough to smack of yet another new achievement.

She made coffee and then went back upstairs to her bedroom, sitting cross-legged on the bed and switching on the television. This was the one room in the house which didn't bear some signs of the devastation the flood had brought with it; downstairs was still a work in progress and the spare room was full of furniture. But here she could relax.

A film maybe. Watching TV on a Sunday morning

seemed like the ultimate luxury. Cass picked up the remote from the bedside cabinet and switched to streaming, flipping through the films on offer. No, not that one. Or that one. Definitely not that; she'd heard it was a weepie. Or that—it was a love story.

The only thing that seemed to drive Jack from her mind was hard work. And the only thing which drove him from her dreams was physical and mental exhaustion. Cass hesitated, looking at her jeans, folded neatly on a chair. Maybe she should put them on and get on with the kitchen cabinets.

The doorbell rang and she climbed off the bed and walked over to the window. Perhaps someone from the village wanted her for something. She almost hoped that it might be a problem which required her immediate attention.

Peering out, she jumped back in horror. Jack's car was parked outside in the lane. Maybe he'd brought Ellie back to renew some acquaintance he'd made here and decided to pop in. Didn't he *know* he couldn't just do that?

Cass watched the front path and saw him stand away from the door, scanning the front of the house. He was alone, and suddenly fear clutched at her heart. Why would he come here without Ellie on a Sunday morning?

She raced downstairs, sliding her feet into her wellingtons when she realised they were the only footwear she had in the hallway. Then she flung open the door.

'Jack…?'

He was making his way back up the path and he turned. Cass's stomach almost did a somersault as suddenly she realised that she hadn't remembered the warmth of his eyes at all. They'd always been so much better in reality.

'What's the matter? Where's Ellie?' Surely the only thing that could bring him here alone was if there was some kind of trouble.

'At Sarah's.' He paused for a moment and then strode back along the path towards her. 'May I come in?'

The temptation to slam the door in his face fought with the need to look at him just a little longer, and lost by a whisker. And she'd opened the door now. Not letting him in would betray the fact that she cared one way or the other.

She stood back from the door in silence and he nodded, wiping his feet and walking into the hall.

'Wow. Quite a difference from last time I saw this.'

Presumably he was referring to the new plaster and skirting boards, and the scrubbed floorboards. All Cass could think about was that the last time he'd been here they'd had something, and now there was nothing.

'It's been hard work.'

'I imagine so.' He seemed a little jumpy. As if there was a point to all of this and he was working himself up to it.

'What do you want, Jack?'

He turned his gaze on her, warm enough to melt chocolate. 'I've come for you, princess.'

No. *No!* What had made him think that he could do this? Leave Ellie with Sarah and pop back for a day spent in bed. Who did he think she was?

'Out.' She glared at him, hoping he'd go before she changed her mind. Her body had just caught on to the idea and was beginning to like it.

'Cass, wait. Can we talk about this?'

'There's nothing to talk about. You can't just drop in whenever you've got a free moment and you think you might like to warm your feet in my bed.'

Reproach flashed in his eyes. 'It's not like that.'

'Okay then, friends with benefits, whatever you want to call it. I'm not interested.'

'Neither am I. Cass, can we sit down…?'

'There's nowhere to sit. The kitchen's full of cupboards, and there's no furniture in the sitting room.' And she wasn't going to take him upstairs to her bedroom.

He rolled his eyes. 'Then we'll do it here.'

'No, we won't. Whatever it is.'

Suddenly he was too close. His lips just an inch away. Cass felt tears begin to roll down her cheeks. 'Jack, stop it. Please...'

'I don't want sex...'

'Stop it!' Didn't he know that friendship was just as much out of the question? She couldn't bear it.

'I want to marry you.'

Suddenly the air began to swim in front of her, distorting everything else. She felt her knees begin to buckle...

Jack managed to catch her before she hit the ground. *Stupid. Stupid.* He shouldn't have just come out with it like that but he was so afraid that Cass was going to throw him out before he got a chance to say it. He settled her in his arms and carried her upstairs, kicking open the nearest door and finding a room stacked with furniture. The other door revealed a large sunny bedroom with light oak furniture and white lace bedlinen.

She was already stirring in his arms and her fingers clutched at his shoulders when he walked over to the bed with her. 'Boots...Jack...'

'Okay. Just relax; I'll take them off.' The room was meticulously clean and tidy, and Jack knew that Cass would probably kill him if he let her wellingtons soil the bed. Sitting her down, he pulled her boots off and then guided her back on to the pillows.

His finger found the pulse in her neck. Strong, even if it was a little fast. His was probably faster.

'I'm all right.'

'I dare say you are. Stay down for a minute.'

She opened her eyes and their pale blue earnestness made his heart lurch. 'I must have just...'

'Have you been eating?' She'd felt light in his arms, and

now that she was lying on her back he could see the line of her hips through the thin fabric of her skirt.

'I...' Her face took on a look of grudging contrition. 'I was putting the kitchen cabinets together last night and didn't stop for supper. I haven't got around to breakfast yet...'

'And so you fainted.' Jack decided not to touch on the immediate reason in case she did it again. He got to his feet. 'Stay there.'

'I'm okay. Really. Just a bit embarrassed.'

Not half as embarrassed as he was, for being such an idiot as to just drop a marriage proposal on her, right out of the blue. But now wasn't the time to mention that, not until she'd had something to eat.

'Stay there.'

'But...'

'No buts, Cass. If you move, I'll... Just don't move.' He tried to put as much authority as he could into his words before he hurried downstairs to the kitchen.

Cass could hear the banging of cupboard doors downstairs. Jack had asked her to marry him?

Maybe she'd got it wrong. Maybe he'd done it on impulse and was regretting it now. Or maybe he'd meant it, and she'd had to go and spoil the moment by fainting. It was her own stupid fault, but the constant hunger for Jack seemed to have overwhelmed everything lately, even hunger for food.

He appeared in the doorway, a glass of milk in one hand and a plate with a couple of croissants in the other. Sitting down on the edge of the bed, he waited for her to sit up before he put the plate on to her lap.

'Feeling better?'

'Yes, much. What were you going to say to me?'

'Eat first.'

How was she going to eat with the words she thought Jack had said bursting in her head like fireworks? She picked up one of the croissants and put it down again.

'I can't.'

He narrowed his eyes. 'Try. C'mon, Cass, I know you can do it.'

'I can't. Really. Jack…' *Please let this be what she thought it was. Please…*

He flashed her a grin. 'I'm glad you can't wait. Don't think I can either.'

'Then get on with it! I'm feeling a little nervous.'

He chuckled. 'Good. I'm feeling a bit nervous too.' Jack picked her hand up from her lap, kissing her fingers, and she nodded him on.

'Cass, you taught me how to believe. And I believe in you. There's only one choice and I've made it. I love you and I want to be with you for the rest of my life. We'll take everything else as it comes, face it together.'

It was everything she wanted to hear. There was only one more question and she had to ask it now, before happiness chipped away at her resolve. 'Are you sure you could be happy? If I couldn't give you children?'

'Wrong question.' He shook his head, smiling. 'If we can't have children *together*, then I can still be very happy. This is how sure I am…'

He reached into his pocket, pulling out a small box. When he opened it Cass clapped her hand to her mouth. The ring inside was beautiful, two diamonds twisted together in a gold setting.

'You're the only woman I'm ever going to want, Cass. You and Ellie are the only family I'm ever going to need. The only question is whether that's enough for you.'

'Me? Are you joking?' He was offering her the whole world and he wanted to know if it was enough?

His mouth curved into a smile. 'I'll let you know when

I'm joking.' He snapped the box shut again and put it back in his pocket.

'Hey! Don't I get to look at it a bit more?'

'I thought you might like to think about it for a while.'

'Jack, ask me again. Please, I know my answer.'

He nodded. He knew her answer too. It had always been this way with Jack. Friends, lovers—they were like two pieces of a jigsaw that fitted perfectly.

He sat on the bed, holding her hands between his. 'Will you marry me, Cass?'

'Yes, Jack. I'll marry you.'

He took the ring out of the box, slipping it on to her finger.

They'd talked for hours, lying together on the bed, side by side. He'd told her his dreams and she'd told him hers. And all of those dreams began slowly to morph into plans.

He was so happy. It felt as if a great weight had been lifted off him, not just the weight of the last months, when he'd struggled to cope without Cass, but the weight of years.

'You want something more to eat?' Jack doubted it. In his remorse at seeing her so thin, he'd raided the kitchen again and she'd worked her way through two sandwiches, a banana and a pot of yoghurt.

'No. I... Were you serious when you said you didn't want sex?' The tone of Cass's voice intimated that she was pretty sure he hadn't been.

'I only want sex under certain conditions.' Her eyebrows shot up and Jack couldn't help smiling.

'Really? Well, you can't just leave me guessing. What conditions?'

'To show how much I love you. To celebrate with you, comfort you, be your companion.' He leaned in to kiss her lightly on the lips, his body burning with need. 'I'm not going to rule out cheap thrills...'

'I like the sound of *cheap thrills*. Would it be quicker to tell me what you *don't* want?'

'Yeah, much.' He eased his leg between her knees. 'I don't want you to be worrying about what time of the month it is, or whether your temperature's just spiked. I want you to see me, Cass. Only me.'

Neither of them had been able to deny that they wanted a child together, but they'd agreed that what they already had was enough. Now was the time to test that out, whether Cass could really leave her own past behind and risk all her broken dreams against what they had now.

'I'd really like that...' She gave him a dazzling smile. 'No expectations, then?'

He wouldn't go quite that far. 'Yeah, I've got expectations. That thing you do... The one that drives me crazy...'

'Which thing is that?'

'Every single one of them. All I see is you, sweetheart.'

'And all I see is you.'

She wound her arms around his neck, pulling him down for a kiss. Then she whispered in his ear, 'Take your clothes off...'

EPILOGUE

JACK FELT AS if he'd been sitting here for hours, although in truth it was probably only ten minutes. He looked around, towards the entrance of the church, and Mimi elbowed him in the ribs. 'Do that again and I'll be having words with you, Jack.'

'You're supposed to be looking after me, not haranguing me.' Jack had asked Rafe to be his best man and he'd refused, telling him that Mimi was the one he'd crewed an ambulance with for seven years. So convention had been thrown to the wind and both Mimi and Rafe sat beside him.

'She won't be late.' Rafe leaned over. 'Cass is never late.'

'She's already late.'

'No, she isn't.' Mimi looked at her watch. 'She's got another two minutes to go. If you don't stop this, so help me, Jack, I'm going to sedate you.'

A sound at the other end of the aisle. There seemed to be some activity in the porch, and suddenly Ellie appeared. It was the second time in six months that she'd been a bridesmaid and, after the petal-throwing debacle at Rafe and Mimi's wedding, Cass had decided that a sparkly wand might go with the pretty pink dress that Ellie had helped pick for herself.

Ellie waved the wand at the assembled company. Their families, their friends and half the village had turned out and squashed themselves into the church at Holme. Every head turned and the organist struck up the wedding march. This time Ellie didn't take fright and started to walk up the aisle, a look of intense concentration on her face.

Then Jack saw her. She had flowers in her hair and her dress fell in soft folds from an embroidered bodice, emphasising the fluidity of her movements. As Cass walked slowly towards him, her hand resting lightly on her father's arm, he was transfixed.

'Stand up, will you?' Mimi hissed the words in his ear, kicking him. Jack wondered whether his legs would be able to support him. Cass was the most beautiful woman in the world and she'd come here to be his wife.

'You've got the rings?' He turned to Rafe in a sudden panic.

'Of course we have.' Rafe propelled him to his feet and Cass smiled at him. And suddenly everything was not only all right; it was touched with more joy than Jack could ever have imagined one man could stand.

She'd made her vows and he'd made his. As they stepped out of the church and into the spring sunshine, a firefighters' guard of honour stood to attention. Miss Palmer was on the station commander's arm and Ellie capered around, swishing her wand. Everyone trooped across to the village green, where two huge interconnecting marquees had been erected, one to accommodate the buffet and the other for dancing.

Jack was by her side all the way, through the speeches, the cutting of the cake, the excited congratulations. Her soulmate. The hero who had saved her and brought her to a place where she was completely happy.

'Do you have a date yet? For moving in?' Martin beamed at Jack.

'A couple of months, we hope. We're taking our time and doing it properly.'

Both Jack and Ellie loved the house down by the river, and Holme was a good place for Ellie to grow up. They'd chosen the new decorations together and when Jack sold his place there would be cash to build a second storey on to the existing extension if they wanted. Cass found Jack's hand and felt his fingers close around hers.

'And I saw the new wall,' Sue chipped in. 'So, no more repeats of last year.'

'It wasn't all bad. Look what I found washed up on my doorstep.' Cass squeezed Jack's hand and he chuckled.

There was one more thing to be done. Jack had made her feel so happy, so loved, that she'd almost forgotten about monthly cycles and calendars. Until last week. She'd been to the doctor and taken a pregnancy test, just to be sure before she went on her honeymoon.

She'd run all the way home to tell him, stopping just yards from the house. He'd told her that he wanted to marry her without knowing what the future held and she couldn't deprive him of the chance to make that ultimate commitment.

Jack led her on to the dance floor. The weather was warm enough for the walls of the marquee to be removed, leaving just a high domed canopy, strung with lights over their heads. When their first dance was over, other couples started to fill the dance floor.

She felt Jack's chest heave in a long contented sigh and she smiled up at him. 'Happy?'

'I don't think it's possible to be any happier.'

She laughed. 'Sure about that?'

'Positive.'

She stretched up, whispering in his ear.

Mimi was watching the couples on the dance floor as suddenly Jack lifted Cass up, swinging her round. Then he set her back on to her feet again, hugging her tight as tears streamed down his face.

'Look.' She nudged Rafe. 'I don't suppose there's a bit more synchronicity going on, is there…?' It had become a joke between the two couples that Jack had set eyes on Cass at pretty much the same moment that Mimi had seen Rafe again.

Rafe thought for a moment. 'No. I don't.'

'Why not? It makes perfect sense.'

'But what are the odds, Mimi? Seriously. It would be wonderful, but…' His gaze wandered over to where Jack was still hugging Cass.

'Trust me, Rafe. Jack's got that same dazed expression on his face as you had last week, when I told you I was pregnant.'

'Really? I didn't look *that* bad, did I?'

Mimi stood on her toes so she could whisper in his ear. 'You were worse. And much more handsome.'

Rafe chuckled. 'Thank you. Would you like to dance?'

'I'd love to dance.'

* * * * *

SUMMER WITH A
FRENCH SURGEON

MARGARET BARKER

To my wonderful family who give me
continual love, inspiration and happiness.

CHAPTER ONE

EVER since she'd been tiny, Julia had always made a special point of trying to appear confident. Well, with three older brothers to boss her around she'd had to be tough to survive. Still, glancing around now at her fellow trainee surgeons, she felt decidedly nervous. Since her disastrous marriage to Tony—who'd done his best to destroy whatever confidence she'd had—her life had been an uphill struggle to even get back to how she'd felt as a teenager, competing against her brilliant medical-student and qualified brothers.

Coming here, to France, to further her surgical career was the first step on her long journey back to self-confidence. And, in fact, looking out of the taxi as she had been driven down the hill just now towards St Martin sur Mer, she'd been in seventh heaven as she'd absorbed the wonderful scenery spread out in front of her. The stunning view had made her forget any apprehension she'd had about taking this big step.

She'd found herself overwhelmed with nostalgia as she'd seen the undulating sand dunes spilling down onto the beach and behind them the small, typically French hotels, cafés *tabac*, restaurants, shops and houses clustered near the high-tech hospital. She'd felt the excitement she'd known as a child when her French mother and English father, both doctors, had brought the whole family here for a couple of weeks every summer holiday.

She brought her thoughts back to the present as the eminent professor of orthopaedic surgery strode into the room. She caught her breath. Wow! Bernard Cappelle looked much younger than she'd expected and very... handsome? She paused, surprised by the turn of her wicked thoughts. It had been a very long time since she'd noticed any man in that way.

He was more than handsome, he was charismatic. Yes, that was more like it. He was oozing the sort of confidence she longed to acquire. Well, maybe, just maybe in another ten years, when she was an eminent surgeon, she would stride into a room and silence would descend as her students stared in awe at their professor of surgery, as was happening now with the great Bernard Cappelle.

If she hadn't made a concrete decision to hold off relationships since Tony had bled her dry of all desire for emotional commitment of any kind she would have allowed herself to fancy Bernard Cappelle.

In your dreams, girl! No chance! She wouldn't let herself even fantasise about him. Good! That meant she could concentrate on making the most of the six-month course without wasting her energy on emotional dreams about an unattainable man who wouldn't even notice her.

The awesome man cleared his throat as he looked around the assembled doctors. Ah, so he was possibly a bit nervous? At least that meant he had a human side.

'Hello, and welcome, ladies and gentlemen. I hope that...'

Bernard Cappelle began by welcoming them to the Hopital de la Plage, which would be their place of study and work for the six-month course. He explained they would study an orthopaedic operation theoretically before they moved on to the practical aspect of observing and assisting in Theatre. They would also be expected to assist with the pre- and post-operative care of the patients and also work in *Urgences*, the accident and emergency department, on occasion if required.

Julia took notes but realised soon enough that she'd read most of this in the brochure she'd studied carefully before applying. So she allowed herself to study the man who was to lead them all to the final exams, which would give them a prestigious qualification that would be a definite help to her in her desire to become a first-class orthopaedic surgeon.

She sat back in her hard and uncomfortable chair, probably designed to keep students awake. There were ten students on the course, Dr Cappelle explained. He'd chosen them from their CVs and was confident from their qualifications and experience that they were all going to give the next six months one hundred per cent of their available effort. He paused for a moment and his eyes swept the room before alighting on Julia in the front row.

'Are you happy for me to speak French all the time, Dr Montgomery?' he asked in heavily accented but charming English.

She was taken aback by suddenly being the centre of attention. Everyone was waiting for her reply. She swallowed hard. 'Yes, yes, of course. My mother is French, my father English, so I'm bilingual.'

'Then if you are happy I will speak in French...' He went on to explain that he was much happier when speaking French. 'And you are not intimidated by being the only lady in the class?'

She sat up straight, trying to look bigger than she actually was. 'Not at all. I was brought up with three brothers who did their best to intimidate me but without success.'

There was a scattering of sympathetic laughter. She was quaking in her shoes but making a valiant effort not to show it. She wished he would take his eyes off her and attention would focus on someone else.

'Excellent!'

A student sitting nearby spoke out in a clear distinct voice. 'Why is it, sir, that women orthopaedic surgeons are few and far between?'

Bernard Cappelle appeared to be giving the matter some thought. 'Good question. Could it be that the fairer sex are more delicate and possibly wary of taking on a profession that requires a certain amount of strength on occasions? What is your view, Dr Montgomery?'

'I have to say,' she continued boldly, forcing herself to display a confidence she didn't feel, 'I'm surprised to be the only woman on the course. I've never found, during my early career so far in orthopaedics, that being female is a disadvantage. When you're operating the patient is usually sedated in some way...I mean they're not likely to struggle with you or...'

Her voice trailed away as her depleted confidence ebbed and flowed.

The student who'd begun the discussion broke in. 'And there's always some hunky big, strong male doctor hovering around a fragile lady, hoping she'll ask for his help so that he can muscle in and...'

She missed the end of his sentence because the entire group was now laughing loudly. Ha, ha, very funny... she didn't think. She waited until the laughter died down before taking a deep breath and speaking in the clear, concise, correct French her well-spoken mother had always insisted she use.

'Gentlemen, you can be assured that I never take advantage of my so-called fragility. My brothers took me to judo classes when I was very young. I was awarded a black belt as soon as I was old enough to qualify and the skills I learned have often come in handy. So, as you can see, I only need to call for help when it's absolutely necessary.'

'Bravo!' Dr Cappelle said, admiration showing in his eyes. From her position in the front row she could see they were sensitive, a distinctive shade of hazel. Phew, she was glad she'd had to practise the art of being strong from an early age. Her show of pseudo-confidence was turning into the real thing, although she realised that had she known she would be the only woman on the course she might have hesitated before signing up.

Well, probably only hesitated for a short while. Looking around, she knew she could handle these young doctors, whatever they tried on. She'd learned a lot about men in the last few years. Basically, they were still boys, feeling as daunted as she was at the prospect of the exacting course they'd signed up to.

'I'm now going to give you a tour of the operating

theatres we use here at the Hopital de la Plage. Some of them will be in use and we won't be able to go inside en masse. May I suggest you make a note of the areas you aren't able to see today so that you can find a more suitable time to inspect them at a later date?'

Before they all filed out, the professor asked them to call him Bernard. He said that he didn't hold with titles in a teaching situation, explaining that it was easier for him to get to know his students if there was always a warm atmosphere, especially in tutorials like today. He looked around the room as if to judge the collective re-action of his students to this unexpected statement.

There was a stunned silence. Julia felt slightly more at ease with the great man when he said that but as she glanced around the room she knew that her fel-low students weren't taken in. Bernard Cappelle some-how managed to remain aloof even while he spoke. She sensed an aura of mystery surrounding him, which made him seem distant, brooding, definitely enigmatic, approachable in a professional situation but with cau-tion. Yes, his students would call him Bernard because he'd requested they do so but at the same time they would be wary of him. So would she but for several reasons, some of them decidedly inadvisable given her past history!

Being in the front row, she went out first and found Bernard walking beside her. He seemed very tall. She wished she'd put her heels on but hadn't realised they were going to trek round the hospital.

'You don't mind if I call you Julia, do you?'

He had such a deep, sexy, mellifluous voice. She was going to have to be very firm with herself to eliminate any sign that she felt an attraction to him. There, she'd admitted it. Well, power plus charisma, plus a barely discernible twinkle in the eye, which undoubtedly accompanied a wicked sense of humour, all added up to a desirable package that she certainly wasn't going to attempt to unwrap. Bernard could teach her his professional skills and knowledge and that was all she wanted from him.

Besides, he was probably married, bound to have a stunning wife waiting for him at home. Although married men were often ready for a fling and flings were another thing totally off her agenda.

'Yes, you can call me Julia.' She didn't even smile, making it seem as if she was doing him a favour.

'Good.'

They were now going inside one of the theatres, which Bernard had told them was not in use that afternoon. There was gleaming, bright high-tech equipment everywhere she looked. She was really going to enjoy working in a place like this.

At the end of the afternoon tour Bernard took them down to the staff cafeteria, where the conversation drifted from the equipment they'd viewed and the endless possibilities of a teaching hospital of this calibre to their previous experience and what they hoped to get out of the course that would be relevant to their future careers.

Somehow she found herself next to Bernard again. She wondered if he felt he had to protect her from the attentions of her fellow students in spite of the fact that she'd made it quite clear she wanted to be treated in the same way as all the men on the course.

'So, do you think you're going to enjoy working here, Julia?'

'I don't know whether *enjoy* is quite the right word.' She took a sip of her coffee. 'I intend to get the most out of it but I realise it's going to be hard work.'

'You look like the sort of person who enjoys hard work—determined, tough, doesn't give up easily. From your CV you seem to have led a busy life both in and outside hospital. Am I right, Julia?'

She nodded. 'I suppose so—at least, that's what people have told me concerning my professional life. I've been focussed on my medical career throughout my adult life.'

'Did that give you enough time for your private life?'

'My private life? Well…'

She broke off. She wasn't going to notify her teacher that she'd come to the conclusion she had a serious flaw in her personality—her inability to handle her time outside the pursuit of her career. Especially in her inability to recognise a complete and utter swine when she thought she'd picked the man of her dreams. She turned her head away from him so that he wouldn't notice the misty, damp expression in her eyes that would give him an inkling of her intense vulnerability since the suffering Tony had inflicted on her.

Looking round the almost deserted cafeteria, she noticed that the majority of her fellow doctors were drifting out through the door, having been told that the rest of the day was theirs to orientate themselves around the hospital or do whatever they wanted.

She had been planning to escape back to the small study-bedroom she'd been assigned in the medical quarters and sort out her luggage. She felt that would be the safest option open to her now, instead of having a discussion about her least favourite subject.

She stood up. 'If you'll excuse me, Bernard, I'm going to make use of this free time to get my room sorted out.'

It sounded trite to her own ears but the last thing she wanted so early in the course was to be interrogated by her boss on the delicate subject of her private life.

As he rose to his full height there was an enigmatic expression on his face. 'Of course, Julia.'

He escorted her to the door. She turned left towards the medical residents' quarters. He turned right towards the theatre block.

She walked swiftly down the corridor. At the entrance to the door to the residents' quarters she found one of her colleagues waiting for her. She recognised him as the one who'd had most to say for himself. Tall, dark and good looking in a rugged sort of way, very self-assured.

He smiled, displaying strong white teeth as he stretched out a hand towards her.

'Dominic,' he said, as he shook her hand in a firm grip.

She reclaimed her hand. 'Julia.'

'I know. Some of us are having an impromptu meeting at the bar round the corner and we'd like you to join us if you could spare the time.'

'Well, my room needs sorting and—'

'Julia, we've all got things to do but…' He broke off and began speaking in English. 'All work and no play isn't good for you.'

She smiled at him. She needed to stop taking herself so seriously and it would be good to get to know her colleagues.

'OK. I'll come but I mustn't stay too long.'

'Don't worry. We're all in the same boat.'

'Ah, it's good to be outside in the fresh air.' Julia revelled in the warm early evening sunshine as they walked out through the hospital gates.

Across the road there were still families on the beach, children running into the sea, which she knew would still be a little chilly in the spring.

'Café Maurice Chevalier,' she read from the sign outside the café restaurant Dominic took her to.

She could see some of her fellow students grouped around a large table outside. Two of them were already pulling up another small table and a couple of chairs. There was a bottle of wine on the table. Someone poured her a glass. Dominic went inside to the bar, returning with another bottle and some more glasses.

Dominic went round the table, topping up wine glasses. They all raised their glasses to cries of '*Santé!*'

'Cheers!' said Dominic, proud of his English.

'Cheers!' everybody repeated, laughing loudly.

Names were bandied about and she managed to put names to faces. Pierre, Christophe, Daniel, Jacques, Gerard and Paul were the most vociferous. Dominic seemed to have been elected leader of the group. Julia was secretly glad she'd got brothers who'd shown her how to join in when she found herself in all-male company.

'This place was here when I was a child,' she said,

during an unusually quiet moment. 'I used to sit outside and watch the sun going down with my parents and my brothers. It's good to be back here.'

'I should think it's good to escape from the attentions of our grumpy old tutor,' Dominic said. 'I saw him deep in conversation with you. How did he come across on a one-to-one basis?'

'To be honest, I don't know what to make of him. All I hope is that he's a good teacher.'

'Oh, he's a good teacher,' Dominic said vehemently. 'But he's a hard taskmaster. Apparently, he went through a difficult divorce and he's sorting out custody of his six-year-old son at the moment.'

'How do you know?' Pierre asked, screwing up his eyes against the glare of the setting sun.

Dominic grinned. 'I came here a week early to get the feel of the place. Unlike Julia, I've never been to this part of France before. I was born in Marseilles. I chatted up one of the nurses—'

Loud guffaws around the table greeted this.

'And found out a lot about Professor Grumpy. There's a rumour that he's going through a bad time at the moment, touchy about his divorce and tends to take it out on his students if they don't come up to scratch. But he's a brilliant surgeon and teacher, much admired by his colleagues.'

'Well, that's all I need to know,' Julia said, putting her hand over her glass as Christophe came round with another bottle.

'Ah, don't be too complacent,' Dominic told her. 'It's also rumoured that he doesn't think women make good surgeons.'

All eyes were on her now. She found herself filled with dread. Not only was she desperate to make a good impression on her new teacher but she was battling with an insane attraction towards him. Could it be true he didn't like women surgeons? So why had she been the only woman chosen for his exclusive course?

She looked out over the beach to the sand dunes at the corner of the bay, breathing slowly until the feeling of dread disappeared. She would cope. She would have to. She turned her head to look up at the magnificent hill behind them. She didn't want negative thoughts to spoil the beautiful sunset that was casting a glow over the hills, just as she remembered from her childhood.

She glanced round the table. 'My tutor in England told me I'm a good surgeon,' she said quietly. 'It's what I want to do with my life. And I'm not going to let a grumpy tutor spoil my career plans.'

A cheer went round the table. She felt she'd been accepted, just as her brothers' friends accepted her.

She stood up, smiling at her colleagues who had now become her friends. 'I've really enjoyed myself but I must go.'

'I'll come with you, escort you back.'

'No, you stay and have another drink, Dominic. It's not far.'

He pulled a wry face, but let her go off by herself.

She walked quickly, pausing as she went round the corner to look up at the sun dipping behind the hills. It had almost disappeared but a pink and mauve colour was diffusing over the skyline. She remembered how she'd once thought it was a miracle that the sun could disappear behind the hills and reappear from the depths of the sea in the morning. Her father had explained about the earth being round and so on but she'd still thought it was a miracle. Still did!

She turned her head and looked out at the darkening sea. There were fireflies dancing on the black waves, illuminating the scene. It was truly romantic, though not if you were all alone surrounded by strolling couples and families taking their children home to bed. She reminded herself that this was the life she'd now chosen, to ensure that she pursued her chosen career to the height of her destiny.

A smile flitted across her lips as she told herself to lighten up. It was a bit early to be having grand thoughts about her destiny.

Oh, yes, she was going to enjoy her evening now that she'd calmed her wicked thoughts and got herself back on the journey that she'd set herself. There would be time enough for romance, marriage, babies and everything else she wouldn't allow herself until she'd established her career.

CHAPTER TWO

ALMOST three weeks later Julia was sitting outside Bernard's office, waiting for her turn to have a one-on-one meeting with him about her progress to date. She was studying the printed sheets that Bernard had handed out at the last tutorial. It was difficult to believe that the first month of their course was almost over. The days had flown by during which they'd all been bombarded with work assignments, essays to write on the theories behind various orthopaedic operations and actual operations to observe in Theatre.

Whilst in Theatre they had to make copious notes, all of which needed to be written up in their own time. The notes then had to be transformed into a coherent observation of the operation, including their own comments and criticisms. These were emailed to Bernard as soon as possible. In no time at all they received an assessment of their work with much criticism from him. She knew she wasn't alone in being the recipient of his scathing comments.

They'd also undertaken sessions in the *Urgences* department, the French equivalent of Accident and Emergency, where they had to do minor operations and treatments on emergency cases, observed and assessed by the director of *Urgences*, Michel Devine. He in turn reported back to the twitchy Bernard.

When Dominic had told everybody that Bernard was reputed to be a hard taskmaster, he had been spot on! She'd been so naive three weeks ago. She hadn't believed she would have to work under such pressure.

Just at that moment Dominic arrived in the corridor and plonked himself down beside her.

'What time's your endurance test?'

She frowned at him. 'Shh. He'll hear you.'

'Don't care if he does. I feel like walking out. It's time he cut us some slack. We're all qualified and experienced doctors, for heaven's sake. Who does he think he is, treating us like—?'

The door opened. 'Good morning, Julia. Dominic,' their taskmaster said, glancing severely at Dominic.

Julia followed Bernard inside and sat down on the upright chair in front of the desk. She wasn't afraid of him, she told herself as he went round to the other side and glanced at the screen of his computer. She reckoned all the information on her was there. Everything she'd ever done since aspiring to take on this arduous course.

He looked across the desk at her and at last there was eye contact with him. She couldn't help the frisson of excitement that ran through her as she looked directly into those dark hazel eyes. Why was she being so perverse in finding herself attracted to this man who'd made the past three weeks such an endurance test for her?

'How are you finding the course, Julia?'

No smile, just that piercing stare that was causing

shivers to run down her spine. Shivers she couldn't possibly analyse.

She took a deep breath. 'It's relentlessly tiring…but exceptionally interesting and frustrating at the same time.'

He frowned. 'In what way is it frustrating?'

'Well, you haven't yet let me loose in Theatre so I can do some actual surgery. I'm getting withdrawal symptoms from all this theorising.'

Was that a brief twitching of the lips or the beginnings of a contemptuous smile on his face? Whatever it was, it died immediately as he looked intensely displeased with her.

'Julia, you will appreciate that I have to make absolutely sure that if I let one of my students 'loose in Theatre', as you put it, that the patient will be in capable hands.'

'Yes, of course, I do appreciate that, but I've had a great deal of experience in Theatre and—'

'So I'm told,' he interrupted dryly. 'Your tutor in London, Don Grainger, gave you an extremely glowing reference, outlining some of the orthopaedic operations you have performed.'

She brightened up at this piece of news. What a treasure Don Grainger had been during her medical-school days and after graduation.

'So,' Bernard continued in the same dour tone, 'during this illustrious career you're pursuing, how much experience have you had of hip replacements?'

Oh, joy! At last she was definitely on home ground! She began to elaborate at length on the hip replacements she'd undertaken, at first assisting before moving on to operating under supervision.

He interrupted to ask questions as she enthused about how she loved to remove the static, painful joint and re-place it with a prosthesis. His questions concerned the types of prostheses she'd used, which she preferred and if she enjoyed following up the after-care of her patients.

'But of course I enjoy seeing my patients after I've spent so much time with them in Theatre. Seeing the patient before and after surgery, making sure they're getting the best possible after-care, is all part of the buzz a surgeon gets.'

'Buzz? What do you mean by this?'

In her enthusiasm for the subject she'd gone into English. Embarrassed at getting so carried away, she began to speak French again to dispel the wrinkles of concern that had appeared on his brow. 'It's the won-derful excitement of taking away pain and suffering and restoring a new, more active lifestyle to a patient. Not exactly what I meant but something like that.'

They were both silent for a few moments. The clock on the wall ticked away the seconds, reminding Bernard he had another student to see. He wished he didn't find this one so fascinating. Was it her enthusiasm for the subject or was it something he shouldn't even be think-ing about every time he met up with her? She was his student, a career woman, and he was a family man. Never the twain should meet!

He put on his stern tutor expression as he stood up to indicate the interview was over.

'Send Dominic in, please.'

She turned and walked to the door, anxious to escape from the inquisition and the conflict of emotions she was experiencing.

'How was it?' Dominic asked as she came out.

She shrugged her shoulders. 'I've no idea how it went,' she whispered. 'Good luck!'

The next day she was still none the wiser. If anything, she was now feeling even more frustrated. She really was getting withdrawal symptoms from being just a cog in the machinery of this difficult course. She needed to actually make a major contribution to an interesting operation in Theatre, feel the buzz of satisfaction she was used to getting when an operation was a success and the patient's state of health vastly improved.

She looked up from the notes she'd been studying as Bernard walked in and took his place at the front of the tutorial room. The chattering between the students died down as ten pairs of eyes focussed on their professor. She thought he looked slightly worried this morning as he glanced around the room.

'Good morning.' A slight nod of the head in her direction as he acknowledged her, seated, as she had been so far this course, in the front row.

Bernard's serious expression didn't change as he began to explain what would happen that morning. They had admitted a patient three days before who had been on the waiting list for a hip replacement. Apparently, the lady in question was from a medical background herself. She had elected to have her operation under general anaesthetic and in the interests of furthering the education of the budding surgeons in Bernard's group she had agreed that her operation should be used for teaching purposes.

'Surgery begins at eleven this morning.' He seemed to be directing his statement right at her.

Why was he still looking at her? She tried to shrink down in her seat. He raised his eyes again to address the now apprehensive students.

'I shall be performing the operation with the help of a qualified and experienced junior surgeon and one of my students.'

He was looking at her again. She swallowed hard.

'I have deliberately given you no warning of this because there will be times in your future careers when you will be called upon to operate at short notice and I wanted to see how you handle the added adrenalin that sometimes causes panic amongst the less suitable candidates.'

He smiled. Thank goodness! It was as if the sun had come out. She shifted awkwardly in her seat, sensing that he was about to make an important announcement.

'The reason I sent out a questionnaire before you arrived here, asking about previous experience of hip replacement surgery, was to ascertain who might be a likely candidate for the first operation of the course. Several of you indicated varying degrees of competence. I consider that some of you would be perfectly capable of being my second assistant this morning.'

He read from a list, Julia holding her breath apprehensively after she heard her name read out.

'There's no need to be worried. We are a teaching hospital with excellent insurance.' His smile broadened. 'There is a stipulation that patients must be chosen with care and must agree to everything that might happen during their surgery. The patient we will operate on this morning is a retired surgeon herself and fully co-operative. Now...'

He paused and looked around the class. 'Who would like the opportunity to work with me this morning?'

Talk about adrenalin pumping! Her heart was pounding so quickly she felt everyone in the room would hear it. This was the opportunity she should seize on. The opportunity she'd asked Bernard for. The old Julia would have been leaping to her feet, desperate for the experience. These days she could feel real fear whenever opportunity knocked.

Seconds dragged by. Nobody had moved. Several throats had been cleared, including Bernard's. She could feel his eyes boring into her. What had her father always told her? Feel the fear and do it anyway.

Her hand shot up, seemingly having a life of its own. Every fibre of her body was warning her to hold off, not to stick her neck out, but this was why she'd come here. To challenge herself and banish her insecurities. She could do this! Raising her eyes tentatively towards the rostrum, she was rewarded by a look of intense pride.

Bernard knew he'd goaded her on that morning. He'd deliberately put her to the test and she hadn't failed him. He'd already seen for himself how knowledge-able she was about her passion but, from what he'd learned during their brief time since she arrived, she was a student who needed her confidence boosted. And this could only be done by subjecting her to difficult and demanding situations that required top-class skills, diligent training, impeccable qualifications and endless energy. The ability to carry on long after your whole body was experiencing real physical weariness, if required.

Though he didn't doubt that intellectually she was probably streets ahead of her louder colleagues he worried that she might not be physically strong enough at times. He would have the same concerns with any female student. A fact that had made him consider hard about offering her a place on this course. If he was honest with himself, he'd only admitted her to the course as a favour to his old friend Don Grainger. Don was no fool. He wouldn't have put her forward to take the course if he didn't think she was a natural surgeon.

But Julia still had to prove herself to him. Although he trusted his old friend, he needed to be in Theatre with her himself to actually make a sound judgement.

He composed his features back to the completely objective, professional tutor he was supposed to be. But it was difficult to hold back the elation he felt now that his plan had worked. The teacher in him wanted to build up her confidence, which he surmised had for some reason taken a knock somewhere along the way. The fact that he found her impossibly attractive must be dealt with as a separate issue, which couldn't in any way colour his professional judgement of her.

'Thank you, Julia. Would you meet me in the ante-theatre at ten-thirty, please? We shall be using the teaching theatre where those of you not required on the lower surgery area will sit on the raised seats behind the transparent screens. You will be able to hear everything, take notes and ask questions at the end of the operation.'

Julia dealt with the moment of panic that suddenly

came over her. She needed to escape and scan her notes. She mustn't leave anything to chance during her debut in Theatre. And she wanted time to check out the patient. That was always important. She wasn't dealing with an abstract. This was a human being who deserved respect so perhaps it would be possible to...

Thoughts tumbled through her mind as she hurried to the door, only to find that Bernard was waiting there for her.

'Would you like to meet the patient?'

She gave a sigh of relief. 'That's definitely on my check list...along with everything else I need to do.'

'Don't worry. There's plenty of time.'

She revelled in his smooth, soothing voice and remembered that he must have had to go through difficult situations to reach the heights of his profession. She had a lot to prove to him so she felt intensely nervous because he still hadn't thawed out with her. Could she work alongside him without making a fool of herself?

She squared her shoulders. She would do the best for the patient, as she had always done, and Bernard's opinion of her didn't matter. Oh, but his opinion of you does matter, said a small, nagging voice in her head.

'You look nervous, Julia,' he said, as if reading her thoughts. 'Take a deep breath. Now let it out. That's better. I wouldn't let you operate on my patient if I didn't think you were capable, extremely capable according to your previous tutor.'

She felt as if she'd grown taller already and much stronger. Her thoughts were clearing and she could feel a list of priorities forming in her head.

He led her along the corridor, speaking now in a gentler tone than he usually used. She felt comforted, supported both physically and mentally. His arm brushed hers as they walked together and she was surprised by the sparks of attraction his close proximity aroused. Not an easy situation to be in. Nervous of Bernard because he would be judging her performance in Theatre, concerned about their patient and surprised at the frequent frissons of attraction towards her boss. This was going to be an intensely difficult situation.

He had a difficult job as tutor to ten students who had begun to regard him as the enemy. But she was beginning to view Bernard differently. Again she felt a tingling down her spine and knew she mustn't give in to this strange insane feeling that was forcing itself upon her.

'You see, Julia, in most hospital situations the surgical team meet the patient before they operate, don't they? So I do like my students to be involved in the pre-operative and post-operative care of their patients, working alongside the full-time hospital staff.'

She felt her clinical interest rising along with the added interest engendered by simply being alongside this charismatic man. On this, her surgical debut day, when she wanted to use her skills and knowledge as best she could, she was also trying so hard not to let her personal interest in him get in the way.

'Yes, as I told you, I would very much like to meet our patient. You said she was a surgeon?'

'An extremely eminent surgeon here in France. As a student I was very much in awe of her.'

'So you've known her a long time?'

He smiled as he looked sideways at his demure companion, looking so fresh, so young, so infinitely...he checked his thoughts...capable. Yes, she was capable. That was all that mattered.

He composed his thoughts again. 'I feel we shall experience full co-operation from our learned colleague. She was a great help when I was a young student in Paris.'

They walked together along the corridor, he adapting his stride to her slower pace. In the orthopaedic ward Bernard led her into one of the single rooms.

'Hello, Brigitte. How are you this morning?'

The patient, who was seated in a comfortable armchair by the window, smiled and put down her newspaper.

'Bernard! I'm very well, thank you, and so relieved that I'm going to have my operation today.'

He introduced Julia as a well-qualified doctor from England who was working towards a career in orthopaedic surgery.

'Julia has had a great deal of surgical experience. She has been mentored by our esteemed colleague Don Grainger and comes to us with his own high recommendations.'

The patient smiled. 'High praise indeed from Don.'

'Well, he's been Julia's tutor since medical school and he wrote in glowing terms about her capabilities. So much so that I've decided to tell my designated assistant to remain on standby in the theatre. I may or may not need him. How would you both feel about that?'

Brigitte leaned forward towards Julia. 'I would be delighted to help you up the career ladder in any way I can, Julia. After the operation—at which, of course, you must assist—we must have a long chat. I truly miss my days in surgery but my arthritis cut my career short. I like to keep up with the latest developments, though.'

Bernard was waiting for Julia's answer. 'And how do you feel about assisting with the surgery, Julia?'

'Very honoured.' She felt confident. Why shouldn't she be, with such generous support from the patient and professor?

'Excellent!' Bernard smiled.

Jeanine, the orthopaedic sister, came in to explain that they were about to prepare their patient for surgery. Did Bernard wish to do a further examination? He said he would like a few minutes to show his assistant the extent of the arthritic damage to the hip. Brigitte, walking with a stick, made her way back to her bed and lay down with a thankful sigh of relief.

She pointed out the most painful areas of her leg, which were around the the head of the right femur. Bernard held up the X-rays so that Julia could see the extent of the arthritic erosion and they discussed the method they were going to use to remove the damaged bone and replace it with a prosthesis.

Leaving the patient to be prepared for Theatre by the nursing staff, Julia still felt slightly apprehensive but at the same time she realised how lucky she was to be given an ideal situation like this in which to move forward, gathering confidence along the way. At the same time she would not only be furthering her career, she would be easing the pain and improving the health of a patient, which was why she and all the members of her family had joined the medical profession.

She walked towards the medical quarters. She needed

a few minutes of peace and quiet to gather her thoughts and focus on the operation in front of her. She no longer felt the need to check her notes. Every bit of knowledge she needed was stored in her brain. She'd assisted at a hip replacement before on several occasions, actually performing part of the surgery with an experienced surgeon hovering nearby, watching her every move, ready to stop or correct anything he didn't approve of.

It wouldn't be any different this time, except that it would be Bernard who would be doing the hovering. And this affinity she felt with him, this desperation to please him was something that unnerved her. It wasn't just that he was her chief in this situation. It was something more than that. Something definitely emotional. An emotional connection. And she was trying to avoid emotion.

Where relationships were concerned she didn't trust herself, judging by her track record. At least she should leave all emotion outside the door of the theatre and concentrate all her training and expertise on doing the best for her patient.

Bernard was waiting for her when she nervously pushed open the swing doors of the ante-theatre. He gave her a smile of encouragement.

'OK?'

She smiled back with a confidence she didn't feel— yet! It would come back to her as soon as she started working. Concentrate on the patient, she told herself. Don't think about yourself. Remember the last time you assisted at a hip replacement. The outcome was excellent. The patient survived to live a useful life—and so did you!

She scrubbed up. A nurse helped her into her sterile gown.

'We're ready to begin, Bernard,' the anaesthetist said over the intercom.

They were ready. Julia was aware of the bright lights as she followed Bernard into the theatre. Indistinguishable faces appeared as blurs through the transparent screen. She made her way towards the motionless figure on the theatre table aware, not for the first time, that going into Theatre felt very much like going on stage.

She was so involved during the operation that she had no time to worry about herself. Her concentration was taken up completely by the task in hand. She found herself working harmoniously with Bernard. Sometimes he would nod to her across the shrouded figure on the table, indicating that she should perform the next stage while he supervised. All the procedures came back to her immediately as her fingers deftly performed what was required.

Time flew by and it seemed only minutes before she was finishing the final sutures. At that point she suddenly became aware of Bernard's eyes on her as they had been during the entire operation. She placed her final used instrument on the unsterile tray, which a theatre nurse was preparing to remove. As she did so she glanced up at Bernard's eagle eyes above his mask. She thought he was smiling but she couldn't be sure as he turned to speak to the theatre sister and began giving her instructions on the immediate after-care of their patient.

There was nothing more for her to do in Theatre. It was all over and she'd survived, and more importantly so had Brigitte. The patient was now being wheeled into the recovery room. As she made her way out through the swing doors, Bernard came up to speak to her.

'I think a debriefing session would be a good idea this evening, Julia.'

As he held open the swing door and followed her out, she allowed herself to admit that the sparks of attraction she'd felt as his gloved hand had brushed hers during the operation had been difficult to ignore. And when she'd looked up once to the eyes above the mask she'd had to take a deep breath to remain focussed and professional.

She looked up at him as they walked together along the corridor. 'Yes, that would be very helpful.'

'Come along to my office about six.'

He was pushing open the door of his office as he spoke as if anxious to be alone again. The door closed behind him and he walked across to his chair. He had to admit to himself that Julia really was a natural. Everything that Don had said about her was true. What Don had failed to mention about his prize student was how attractive she was.

What was it about Julia that made him feel so physically moved when they were together? Even in Theatre, the place where usually he was at his most professional, he'd felt sparks of attraction. That time when he'd passed her an instrument and their gloved hands had briefly touched... He shouldn't be thinking like this!

He had a difficult ex-wife to deal with, a wonderful six-year-old son who should be his priority. He shouldn't even be allowing these insane thoughts to enter his mind. He leaned back in his chair and took a deep breath. That made it worse because he was sure he could still smell that subtle perfume that lingered around her.

Was he going mad? He switched on his computer and forced himself to begin writing up his notes on the operation.

Walking down the corridor, Julia had no idea what impression she'd given Bernard during the operation. He'd given her no indication of his assessment of her performance as he'd closed the door, seemingly anxious to get away from her.

Her confidence, which had been high in Theatre, was now wavering but she reminded herself of the way he'd reassured her all the way through the operation. Now that she had time to reflect, she thought he'd even smiled into his mask on occasion and nodded approval as she'd used her initiative. And she was almost sure she'd heard him whisper, 'Well done!' as she'd finished the final suture—or had she imagined that?

But did it matter what Bernard thought of her performance? If she was satisfied that she'd given it one hundred per cent and made life easier for her patient then that was what really mattered, wasn't it? Seeking approbation from Bernard was not why she'd come here.

She walked away purposefully. She would make notes, be ready to ask questions and take the criticisms that would help make her a better surgeon in the future.

At six o'clock she was standing outside Bernard's office, waiting for the second hand to reach the top of her watch.

'Come in!'

He was sitting at his desk. He stood up and came towards her as she closed the door, motioning her to sit in one of the armchairs placed near the window. He took the other one and opened a file of notes. She put her briefcase on the floor at the side of her chair after taking out her own small laptop.

'So how do you think the operation went, Julia?'

She cleared her throat and launched into the questions she'd prepared, going through all the steps of the operation from the first incision to the final suture.

He answered all her questions carefully and lucidly while she made notes on her laptop.

She leaned back against the back of the armchair as he answered her final question, and looked across at him. The expression on his face gave nothing away for a few seconds until he relaxed and gave her a studied smile.

'Excellent! I like a student who has everything under control both during and after the operation. I've no doubt you'll make a first-class surgeon.'

She breathed a sigh of relief. She'd sensed his approval but until that moment she couldn't be sure she hadn't been imagining it.

She smiled back. 'Thank you, Bernard. So, do you have any questions for me?'

'Just one.' He hesitated. He really shouldn't say what was uppermost in his mind. But he planned to be very careful if he felt himself giving in to the wrong emotions.

'It's been a long and intense day. Your trip shouldn't all be about work, however. You are a visitor to France after all, so may I buy you a drink at the Maurice Chevalier?'

She hesitated for a couple of seconds. She doubted very much that Bernard had extended this invitation to any of her fellow students, but his offer had been very formal. She would be foolish to try and read too much into it. Finally she smiled and nodded her agreement.

As she closed her laptop and put it back in its case she was aware of the now familiar tingling feeling running down her spine. Apprehension?

Yes, but it was something more than that, she admitted as she felt the light touch of Bernard's arm as he ushered her out through the door.

CHAPTER THREE

THE Maurice Chevalier was deserted when they first arrived. Julia breathed a sigh of relief. The last thing she wanted was to seen by her fellow students socialising with their tyrannical boss. She had mixed feelings about her motivation in accepting his offer to buy her a drink. Yes, he was thawing out towards her. But would her colleagues think this was favouritism? And should she be alone with him in a social situation given the insane feelings she'd been experiencing?

Very soon a trickle of sunset worshippers gradually filled up most of the tables overlooking the sea. She folded her white cashmere sweater on her lap as she sat down and breathed in the scent of the sea and this unspoiled stretch of the coast that she loved so much.

It was turning a bit chilly now that the sun had disappeared behind a cloud so she would soon have an excuse to wear the new sweater that she'd fallen in love with when she'd been doing some last-minute panic buying in London . She didn't usually spend so much on clothes but she'd salved her conscience by convincing herself that anything that would boost her depleted confidence was a definite asset.

'What would you like to drink, Julia?'

'I'll have a Kir please, Bernard.'

He nodded before going inside to the bar, returning shortly with her crème de cassis and white wine aperitif and a pastis with ice and water for himself.

She smiled as he placed the drinks on the table. 'Thank you. I used to come here as a child with my parents and brothers when we were on holiday. My mother used to drink Kir. I knew it was a very grown-up drink but she allowed me a small sip. I loved the taste of the blackcurrant juice mixed in with white wine. As soon as I was old enough I tried one for myself and that became my favourite aperitif in the evenings.'

'To your grown-up Kir, Julia.' Bernard smiled as he raised his glass to her. He thought she looked so lovely now with the sun low in the sky on her face. What an enigma she was! To think that she had performed so self-assuredly in Theatre today and yet here she was reminiscing so naively about her childhood.

She smiled back as she took her first sip. 'Mmm! So reviving after a long day in hospital!'

'You deserve it after your performance this morning. I was proud of you—I mean, you're one of the students I selected from a large number of applicants who wanted a place on the course so it's good to know you didn't let me down.'

He hastily drank from his glass of pastis with ice, adding some water so that he wouldn't become too exuberant. He didn't want Julia to misinterpret his remarks. She might think he…well, he fancied her in some way. Perish the thought, he lied to himself, knowing full well that she was a most attractive woman and he'd better be careful or he might go overboard in his admiration.

But putting that aside, he told himself sharply, trying to leave his admiration out of the equation, whenever he discovered a talented student he found it very satisfying, euphoric almost! But he'd better hold back with the praise so that Julia would work hard throughout the course and not let him down. And he must also be aware that his delight in her achievements had to remain totally without emotional attachment.

Nevertheless, it was certainly true that he found himself drawn towards her in a way that a professor shouldn't think of his student. They were both adults, yes, but he mustn't let this attraction he felt affect his professional judgement of her during the months of hard work ahead.

He looked across the table. 'So tell me, Julia, what made you apply for this course?'

She hesitated before answering. 'Well...er...having survived a disastrous marriage that had been a total mistake, I felt it was time to make a fresh start and get on with my career. My family background also contributed to my decision. Mum and Dad, who'd planned to be surgeons when they were in medical school, had then taken a more practical route to become general practitioners because they fell in love, married when my eldest brother was on the way and...'

She broke off and took a deep breath. 'Sorry, Bernard, you don't need to know all this.'

'Oh, but I do. It's fascinating! Your story is similar to mine, in fact. I too come from a medical background where my parents gave up their ambitions in favour of family life. Please go on.'

She felt relieved she wasn't boring him. 'Well, as I

told you before, GP parents and three brothers, now surgeons, meant I had to be a high achiever to get myself heard in the family. Fortunately I enjoyed studying my favourite subjects. Only when I hastily married Tony after a whirlwind courtship and found it so difficult to find the time for study did I question the sanity of becoming a surgeon.'

She leaned back against her chair, her eyes temporarily blinded by the sun low in the sky, setting behind the hillside that swooped down into the sea. She delved into her bag for her sunglasses.

'That's better.'

She paused to gather her thoughts. How much should she tell him? He was a good listener, seemed interested, but was he simply being polite?

'At times I despaired of my exhausting role of wife, stepmother, medical student...'

'So you hadn't qualified when you married. Why didn't you wait until...?'

'I thought I was madly in love! I'd never been in love before and the wonderful euphoric sensations I experienced when I first met Tony swept me along. For the first time in my life I entered a world that was quite different from my own.'

Bernard looked puzzled as he watched the vibrant expressions on her face. 'In what way was it different?'

'Tony was a very successful man, having made enormous profits in the building and property business, proud of the fact that he'd come from a deprived background and made something of himself. Money meant everything to him. He lived and breathed doing deals, buying expensive clothes for himself, for the children and for me. He told me he'd outgrown his first wife, she was lazy, an ex-model who'd let herself go and wouldn't keep up with his aspirations so he'd set her up in an expensive house where she could bring up their two children. He'd bought a luxurious flat in London where he could continue his wheeling and dealing.

'I found out later that his wife had divorced him because of his womanising, realising that she was happier without him. She'd been hoping for a huge divorce settlement but she was still waiting. Of course, I didn't know any of this when I first saw him at the opera.'

'The opera?'

She smiled. 'Oh, it was a business deal he was doing with a client and he clinched it by taking this man and his wife to a performance of *La Bohème*. Anyway, I'd gone along with a group of fellow medical students and we were queuing at the bar in the interval, trying to get a drink.

'Tony was in front of me and put on the charm when he gathered that we were all medical students. He insisted on buying everybody a drink before whisking me off to his table and introducing me to his business friends as a young doctor. With the benefit of hindsight I know I shouldn't have allowed myself to be swept away by an unknown man who liked to flash his cash but I was still young, impressionable, and having had a cloistered childhood this whirlwind from another exciting world seemed the epitome of sophistication.'

'But what about your own friends? Didn't they think…?'

'Oh, they were happy to accept the free drinks but they thought I'd gone mad…which actually I had, for the first time in my life! I'd always been so careful to toe the line and do everything my mother and father told me…especially my mother. She'd insisted I mustn't marry until I was well established in my career. She used to constantly tell me about how she'd sacrificed her ambitions and forced herself to be content with life as a country GP, married to a GP, struggling with a huge workload whilst bringing up a family.'

She looked across the table at Bernard, who was hanging on her every word. She took a deep breath as she remembered her totally out-of-character stupidity in those early days of her relationship with the charismatic but totally unreliable Tony.

'You see, I was totally blown away by Tony's charismatic aura. I'd never seen anyone like him before except on TV or in a film. Looking back and remembering, I can't believe how gullible I was in those days. I feel as if I'm remembering something that happened to someone else, a little sister if I'd had one, someone with no experience of real life—which, in a way, was exactly how I was. I couldn't take my eyes off this tall, handsome character in the well-cut, expensive suit who seemed to demand attention from everybody who was listening to his deep, sexy voice.'

She paused as the weird memories from her past came back to her.

She took a deep breath as she watched Bernard's reaction. Yes, he was a good listener and definitely seemed to want her to continue.

'Tony was proud of the fact that he was a self-made man who'd come from a poor background. At the time I just couldn't help admiring him and then the admiration blossomed into something more dangerous and I fell for him, hook, line and sinker, whilst enjoying the fact that he seemed attracted to me.'

'So he was impressed by the fact that you were a medical student?'

'Oh, he thought I was a good catch. He told me during our disastrous marriage that he'd thought I must be from a wealthy family because we were all doctors. How wrong he was! Our education was the top priority to my parents and that made a big hole in the family budget.

'What I didn't realise was that his business deals were getting fewer and further between and he needed to find a wealthy wife to help keep him in the lifestyle he'd got used to during his successful years. My parents met him for the first time at our registry office wedding. My mother could hardly disguise her dislike of him and she made no secret of the fact that I'd let her down badly. That hurt...that really hurt.'

Her voice faltered as she remembered the angst she'd suffered, knowing full well that it was all her fault, knowing she'd hurt her mother who'd given up so much to raise her family. She shifted in her seat, pulling the sweater around her shoulders as she glanced away from Bernard towards the beautiful seascape in front of them. Maybe she should stop talking about her past and give him a chance to recover from his busy day.

'Bernard, you're a good listener but I don't want to bore you.'

'Please continue! I'm fascinated. I can see where you're coming from now. I do like to take an interest in the background of my students. As you say in England, it helps if I know what makes them tick, isn't it, Julia?'

'Yes, you got that exactly right, Bernard. You're finding out what makes me tick.'

He leaned across the table. 'I can tell you already, having known you only a couple of days. You're aiming for the top and it isn't easy, believe me. You'll reach the next peak and what will you find? Another peak to climb!'

He broke off. 'Please do go on. So you married this man from a different world? Were you happy at first?'

'Well, for the first few weeks of our marriage Tony boasted to all his associates—I won't call them friends because they were mostly hangers-on intent on helping themselves to his dwindling cash—about his clever young wife who was going to be a doctor. But the problem was that he thought I could pass my exams without spending time studying, be the perfect stepmother to his children when they came to stay at weekends, be a good hostess to his clients—and I quickly realised it wasn't possible. That's when it all turned nasty. His attitude completely changed. He seemed to think that by shouting at me he could turn me into superwoman, perfect in everything he wanted me to do for him.'

'You have another saying in England—marry in haste, repent at leisure. Isn't that right?' Bernard was watching her reaction. 'Was that what happened?'

'Exactly! He changed completely once the ring was on my finger and he realised my family hadn't endowed me with money. One of the things he told me before we married was that having fathered twins who were then five, a boy and a girl, he didn't want any more children.

It was a struggle to come to terms with that because I'd always hoped I would have children of my own when I'd established my career.

'I subjugated my own desires for parenthood by immersing myself in taking care of my stepchildren. I loved those two as if they were my own and it was a terrible wrench when we split up and I lost all contact with them.'

Bernard noticed the emotional waver in her voice as she said this. Yes, he could see she would adore starting a family. Warning bells were ringing in his head. He mustn't get too familiar with her.

'So what caused you to split up?'

'It was pressures of my work and trying to take care of my stepchildren. Tony, not being from a medical background, just didn't understand. I adored the children, bonded with them and began to put them before my medical studies, but Tony was still dissatisfied with the amount of time I could spare him. He began to look elsewhere.

'Everything came to a head one fateful weekend just six months after we were married. I was trying to get to grips with some revision in the study and was working on my computer when he flung open the door and told me to leave all that medical stuff and get into some expensive clothes. It was important that I should get out of my scruffy tracksuit and tart myself up so that I looked drop-dead gorgeous. He'd been speaking to a prospective client and he was taking him and his wife out for lunch. The wife, apparently, was a real doll and knew how to dress so I'd better make the effort.'

She took another deep breath as the awful memories of that occasion came flooding back.

'I pointed out that I had an exam on the Monday and I needed to study...'

She broke off as she remembered how miserable she'd felt. Bernard put his hand across the table and laid it over her slender fingers. 'Julia, you don't have to tell me if it's too awful to remember.'

She swallowed hard. The touch of his fingers and his obvious concern for her unnerved her. Careful! Be very careful. Don't mistake sympathy with emotional involvement.

'Tony told me he was fed up with seeing me studying. I was no fun any more. And then he blurted out that he'd met somebody else. He wanted a divorce.'

'So...what did you do?'

'To be honest, I'd had enough and it was a blessed relief to think that I could walk away from the hell that my life had become. I asked him to have my things sent to the medical school. He said he would make all the necessary arrangements for my stuff to be sent wherever I wanted. I took my laptop and a few books, went back to the medical school and tried to concentrate on the exams looming after that disastrous weekend.'

'You must have felt...'

'I felt relieved to escape from Tony.' She shivered at the bad memories that still haunted her, often preventing her from sleeping in the night. 'But terribly sad to lose contact with the children.'

They sat for a few moments in silence. Bernard had been deeply moved by the story of her marriage. He could see how she would need her confidence to be boosted at every possible moment. But he mustn't go overboard. Mustn't allow emotion to take over. Yet he didn't want to cut short the evening and they both needed a meal after their long day.

'Let's go inside and have something to eat. That's if you'd like to,' he added. 'Maybe you've got other plans tonight, meeting up with friends from the group or...'

'No plans tonight except to relax.' She smiled up at him. He was already standing, looking down at her.

He led the way. Inside, the warmth of the sun had made the place feel cosy and inviting. He held out her chair for her. The waiter came along and Bernard asked what the *plat du jour* was.

'Always best to get the main dish that's been cooked that day in these small places, don't you think?'

She felt very comfortable with him as he ordered the coq au vin for them. It came in a large casserole dish. Bernard dug the large serving spoon into the centre and helped her to a generous portion.

'Hey, steady on!' she said, reaching across to touch his wrist. A shiver went down her spine, a quite different shiver to the cold one she'd experienced outside. She felt they must have met somewhere before in a former life. She put both hands back in her lap.

'Did you live near here when you were a child, Bernard?'

He passed her plate across to her. 'I was born just five miles from here, up there in the valley beyond the hills. My grandparents were farmers. The farm is still there, but my father decided he wanted to be a doctor. He went off to medical school in Paris—like I did—and after qualifying he did a course in general practice so that he could come back to our village and fill a very real need. He set up practice in a room at the end of the house and my mother acted as receptionist and nurse besides running the family. She had trained as a nurse in Boulogne but she was born in the village.'

She swallowed a spoonful of the delicious chicken casserole. 'Did you have brothers and sisters?'

He shook his head sadly. 'No, my mother wanted to have more children but it didn't happen. She died of ovarian cancer when I was six.'

'That must have been awful for you and your father. However did you cope?'

'My father employed a lady from the village to help out as nurse, receptionist and housekeeper but it was hard for him to adapt. He also employed her daughter Marianne to help her mother with the housekeeping and look after me. She's still working up there at the farm just as she did when she was sixteen. She took care of me from the time I was six and when she married in her late teens her husband moved in to work on the farm. They became part of the family.'

He hesitated for a moment as if to compose himself. 'I was fifteen when my father died. He'd never been the same since my mother's death. He went through the motions of being a competent doctor but one harsh winter he succumbed to a bout of influenza that turned to pneumonia. I think he simply lost the will to live without my mother.'

They were both silent for a while, engrossed in their own thoughts as the delicious, home-cooked food revived them.

Bernard cleared his throat and put down his spoon.

'I always wanted to marry someone who would be my soul mate as my parents had been together,' he said huskily. 'But it didn't happen. Like you, I was mistaken about the partner I chose—or did she choose me?'

He gave her a whimsical smile. 'If only I could turn the clock back. Apart from the fact that I wouldn't have had my wonderful son, Philippe, if I hadn't met Gabrielle.'

She leaned back in her chair, watching the sad expression that flitted across his face. The young families around them were departing now, mothers ushering their offspring out of the door as fathers paid the bills. It was all so nostalgic. Why couldn't she have replicated something like this? Why couldn't Bernard?

It wasn't just that both of them were career minded, both aiming to climb the peaks to the top of their chosen profession. It was possible to have a career and a family—but not yet! The timing was wrong. She mustn't get ideas about the rapport building up between them. She mustn't fantasise about developing a meaningful relationship with Bernard.

'How often do you see your son?'

'As often as I can escape from my work. I'm going to Paris this weekend to see him. Philippe lives with Gabrielle in her mother's house, which is very convenient. His grandmother dotes on him and has been a tower of strength to all of us when my wife was...well, lacking in maternal instinct and hell bent on—'

He broke off. 'No, you don't want to hear all the sordid details of our less than perfect marriage.'

She wanted to say, Oh yes, I do. She liked to hear about other people making mistakes in their lives. It made her feel in some way that she wasn't the only naive idiot where relationships were concerned. But she remained silent

'I'll get the bill.' He signalled for the waiter. Suddenly he was turning back into the professional as his thoughts turned to the work ahead.

'I've asked Dominic to assist me tomorrow in Theatre. He came to me this afternoon and said he would be happy to assist. It just so happens I've got to do a knee replacement tomorrow morning so I'll be able to put him through his paces. He's had a lot of experience but wasn't brave enough to volunteer for the first operation of the class.' He stood up and moved round to hold the back of her chair. As they walked to the door he said, 'Thank you for setting the ball rolling today, Julia. You'll be a difficult act to follow.'

As they walked back together towards the hospital she was aware of his hand hanging loosely by his side. She so wished he would take hold of hers but she realised he was in professional mode again. Just as well when she'd decided to keep a rein on her own emotions.

'I've got to do some work,' he said briskly, not trusting himself to relax his guard as they stood together outside the main door of the hospital. He did have work to do in his consulting room but he was trying to ignore his real feelings. What he wanted to do was whisk her back to his rooms in the medics' quarters and... No, don't go there, he told himself as he looked down at her beautiful face turned up towards his.

'So have I,' she said quickly, knowing full well that all she wanted to do was have a hot shower and climb into bed. The shower should help to take away the mad emotions running through her mind and her body, but would she be able to sleep?

'Goodnight, Julia. See you tomorrow.'

He bent down and brushed the side of her face with his lips, telling himself they were off duty now and hospital protocol had no place in this private moment. He mustn't give anyone cause to think that he was favouring one of his students because he wasn't. But he couldn't bear to let her go without some brief contact. Anyway, it was normal to exchange kisses on the cheek in France after spending the evening with a pleasant companion.

She walked quickly in the opposite direction from his consulting room, taking the long way round to her study-bedroom in the medics' quarters. She didn't look back.

He watched the slight, slim figure in the beautiful white sweater and figure-hugging black trousers turning the corner at the end of the corridor. He'd better wait a few moments before he made his way to his own study-bedroom, where he planned to sleep that night. He felt too tired to drive out to the farm and he'd had a couple of glasses of wine with the meal. He could go and do some work in his consulting rooms but he didn't think it would be easy to concentrate tonight.

He realised the nurse on Reception was watching him. He hoped he'd given Julia enough time to disappear into her room.

He let the water cascade over him as he soaped himself with shower gel. His mind was buzzing with conflicting ideas. It was going to be so difficult to keep his growing admiration for Julia under control. He had to remain totally professional. But that was easier said than done.

He stepped out of the shower and reached for a towel. He'd hoped the hot water would help to put him in a steadier mood. It had been a long time since he'd felt like this. As he dried himself and threw the towel towards the laundry bin he recognised the symptoms only too well. It wasn't necessary to have medical qualifications to recognise that he was very attracted to Julia. And he wanted to go along with this mad, wonderful feeling. But it could be disastrous!

He climbed between the cool sheets, kicking at the corners where the maid had tucked them in. That was better. One of the perks of being a consultant was that you had daily maid service and a decent-sized room. He thought of the tiny room where Julia would be cloistered and hoped she was comfortable. She would have forgotten all about him and knowing how conscientious she was she would be reading up about knee-replacement operations.

He put his hands behind his head and leaned back against the pillow as he thought about how she had suffered with her marriage. He would have liked to talk about his own marriage with her but had decided against it even though he just knew she would have lent him a sympathetic ear. But he'd never told anyone the full story of what had gone wrong with Gabrielle. He'd been every bit as gullible as Julia! But at least he had his adorable son, Philippe, to dote on—the one good thing to have come from that ill-advised union.

Which reminded him about the latest bombshell his ex-wife had dropped recently. She was planning to get married again. The prospective husband was rich apparently but also considerably older than she was with grown-up children from a previous marriage and he didn't want a young child around the house. So she'd asked him to have Philippe live with him.

Bernard knew he would be absolutely thrilled at having Philippe with him. He'd already planned ahead so that the new arrangement would work. Philippe could stay at the farm during the day with Marianne, go to the local school as he'd done, make friends in the village. He felt the excitement rising at the prospect. But it was tinged with apprehension about how Veronique, Gabrielle's mother, would react.

His ex-wife hadn't yet told her mother of her plans. It would be too cruel to simply take Philippe away. He was like her own son and she'd poured all her considerable maternal love into his upbringing to the age of six. He would have to make sure Veronique came over to see Philippe and that he took his son to Paris as often as he could.

He could feel the doubts creeping in already and knew that if he was really honest with himself the situation was far from solved. Ah, well, he'd have to contend with that problem this weekend when he went to Paris. Meanwhile, he'd better try to get some sleep.

He allowed himself to think about Julia as he closed his eyes, alarmed at the physical reaction surging through his body. If only he'd been able to bring her back here, make love to her and then fall asleep with her in his arms.

He knew that it was going to take an effort on his part but he had to stop thinking like this, definitely try

to see her only in a professional situation. Yes, that was
what he should do. But whether he could keep to this
resolution was a different matter.

CHAPTER FOUR

As Julia showered in the tiny bathroom tucked away in the corner of her study-bedroom her thoughts turned to the day ahead. Hard to believe she'd been here more than a month. The last five weeks had flown by so quickly as she'd tried hard to put all her energy into adapting to her new situation.

She stepped out of the shower and grabbed a large fluffy towel. A whole weekend stretched ahead of her. Two whole days when she was going to try and catch up on her sleep, do some work on the notes she'd taken during Bernard's tutorials and then spend some time outside in the glorious June sunshine.

For the past few weeks she'd spent far too much time indoors, in Theatre and in the wards, seeing the pre-operative and post-operative patients in her care. On two occasions she'd been called in to help out in the *Urgences* department, the French equivalent of Accident and Emergency. She'd enjoyed all her work, giving all her energies and expertise to the patients and ensuring she learned and made notes on every important medical experience to store up for future reference.

But as she pulled on her jeans and a favourite old black T-shirt she knew she'd neglected her own health and strength in her desire to embrace every situation in her new life. It was something her parents had constantly chided her about. But it had been a case of 'Do as I say, not do as I do.' She'd long ago realised she was inherently disposed to using up her energy and then falling back on her frazzled nerves with an empty tank of petrol—just like her parents and brothers.

Nevertheless, she had work to do this morning before she could play. She sat down at her desk and reached for her laptop and the notebook that was always in her bag. She tried to put as much information straight onto the laptop but in many situations where she had a hands-on approach this was impossible.

She particularly enjoyed Bernard's tutorials because they seemed to be the only times she saw him nowadays—when they were in a professional situation. He'd definitely thawed out with all of his students and she'd noticed he'd gained their respect now that they appreciated how much he wanted them all to succeed.

She'd been particularly amazed—and gratified!— when he'd praised her in front of all the students, saying she'd made him reassess his opinion of female orthopaedic surgeons. 'I've no doubt now that Julia is inherently talented and a natural at this type of surgery.'

She'd been delighted by his praise, but slightly apprehensive. She worried that her fellow students would tease her for being teacher's pet. She needn't have worried on that score because they crowded aound her at the end of the tutorial, congratulating her. Those who'd watched her debut performance were especially complimentary.

Dominic had actually kissed her on both cheeks,

and as she glanced at their tutor on the rostrum she'd seen him frowning with disapproval. Strange. She didn't know what to make of that. Dominic was ever the flamboyant one of the crowd and she'd made a point of discouraging any advances. While she enjoyed spending time in Dominic's company, if she was honest with herself it was Bernard's attentions she longed for.

She wondered what he was doing this weekend. She knew he'd been off to Paris to see his son on the weekend after they'd enjoyed supper together at the Maurice Chevalier. She'd looked forward to his return but on the Monday morning, as they'd worked together, he'd seemed distant, preoccupied even. During a coffee break, when all her colleagues had been with them, she'd plucked up courage, hoping to break the ice, and asked him if he'd enjoyed his weekend. He'd answered briefly that, yes, it had made a change from hospital life.

From the pained expression on his face she'd deduced it hadn't been a total success. But there had been something else in his manner towards her. Without being overtly cold, he was putting her at arm's length, as it were. Making it obvious that perhaps he regretted being so warm towards her after her debut performance in Theatre. At least, that was how she'd taken it. So she'd thrown herself into her work and reined in her emotions, which, yes, she admitted it now, had been getting out of control.

But it hadn't been easy. She was still plagued by embarrassing thoughts about him. Thoughts that had nothing to do with real life and never could become reality...could they? She was like a teenager with a crush on the teacher! She should get out more, which she was definitely going to do this morning after she'd done some work on her notes.She sighed as she opened up and began reading the scribbled notes, remembering how she'd hung on every word as Bernard had delivered an off-the-cuff mini-lecture about performing amputations a couple of days ago. The importance of preparing the patient both physically and mentally. And then the after-care, the importance of listening, referring the patient to the best professional care. She'd been totally enthralled by his sympathetic approach, by the stories he'd told them about his secondment as an army surgeon in a war zone overseas. Some of his descriptions of what that had entailed had brought tears to her eyes because she'd found herself thinking she was so glad that he hadn't had to have a limb amputated.

That beautiful body of his—well, she assumed it was magnificent beneath the well-cut suits. Occasionally when he took off his jacket and rolled up his sleeves in a practical situation she'd seen muscles that looked as if they should be on one of those statues she'd seen when she'd wandered around the Louvre in Paris.

She made a determined effort to gather her thoughts and get back to the real work in hand.

A couple of hours later she got up from her desk and pulled on her jeans and a T-shirt. Scraping her long blonde hair into a ponytail, she hurried out of her room, anxious to get on the beach before it got too hot.

In a room not too far away down the corridor that was reserved for senior staff Bernard was also working on his laptop. He was transcribing notes for a paper he had to deliver at a conference in Paris soon. He'd been putting it off as he'd had to spend a lot of time with his students during the last month. They were an intelligent group and the work was enjoyable but time consuming.

He glanced at his watch. Good thing he'd started early that morning. He'd still have to finish off the paper while Philippe was here. He'd promised to take him to the beach. Perhaps if he took him there this morning they could go up to the farm, have lunch and then he could work for a couple of hours while Marianne took care of Philippe.

He phoned the farm. Marianne was delighted with the arrangement he proposed. 'Yes, take Philippe to the beach for the good sea air before you come out here for lunch. Your rooms are ready, of course. See you soon, Bernard!'

He started to get ready for the arrival of his son. Philippe's car, driven by the uniformed chauffeur, would arrive soon from Paris. This was one of the perks that Gabrielle had got used to since she'd begun dating the wealthy Frederic—her soon-to-be husband.

Julia walked briskly down to the beach. As the warm summer breeze fanned her cheeks she felt reinvigorated. This was exactly what she needed today. Fresh air. No work. No worries!

She skipped down the wooden steps that led onto the sand and broke into a gentle jog. As her breathing improved to a steady rhythm she increased her pace to a gentle run. Mmm, it was good to know her limbs hadn't seized up as she worked endlessly in hospital! She ran towards the sea and began to follow the shoreline.

'Julia?'

She turned at the sound of a man's voice. A little way up the beach a man in a T-shirt and shorts was digging a moat round a sandcastle. A child was helping him.

'Bernard?' She stood still, panting to get her breath back.

Bernard stopped digging and leaned on his spade. 'I don't mean to disturb your run but I'd love you to meet my son.'

She smiled as she walked up the beach towards him. He came towards her. Her heart, which had increased its rate due to her running, was now beating even more rapidly.

The young boy followed behind.

'Hello.' She smiled down at the young boy who turned to his father, looking up at him adoringly whilst waiting to be enlightened as to who the lady was.

'This is Julia, Philippe.'

Philippe extended his hand towards her. 'Hello, *mademoiselle*.'

She gave the charming boy a big smile. 'Oh, please call me Julia,' she said in French. 'Have you come from Paris this morning?'

Bernard watched her easy rapport with his son. It gave him a warm feeling but warning bells rang. Julia was only here for six months. He mustn't allow a rapport to build up between them. Philippe would be sad when she had to leave. So would he!

'Yes, I came by car. Are you a doctor here, like Papa?'

'Yes, I'm a doctor but I'm also a student on the course

that your father is in charge of. I'm learning how to improve my surgical skills.'

'Oh, yes, Papa has told me all about it. I'm going to be a surgeon when I grow up.'

'Are you?'

'Papa tells me I'll have to work very hard if I want to be a surgeon. Papa works hard all the time. Look at the castle he's building for me, Julia.'

'It's beautiful! A real work of art.'

'What's a work of art?'

'Well, it's something that's beautiful.'

'I've been digging the moat round it and piling the sand on the castle while Papa made the work-of-art bit at the top. I'm going to run down to the sea now and bring back some water in my bucket.'

Julia smiled down at the eager young boy. 'If you start digging a channel down to the sea, the incoming tide will flow into it and come all the way up to the moat round your castle.'

Wide eyes stared up at her in amazement. 'Will it really, Julia? Will you help me?'

She'd been totally unaware that Bernard had been watching with mixed emotions the two of them getting on so well together. He could feel the poignancy of the encounter and the feelings he was experiencing were difficult to understand.

She glanced across at him, her maternal instincts making her want to spend time with this adorable child but at the same time wondering how Bernard would feel. To her relief he was smiling fondly at the pair of them.

'That's a brilliant idea, Julia. Are you sure you can

spare the time? I know your tutor has a reputation for pushing you hard!'

She smiled back at him. 'I'm giving myself the whole day off to recharge my batteries.' She turned back to the little boy, who was still waiting for her answer. 'I'd love to help you, Philippe. Have you got a spare spade?'

Bernard picked up a large plastic bag and passed her a spare spade.

'Thank you.'

His hand, covered in sand, felt rough as it touched hers. She looked up at him and her heart seemed to stand still. She allowed herself to look into his eyes for a second longer before she turned back to his son.

'Come on, Philippe. Let's show Papa how hard we can work together.'

Bernard leaned against his spade as he watched Julia take his son to the edge of the sea. As they sprinted together she looked so young. Her long blonde hair had escaped the band she'd tied round it and was flowing over her shoulders. He couldn't help thinking how much more attractive she looked now than when she had to imprison it in a theatre cap. And, heaven knew, she had a serious effect on him in Theatre even without that tantalising hair showing!

He shouldn't be thinking like this. How many times had he reprimanded himself for breaking his self-made rule of no commitment ever again? And before his eyes he could see the rapport developing between Julia and Philippe.

They were digging their channel now. The tide was coming in and beginning to trickle into it. Throwing aside all his reservations about relationships, he ran down the beach to join them. This was what he needed. Some carefree relaxation. If Julia could give herself a day off, so could he.

The channel grew much quicker now with three of them working together. In no time at all it had reached the moat of the castle and water was trickling in, slowly at first and then more quickly.

Bernard put the finishing touches to the crenellated edge at the top of the castle before reaching into the bag for a small boat.

'Here you are, Philippe. See if your boat will sail round the castle now.'

'Oh, it's brilliant! Look at my boat, Papa!' The little boy was clapping his hands with delight, stopping occasionally to push the boat if it got stuck in the side of the castle. 'Round and round and round and...'

'That was a brainwave of yours, Julia,' Bernard said quietly. 'I can see you've done this a few times.'

She smiled. 'I have indeed. And on this very beach. But the tide's coming in very quickly now so Philippe had better make the most of it. Not long before you'll have to pack up and leave. I'll help gather up your things.'

Together they gathered up the plastic beach toys and Bernard stuffed them back into the large bag. A particularly strong surge of water flooded the moat and he called out to Philippe that they would have to go now.

'No, Papa, I don't want to go!'

Another surge of water swirled around Philippe's ankles. 'OK! I'm coming.'

Philippe ran to his father for safety, putting his arms around his legs. Bernard hoisted him up onto his shoulders and picked up the bag then they all hurried up the beach.

'I've got my car parked on the promenade. I'm taking Philippe up to my farm. Julia, can I give you a lift back to hospital or are you going to keep running on the path up there now that the tide will soon be in? Alternatively...'

He hesitated only a second before putting to her the idea that had been forming in his mind.

'Would you like to come up to the farm with us as you've given yourself a day off from the tyranny of your endless work schedule?'

'Oh, Julia, please say you'll come! I can show you the sheep and the cows and the—'

'That sounds really exciting, Philippe.' She shouldn't accept this invitation but she desperately wanted to. She salved her conscience by telling herself that it would be good for Philippe to have someone other than his father to amuse him. 'Thank you, Bernard, I'd love to see your farm.'

'Hurrah!'

Bernard had already justified his invitation by telling himself that Julia obviously loved children and might like to amuse Philippe while he got on with some work that afternoon. He led the way up the steps and along the promenade to the car.

Philippe had slipped his little hand inside Julia's and was chatting happily to her about the farm, the animals and all the other delights of the place that was his home when he was with his beloved Papa.

'You don't mind sitting in the back, I hope? Philippe

is happier there if he's got someone to talk to and you both seem to have a lot to discuss.'

'Oh, we've got a lot to talk about, haven't we, Philippe? So, did you drive yourself over from Paris this morning?'

Philippe giggled. 'I'm only six.'

'Oh, I thought you were much older.'

'Philippe is six going on sixteen, actually.'

She smiled, positively glowing at the attentions of father and son. Bernard was leaning through the door of the car, checking on Philippe's seat belt and pointing out hers. He was very close as he leaned across to check on both of them. As he straightened up and prepared to close the car door their eyes met and Julia felt a frisson of pure excitement mingled with apprehension running through her. She felt emotionally warm and cosseted and decided to simply go with the flow for a few hours. No point worrying too much about where all this might be leading

There was absolutely nothing wrong with them being friends, she decided. But as she looked up at the expression on Bernard's face she held her breath.

His expression was one of total admiration as he looked at her and she could feel her confidence zooming higher. Bernard was so good for her professional confidence. She remembered how he'd praised her in front of her colleagues. That had given her ego a much-needed boost after the knocks she'd taken in the past. This was what she needed, a totally platonic friendship. The fact that she was only here for just over four more months and shouldn't be building a rapport with Bernard's son was still at the back of mind, but for today she shelved the problem. A day off was a day off from worry.

Bernard drove them out onto the main road.

'I'm going to drive as soon as I'm old enough, Julia. Thomas was explaining about his car this morning when we came down this hill. It's such a clever car, it changes gears all by itself. Papa has to change his own gears in this car, don't you?'

'It makes me feel more in control.' Bernard shifted down a gear as the hill grew steeper.

'Thomas says he'll teach me to drive when I'm older.'

Bernard remained quiet. Who knew what the future held? There were so many hurdles to negotiate in the new situation that his ex-wife had thrust upon them.

Julia was also confused about the man Thomas but she didn't want to ask questions. It was Philippe who provided a clue.

'Thomas took his cap off when we got outside Paris. Mummy likes him to wear it when he takes us shopping. He's Frederic's chauffeur.' He leaned towards Julia. 'I think Mummy is going to marry him soon—well, she keeps telling me she is. I hope we don't have to move into his house. It's so quiet and Frederic won't let me use his computer. I was only looking at it one day when he came in and he got really cross with me. I wasn't going to play games on it or anything like that.'

Bernard pulled into a parking area saying that this was a good place to admire the view. There was a tight feeling in his chest. The revelations that his son made every time he saw him made his heart bleed. The sooner he finalised the custody preparations and got Philippe over here, the better. He got out of the car and opened the back doors.

'Wonderful view, isn't it?'

Julia heard the emotion in his voice and saw the sad expression in his eyes. She could only guess at the situation that had developed in Bernard's life and he was obviously deeply concerned about his son's welfare.

Bernard was taking hold of Philippe's hand as he jumped out onto the grass. 'Keep hold of my hand, Philippe. I don't want you to roll down the hillside and end up in the sea.'

Philippe giggled. 'That would be fun!'

'Do you know, Philippe, I used to stand here admiring the view with my *papa* and mummy when I was younger?' Julia said.

'Really! Papa told me that you live in England.'

'Oh, I do live in England but we used to spend our holidays in France. My mother is French and my father is English. My mother was keen we should speak French all the time when we were in France so we would enlarge our French vocabulary.'

She broke off as she noticed the puzzled expression on the young boy's face. 'Sorry, Philippe, I keep forgetting you're only six. What I'm trying to say is that we needed as much practice as we could get to make sure we spoke good French. My grandmother lived over those hills there in Montreuil sur Mer.'

She pointed her finger towards the hills they'd travelled over so often.

'We used to stay with her when I was small and after she died we continued coming over to France and staying here on the coast for our holidays.'

Bernard was smiling across at her appraisingly.

She smiled back. He looked like a man who was also taking a day off from his worries.

'Philippe is so intelligent I'm speaking to him as if he were much older,' she said quietly.

'I entirely approve. I do the same myself. Expand his knowledge as much as you can if he's interested. If he gets bored he'll switch off. It's a fascinating world if he's with the right people while he's growing up.'

Philippe was anxious to be included in the conversation again. 'So, Julia, when did you learn to speak French properly like you do now?'

She thought hard. 'I sort of learned it alongside learning to speak English—as a child. It seemed natural to speak English to my father and French to my mother. My brothers learned in the same way.'

'How many brothers have you got?'

'Three brothers, all older than me.'

'They must be very old. Are they as old as Papa?'

'My eldest brother, John, is about the same age as your father, I think. One time when we were standing here John started walking down that steep slope when my parents weren't looking. His trainers slipped on the wet grass and he tumbled a long way down the field until he managed to stop.'

'Was he hurt?'

'No, but his clothes were all grass stained and muddy. My mother wasn't too pleased.'

Philippe giggled. 'It must be fun, having brothers to play with. Frederic, Maman's fiancé, has got a few grown-up children but I don't think he likes them very much. They don't come to see him. He's very old, you see, and he gets tired.'

Julia looked across at Bernard. As their eyes met she could see his desolate expression deepen. Poor Bernard! She wanted to lean across the top of Philippe's head and give him a big hug—in a totally platonic, friendly way, of course. She mustn't lose sight of the fact that she'd come out to France for a fresh start and here she was becoming involved with another ready-made family, just as she had with Tony.

But Bernard wasn't like Tony. Nobody could be as bad as Tony. But what did she know about men? Only that if they wanted you they were charming and attentive at first. When they were fed up with you they moved on to someone else.

'Come on, let's all get back in the car. There's a storm brewing up over the sea.' Bernard was pointing out towards the horizon. 'Can you see the white flecks on the top of the waves, Philippe?'

'Yes, it's so exciting. The white flecks on the waves look like white horses riding over the waves. Oh, look up there, Papa! The sky's getting all dark. Where's the sun gone? Can't we wait here till it really arrives, Papa?'

'It's better to get to the farm so we don't get wet.'

Bernard drove over the brow of the steep hill and started down the other side. The road was narrow with tortuous bends. He drove carefully because the rain was now pelting down and hailstones were bouncing on the slippery road.

'I remember coming over into this valley as a child and seeing that village down there! Difficult to see it in all this rain but I know it's there.'

Bernard switched on the car lights, hoping that if another vehicle drove towards him it would also have its lights on.

'We can't see the farm in this bad weather but we'll soon be there. It's on the other side of the village.'

It was a difficult but short drive down the hill. The rain began to ease off as they drove through the village. Bernard pointed out various landmarks—the village school, the *tabac*, the *alimentation*, which sold groceries.

'There's no *boulangerie* these days. A van comes over from the next village and delivers the bread to the *dépôt de pain*—that building over there, which doubles as the newsagent.'

They were soon driving out of the village towards the farm. The gate was open. Smoke was curling from a chimney.

'Strange to see smoke from a chimney in June,' Julia said.

'We have an ancient wood stove in the kitchen, which is never allowed to go out.'

'I help Marianne put wood on the stove when I come to stay with Papa. Look, there she is.'

A plump, middle-aged lady was coming towards the car, carrying a large umbrella.

Bernard got out and took charge of the umbrella. 'Philippe, you go into the house with Marianne. I'll bring Julia under the umbrella I've got in the boot of the car.'

She felt a firm arm going around her waist as she moved towards the kitchen door. They were sheltered from the rain by the umbrella but as she splashed through the puddles she glanced down at her mud-splashed workout clothes.

'Oh, dear,' said Bernard. 'Looks like your clothes have taken a bit of a beating.'

Julia laughed. 'Are you trying to say I look a mess?'

His grip tightened around her waist as he steadied her advance towards the kitchen door. Rain was dripping from the edge of the umbrella all around them but for a brief moment she felt as if they were the only people in the world. He'd pulled her to a halt and was looking down at her with such a strange expression on his handsome face. She felt her heart beating madly.

She knew this was another of those magic moments in life that she would never ever forget. For a brief moment she allowed herself to think that nothing else mattered except this magic feeling that was running through her.

'Papa, hurry up!'

'We're coming, Philippe.'

CHAPTER FIVE

JULIA wiggled her bare toes in front of the lively flames in the wood-burning stove as she sipped the mug of hot coffee that Bernard had just put into her hands before settling himself amongst the squashy cushions beside his son.

'I can do that, Julia!'

'Do what, Philippe?'

She looked across at the other side of the stove and watched as the small boy wiggled his toes much faster than she could. He was curled up in a corner of the old sofa, snuggling up to Bernard, who was looking more relaxed than she'd ever seen him.

She smiled at the pair of them. 'You're much more supple than me, Philippe.'

The young boy giggled. 'That's because I like running about in my bare feet. Maman won't let me go without shoes in Paris but when I come home—I mean to this home, my real home—Papa doesn't mind, do you?'

Bernard put his coffee mug in a safe place on the hearth out of reach of Philippe's arms, which rarely stayed still when he was enjoying himself.

'That just depends on the weather. It wouldn't be a

good idea to wade across the farmyard while it's still raining, would it? You saw the state of Julia's jeans and shoes when she came in, didn't you?'

Philippe put his head on one side while he considered his father's words. 'You know, Papa, I think Julia should have taken off her things in the car so she wouldn't have spoiled them.'

'Maybe I didn't want to arrive in the kitchen half-dressed.' She took another sip of her coffee, feeling a nice, warm, thawed-out feeling creeping over her.

'Oh, it wouldn't have mattered, would it, Papa? You see people with no clothes on all the time, don't you?'

Bernard looked across at Julia with a whimsical expression on his handsome face. 'I do indeed, son. But not usually beautiful young ladies like Julia. I have to say, though, that Julia's own trousers are a much better fit. Kind as it was of Marianne to wash them, these baggy jeans tied up with an old belt look most comical on her.'

She gave him a wry smile. 'Oh, very funny! Are you trying to tell me I look frumpish now?'

'Julia, you would look good in an old sack.'

She felt overwhelmed by the admiration that shone from his eyes. She realised he was flirting with her, probably feeling safe because his son was with them.

Philippe was obviously enjoying being part of a grown-up conversation. Suddenly, he jumped up.

'Shall I get a sack, Papa? I know where Gaston keeps a whole pile of them in the barn. We could cut some holes for her arms and then Julia could put it over her head. Then we could all play at dressing-up, couldn't we? Would you like that, Julia?'

She pretended to be considering the offer, keeping half an eye on Bernard, who looked as if he was going to say something outrageous. Keeping a serious expression on her face, she said, 'I think you might get a bit wet, Philippe, if you go out to the barn.'

'Oh, yes, the rain!' Philippe stared across at the kitchen window where the drops of rain seemed even bigger as they lashed at the panes of glass. 'When will the rain stop, Papa?'

Bernard shrugged. 'Soon, I hope. We'll have to play a game that doesn't involve going outside until the weather improves. Would you like to find one of your board games that the three of us could play together?'

He looked up at Marianne, who'd just returned from organising the washing in the utility room alongside the kitchen and was waiting to say something to him.

'Bernard, I heard you talking about the weather. I was about to suggest we have an early lunch because the weather report says things are likely to improve…'

Julia gathered that the weather report on television had predicted there would be dry weather and sunshine in the afternoon. Marianne had a chicken casserole in the oven, which she could serve up in a few minutes.

'Excellent! Let's have an early lunch.' Bernard stood up and moved across to Julia. 'Be careful you don't trip up in those baggy pants.'

He held out his hand, which she took, not because it was required to steady herself but simply for the feel of those firm, enticingly capable fingers in an off-duty situation. Marianne said she'd laid the table in the dining room. Bernard, still holding her hand, led her down a stone-flagged corridor to the front of the house, which had a good view of the garden.

Philippe skipped along beside her, chattering all the time. She was glad none of the young boy's conversation required an answer because she had suddenly become overwhelmed by the warm feeling of the intimacy that was developing between the three of them. She felt she was enveloped in a family situation that seemed perfectly natural.

'I want to sit next to Julia, Papa!'

'That's strange, so do I.'

'She can sit between us, can't she?'

Bernard led her to the table where a beautifully laundered white cloth had been placed. The silver cutlery shone in the light from the chandelier hanging over the centre of the large round table.

'It's not often we need to have the light on during the day,' Bernard said, glancing out at the darkened garden with low black clouds overhead.

He held out a chair for her. Philippe sat down quickly beside her. Bernard smiled. 'It's a good thing we have a round table. My grandparents bought this table for my parents when they were first married.'

Marianne bustled in and placed the chicken casserole in front of Bernard.

'Enjoy your lunch!'

'Thank you!'

Bernard began serving out portions of the delicious casserole. Throughout the meal the warm rapport between the three of them continued. The conversation flowed, the food was exceptionally good and only

Philippe noticed, as he put down his dessert spoon, preparing to leave the table, that the rain had stopped.

'Papa, the weather report was correct. Here's the sun!'

He waved his arms excitedly at the sun, which was now shining through the windows as they left their places in the dining room.

Julia was feeling replete, having enjoyed a good helping of the chicken casserole and farm-grown vegetables followed by a home-made apple pie. Philippe had enjoyed joining in the conversation and she found she loved the sound of his young voice making interesting comments, asking questions, always giving a positive aspect to what they were discussing.

He seemed older than six but that was possibly because he'd had to get used to different situations during his short life. She hoped Bernard would elaborate at some point about why his marriage had been as disastrous as he'd implied. It couldn't have been his fault. He couldn't have brought about a divorce...not with his generous personality and wonderful parenting skills. His wife must have been in the wrong.

She remembered how, glancing up at Bernard as she'd finished her apple pie, she'd seen him looking at her with an enigmatic expression. Had he any idea how overwhelmed she was by the warmth of the situation they'd created that day, just the three of them? It was the first time she'd felt she belonged somewhere since she'd left her own family home.

Bernard suggested a grand tour of the farm, if he could enlist the help of his son as a fellow guide perhaps? After all, he knew the interesting places as well as his father now that it had become second home to him.

Philippe readily agreed to help his father show Julia around. They started with the barns. The smell of the hay in one barn took her right back to her own childhood.

'My brothers and I had some friends who lived on a farm. We used to spend lots of time there in the school holidays and the barns were wonderful places to play hide and seek in.'

Philippe said children in France also played that game but he hadn't got any friends to play it with when he was here and there weren't any barns in Paris.

Oh, dear! Julia wished she hadn't started talking about her childhood. Obviously, neither Bernard nor his son had experienced the enjoyable if sometimes chaotic family situations she'd had. Once more she thought how sad for Bernard that his marriage had been a disaster. He was a brilliant father.

They walked up the hill to see the sheep grazing on the hillside and talked to Gaston, Marianne's husband, who was mending a wall. The affable, middle-aged man was happy to show them his wall-making techniques and smiled encouragingly at Philippe, who was a willing pupil.

'We'll have you up here, helping me out, when you're a bit bigger,' he told Philippe. 'Would you like that?'

'I'd like to stay here all the time. It's much better here than in Paris.'

As they were going back down the hill, Philippe skipping happily ahead of them, Bernard spoke quietly to Julia.

'You've no idea how relieved I was when Philippe just said he'd love to live here.'

'I'm sure he would. It's a wonderful place for a child.' She hesitated. 'You aren't thinking of...?'

'I'll tell you later.'

Philippe was running back up the hill. 'Papa, Julia, look, there's a rabbit by the side of that wall. Can you see it? Oh, look, there's another one.'

She couldn't help thinking that she didn't want this day to end. How wonderful it would be to spend more time with Bernard and his son. She tried not to think too far ahead. This was a one-off day. A day to cherish and not to look into the future.

Bernard handed her a glass of Kir as they sat together in the conservatory, which was bathed in the evening sunlight. Philippe had gone to bed without protest, being completely exhausted by the activities of the day. But not too exhausted to listen to the bedtime story he'd requested from Julia.

She took a sip of her Kir before placing the glass on the small table beside her wicker chair. 'You know, Bernard, little Philippe fell asleep when I was only two minutes into the story. Doesn't say much for my reading, does it?'

'Oh, I don't know. He was almost asleep when I lifted him out of the bath. I gathered you'd be downstairs in the land of the grown-ups within half an hour. What took you so long?'

She raised an eyebrow. 'Need you ask? Marianne intercepted me to check I had everything I need in the guest room. You are all being so kind. I hadn't intended to stay but you both convinced me I had to.

'Then there was your son beseeching me to have breakfast with him and you telling me that you didn't want to drive back to the hospital and... I could have got a taxi, you know.'

'I know,' he said languidly. 'But I wanted you to stay and I got the casting vote.'

He moved his chair closer to hers. 'I wanted to have time to talk to you in an off-duty situation. I don't want to think about the hospital tonight. And...well, I just wanted to be with you. I like being with you.'

He leaned across and cupped her chin with his hands. Slowly, he lowered his head and kissed her on the lips, a long, lingering, deliciously wicked kiss.

As he drew back she reflected that she would have preferred the kiss to have lasted much longer, but that would do for now. It had whetted her appetite for more, more of...well, more of everything where that had come from. But she conceded it really was not part of the plan for a new start in life. Except men like Bernard wouldn't wait for ever while she achieved all her ambitions and then told him he was definitely the man for her.

'What are you thinking?' he breathed.

She looked up into his expressive hazel eyes. For a brief moment she longed to tell him. To ask him if he could possibly understand her yearning to start a relationship with him whilst having to cope with her sensible reluctance to change her ambitious plans. She couldn't have it both ways...or could she?

She hesitated before moving on from her impossibly romantic thoughts. 'I was thinking how peaceful it is out here. This afternoon you said you were glad Philippe loves this place. Are you planning he should spend more time here?'

He leaned back in his chair. 'The fact is, the situation has been rather thrust upon me. Gabrielle is going to marry Frederic, a rich, retired businessman much older than she is. He's got grown-up children and finds Philippe too much trouble when he's around their Paris house. Gabrielle has asked me to have Philippe to stay with me permanently.'

'But that would be good for you, wouldn't it?'

He gave a big, contemplative sigh. 'It is my dearest wish to have my son living with me. There are a few problems to be sorted before we can go ahead. Gabrielle, of course, is anxious to be able to get on with her wedding plans without having to think about what to do with Philippe.'

'But surely, as his mother... I mean I don't understand. Bernard, you've hinted that your marriage was a disaster but you haven't told me why. Is your ex-wife to blame for...?'

'I should never have married Gabrielle. She was totally wrong for me right from the start and for that I blame myself.'

He splashed some more iced water in his pastis and raised it to his lips, the ice clinking as he took a much-needed drink. If he was going to be seeing more of Julia in an off-duty situation then he owed it to her to fill her in on his background. She was watching him now with a wary expression on her face, as well she might if she suspected half of what he was going to tell her.

He trusted her implicitly. He didn't know why because he hadn't known her for very long. But it was long enough to know she was his kind of woman. Whereas Gabrielle certainly was not and never had been.

He leaned back against the cushions and stared up at the ceiling where a fan was whirling round above his chair, bringing welcome cool air to the warm evening.

'My only excuse for even talking to Gabrielle was that I was young and inexperienced. I met Gabrielle Sabatier in Montmartre. I'd gone with a crowd of fellow doctors to celebrate the fact that we'd all qualified in our final exams. Gabrielle was working as a waitress in the restaurant where we were having supper. She told me later that evening…' he paused as a sudden vivid recollection of that seedy flat in a narrow street forced itself upon him '…that she needed a wage to pay her rent while she was searching for employment as an actress, having just finished drama school.'

He got up and walked over to the window, looking out across the lovely garden so lovingly cared for by Marianne and Gaston, and beyond the garden wall the hills bathed in evening sunlight. He'd always loved beautiful things in his life. How could he have fallen victim to the tawdry life that Gabrielle had introduced him to?

Julia moved swiftly across the room and stood in front of Bernard, looking up at him, her eyes full of emotion as she recognised he was undergoing some sort of crisis.

'Bernard, you don't need to tell me about your past life if it distresses you. Come and sit down again.'

'If only…' He enfolded her in his arms, bending his head so that their cheeks were together.

She could feel the dampness of his cheek as he struggled to contain his emotions. She remained silent for a few seconds, feeling his heart beating against hers, experiencing a longing she'd never known before.

And then he kissed her with an urgency that thrilled her through her whole being. This was the man for her, with all his past problems, with all his future ahead of him to sort out which way he would turn. She longed to be a part of his life.

Gently he released her from his arms and stood looking down at her, the evening sunlight bathing the two of them as if blessing their emotional embrace.

'Julia, I want to tell you everything about my liaison with Gabrielle. Things I've never discussed with anyone before. I feel...I feel you will understand why I have such a lot of emotional baggage to contend with.'

He took hold of her hand and together they walked back to their seats. He settled her and moved his chair even closer. She took a sip from her glass and he reached for the bottle of crème de cassis to top her glass up.

'You see, I'd never met anyone like Gabrielle in my life. I thought I'd fallen in love with her even while she was serving on at the crowded table in Montmartre. My friends were joking, saying she fancied me. Well, I was overwhelmed by this vivacious, sexy creature, as were all my friends.'

Julia couldn't help jealous vibes disturbing her. Oh, dear, she was becoming more involved than she'd ever meant to be. Maybe she should insist he keep it all to himself? His past was something she didn't want to think about.

'Gabrielle asked me to wait until she'd finished work

and go back to her flat with her.' He paused and drew in his breath. 'I knew what would happen. I wanted it to happen. Yes, we became lovers that night and I was too enamoured to see what she was planning.'

'Which was?' As if she couldn't guess!

'She thought I was a good catch. A young doctor with a safe, well-paid career ahead of him. A meal ticket for life! Sorry, I don't want to sound bitter but...anyway, weeks later when she told me she was pregnant, like the idiot I was, I agreed to marry her.'

Julia felt a pang of sympathy for the young, inexperienced Bernard. She leaned across and squeezed his hand. 'It often happens to young men, even experienced men.'

He flashed her an endearing smile of gratitude. 'I hope Philippe has more sense when he starts growing up. Anyway, it transpired she'd been brought up in relative luxury in the sixteenth arrondissement of Paris, in between the Bois de Boulogne and the river Seine—in a very pricy house. Her father had been a successful businessman until he overextended himself, went bankrupt and took an overdose, after ensuring that his widow would keep the house, albeit living a frugal lifestyle with Gabrielle, her only child.'

'Did you ever think that Gabrielle had been traumatised by the death of her father?'

'Oh, I'm sure she was. Her response to the tragedy had been to turn herself into an even harder, more ruthless character. But I didn't know that when I agreed to marry her.'

He splashed more water into his glass as he tried to remember exactly how it had been. Julia was right in saying that Gabrielle must have been traumatised by the suicide of her father.

'Believe me, I've made so many allowances for her behaviour…but each time she disappointed me with her responses. Anyway, a few weeks after we were married Gabrielle told me she'd miscarried. I insisted on taking her into hospital where tests proved that she'd never been pregnant in the first place. She knew I'd seen through her plan. We became like strangers when we were together. She began to show her true colours, nagging me to rent a house in the prestigious area where she'd grown up and her mother still lived. I told her I couldn't afford it. I was at the very beginning of my medical career, working all hours I could, and I couldn't take on any more expense. I was exhausted most of the time.'

There was a sound of someone coming down the corridor. Bernard sat up his chair as Marianne appeared in the doorway.

'I'm going to prepare supper for Gaston now, Bernard. You're absolutely sure you don't want me to cook supper for you?'

Bernard smiled. 'We're not hungry yet, Marianne. I'm going to make an omelette and salad later on.'

'Well, if you're sure.' Marianne turned to Julia. 'I've put your jeans in the guest room. I do hope you have everything you need in there.'

'Thank you so much, Marianne, for everything.'

'You are most welcome. See you tomorrow.'

As the footsteps receded down the corridor Julia asked Bernard where Marianne lived.

'She and Gaston live in the old surgery at the end

of the house. After my father died we had it converted for them so they could be on site while I finished my schooling and moved to Paris to train as a doctor.'

They were both silent as Julia digested this information, thinking to herself that Bernard hadn't had an easy life. Perhaps that was one reason why he'd fallen in love so easily and so quickly with someone who'd appeared on the surface to be the girl of his dreams.

'So what happened after Gabrielle knew you'd seen through her machinations?'

'Oh, she started to make my life hell. There was I, trying to establish myself as a reliable junior doctor at the hospital and she just never stopped nagging while I was with her. I tell you, I was tempted to walk away from this disastrous marriage but I decided the honourable thing to do was to stick it out. In our family background marriage was a lifelong contract, not to be broken.'

'Didn't she work?'

'She got a small part in a TV soap and told me she'd got a long contract. But actually it was only for three months, to be reviewed. On the strength of that I gave in to her demands that I rent the house she wanted. We moved into the house. Two weeks later Gabrielle admitted her contract had been terminated. I phoned her director to enquire what had happened. He said she was temperamental and unreliable. Hah! What a wise man. If only I'd had the sense to see through her earlier.

'Anyway, I continued to work long hours and began to climb the career ladder. I was earning more and just able to scrape the rent together. Then one day when I returned home there was a note saying she'd left me.'

'How did you feel about that?'

He looked across and smiled. 'If I'm honest, I felt relieved. It was as if a burden had lifted from my shoulders. I assumed she'd met somebody…and I was right. But two months later she returned. She'd had an affair with a married man who'd promised to leave his wife but he'd gone back to her. She begged me to forgive her. I was too busy with my all-absorbing work at the hospital to contemplate divorce.' His voice dipped as he resumed a tone of resignation. 'I took her back.'

'Was she grateful?'

'She seemed to have changed. She even turned on the charm. I should have realised she was up to something. She began begging me to make love to her. I insisted she stay on the Pill. A baby at this stage of our fragile relationship would have been unthinkable.' He breathed out. 'And guess what?'

'She stopped taking the Pill and became pregnant?'

He gave her a wry grin of resignation. 'Why weren't you there to say that when I took her back! I saw right through her but it was too late. It was the last straw. Even though I'd always longed for a family, I knew I couldn't afford the added expense unless I earned more. I told her I was going to apply for a prestigious surgical appointment in St Martin sur Mer. If I was successful we would move there.'

'How did she feel about that?'

'She said she wouldn't leave Paris. I told her that if I was successful in getting this appointment I would support her and the baby, whether she came or not. When I told her I'd been successful she flounced out and went to live with her mother but not until after she'd demanded a large monthly sum to be paid into her bank account. The one good thing that came out of her move back to her mother was that there was a steadying influence in her life. Veronique Sabatier is a saint! How on earth she came to give birth to a daughter like Gabrielle I cannot imagine.'

'So Philippe has had a good grandmother to care for him?'

'Absolutely! What a relief. As soon as he was born I loved him with the all-consuming love that only a parent knows. And now...'

He spread his hands wide. 'I'm going to be able to have him with me always—well, until he's a grown man and leaves the family nest.'

She saw the loving expression in his eyes as he drew her to her feet, holding her close to him. 'Thank you for listening to me. I've never told anyone the full story of my disastrous marriage.'

And then he kissed her, this time more slowly, taking time to savour the joy of being with her. Neither of them was thinking beyond the next moment. The present was all that mattered.

He released her from his embrace, looking down at her with an expression of love on his face.

'Let's go and have supper together,' he said, his voice husky as he struggled to come to terms with the fact that all he wanted to do was lift her into his arms and carry her upstairs.

He put his arm around her as they walked towards the kitchen. She revelled in the connection that existed between them, wondering at how much their relationship had developed during the day. How much more could it develop before she found herself hopelessly in love and unable to sort out her conflicting emotions?

CHAPTER SIX

JULIA lay back against the goosedown pillows. She'd been able to tell it was goosedown as soon as she'd laid her head on the softness that had moulded itself around her head. Mmm. Everything about this room was luxurious, well appointed, but probably rarely used—she hoped! The idea of Bernard having a guest room like this made her think that he wanted to impress the girls he showed in here.

But then did he leave them here all by themselves to admire the room? Almost as soon as he'd shown her the superb bathroom, fluffy towels and expensive soap he had left!

But not before that goodnight kiss. Her legs began to feel weak again, even though she was now lying down. She'd been hanging on to her excited emotions, trying hard not to show her real feelings because she knew she simply couldn't have controlled her desire to make love with him.

When he'd taken her in his arms once more, just outside the door to her bedroom, she'd gathered her thoughts together in something of a panic. She'd wanted him physically, desperately, but her rational self had told her not to go there, not to upset the relative calm of their relationship, which worked with the current situation of professor and student. She'd made mistakes before when she'd allowed herself to give in to her passionate nature.

Yes, he'd kissed her gently at first and her wickedly fluid body had reacted with instinctive longing. Oh, yes, she wanted this man…oh, so desperately. But almost as soon as he'd started to kiss her with real urgency he'd pulled away and whispered, 'Goodnight, Julia,' in that deep, sexy voice. And before she'd known what had happened he had been striding away from her to his own room.

Shortly afterwards, in his room not too far away, Bernard, lying back against the pillows, was wondering why he hadn't stayed to make love with Julia, cursing himself for doing what he'd considered to be the right thing. He remembered how she'd felt in his arms. She'd given every indication that she'd wanted him to make love to her. He hadn't misread the signals. Would it really have complicated their relationship too much at this stage if he'd given in to his true feelings?

He rolled onto his side, waiting for the waves of desire to calm down. The cold shower he'd just taken hadn't helped as much as he'd hoped. He'd only known Julia a few weeks but he knew that he was falling in love. Being in love with a student—any student—wasn't an easy situation to be in.

Yes, they were both adults, so there was nothing untoward about the situation. Nothing that the hospital board of governors could possibly frown upon so long as they were discreet. It was more the problem of handling the emotion for the next few months before Julia finished the course and took the final exams.

For the final month he would find it easier. With the exams over he could relax. He would already have assessed her performance as a student during the course. A panel of external examiners would mark the exam papers and listen to her answers to their questions in the viva voce exam.

Thinking rationally, as he hoped he was doing now, helped to sort out his confusing thoughts. He realised she was the most talented student he'd ever had to deal with. He mustn't do anything to put her off track because she was obviously very ambitious and had a lot to live up to, coming from a prestigious family background like hers.

There was also the problem of her having been hurt by that dreadful ex-husband who seemed to have been hell bent on destroying her confidence. Since she'd arrived here, he'd been trying to build up her confidence again so she could realise her full potential.

Yes, he'd seen her blossoming into an excellent surgeon, relaxing with her fellow students and having an easygoing friendship with him. She already seemed to be more in control of her own life. He'd admired her when she'd first arrived but this increasingly self-confident woman was becoming more and more irresistible to him.

He turned on the bedside light again, knowing that it would be impossible to sleep, with Julia only a short distance away. The moon was shining through the open window onto his huge bed where he should have brought Julia if he'd given in to his true feelings. He gave an audible sigh as he wondered if she was lying awake staring at this same moon and if so, what was she thinking?

He'd been flirting with her all day so why did he have to rationalise himself out of going ahead with his natural instincts? He didn't even know how she would have felt if he'd suggested she sleep with him. As he'd held her in his arms on the pretence that he had simply been saying goodnight she'd been so wonderfully pliant. He'd felt every curve in that vibrant body reacting to his caresses. But he'd forced himself to leave her.

With the occasional dalliance making his off-duty time more interesting for a while he wouldn't usually have thought twice about making it obvious he wanted to sleep with her. If the woman was willing, they would go ahead. But it didn't mean anything. It was an experience that they both enjoyed as mature adults free of any committed relationship. He'd always checked that they weren't involved with a partner.

But Julia was special, the most wonderful woman he'd ever met. The only woman in his life who made him feel that he had to sacrifice his own feelings so that he wouldn't spoil her future potential. She was like a precious flower that he had to nurture.

The sun was shining in through the gaps in the chiffon drapes at her window. Julia stirred and cautiously opened her eyes, unsure of her surroundings. She'd lain awake half the night but the sleep that she'd just been enjoying had been very deep and she was reluctant to return to reality. Somewhere in a nearby room she could hear a child's voice singing.

So, she hadn't dreamed she was in Bernard's farmhouse. She hadn't imagined that wonderful day they'd spent together.

She sat up quickly as she heard gentle tapping on her door.

'Julia, can I come in?'

'Of course, Philippe!'

She pulled the robe from the bedside chair to cover her shoulders. Even as she did so she remembered how impressed she'd been when Bernard had produced the cream silk, extremely feminine robe last night. But then the inevitable moment of jealousy as to who'd worn it before her had threatened to invade her happy mood.

Philippe stood beside her bed, smiling. 'Marianne has sent me to tell you that breakfast is ready.'

The young boy described the delicious breakfast that Marianne had prepared and Julia listened, smiling at him. She raised her head as she became aware that Bernard was now standing in the doorway. He was wearing a dark blue towelling robe that covered most of him except for his athletic, muscular calves and bare feet. His dark, sleep-tousled hair was still damp from his shower and he was looking wonderfully handsome with the sunlight on his lightly tanned face.

'No need to hurry, Julia. I've brought you some coffee. Marianne is still making preparations downstairs so take your time.' Bernard placed a small tray with a cafetière and a delicate porcelain cup and saucer on her bedside table. 'Philippe insisted it was time to wake you.'

'Julia was awake when I knocked on the door, weren't you?'

'I was indeed, Philippe.'

Her eyes met Bernard's over the top of the small head and she felt her heart turn over. The warmth and love she'd felt yesterday had returned as she became wrapped up once again in this idyllic family situation.

Bernard retreated again to the doorway and held out his hand towards his son. 'Philippe, come with me while Julia gets herself ready.'

'Can't I stay and run her bath for her, like I do for you, Papa?'

'I think Julia will be happy to have a few quiet moments to gather her thoughts for the day ahead, so we'll see her when she comes downstairs.'

After they'd gone, she enjoyed a leisurely soak in the bath, balancing the delicate coffee cup in the small tiled alcove of the wall. It made a welcome change from the hurried shower she took most mornings in her tiny en suite.

When she got herself downstairs fully clothed in her workout gear from the previous day, the smell of freshly baked croissants drew her to the kitchen. Bernard was reawakening the dormant flames in the wood-burning stove. He closed the stove door and turned as he heard her coming in.

He put down the poker on the hearth and came across to pull out a chair for her at the table. Philippe ran inside from the kitchen garden and jumped up onto the chair beside her and began to eat enthusiastically. He urged Julia to join him and, smiling, she reached for a still warm croissant.

Julia was halfway through her croissant, spread liberally with the home-made apricot jam, when she saw Bernard answer his mobile.

'Bernard Cappelle.'

She saw him frowning. From the ensuing conversation she gathered it was an urgent call from the hospital.

'Of course. I'll be there as soon as I can.'

He looked across the table at her. 'That was Michel Devine from the emergency department. There's been a road traffic accident on the motorway, involving several vehicles. He's asked permission to call in as many of my students as possible to help with the patients who will be treated at the hospital. Are you willing to…?'

'Of course.' She was already pushing back her chair.

'Michel, I've just spoken to Dr Julia Montgomery and she says she's available.'

Minutes later they were driving down the hill towards St Martin sur Mer. Bernard had asked Marianne to take charge of Philippe, who would have to stay at the farm for another day. Philippe had been delighted at the prospect of a whole day with Marianne and Gaston on the farm and another night with his father.

Julia could see a couple of ambulances arriving outside the hospital as Bernard carefully negotiated his way through the traffic at the foot of the hill. The porter in charge of the hospital gateway directed several vehicles to the side so that Bernard could come through and park.

Inside, Michel was organising his staff. A triage system was being set up so that patients were assessed as soon as possible after their arrival.

A nurse was handing out white coats to the arriving medical staff. Julia pulled hers on and reported to Michel Devine for instructions. He asked her to check out the patient in the first cubicle.

'The paramedics have put a tourniquet round his bleeding leg to stem the flow but we need to do something more effective now we've got him here,' he told her tersely. 'There's a nurse in there who'll help you while you assess what needs to be done, Dr Montgomery. It's obviously a serious orthopaedic problem, which is in your field of expertise.'

She moved through the curtain to the cubicle and went in to take charge of the situation. The young man's eyes pleaded with her to help him as she took hold of his hand. He was lying on his back, his hands clenched over the bloodstained sheet that covered him.

She spoke to him in French, making her voice as soothing as she could. He was obviously in deep shock. Glancing down at the notes the nurse handed to her, she saw that his name was Pierre. She noted that sedation that had already been given at the scene of the traffic accident.

Gently peeling back the sheet that covered his injured right leg, she could see that this was a very serious problem. The right leg had been badly damaged and would require immediate surgery. She was already making a swift examination of the damaged tibia and surrounding tissues when she sensed that someone else had joined her in the cubicle.

Relief shot through her when she heard Bernard's voice behind her. He moved to her side and leaned across the patient so he could form his own opinion.

'I'll make arrangements for immediate surgery,' he told her.

She nodded in agreement. 'Are those Pierre's X-rays?'

Bernard was already flashing them up on the wall screen. She swallowed hard as she tried to make sense of the crushed pieces of bone. From the knee downwards, the leg seemed to resemble a jigsaw puzzle. Was it still viable? It was going to require some expert surgery and after-care if their patient was to be able to walk on it again. Maybe amputation followed by the fitting of a prosthesis might be the only option. A decision would have to be made during surgery.

She held Pierre's hand as Bernard made a swift call to the surgical wing.

'*Ma femme*, my wife,' the young man whispered. 'Monique. *Je veux...*' His faint voice trailed away as tears started trickling down his bloodstained face.

Even as Pierre was asking for his wife, the nurse, at the other side of the cubicle, was looking directly at Julia. 'The information is in the notes, Doctor.'

Glancing briefly down at the notes, Julia learned that his wife, who was seven months pregnant, had been unconscious since the accident. She'd been sitting beside Pierre in the passenger seat when the vehicle had crashed through. Their patient had cradled her in his arms until a doctor had arrived and taken her away in the first ambulance. She was already in the obstetric suite, undergoing an emergency Caesarean.

'Julia, I'd like you to assist me. Theatre Sister is making preparations for us.' Bernard went on to instruct the nurse about premedication for the patient. Julia was glad he was cool and calm because she knew that was how she must be—totally professional so that she could do her best for the patient.

Bernard came across to speak to Pierre, explaining the serious condition of his leg. Julia held her breath as the subject of possible amputation was broached. Pierre looked at her and then at Bernard.

'Is that a possibility? Can't you...?' His voice trailed away.

'Pierre, we'll do all we can to save the leg, but if it's too badly damaged it would make more sense to amputate. Prostheses these days are excellent and you would be taught to walk. I hope it won't come to that but the decision can't be made until we find the full extent of your injuries. Do you understand?' he added gently.

Their patient closed his eyes for a moment. Then in a clear voice he declared that he fully understood and would accept their decision, whatever it was.

Carefully, Julia withdrew her hand from the patient's grasp. 'I've got to leave you for a short time, Pierre. You'll soon be going to sleep but I'll be up there in Theatre with you and I'll see you when you come round from the anaesthetic.'

'*Merci*,' he whispered. 'Thank you, Doctor.'

She swallowed hard to force herself to be totally professional, aware of his sad eyes on her as she followed Bernard out of the cubicle.

There was no time for a break during the day. Julia assisted Bernard with Pierre's long operation and found herself scrubbing up for the next patient almost immediately. They were supported by a good team from the surgical orthopaedic department, each member adding their expertise to the operations that were performed.

In the early evening, when she and Bernard could finally take a break, he drew her to one side for a quiet debriefing. They were still both in theatre greens up in the recovery room, having just despatched their final patient to one of the orthopaedic wards.

As Bernard started to speak she sank down onto a plastic chair at the side of the water cooler and reached out to take a plastic cup.

'Here, let me do that for you.'

'Thank you.' She flashed him a grateful smile as she took the cold water from him.

Their hands touched and she felt a frisson of energy running through her at the contact. She drank deeply and didn't stop until she'd finished all of it.

'That's better! I feel almost human again.'

Bernard smiled. 'Michel just called to say the emergency department has dealt with all the accident patients that were assigned to this hospital. He's very grateful for our help and suggests we go off duty.'

'Well, if you're sure they can cope, I'd love to go off duty.'

'I'm absolutely sure. Besides, you look completely whacked, Julia.'

'Thanks very much! That's just what a girl needs, to be told she looks as exhausted as she feels. Still...' She sat upright, threw the plastic cup into the bin and stood up. 'There's nothing that a shower and a change of clothes can't put right.'

'How about supper? That would be reviving, wouldn't it?'

What exactly was he suggesting? She couldn't do anything to stop the anticipation running through her.

'Well, what do you say, Julia? Why don't you come back to the farm with me? I've got to return there as soon as possible because Philippe will be getting impatient. If you're with me, he'll be over the moon.'

He was waiting for her answer. She was very tempted at the prospect.

'Well?'

'Why not?' She didn't like the sound of her breathless voice, which completely gave away her confused emotions. She'd meant to sound so cool, as if this was just an invitation to a friend's tea party.

'Good! I'll call Marianne and tell her you're coming so she can get your room ready.'

'Oh, there's no need to—'

'Yes, there is! Because if you think I'm driving back to the hospital again, you're mistaken. And don't start talking about taxis. There aren't any out in the countryside. This isn't London or Paris, you know.'

She laughed and suddenly it was as if the sun had come out from behind the clouds. They'd been in a windowless theatre all day but she could almost breathe the vibrant country air that she would experience when they escaped together.

He put a hand in the small of her back. 'Can you be ready to leave in half an hour?'

'I'll try. I've got to spend a few minutes in Intensive Care with Pierre. I promised I would when he came round from the anaesthetic at the end of his operation.'

'I'll come with you to make sure you don't stay too long. The intensive care staff are experts, you know, and the orthopaedic staff are also checking on our patient.'

'Oh, I know he's in good hands but a promise to a patient is a promise.'

He bent down, cupping her face in his hands and kissing her gently on the cheek. 'You're not becoming emotionally involved with a patient, are you, Doctor?'

She felt a fluttering of desire running through her body. That was only a chaste kiss, for heaven's sake. She moved to one side as the swing door opened and a nurse walked in.

'We can continue this discussion as we go along to see our patient,' Bernard said gravely, leading the way out into the corridor.

Sister in Intensive Care gave them a brief update on Pierre's condition as soon as they arrived. He was on continual intravenous infusions of blood and breathing normally now after the initial difficulties following the general anaesthetic.

'It was a long operation,' Bernard said. 'Has he asked for details?'

'He's still very confused and the morphine keeps him semi-sedated. But he'll be pleased to see you so that you can explain what you actually did.'

Julia picked up the notes. 'Let's go and see him.'

Pierre's eyes were closed and he was lying on his back. His injured leg was up on pillows, covered by a cradle.

'Pierre,' Julia said gently.

Their patient opened his eyes and a slow smile spread across his face.

'Thank you,' he whispered. 'You did save my leg, didn't you?'

'Yes, we did,' Bernard said.

'And my wife, *ma femme*?'

Sister smiled broadly. 'I was just coming to tell you. I've had a call from Obstetrics. You have a beautiful little daughter, Pierre. She's very tiny because of being premature so she'll need to stay in hospital for a few weeks.'

'Et ma femme?'

'Monique is very weak so she'll be staying in hospital for a while until her strength returns.'

'You'll all be in hospital for a while,' Julia said. 'We'll arrange who can visit who as soon as possible.'

Pierre breathed a deep sigh of contentment. 'You've all been so good to us.'

As they walked back down the corridor and out through the front door, Julia looked up at Bernard. When they'd left Intensive Care he'd waited while Julia popped back to her room to change and pack some nightclothes. She met him at the hospital entrance.

'It's at times like this I remember that I love being a doctor,' she said quietly, lengthening her stride to keep pace with him.

He took hold of her hand as they continued walking towards the car park.

She glanced around to see if anyone was watching.

'Don't worry,' he said, as if reading her mind. 'We're off duty. We can do anything we like.'

'Anything?'

He grinned. 'Why not?'

CHAPTER SEVEN

As BERNARD drove up the narrow, winding road that led to the top of the hill above St Martin sur Mer, Julia could feel herself relaxing already. She leaned back, studying Bernard's firm hands turning the steering-wheel as he negotiated one of the bends. A white sports car was coming towards them, a young couple laughing together as they passed within inches of their car, driving much too fast on that potentially dangerous section of the road.

Bernard eased off the accelerator just in time as he realised the other car was going to encroach on their side of the road. The blaring music from the young couple's car became fainter as it disappeared down the hill.

He breathed a sigh of relief as he continued up to the top of the hill. 'They wouldn't drive with such abandon if they'd seen the damage that sort of driving can do.'

'I was thinking exactly the same. Michel told me the multiple crash we assisted with was caused by a van driver using a mobile phone as he was overtaking a car. He lost control of his van, ploughed through the central barrier and vehicles piled up around him.'

'Including our Pierre and his wife,' Bernard said

quietly. 'I'm so relieved it was possible to save them. The result of good teamwork throughout the day— paramedics, nurses, doctors, everybody.'

He took a deep breath as the enormity of the events finally hit him now that he'd left hospital and was able to assess the situation.

His voice wavered with emotion when he spoke again. 'Pierre and Monique had only been married a few months and that precious baby was a much-wanted child.'

Julia swallowed hard. 'All babies are precious.'

Bernard could hear the gentle, emotional tone in her voice as she said this.

'You love babies, don't you?'

'Yes, of course I do.' She hesitated. 'I'd love to have my own baby. But not until the right time,' she added quickly. 'I need to feel I'm in charge of my own life first.'

He eased the car over the brow of the hill. 'Since you arrived I've sensed you're becoming more and more in charge.' He changed gear as the road flattened out. 'But, Julia, you mustn't be too inflexible. Who was it that said life is what happens when you're making other plans?'

Julia thought for a few moments. 'I don't know who said it but it's very true.'

They were sailing down the other side of the hill now, into the green, spring-awakened valley. She could feel the connection between them growing stronger by the minute.

She clenched her hands as the truth of everything that had happened since she'd met Bernard hit her. This was the sort of man she wanted in her life. She drew in her breath. This was the actual man she wanted in her life. But even as the realisation came to her she reminded herself that the timing wasn't right.

She'd planned to make a fresh start. This was why she'd left the old life behind. She shouldn't be thinking of veering off course. She'd done that before and look where that had landed her!

But she needn't change direction if she was careful. There was no harm in enjoying the present without taking too much thought about the future. She needed the fun and enjoyment of being with Bernard. He lifted her spirits. So, all things considered, she could make her present situation work…couldn't she?

As they drove through the farmyard gates, she determined to enjoy the evening whatever happened. She was going to focus on the present and let the future take care of itself for now.

Bernard switched off the engine and reached a hand across to take hold of hers. 'You're very quiet all of a sudden. What are you thinking?'

'I was thinking about how much I'm looking forward to seeing Philippe.'

A little whirlwind dashed out through the kitchen door, tearing towards the car.

Bernard laughed. 'You've got your wish.'

'Papa! Julia! I was waiting for you to arrive. Marianne! They're here.'

Bernard suggested the three of them have an early supper together at the kitchen table. He explained to Marianne that both he and Julia hadn't had time for lunch and also they both wanted to spend as much quality time with Philippe as possible before he went to bed.

The supper was a riotous success with Philippe excited and happy to have the undivided attention of two doting adults.

'Would you like some more pie, Philippe?'

Bernard was already slicing through the pastry to the succulent guinea fowl underneath in anticipation of his son's answer. Marianne's pie was a family favourite.

Philippe grinned and held out his plate. 'Yes, please.'

'You must have had a busy day to give you a good appetite like this.' Bernard put a generous slice on Philippe's plate.

'It was brilliant!' Philippe recounted the day's happenings, including feeding the hens, collecting the eggs still warm from the nests, helping Gaston mend a wall and milking the cows.

'And you helped me with the pastry,' Marianne said as she came in with a platter of cheeses from the larder and placed it on the sideboard. 'I'll leave this here, Bernard, for when you're ready for your cheese course. I've also left some desserts in the fridge, if you wouldn't mind helping yourselves. I'm going over to see my sister in the village tonight.'

'Of course, I remember now. It's her birthday. You should have reminded me and gone earlier. Thank you for this excellent supper. Go off and have a great evening.'

Julia came down to the kitchen after putting Philippe to bed to find that Bernard had finished clearing up.

The dishwasher was whirring away in the background as he came towards her and handed her a glass of wine.

She gave him a wry grin as she took the glass from his hands. 'I try to stick to the rule that I don't drink after supper if tomorrow is a work day.'

'Ah, rules were made to be broken. This is only a *digestif*. Something to round off a delightful dinner.' He raised his glass to his lips. 'Here's to good food, excellent wine and congenial company.'

She took a sip of her wine, feeling suddenly shy now that they were alone.

'How was Philippe when you left him?' he asked.

'Trying hard not to fall asleep before you've been up to see him.'

He put his glass down on the sideboard. 'Don't go away. Take your wine into the conservatory and I'll be back shortly. And, Julia...?'

'Yes?'

'Don't fall asleep. I know you must be tired but...'

She laughed. 'I've no intention of falling asleep.'

As she settled herself on the comfortable, squashy-cushioned sofa she knew she hadn't felt this happy for a long time. Yes, she would go with the flow again tonight. She'd seen enough misery during the day. She was going to seize the moment and not think about tomorrow. If Bernard held her in his arms tonight as he'd done last night, she was going to make sure that this time she gave him the right message. She wasn't going to let him give her a goodnight kiss and leave her languishing in her lonely bed, thinking about what might have been.

* * *

'Philippe's asleep,' Bernard whispered as he sat down beside her on the sofa a few minutes later, putting his arm around her and drawing her against him.

She could feel the instantaneous awakening of her whole body. In the short time he'd been away from her she'd been fighting against weariness. But as soon as she felt his arm around her she was totally wide awake. She could feel every fibre of her body quivering with anticipation as he bent his head and kissed her, oh, so gently. She parted her lips to savour the moment. His kiss deepened.

This was the first time he'd kissed her with such glorious abandon. She responded in equal measure. She gave an ecstatic moan as his hands began to caress her breasts. Deep down inside her she felt herself melting, becoming entirely sensual, fluid, unwilling and unable to control the rising desires inside her.

Suddenly he broke off and leaned back against the sofa. His breathing was ragged as he looked questioningly into her eyes.

'Julia, I want to make love to you so much but we need to discuss what this will mean to our relationship. I'd love to settle into a serious long-term relationship with you but I don't think that either of us could make the commitment necessary. You've got your career to think of and eventually you will want a husband and a family of your own. I'm not sure after my last experience that I will ever be able to offer that to you, and I know that would be a great disappointment to you.'

She hesitated. 'Yes, it would. You have your son. I've always wanted children when I've established my career. My first marriage was a disaster but I adored my stepchildren. It was so hard to walk away and never see them again.'

Her eyes misted over. Bernard moved closer again, taking hold of her hand and kissing the palm very gently. 'I want you to have the experience of your own children because you have so much maternal instinct to draw on. Philippe already adores you.'

'I know. Getting close to Philippe worries me in many ways. Not only will I miss him terribly when the course finishes and I have to return to London, I'm also concerned about him getting used to me being with you. After what he's experienced with his own mother, I'd hate to cause him any more upset.'

'We could have a compromise relationship, don't you think? A short-term affair while you're here in France?'

He put his arms around her, drawing her closer, his eyes probing hers, willing her to agree.

She gave him a gentle smile. 'I think a short no-commitment affair would be fun. We should live one day at a time, enjoy being together and not think too far ahead.'

'Oh, my darling Julia...'

His lips claimed hers and the passion of his embrace deepened.

Briefly, he paused and looked into her eyes, silently questioning if she wanted him as much as he wanted her.

'Yes, oh, yes,' she whispered.

He smiled, the most wickedly sexy smile she'd ever hoped to see on his handsome face as he scooped her up into his arms.

* * *

Julia opened her eyes and for a brief moment she felt unsure of her surroundings as she struggled to leave the dream she'd just enjoyed. Moonlight was flooding through the open window and there was a scent of roses, damp with dew. This room looked out over the garden.

And then she remembered. It hadn't been a dream. The lovemaking had all been real. The gentle caresses that had become more and more irresistible to her. Her own hands had explored that wonderful athletic, muscular body, longing for Bernard to take her completely. And then when she'd felt him inside her she'd felt completely at one with this wonderful man who had been taking her towards the ultimate ecstasy. They had climaxed together in a heavenly experience when they'd clung to each other, feeling that they would never be separated.

'Are you awake?'

She heard his deep, sexy voice from the other side of her pillow. They'd slept together, very, very close. His bed was enormous and there was space all around them.

Gently he pulled a crumpled sheet around her. She realised they were both naked. The rose-scented breeze had probably wakened her.

He raised himself up on one elbow, looking down at her with a heart-melting expression in his eyes that made her feel she was absolutely special to him.

'Your skin feels chilly,' he murmured, his hands roaming over her in the most tantalisingly erotic way.

For a brief moment she thought he might leave her and go across the room to close the window. But, no, he'd had a better idea!

She moaned with desire as he covered her body with his own. This time their lovemaking took her to heights of ecstasy she'd never imagined existed.

As they lay back against the pillows, their arms still around each other, she could feel her body tingling with the excitement of a joyful consummation.

'Are you still cold?' he whispered.

She laughed. 'I think we should both run barefoot on the dewy grass outside to cool off.'

'You look wonderful when you're totally abandoned. You should stay like this all the time, no problems, no rules…'

'No tomorrow,' she whispered, as she realised they were both longing to make love again…

It was the early morning sun shining in through the still open window that woke her up this time. And this time she knew immediately where she was because she was still clasped loosely in his arms. Mmm, what a night! It had definitely not been a dream. In her wildest dreams she could never have imagined all that. Maybe she'd died and gone to heaven.

So, what now?

CHAPTER EIGHT

JULIA switched off her computer. In the past few weeks since that idyllic night she'd spent with Bernard her life had revolved around work. He seemed intent on working through the syllabus in great detail, with her and the rest of the students using practical sessions in Theatre and theoretical tutorials.

Her mobile was ringing.

'Julia, are you free this evening?'

Was she free? If she wasn't she would make sure she cancelled whatever it was that stood between her and an evening with Bernard. She'd seen precious little of him recently in an off-duty situation and was beginning to think he regretted suggesting a short-term affair. Or maybe he just didn't have the time.

'I'll just check.' She paused just long enough to flick to the right page in her diary. Totally devoid of any social engagement. 'What did you have in mind?'

'I need to talk something over with you. Actually, I feel I owe you an explanation as to why I've been a bit distant recently.'

He paused and cleared his throat.

She waited. Was he going to explain why he'd seemed somewhat distracted whenever they'd been together?

He sounded unusually nervous when he spoke again. 'It was a pity I had that phone call from Gabrielle so early in the morning when you were staying with me. Having to take Philippe back to Paris that day wasn't what I'd planned but my ex-wife can be very difficult if she doesn't get her own way.'

She waited again as he paused, not wanting to interrupt the flow. She remembered she'd crept out of his bed and gone to the guest room early in the morning before anyone else had woken up. So she'd been surprised when Bernard announced at breakfast he had to take his son back to Paris and had cleared his commitments at the hospital for a couple of days. Michel would be in charge of his students—who, of course, included her—and he would give them on-the-spot tuition in the emergency department.

'Frederic, Gabrielle's future husband, wanted to legally clarify the situation on custody of Philippe, to make sure that he wasn't going to be involved in any way and that I was going to take charge of my son. It's been hell sorting everything out for the past few weeks. I don't know who's worse to deal with, Gabrielle or Frederic. They deserve each other! Anyway, are you free to have dinner with me this evening?'

'Yes…I'd love to.'

No point in hiding her feelings. He sounded much more like the man she'd found so intriguingly irresistible when she'd first arrived.

'Are you in your room?'

'Yes, I've been working.'

'I'll reserve a table at the hotel restaurant for eight o'clock. Meet me in Reception about half past seven.'

* * *

He breathed a sigh of relief as he put the phone down. The past few weeks had been difficult for him. Besides coping with Gabrielle and Frederic's demands, going over to Paris every weekend, he'd also been trying to sort out his feelings for Julia. He'd had to make sure he remained dispassionate about her in his professional dealings. The fact that he'd convinced himself he could handle a short-term relationship before they'd made love that night didn't make it any easier. The practicalities of a relationship between professor and student took some careful handling.

Also she'd had a disastrous marriage. He couldn't be flippant about any relationship that grew between them. It had to be what they both wanted. Now there were other practical considerations. With Philippe's imminent arrival it was going to be difficult for them to see each other. Julia had spoken the truth before as well—if she became an item in his life Philippe would come to regard her as a mother figure. He suspected he already did but to what extent he couldn't be sure. So if she walked out of their lives—as well she might now that her confidence had returned and she was very much in demand—his son's heart could be broken as well as his own!

The fact remained that they ultimately wanted different things out of life. She deserved a husband devoted to her and children of her own. Was he the man to take that risk again? He'd vowed to himself while he was going through the hell that Gabrielle had created during Philippe's early childhood that he would never have another child. Even though he adored Philippe he still remembered the problems associated with having

a baby. Could any partnership remain a loving relationship while the parents coped with the problems that
babies posed, especially career-minded parents battling
with everyday work situations?

He sighed as he went into the shower to prepare for
this important date. He'd decided he would stay in the
medics' quarters tonight and had brought a casual suit
to change into.

He was relieved to see her welcoming smile when he
went into Reception. He'd almost forgotten how beautiful she was when she wasn't shrouded in a white coat or
a green theatre gown, or else frowning over a problem
that needed explaining in a tutorial. She was wearing
some kind of silky-looking cream dress and heels. That
made a change from the T-shirt, jeans and trainers that
seemed to be standard uniform among his students.

He felt a flicker of desire running through him as
he noticed how sexy she looked with the dress accen-
tuating her slim figure yet clinging to the curves of her
breasts and hips.

He took a deep breath to steady his emotions as she
began to move towards him. She seemed to glide in
those strappy high-heeled sandals that made her ankles
look so slim. The skirt skimmed her knees, hiding those
fabulous thighs, which he knew were oh, so tantalising.

'Julia, you look stunning!'

He rested his hand on the back of her slim waist to
guide her out through the door, aware that they were
being watched by various members of staff. He would
reserve his kiss of welcome till later.

He raised his hand. 'I think that should be our taxi.'

Checking with the driver, he helped her inside. They sat slightly apart on the back seat as the taxi drove off towards the seafront.

Julia could feel her excitement mounting. Glancing sideways, she saw her handsome escort was watching her. She smiled at him. He moved closer, took hold of her hand and kissed her briefly on the lips.

Her fingers tingled as his hand closed around hers. Mmm, they were on course again! She didn't know where they'd been but she knew, or rather she hoped she knew, where they were going.

The hotel was one of the older buildings at the far end of St Martin's seafront. She remembered reading about it in a good-food guide. It certainly looked like a very smart sort of place from the outside.

A uniformed man came to open the car door for her as Bernard was paying off the cab. Inside the ambience was relaxed and welcoming. They were shown into the dining room with a small discreet bar near the entrance. Their table by the window was ready. She sat down, her eyes catching a glimpse of the darkening sky over the sea. The sun had already dipped into the sea and the pink and blue twilight seemed so romantic.

She looked across the table at Bernard, her heart brimming with emotion, feeling so close to him again. He was ordering a bottle of champagne.

'What are we celebrating?'

He smiled. 'The end of an era.'

She gave him a questioning look.

'I'll tell you when the champagne arrives...ah, here we are.' He was glancing at the label. 'Fine. Yes, open it, please.'

The popping of the cork, the fizzing in her glass. She was intrigued, impatient for him to enlighten her.

'Here's to the future,' he said enigmatically, holding his glass towards hers. 'I've finally settled everything with Gabrielle and Frederic but it's been difficult dealing with them. They're going to be married next week and Philippe is safely tucked up in bed at the farm. Marianne is over the moon to have him finally living back home where he should be.'

'So, what was the problem?'

'Problems!' he corrected her. 'Where shall I start? Everything had to be legally sanctioned as regards Philippe. Gabrielle wanted him to be privately educated but I insisted I wanted him to have the same upbringing I'd had out here at the village school. I want him to enjoy the countryside. To bring his friends back to the farm whenever he wants to.'

'What did Gabrielle think of that idea?'

'Well, of course, neither she nor Frederic want to be involved in bringing him up themselves but they wanted him to be taken each day to a private school about twenty kilometres from the village where he would mix with "decent children," was how she described it to me. She pointed out that she wanted him to have the best education possible so he would be a success in life.'

Julia watched him take a drink from his glass, noticing the perspiration on his brow and the set of his jaw as he swallowed hard. It hadn't been an easy time for him, she surmised.

He put down his glass. 'I pointed out that Philippe had set his heart on being a surgeon like me and the village school had given me a good education, preparing me for eventual admission to the excellent lycée in Montreuil.'

'Did that satisfy her?'

'Well, Frederic and I had to convince her that the medical profession was well regarded. She pointed out that we'd had money problems when we were first married. I explained that the early days of a profession are always difficult financially but unless Philippe becomes hampered by a difficult marital relationship—as I was—he would be a success.'

'I bet you enjoyed saying that to her!'

'I certainly did. It also shut her up. She didn't want me to start making revelations to Frederic of how she'd made my life hell when we were first married. Oh, the poor man doesn't know what he's in for. I actually feel sorry for him. Still, it's not my problem any more!'

He smiled across the table at her. 'Anyway, let's order. What are you going to have, Julia?'

She picked up the menu that the waiter had left with her. She chose moules marinières as a starter, followed by a locally caught fish, with added prawns.

'This is pure nostalgia for me, Bernard. As a child I loved the fish dishes I ate when we were here on holiday—unlike my brothers, who always asked for steak frites.'

'Ah, yes, there used to be a small wooden café on the edge of the beach that served the most delicious steak and chips.'

'That's the one!'

They relaxed into their memories of St Martin sur

Mer, which they both agreed had been an idyllic place for children.

'It still is,' Bernard said. 'And the surrounding countryside is the healthiest environment to bring up a child. You've no idea what a relief it is for me to know that Philippe will breathe in clean air every day when he goes to school instead of fumes from traffic.'

'You're very lucky.'

'I am now,' he said, his voice husky.

He reached across the table and squeezed her hand. She felt desire rising up inside her. Did he mean what she hoped he meant?

Their meal was beautifully served. They took their time, caught up once more in their conversation, which flowed so easily.

Bernard told the waiter they would take coffee on the terrace. He took her hand as they went out of the dining room and relaxed in the cushioned wicker chairs by a small table overlooking the sea.

He was intensely aware that this was the first time they'd been alone since they'd made love on that idyllic night they'd spent together. It had been almost too perfect for him. She could be the woman of his dreams, but there were so many reasons why he had to be careful with her.

He took a sip of his coffee. 'You know, you've changed a great deal since you first arrived, Julia.'

'Have I?'

'You've become much more confident and your confidence seems to grow day by day.'

'I'm certainly enjoying the course...in an exhausting kind of way. So much work to get through and then the exams looming at the end of it all.'

'I don't think you need to worry. Hard work plus natural talent for your chosen profession will bring success.' He paused, trying to make his question sound as innocent as possible. 'What have you planned to do after the exams?'

The question, out of the blue, threw her completely. 'Well, I'd planned to go back to London. Don arranged for me to have a six-month sabbatical from the orthopaedic department. I enjoy my work there and it's a good springboard from which to climb higher up the ladder, either in my own hospital or wherever a promotion should arise. I've always been ambitious but...'

He waited, watching her struggle to find the right words. He sensed what she would say even before she spoke again.

'I can't help my longing to have a child, well, a whole family really. And fitting that in with the demanding career I've also set my heart on is confusing. I'm really beginning to appreciate my parents' dilemma. I wonder if I'll have time to fit in everything I want to do with my life.'

He watched her trying to deal with the conflicting thoughts running through her mind. Since telling Julia he wasn't sure about being able to marry again and have more children, he'd had time to think. Marriage and parenting with Julia would be a totally different experience from what he'd had with Gabrielle. If they split the responsibilities fifty-fifty, they could both continue their careers.

But such a situation would require total commitment

to each other as well as the child. Marriage really was the only way. But if he told her he'd changed his mind about children and asked her to marry him, would she agree simply to have him father a child? He had to be sure she loved him first and foremost before he thought so far ahead.

That was why he'd needed some space from her after falling so hopelessly in love during that night they'd spent together at the farm. The struggles he'd endured with his ex-wife and her new partner had given him time to think about his relationship with Julia.

She was watching his serious expression. 'You're very quiet. Is something troubling you?'

'No, definitely not. Except…' He took a deep breath, almost frightened to say what was on his mind. His feelings were intense and raw, he could even feel them manifesting themselves in every part of his vibrantly awakening body. Would she feel the same way?

'Will you excuse me for a moment?'

He was already walking back into the dining room. She sat very still. Through the open door she could see him talking to the head waiter and decided he was paying the bill.

Darkness had fallen. She looked out across the bright lights beside the seafront. There were palm trees planted at the edge of the beach, which looked wonderful in summer but took a beating sometimes during the winter.

She was so captivated by the view that she didn't notice him come back to the terrace. He took her hands and drew her to her feet. He was grinning in a boyish, mischievous way.

'I've got the option on the bridal suite for tonight. I thought it would be a perfect place to relax at the end of our busy day. You won't have to creep out before dawn so as to avoid being seen in my bed either. A discreet chambermaid will bring breakfast in bed too, if you'd like. What do you say?'

She giggled. 'I'd say you'd gone mad. Why the bridal suite?'

'Because that's the only room vacant tonight.'

'Oh, don't spoil it. I thought you wanted to lavish loads of money on me because I'm worth it.'

If she only knew! He wasn't going to tell her the real truth—that there actually were a couple of much cheaper rooms available.

'So, you're happy to stay here?'

'I'd love to check out the bridal suite. I've never slept in anything like a bridal suite in my life.'

He put his arm around her waist and led her to the door. 'Who said anything about sleeping?'

She really was confused this time when she awoke in the middle of the night. At first she thought she was in Bernard's bed at the farm. His head was certainly on the edge of her pillow. She put out her hand to touch the thick, dark hair. And then she remembered.

The first and last time they'd spent the night together had been fabulous but this time…! Her body was still tingling with the most consummately passionate experience…or was it experiences? They had been in each other's arms from the moment they'd stepped across the threshold of this sumptuously exotic room.

By the time she'd reached the top of the stairs with

his arm around her waist her legs had turned to jelly. Every fibre of her body had been crying out for his love-making, his wonderful, creative, heavenly lovemaking.

He opened his eyes and smiled his slow, sexy smile that told her the night was still young. They had hours and hours before daybreak and reality. When they would both try to come back to earth. But for the moment there was no tomorrow...

Julia said that, yes, she would love to have breakfast in their room when he asked her.

He picked up the bedside phone in one hand and reached for her with the other. 'Oh, no, you don't escape this time. Room service, please. We'd like to order two breakfasts please to room... Oh, great, thank you.'

He put down the phone. 'They knew we were in the bridal suite. We didn't make that much noise, did we?'

She laughed. 'I don't remember.'

'Oh, well, in that case, let me remind you...'

'Not now. What about the chambermaid?'

'Oh, never mind the chambermaid.'

'I'm going for a quick shower.'

'Spoilsport,' he said carefully in English.

She waved a towel at him from the door to the bath-room. 'Your English is definitely improving. You must have a good teacher.'

'And your surgical skills aren't too bad either since you found yourself a good teacher.'

'Sorry, what was that?'

'Not important.'

He settled back against the pillows to await her return, feeling blissfully happy with the way things had gone since his sudden daring idea to take a room here. If he could ever be sure that she really and truly loved him for himself and didn't just regard him as a baby maker, he would ask her to marry him. He'd been very careful to ensure she knew he believed in using a condom. An unplanned pregnancy wasn't what either of them needed.

But what about his dread of going through the early days of a new baby? Even the most loving relationship must be affected. His parents had survived and remained in love, but would he and Julia be able to replicate that when they were both ambitious and in difficult and demanding work situations?

For the moment Julia needed to concentrate on her work at the hospital and her exams. But a little light relief in her off-duty time would help to relax her and prevent too much tension, wouldn't it? He smiled to himself as he heard the taps had stopped flowing in the bathroom. She would soon be back in his bed and he would be able to check she wasn't becoming tense again.

There was a knock at the door. He'd have to wait.

Groaning with frustration, he rose to admit the waiter...

CHAPTER NINE

THE summer was moving along too quickly. As she switched off her computer Julia realised that they were more than halfway through the surgical syllabus that Bernard had set for them.

She got up from her chair and walked across her small room, which was now so familiar. It had become home to her and apart from the occasional night up at the farm this was where she'd lived all the time.

And there'd been that completely heavenly night in the bridal suite! She would never forget that. She was beginning to think it might have been a one-off but she hoped not.

She bent to straighten the sheet on her bed, which was exactly as she'd left it that morning before she'd gone down for a practical tutorial in Theatre. As she leaned across the bed to take hold of the sheet she decided to lie down and take a short break before the evening. It had been a long day, a hot day apart from her time in Theatre when Bernard had insisted the air-conditioning be turned up to full.

She stared up at the ceiling. He'd seemed sort of tetchy today. He often seemed a bit irritable when he was teaching and operating at the same time. She could understand it. She could well imagine how she would feel if she had to do the same. Maybe that would happen when she became a more qualified and experienced surgeon.

The life of a surgeon was a demanding one for sure. No wonder Bernard seemed like two people sometimes. There was the man who could relax when they were together. Ah, she loved him so much when they were alone! But she worried about him when he was working. Was that natural when she wasn't sure where this relationship was going? Worrying about her man with a kind of wifely instinct? Also worrying about his child, who was becoming more and more attached to her every time she saw him?

Her mobile was ringing. Maybe it was Bernard, cancelling their date for tomorrow. It had happened when he'd told her there was an emergency he had to deal with.

'Julia, are you free this evening?'

She sat up, alert and excited by this turn of events.

'Yes; just finished writing up this morning's op. Do you think you could explain that new way you demonstrated of closing up the patient? When I was writing it up just now I—'

'Of course I'll explain but not now. I've just finished so I'm driving home in ten minutes. I thought we could all make an early start together on our day off tomorrow. Can you make it?'

'Yes, but I'll need to pack a bag. Where are we going tomorrow?'

'Oh, let's decide this evening. See you in ten, OK?'

She leapt off the bed and started throwing things

into her overnight bag. Typical Bernard! He could be so impulsive at times—like booking them into the bridal suite.

She forced her mind not to think about that particular occasion because she wouldn't be ready in ten minutes if she did. She could think about that later when they were alone in his bed.

He smiled and came towards her as she arrived in Reception.

'Well done! I knew you could do it.'

'Why the rush?'

'No reason. Just impatient to leave my daytime self behind and put on my off-duty persona.'

He put a hand on her back as they walked out towards the staff parking area.

'Ah, so you admit you're a different person in hospital from the impulsive man you can be off duty?'

'Absolutely! Guilty as charged. And to think you noticed!'

'Difficult not to.' She got into the passenger seat.

Bernard closed her door and went round to the driver's side. He started the engine and then placed a hand over hers. 'Which of my personalities do you prefer?'

She smiled up at him, feeling the familiar stirrings of desire simply by being close to him.

'Definitely the off-duty man. The other one can be a bit of a temperamental tyrant when he's in Theatre.'

He bent his head and kissed her on the lips. Drawing away slightly he murmured, 'Ah, so you noticed? It's only an act I put on to keep the students on their toes.'

'Well, this student was certainly on her toes today.'

'I noticed. That's good!'

He put the car in gear and moved out towards the front gates. 'So the work's going well, is it?'

'Exceptionally well. If you could give me a few minutes' private tuition tonight on that point I mentioned when you phoned?'

'Oh, I can certainly give you my full attention later on when we're alone.' He changed gear as they began a steep ascent.

She felt her body reacting already to the thought of the night ahead and she sensed he was in a similar mood. His voice had been definitely sexy as he'd said 'when we're alone'. She couldn't wait for the personal tuition.

Sitting around the kitchen table with the excitable Philippe chattering to her, she relaxed completely.

Marianne had bought mussels from the fish merchant who delivered to the village on Fridays and she'd been delighted when Bernard had phoned to say that Julia was coming that evening. The housekeeper placed the steaming, aromatic dish of moules marinières in front of them now.

'Bernard, I think this is one of Julia's favourite dishes, am I right?'

'Marianne, you're amazing!' Julia said. 'You remembered!'

'Well, it's my favourite, also,' Philippe said. 'May I have that big one there, Papa?'

'Of course!'

Bernard beamed round the table, a feeling of total happiness descending upon him. This was how every working week should end. Sitting at the table with his son and his beautiful, talented...what was Julia to him exactly? Certainly he shouldn't take anything for granted. There was nothing permanent about the situation, even though he wished it could go on for ever.

He glanced across at her and saw she was watching him with those eyes that sometimes looked so questioning, as if she wasn't sure of something, as well she might be. She was the most wonderful woman he'd ever met but he still couldn't allow himself to think of her as being a permanent fixture in his life. He still felt unsure of the future. There were still so many problems to iron out before he could be sure she would always be there.

Bernard put the pencil down on his notepad. 'So, does that answer your question?'

'Yes it does, Professor. That's what I put in my notes but I had to be sure.'

He gave her a sexy grin. 'So may I forget my academic commitment to a demanding student and relax again, Dr Montgomery?'

She giggled as he put his arms around her and drew her into their first embrace of the evening. They were still downstairs in the conservatory but they were alone at last with the whole of the night ahead of them.

'Marianne has put your things in the guest room,' he said solemnly.

'Do you think she understands the situation?'

'Well, if she does understand what's going on, she's more clued up than I am,' he said enigmatically.

He took a deep breath. 'Of course she assumes we sleep together at the beginning of the night...well, not so much sleep but… Yes, of course she understands the situation. She also understands that you creep along to the guest room in the early hours before Philippe wakes up.' He hesitated. 'You don't have to do that, you know.'

'I just feel that…it's simpler this way. I don't want to confuse him.'

Bernard drew in his breath. He surmised she didn't want it to be taken for granted that she would always be there. She'd come out to France to make a new start, hadn't she? That had been her initial idea. Now that she'd found her confidence, she may well decide to spread her wings and fly away at the end of the course. She had the whole of her life in front of her. He must never take her for granted.

He drew her closer in his arms. 'Let's go to bed.'

Their lovemaking had been unbelievably tender. Afterwards he held her in his arms so tightly it had almost been as if he was going to keep her there, safe, in the place she loved to be. But there was something different tonight. She sensed a certain melancholy in the moment.

Bernard lay with his arms around her, trying not to dispel the mood. Their consummation had been heavenly as always but almost immediately afterwards reality had forced itself upon him. This relationship was all too good to be true so far. He wanted to make it go on for ever…but only if that was what she wanted. He couldn't burden her with the question of commitment to him when she was coming up to the difficult weeks before the exams and the end of the course.

And he could definitely not bring up the subject of

babies. If he told her he was beginning to think he'd love to father a baby with her, how could he be sure it would be him she wanted or a baby? She could be very loving, but so had Gabrielle been when she'd wanted her own way.

But the wounds of his suffering still hadn't healed properly. The thought of spoiling their idyllic relationship by commitment, pregnancy and a small baby to care for, along with dual careers in surgery, was a very daunting one. Julia had come over to France to make a fresh start on her own. Did he have the right to impose a different kind of life on her? He couldn't bear to spoil the brilliant future that lay ahead of someone so talented.

Julia woke in the early morning and stretched out her hand under the sheet. Bernard wasn't there. Of course he wasn't. She'd made an early departure from his bed last night. He'd seemed tired, less communicative after they'd made love, so she'd decided to come along here to the guest room to get a whole night's sleep before their day out.

He'd kissed her tenderly, lovingly when she'd explained, but he'd seemed somewhat distant, as if he was standing outside their relationship and being totally dispassionate. Maybe she should have asked him if he was worrying about something but she'd sensed he wouldn't have told her. He could be a very private person when he wanted to be. But she loved him, oh, how she loved every facet of his enigmatic character.

She sighed as she switched on the bedside light. Almost seven o'clock. The little whirlwind would come charging in soon.

Bernard had heard Philippe chattering to Julia in the guest room. He'd woken very early today, which was unusual. Last night had been wonderful, holding her in his arms, making love to her, knowing they would be together today. He wasn't going to worry about where their relationship was going. He would simply accept that they made each other happy and now wasn't the time to think too far ahead.

'So where are we going today, Papa?'

Philippe stretched his little arm across the table. Bernard reached forward and wiped away some of the jam and croissant crumbs that had collected on the palm of his son's hand with his napkin. Then he gave the still sticky hand a squeeze.

'Would you like to go out in the boat?'

'Yes, oh, yes, let's go in the boat, Papa! Out to the island?'

As Bernard steered his boat across the sea he could feel the cares of the past week disappearing. He could hear Philippe chattering happily to Julia, who was pointing out landmarks on the now distant shore. She too seemed happy to be out in the boat, reminiscing with his son about her childhood holidays in this area.

'Oh, we didn't have our own boat,' Julia was explaining to Philippe. 'We didn't live over here in France so my father used to hire one sometimes. My brothers always wanted to steer it and I was always the last to have a go…and then only under strict supervision.'

'What's supervision?'

'It's when a grown-up watches you the whole time you're holding onto the wheel and—'

'Papa, will you supervision me while I'm steering the boat? Or Julia could supervision me, couldn't she?'

Bernard turned, one hand still on the wheel. 'Pass me that wooden box. If you stand on that, I'll supervise you while you hold on to the wheel. At least we've got a clear route ahead of us. Nothing for you to bump into at the moment.'

Julia helped Philippe onto the box and stood at the other side of him while Bernard kept a light hand on the wheel.

'No need to turn the wheel, Philippe. We're going straight ahead towards that island.'

'That's our island, isn't it, Papa?'

'Technically, no, but…'

'What's technically?'

'We don't own it but we're allowed to go there.'

'But we've been there lots of times so we can pretend it's ours.'

Bernard stooped and planted a kiss on his son's head. 'We can pretend anything we like today.'

His eyes met Julia's as he raised his head. He could feel a lump rising in his throat as he saw the wistful expression in her eyes. Did she feel the same way as he did about the day ahead? Just the three of them, pretending to be a family?

As they neared the shore, Julia helped Philippe down off the box again so that Bernard had full control of the boat. As they reached the shallows she took over the wheel, as they'd discussed, so that Bernard could jump out and tie up the mooring rope.

'I always wanted to tie up,' she said to Philippe. 'But my brothers got there first. My father would be steering the boat and my mother holding tightly to my hand.'

'It's more fun being a boy, I think.'

'Well, I did used to think my older brothers had a lot of fun. But I always had fun too.' She was holding the young boy's hand as they stepped barefoot into the shallows, holding their sandals so they didn't get wet.

Bernard was holding out his hand to take their sandals as they reached the shore. They walked up the beach to settle themselves under the shade of the trees. Bernard started bringing their things from the boat.

Philippe was already stripped off and running into the sea. He'd insisted on wearing his swimming trunks from the moment he'd got dressed that morning.

'Come on!' he shouted happily.

'Is the sea warm?' Julia asked as she stripped to the bikini she was wearing under her shorts.

'Very hot, hot, hot. Come and try it.'

'OK, I will.'

Bernard took hold of her hand. 'It's going to be a scorcher today.'

She revelled in the touch of his fingers enclosing hers. 'Last time I was here it rained all day and we played under the trees, wearing our mackintoshes.'

He drew her closer, feeling a frisson of desire at the closeness of her bikini-clad figure. 'How old were you?'

'It was years ago! I don't remember. I...' She glanced

at the small boy in the sea. 'We'd better go and supervise Philippe.'

Bernard laughed. 'Supervise seems to be the word of the day. I'm glad there's nobody to supervise you and me today. I'm feeling positively reckless.'

She laughed as, still holding her hand tightly, he set off down the beach.

'If only the rest of your students could see you now, Professor!'

'Papa, there are some little fish nibbling at my toes. Look, look, they're everywhere in the water. Julia, come here, can you see them? What are they?'

'Well, my English father used to call them sticklebacks. My French mother simply called them little fish, like you do.' She wiggled her toes. 'They tickle, don't they?'

'Let's swim, Papa. I can swim, Julia. Watch me!'

One each side of him, he proudly swam out towards the deeper water. 'We won't go too far out,' Bernard said to Julia as they swam alongside. 'Philippe loves swimming but he'd go on swimming till he felt tired. He forgets he's got to go back.'

'Yes, but you always put me on your chest, Papa.'

'See what I mean?'

Bernard's arm brushed against hers. The water further out was colder than nearer the shore but even so she felt a warm glow stealing over her. Just being close to him in any situation was one of the joys of their relationship. Again she found herself wondering how long they could be together like this before decisions about the future had to be made. Well, there were no decisions to be made today. Enjoying the moment was her primary concern.

'Time to go back.' Bernard steered the other two around so that they were all swimming back towards the shore.

Bernard had brought everything they needed for a barbecue. He quickly built up the sides with the large stones they'd gathered and got the fire going underneath before placing the metal rack over it.

'I've never tasted such delicious chicken drumsticks,' Julia said, tearing at a piece with her teeth. She looked across at Bernard, who'd just put more chicken on to grill. 'Mmm, you must be a very experienced chef, sir.'

'Papa always cooks lunch when we come here. Why does lunch taste much better out in the open air than inside, Julia?'

She laughed. 'Good question! I've often wondered about it.'

Bernard dropped some more food on Philippe's plate. 'On this particular island it's because we've all been swimming, which is marvellous for inducing an appetite, and the sun is shining through the trees and we're all happy.'

'And we're going to stay here all night in Papa's tent and wake up in the morning to start swimming as soon as the sun comes up.'

'Oh, not this time, Philippe. I didn't bring the tent. Anyway, it wouldn't be big enough for three of us.'

'Yes, it would! Julia and I don't take up very much room, do we? Well, do we really need a tent? It's warm enough to sleep here under the trees.'

Philippe snuggled up to Julia, wiping his sticky hands on a nearby patch of grass. 'You'd like to stay here, wouldn't you, Julia? I bet you stayed here all night when you were here on holiday, didn't you?'

'No, I'm afraid we didn't. Why don't you just close your eyes now, pretend it's night-time and have a short sleep? You look sleepy to me.'

Philippe stared at her. 'How did you know I feel sleepy?'

'Because you got up very early and you've had a busy day that included a long swim. That's always exhausting.'

She was already tucking a dry towel around the small boy and lowering her voice. He snuggled closer into her side. 'You will wake me, won't you, Julia? I don't want to wake up and find it's all dark and I've missed the rest of the day. It's such a nice day. I don't want to miss anything. Don't leave me, Julia…'

His voice drifted away as his breathing steadied and his eyelids drooped.

Watching her, Bernard felt the urge to put his arms round his two favourite people and keep them here with him for ever. He could build a camp here under the trees and blot out the rest of the world and its problems. What a wonderful mother Julia would make when she had children of her own. But she was also born to be a talented surgeon. He forced himself away from the problem. Today they belonged together and the future was the future, something to think about tomorrow.

He sat down on the sandy, grassy slope and reached towards her, careful not to disturb his son sleeping nearby, visible to them through the long grassy fronds.

Lowering his head, he kissed her gently on the lips. His kiss deepened. She clung to him, aware of the poignancy of this tender moment. One day in a family situation with Bernard had made her sure of what she wanted in life—career and motherhood, hand in hand. If she could have both options with Bernard that would be perfect. But there were so many obstacles to clear before that could happen. Could she convince Bernard to take a chance on them?

He was pulling her to her feet, leading her to a shadier spot a short way into the trees.

'It's OK, we can see Philippe from here. He's exhausted so he'll sleep until we wake him up.'

She couldn't dispute that even if she'd wanted to, which she didn't! Her passion and desires were rising up inside her as his hands caressed her into a mounting frenzy of uninhibited lovemaking.

Only as she felt the onset of her climax did she attempt to stifle the moans that were rising in her throat. She mustn't cry out, mustn't wake the sleeping child…

'Julia, it's time to wake up.'

She opened her eyes to see Bernard kneeling beside her. The sun was slanting down in the sky. She glanced across at the still sleeping Philippe.

'How long have we been asleep?'

He gave her a sexy grin. 'Too long. There's a boat coming over. Look. I've started packing up. Would you wake Philippe?'

As she sat at supper much later that night in the kitchen, she knew she would remember this day for the rest of her life. Whatever happened in the future, the days, months and years of uncertainty stretching ahead of them, she would never forget what a blissful day she'd enjoyed before she had to go back to reality and deal with the problems that lay ahead.

CHAPTER TEN

THE end of the course was fast approaching and exams were looming. Concerned as she was about the state of her relationship with Bernard, Julia was just as worried about her performance in these tests. Succeeding at this course had been her reason for coming to France. Bernard had proved a delicious distraction.

As the warm water from the shower cascaded over her body she allowed herself to look back on those halcyon days of high summer when Bernard had taken her out in his boat to 'their' island. Mostly Philippe had been with them, which was always fun. On two occasions he'd been in Paris for the weekend, staying with his grandmother who was always asking for a visit. So they'd gone alone to the island, sleeping overnight in the small cabin on the boat.

She sighed as she patted herself dry with her towel. For the last couple of weeks it had been nose to the grindstone the whole time, revision for the written exams and preparation for practical theatre work. There wasn't much she could do about preparing for the viva voce where a panel of examiners would ask her questions. Either she would satisfy them with her answers or she wouldn't.

She glanced out of the window as she finished dressing. The branches of the tall oak tree at the side of the hospital garden were being buffeted around by a high wind. The leaves had turned an autumnal gold in the past week and some of them had been blown away already. Here in the hospital, where the air-conditioning had been switched to central heating, she would be warm.

After a quick coffee and croissant in the cafeteria, she made her way along the corridor to the orthopaedic ward to see the patient she was to operate on that morning. This was the part she really enjoyed; meeting with the patient, the human aspect of surgery. When he was anaesthetised on the table the situation would change. Especially this morning when there would be an examiner watching her every move.

'Good morning, Vincent. How are you?'

Her patient, a middle-aged man who looked younger than his age and had told her he still wished he could play football, smiled broadly as she arrived at his bedside.

'I'm good, thank you. But I will be happier when the surgery is over.'

She patted his hand in sympathy, secretly thinking exactly the same as he did. How happy she'd be when the operation was over!

'I just called in to check you're OK about everything. We really do appreciate you giving your consent to allow your operation to be assessed by an examiner and performed by someone who is currently qualified to do the surgery but aiming for a higher qualification.'

'Of course it's my pleasure! I'm happy to be of service to the hospital in any way I can. Professor Bernard explained to me about... Ah, but here he is.'

Julia glanced up and saw that Bernard had joined them. 'Hello, Vincent, hello, Julia. Yes, I've explained the exam situation to Vincent.'

Vincent pulled himself up against his pillows. 'Yes, I know I'm in capable hands. Dr Julia will do my knee replacement, with a more senior surgeon by her side, who I hope will be you, Professor.'

Bernard smiled. 'Yes, that's correct. Theoretically I could intervene and take over if I felt it necessary. But in this case I'm sure that won't happen. I've worked with Dr Julia many times and she is exceptionally experienced and talented.'

Vincent gave him a cheeky grin. 'And also very beautiful!'

The two men laughed together boyishly.

'Without doubt,' Bernard said, his eyes meeting with Julia's. 'Beauty isn't a prerequisite for a surgeon but I think it helps the patient to be cared for by someone beautiful on the morning of their operation.'

To her dismay she could feel a blush rising on her cheeks as her eyes met his. 'I was just about to check that the results of all our pre-op investigations will be made available to the examiner.'

'You're in charge,' Bernard said solemnly. 'I'll leave you to it.'

She was carrying copies of her patient's notes as she left the ward some time later. Everything was in order. The left knee had been prepared for surgery. The paperwork concluded. The results of Pierre's blood tests were to hand. No problems with his haemoglobin or electrolyte balance. He was a man in excellent health apart from the knee injury, which he'd told her had meant he couldn't play football any more, not even for the local team in his village.

As soon as she walked into Theatre a feeling of confidence and capability flooded through her. She was vaguely aware of a stranger at the back of the room who was obviously the examiner. But there was no reason for that to make any difference to her performance. She'd performed a total knee replacement before. No need to worry about the outcome.

The anaesthetist nodded. Everything was OK with the patient's breathing under the anaesthetic.

With a steady, sterile, gloved hand she took the scalpel she'd asked for from Bernard and made the first incision.

'How did it go?'

She looked up at Dominic, her fellow student, who was walking towards her in the corridor as she tried to slip away for a desperately needed coffee at the end of the operation.

She stopped to chat to him. He looked terribly worried and nervous.

'It went well. No need to worry. You'll be fine. I was introduced to the examiner at the end. He was absolutely charming but he gave nothing away.'

'Didn't you ask him how you'd done?'

'Of course I didn't! Bernard's talking to him now. I needed to get away. You're on this afternoon, aren't you?'

'Can't wait!' he said gloomily. 'Can't wait till it's all over.'

'Have you got a nice, co-operative patient?'

He smiled. 'Oh, she's very nice. Couldn't be more helpful. And I know I can do a good job. I'm just on my way to check on her. Thanks for the pep talk, Julia. Just one more question.'

'Yes?'

He hesitated. 'Will you be staying on in France or going back to England once this course is over?'

She drew in her breath. 'I'm still not sure. My consultant in England is waiting for me to let him know. He's still under the impression I'll be rejoining the orthopaedic firm.'

Dominic grinned. 'And your consultant in France is hoping you'll stay here?'

'No comment! Good luck!'

She turned and walked away. She had to make a decision soon about what she should do. But she was still not sure where Bernard stood on their future and she was afraid to ask. She knew she wanted to continue with her career but she also wanted to continue her affair with Bernard. If he would only put into words how he felt about her. Give her hope that their affair could become more permanent…possibly leading to marriage?

She walked on, head down so that she could think without having to break off and talk to someone. Marriage would be a step too far for Bernard. He didn't want children and she did. Could she persuade him to change his mind about that? But then he might think she only wanted him to father a child, wouldn't he?

She banished the thoughts from her head. If only Dominic hadn't opened up all her doubts and fears about where she and Bernard were heading. Perhaps she should phone Don in London and talk it over with him. And if Bernard was still keeping her guessing she'd book a seat on the train and go back to London. Couldn't do any harm. It might even make Bernard tell her how he really felt about her.

Her confidence about her career prospects continued to grow as the exam period continued. It had been a couple of weeks since she'd operated on Vincent and he'd made excellent post-operative progress. In fact, the orthopaedic consultant in charge of his outpatient care had told her earlier that day that he'd seen him in his clinic, walking extremely well with the aid of a stick in physiotherapy. The consultant had told her he wouldn't need the stick for much longer.

Yes, she was delighted with the news. And also relieved that the other operation she'd performed under examination, which had been the required emergency operation, had also gone very well.

She'd known that she was theoretically on call for the whole of the examination period except when she was actually doing a written exam, doing an exam operation or taking the viva voce. She'd been relieved that when the actual emergency call had come she'd been well rested after a good night's sleep in her room and ready to spring into action.

As soon as the call had come from Michel in *Urgences*, asking her to go immediately to Theatre where an emergency case and an examiner were waiting for her, she'd felt herself to be on top form. A teenage girl had been rescued from a burning car. Unable to move from the damaged passenger seat, she'd been pulled out by her friends through the side window. Her patient's ankle was badly shattered as part of the engine had smashed through the front of the car, crushing her foot.

Quickly assessing that she would have to pin the ankle to realign the shattered bone, she'd simply got on with the job, hardly aware until later that she'd been examined.

After that, the written exams hadn't caused her any problems. Everything in the syllabus had been covered by the questions, which meant there was a variety of choice.

Her phone was ringing. 'How did the viva voce go this morning?'

'Bernard, I thought you would know more than I do!'

'Well, if I did I wouldn't be asking, would I?'

'And if you did you wouldn't be telling either! Oh, the distinguished panel were very civil, very cool, didn't ask me anything I couldn't answer. All in all I actually enjoyed it.'

'Good! You haven't forgotten the party tonight, have you?'

'Of course not.' She sprang off the bed and dashed over to her wardrobe, flinging wide the door. 'I hadn't forgotten but I'm running late. What would you like me to wear?'

'How about that sexy nightdress you brought with you the last time you were here?'

'Oh, you mean that flimsy bit of silk I picked up in the boutique on the seafront? It's still in the bag it came in, as well you know. One day I'll wear it—when I'm allowed to take it out of the packaging!'

'I thought there wasn't much point when I was only going to take it off as soon as you got within reach.'

She heard him chuckling down the line. That was more like the Bernard she knew and loved. The last few weeks had been a tense time for both of them with little time for frivolous exchanges that had nothing to do with exams.

'I'll drive you over to the farm in about half an hour. OK?'

'Fine! How are my fellow students getting out?'

'I've paid for a minibus there and back. I don't want to have to worry about drunk driving amongst my students. I want everybody to enjoy themselves now that the exams are finished.'

Marianne had done them proud! As Julia surveyed the buffet supper the housekeeper had laid on for them she felt she had to quietly congratulate her.

'Oh, I enjoyed it, Julia,' Marianne said as they whispered together in the kitchen. 'And two of my friends from the village came out to help me.'

'They're the ladies who were serving drinks earlier, I presume? Honestly, Marianne, I would have been out to help you today but I didn't finish my last exam until this morning.'

'Julia, I didn't expect you to help when you've been so busy at the hospital. Bernard told me you were giving all your energy to the exam. That's why we haven't seen you out here for a while. Philippe was so excited when he knew you were coming. And I'm glad you read his bedtime story before he went to sleep. I'd hoped you'd give him some time.'

'I've missed him so much. I just love him to bits. He's...very special.'

Marianne gave her a searching look. 'He feels exactly the same about you, Julia.'

Julia swallowed hard. She knew the implication was that she shouldn't take that love lightly, that she shouldn't break a young boy's heart. Now that she'd finished her exams, all the emotional problems of her relationship with Bernard had begun crowding in on her again.

'Are there any more of those canapés, Marianne?'

It was Bernard, putting an arm round her waist as he rescued her just in time.

'Lots more in the oven ready to come out.' She raised her voice. 'Gaston, get the canapés out, please!'

'What were you two whispering about?' Bernard handed her another glass of wine as he steered her towards the window seat in the sitting room.

Julia smiled. 'I was congratulating Marianne on the marvellous buffet supper.'

'Oh, she loves having a party here. It doesn't happen as often as she would like. Thanks for putting Philippe to bed. He'd been waiting to see you all day, apparently, and I was too tied up with my guests to help you. I popped upstairs to his room just now and he's out for the count. I don't think we'll hear from him, in spite of the noise, until the morning.'

He wondered if she knew how nervous he'd been feeling when he'd said that. He'd decided, really decided, against all the odds that he was going to tell her how he really felt about their relationship tonight. He found himself holding back on the wine. He wanted to remember this night even if...no, he was going to be positive. He had to know the truth, whatever it turned out to be.

'I want to make a toast, everybody!' Dominic was standing in the middle of the room, raising his glass in the air. 'I think I know I speak for all of us on the course when I say that we've had the best professor guiding us every step of the way. I've learned a lot, rediscovered areas of surgical technique I'd forgotten and grappled with the new techniques Bernard has taught us. Whatever my exam results, I'll always be a better surgeon than I would have been and a much better all-round doctor. So, fellow students, please raise your glasses to Bernard, the finest surgical professor we could possibly have wished for!'

Glasses were raised high. The wine flowed. The conversation turned to what everybody was going to do now it was all over. Most of them were going back to the hospitals that were still holding their jobs open for them. The general consensus was that promotions were imminent if their exam results were good. Others were more pragmatic. They would pick up where they'd left off, happy that they'd had the experience to widen their knowledge of surgery.

'How about you, Julia?' Dominic asked. 'Have you made up your mind at last?'

She cleared her throat. She felt nervous with Bernard standing so close to her, listening to every word she was saying. They'd moved to be with the group in the centre of the room but his hand was still lightly on the small of her back.

'I'm keeping my options open for the moment,' she

said quietly. 'I'll have to return to London to discuss my future with my tutor, whatever I decide to do.'

'When will you go?' Dominique asked.

She hesitated. They were all looking at her, including Bernard whose expression was totally enigmatic. They hadn't discussed this and she now wished they had. She hadn't had time...or had she simply been avoiding this conversation?

'Well...I've reserved my seat on the Eurostar tomorrow. I'm going to London for a few days to talk things over with Don.'

Bernard swallowed hard, trying not to convey any emotion at the announcement. He should have known this would happen. This now confident young woman who'd come out here for a fresh start and made such an impression on all her colleagues. She was ready now to fly away and get on with her successful life. She was ready to combine career and motherhood whenever the time was right. And even if he'd told her he'd changed his mind about having a commited relationship again, it wouldn't have made any difference.

She didn't need him to be her husband and father her child. She was so charismatic, so utterly desirable, so talented, so sexy she could take her time in choosing the right partner for herself.

As he watched her fellow students crowding round her, wishing her well in the future, he knew that he'd lost her. She was going back to London tomorrow and she hadn't told him. Just for a few days, she'd said. But once she got back there she wouldn't return. Her colleagues over in London would gather around her, just as her French colleagues were doing now, and Don

Grainger would persuade her to return and climb the career ladder under his tutelage.

He had to let her go back to London. He mustn't try to dissuade her. It would be selfish of him to try. She was off the course now. Her reason for being here finished. Her exam results would reach her electronically, wherever she happened to be.

CHAPTER ELEVEN

JULIA breathed a sigh of relief as Dominic finally weaved his way across the farmyard to join his colleagues in the waiting minibus. She thought he'd never go so she could be alone with Bernard and explain why she hadn't told him she was leaving for London tomorrow.

She looked around the room but Bernard had disappeared while she'd been listening to Dominic's endless talking. Where was he?

'Ah, there you are, Bernard.'

He was coming through the door. She smiled and moved towards him but stopped in her tracks when she saw he was carrying her overnight bag.

His expression gave nothing away. 'I think it's best for you to go back to the hospital tonight. You've got an early start tomorrow. I've told the driver of the minibus you'll be going back to the hospital and will be with them as quickly as you can.'

'Bernard, I wanted to explain the situation to you tonight. I'm only going to London for a few days.'

'So you said. I'll wait to hear from you. Let me know your plans when you've discussed things with Don.'

He was moving closer, still holding her bag. 'I'll take you to the coach.'

He really meant it! She'd better go gracefully without trying to explain now. Maybe this was his way of ending their short-term relationship. Perhaps he was relieved to have an excuse to end it so easily.

She'd never thought it would end like this. But she'd never been any good at understanding men. She must have got it wrong again!

Her colleagues in the minibus had started to sing now.

Julia winced at the noise disturbing the peace and quiet of the valley but she needn't have worried. Everyone fell silent as she and Bernard reached them. Dominic made a space on the front seat for her and took her bag. For the sake of appearances she smiled at Bernard. He smiled back but it was a wintry smile that was there to pretend that all was well.

The driver was anxious to get going. Everyone started calling their thank-yous and goodbyes.

She doubted very much that Bernard could hear her saying goodbye to him. He gave a wave of his hand and walked back up the farmyard.

She woke in the early morning of a grey dawn. Even the clouds through the window added to her dark feelings. She stretched out her hand towards the other side of the bed. The sheet was cold. She knew he wasn't there. She'd come back to her room at the hospital. Correction! He'd sent her back to her room.

She propped herself up on her pillows and checked the time. She'd set her alarm when she'd got back last night. It would soon be time to get up and make final preparations for the journey.

She remembered the awful journey in the minibus last night. Her friends had become mercifully quiet after she'd joined them. They'd had the decency not to ask questions and they hadn't sung any more. But she'd been very relieved to get to her room and close the door on her own little sanctuary.

Her alarm was sounding. Time to get up. She threw back the duvet. She'd asked the hospital domestic staff to keep her room for a further week until she got back from London. But now she was unsure whether she would return. Her emotions were in turmoil and now wasn't the time to try and sort them out. She determined to go back to London to make her decision.

CHAPTER TWELVE

She stepped down from the Eurostar at St Pancras, marvelling at the speed with which she'd been transported from Calais–Frethun. Only an hour ago she was stepping on the Eurostar in France and now here she was making her way through the crowds, hearing English voices. She got a taxi after only a short wait and gave him the name of her hospital.

'Are you visiting a patient?' he asked her conversationally.

'No.' She climbed into the back seat.

Usually she enjoyed chatting with cab drivers as they struggled through the London traffic jams but today was different. She felt different, spaced out, unreal. Maybe when she was back amongst her colleagues in the orthopaedic department she would be able to make sense of her future. She'd gone away with such high, ambitious hopes. She hadn't been looking for an all-consuming relationship that had turned her world upside down and forced her to examine her dreams.

She wished she'd been able to say goodbye to Philippe. She forced herself to ignore her feelings of guilt about him. He'd come to regard her as a second mother figure and if she stayed in England he would feel she'd abandoned him. And she would miss him more than she dared think about just now. And as for Bernard... If their affair was over...

Her eyes misted over as she searched in her bag for a tissue to blow her nose.

One step at a time.

She felt a surge of apprehension as she paid the driver and looked up at the tall façade of the building that had been her home and workplace as a medical student and then a qualified doctor. It usually felt as if she was coming home again but this time was different.

'So, you'll get your exam results in a couple of weeks, I understand?' Don smiled across the desk at her. 'I was so relieved to get your email this week to say you were coming back to report on the course.'

'Thanks for your reply. I'm glad you were free to see me this morning.'

'I would have made time for you, Julia.' The consultant hesitated, running a hand through his steel-grey hair as he observed his star pupil. Something told him that she wasn't feeling her usual positive self.

'Would you like more coffee? You must be tired after your early start this morning.'

'No, thanks.'

She sat up straight against the back of her chair as she tried to brighten herself up. In the background she could hear the hum of the endless traffic outside on the forecourt of the hospital. An ambulance screeched to a halt and the siren stopped. It was weird. She should be feeling nostalgic by now.

'I've kept in touch with your progress over in France,' Don told her in a casual, friendly tone.

She managed a tight smile. 'I thought you might.'

'Oh, yes. I wasn't going to let you slip through my fingers. I've invested a lot in your training. Seen you grow up from student days. I'll be retiring soon, you know, well, in a couple of years.'

'No, I didn't know. You'll be missed here.'

'Oh, nobody is indispensable. Anyway, to go back to my progress reports from France, your professor, Bernard Cappelle, seems to think very highly of you. When I spoke to him a few days ago he told me you'd made excellent progress and he had high hopes for your exam results. From the way he spoke it seemed you might be staying on in France.'

Her heart gave a little leap of excitement but she remained silent, waiting for him to continue.

He carried on, wondering why she wasn't making any comment.

'That's why I'm so delighted to see you here in London today. There's the possibility of a promotion in the department, and then when I retire in two years my vacancy will be up for grabs. I've no doubt that, having excelled on the prestigious course at St Martin, you would be a strong candidate.'

He broke off. 'Julia, I think you should take a rest for a few hours to recover from the journey. I've asked Housekeeping to prepare your old room in the medics' quarters. My secretary has the keys. Let's meet up here in my office about four this afternoon.'

He stood and walked round the desk. She remembered how he'd been a father figure to her when she'd gone through the messy divorce days. He wasn't fooled by the brave face she was trying to effect. He held out his hand as she stood up, making a valiant effort to keep going.

She grasped his hand. 'Yes, you're quite right, a rest would be a good idea. I'll be back at four. Thanks, Don, for—'

'For treating you like one of my daughters.' He grinned. 'When you've got four girls at home you become an expert at sensing when something is not quite right.'

She smiled back, knowing she hadn't fooled him. She would have to sort out her problems, emotional and career-wise, before she came back.

She fell into a troubled sleep the moment her head hit the pillow. But the dreams that haunted her throughout were worse than being awake. She was dreaming that Philippe was seriously ill, that Bernard wasn't there with him, that he was on the island looking for her, calling her name, but she was calling out to him from the sea where she felt as if she was drowning. The water was over her head but her arms and legs weren't working properly… She managed to struggle up from the depths of her sleep. Relief flooded through her as she realised she was safe in her room. She was wide awake now and her mind had cleared. She knew she had to speak to Bernard as soon as possible.

He wasn't answering his phone. She tried several times. She'd get hold of Michel Devine in *Urgences*.

'Michel?'

'Michel Devine.'

His abrupt manner and the background noise told her he was on duty.

'It's Julia.'

'Ah, Julia. I thought you were in England. Bernard told me—'

'I'm trying to call him but he's not answering.'

'He's up in Paediatrics with Philippe—that's why he's not answering. I'll get a message to him if—'

'Is Philippe OK?'

'We're not sure. Bernard brought him in this morning. He's going through tests for meningitis.'

'Oh, no!'

'Don't worry, Julia. Philippe is in safe hands and Bernard is constantly with him at his bedside. What message shall I give Bernard?'

'Tell him...tell him I...tell him I'm coming back tonight. Thanks, Michel.'

She glanced at her watch as she zipped up her bag. Good thing she hadn't unpacked anything except her toothbrush. She went out into the corridor. She'd contacted Don, who'd agreed to see her earlier that afternoon.

He was waiting for her in his consulting room in Outpatients. A couple of patients were waiting outside as she went in and closed the door.

'Thanks for seeing me at such short notice. I'll make it brief because I know you've got patients waiting.'

'So why the change of plan, Julia?' He got up from his desk and moved over to the window where there were a couple of armchairs and a small table. 'Have you had any lunch?'

'I'll get something on the train.'

'The train?'

'I'm going back. Bernard Cappelle's son is ill with suspected meningitis. I have to be there with them. Sorry, Don, but it's put everything in perspective, coming back to England. I wasn't sure what it was I wanted but now I am.'

For a moment the consultant stared at her before he realised the reason behind her strange behaviour.

'Ah, I get the full picture now. I have to say I wondered if there was something going on between you and Bernard. So you're an item, to quote my daughters, are you?'

She hesitated. 'Yes, we've built up a relationship, a complicated relationship, and I don't know where it's going, but...' She stared across the small table at Don. 'I shouldn't be burdening you with all this.'

'Julia, you are talking to an expert in the affairs of the heart and in my opinion you've got it pretty bad. So I'm all agog to hear what you're going to do about it.'

She hesitated. 'I've got to think about it.'

'What's there to think about? You're obviously head over heels in love with the man. Call me an old romantic but you shouldn't turn your back on that sort of relationship.'

'But, Don, remember when I was going through that awful divorce and I told you I'd never trust my own judgement of character again? I was trying to be rational this time, taking my time to think through the problems of marrying Bernard and carrying on with my career.'

'You were too young when you married that obnoxious man. You'd had no experience of people like that.

Now you're an extremely intelligent and experienced woman. I'm sad to see you going back because I had great plans for your future here. But you've got to go back and stay there with Bernard. You obviously love both him and his young son. Let me know as soon as the boy has been through all his tests at the hospital.'

The journey seemed much longer on the way back. She was amazed to see Michel Devine waiting for her at St Martin station. She'd told him the time her train from Calais–Frethun would arrive.

'How's Philippe?'

'Still having tests.' He opened the car door for her. 'Bernard is with him the whole time but the paediatric department is firmly in charge.'

'I just hope it's not meningitis.'

'If it is, he's in the best hospital to deal with it. And he's got the best father to lavish attention on him.'

'Thanks for picking me up, Michel.'

'I thought you might be shattered after going there and back in the space of a few hours. I thought of sending a taxi for you but I'm going off duty now and I can get you back to the hospital myself.'

'Well, it's much appreciated.'

'I'm so glad you've come back. You definitely belong over here…with Bernard. As a widower of three years, I was pleased when I saw you and Bernard getting on so well. A good relationship like yours is worth sticking to. My wife and I were only married for three years before she lost her battle with cancer. While she was alive were the happiest days of my life.'

She swallowed hard as she heard the raw emotion in

his voice. They were drawing into the forecourt of the hospital.

'Thanks, Michel. I'll go straight up to Paediatrics.'

He switched off the engine and came round to help her out. 'I'll put your bag in Reception till you need it, then I'll go off duty.'

'Thanks for the advice.'

He gave her a sad smile. 'What advice?'

'Not in so many words but you nudged me in the right direction.'

'I hope so.'

CHAPTER THIRTEEN

JULIA pushed open the swing doors that led into the paediatric ward. It was late in the evening now and most of
the children had been settled down for sleep. The lights
had been dimmed in the main ward. She could see the
ward sister walking towards her now.

'Ah, Caroline!'

She was glad they'd met socially during the summer.
She also knew that she was one of the most experienced
and well-qualified sisters in the hospital.

She began to relax. 'How is Philippe?'

Caroline frowned. 'I'm afraid the tests are still in-
conclusive. Bernard is with him. He's been here all day.
I thought you were in England, Julia.'

'I made a brief visit to see the boss of my department. I'm back now. Change of plan. Where is...?'

'Let me take you to his room.'

Caroline took her to a room near the nurses' station.
The door was slightly ajar. She pushed it open.

'A visitor for you, Bernard.'

He was sitting by Philippe's bed, hunched over his
son, his head resting in his hands, his elbows on the
sheet. He turned his head and for an instant she saw a

flash of welcoming light in his eyes before the mask of total dejection returned.

'I thought you were in England.'

Sister went out and closed the door behind her as Julia approached the sick child's bed. Bernard stood up, running a hand through his dishevelled hair. She could see that he hadn't shaved that day. The dark stubble she'd noticed he always had in the mornings was now much more prominent—positively designer stubble, she couldn't help thinking. She longed to draw him against her and hold him there but sensed the cold aura surrounding him.

'I came back,' she said lamely. 'I was worried about Philippe.'

She leaned across the small patient now, automatically reaching for his pulse. It was racing along too fast, almost impossible to count the beats. His skin was dangerously hot.

'What's the latest?'

Bernard handed her the notes. She was still scanning the test results as one of the doctors on the paediatric firm came in.

'What's the latest news from Pathology, Thibault?' Bernard asked, his calm voice belying the obvious anxiety that cloaked the rest of him.

'A glimmer of hope, Bernard. The latest blood sample gave negative results for meningitis. I'm going to take another sample now.'

She stood beside Bernard as the blood sample was taken.

'It could be septicaemia, couldn't it?' he said to the

young doctor as he prepared to return to the pathology laboratory.

'Or it could be the antibiotics beginning to kick in,' Julia said quietly, thinking out loud.

The three of them pooled their ideas, each anxious that the dreaded diagnosis of suspected meningitis should be proved to be wrong.

'We'll just have to hope, Bernard,' Dr. Thibault said gently. 'Tonight is the crucial time. As you know, if we don't have an improvement in your son's condition by tomorrow morning there is a chance that—'

'Yes, yes,' Bernard said, his voice wavering now. He didn't want to contemplate that his son's illness could be fatal. 'We can beat it! This is the twenty-first century and we'll pool our skills to save Philippe.'

'If I might suggest, Bernard,' the young doctor said, carefully, 'you've been here all day and you must be tired. I think I could arrange for you to take a break if you would approve of that?'

'I can't leave Philippe at this stage.'

'I'll call the path lab and ask them to collect this blood immediately. I can stay here with your son for the next hour.'

Julia looked across the small table at Bernard. The canteen had been deserted when they'd arrived but she had phoned the kitchen and the staff cook on night duty had turned up to prepare some food.

Chicken and vegetable soup had been placed in front of them, along with a crusty baguette heated up in the oven and a basket of fresh fruit—apples, oranges and bananas.

It wasn't until they'd started to eat the soup that they both realised how hungry they were.

'Did you have lunch over in England?'

She put down her spoon, having polished off her first helping. 'There wasn't time. I meant to get a sandwich on the train but I wasn't hungry. I'm hungry now.'

'There's more soup in this casserole,' Bernard said, dipping in with the soup ladle the waitress had left on the table.

It was only when she'd finished the last piece of her apple that her brain seemed to function again.

'Dr Thibault was quite right to send you off for a break. You looked terrible when I first got here.'

'Thanks! You weren't looking your usual self either.' His eyes seemed to be boring into her. 'Care to tell me why you're here?'

'I told you; I was worried about Philippe.'

'And?'

'Bernard, I don't think we should talk about this until we've got through tonight.'

'We? You don't have to stay, Julia.'

'Oh, but I do. I can't rest until I know that…that he's out of danger.'

Bernard stood up. 'Neither can I.'

She must have dozed off in the high-backed armchair beside Philippe's bed. Bernard, at the other side, was wide awake, she could see, sponging his son's chest with cold water.

As he dabbed it dry he looked across at her. 'The rash isn't so pronounced. It's disappearing in places. I'm beginning to hope it's septicaemia.'

'Still dangerous,' Julia said quietly. 'But easier to treat than meningitis.'

Bernard nodded. 'He's opening his eyes... Julia!'

She jumped up from the chair and went round the bed. 'Philippe?'

'Where am I?'

Julia could feel tears of joy pricking her eyes as she heard the weak little voice. A tear trickled down her cheek as she leaned over Philippe, taking hold of his tiny hand. She'd been right to come back here. This was where she belonged.

Philippe was propped up against the pillows, eating a small carton of yoghurt. It was what he'd asked for as soon as he'd begun to feel stronger. Since the amazing recovery in the early morning he'd gradually gathered strength. The diagnosis was confirmed, septicaemia. His treatment and medication had been adjusted accordingly and there was every chance now that he was going to have a full recovery within days.

'Papa, can we go home? I want to see the cows. Gaston will need some help with the milking today.'

'We'll need to stay here for another night at least.'

'But you'll both stay with me, won't you? Julia, you can stay, can't you? You won't leave me, will you?'

She looked at the anxious eyes of this young boy who meant so much to her and across the bed to his father whom she loved more than she'd ever imagined possible.

What would she do if he didn't want her any more?

CHAPTER FOURTEEN

SHE'D spent the night in the guest room. On Bernard's instructions Gaston had moved another bed into Philippe's room before they'd all arrived back from the hospital yesterday. Bernard had insisted she get a good night's sleep.

'You've spent the last three nights in an armchair so you must get a proper rest tonight,' he'd told her.

She'd argued that so had he. They could take turns at caring for Philippe during the night.

But Bernard had been adamant that he wanted to do the night watch. As she pulled the curtains fully back and fixed the ties, she raised her face to the morning sun. There was little heat now in the late autumnal rays but it was soothing to her nerves. Bernard had been right. She did need a good rest. Her nerves had been totally frazzled over the last few days since Philippe had become ill.

And the journey to London and back had tired her more than usual. Well, the discussion with Don Grainger had set her thinking.

She sighed as she looked out over the garden. The fallen leaves on the lawn. The roses drooping and waiting to be dead-headed. She'd pushed the emotional problems that still existed between Bernard and herself to the back of her mind until they were absolutely sure Philippe was out of danger. And she didn't want a discussion while Philippe was the main priority in Bernard's life.

Maybe she should simply go back to her room in the medics' quarters at St Martin? Marianne and Gaston were taking care of all the practicalities of the situation. Was she really needed here?

'Julia, I've brought you some coffee.'

She raced to the door at the welcome sound of Bernard's voice.

He was standing outside in the corridor, carrying a small tray, the expression on his face totally unreadable.

'How's Philippe?'

'He had a good night. In fact, so did I. I slept until Marianne brought the coffee tray just now. She's taken over to give me a break. I feel that now Philippe is out of danger and you're back from London we should talk. My place or yours?'

For the first time for days he looked relaxed again. There was a half-smile on his face but still that awkward coolness that had to be resolved if she was to convince him that she'd made a mistake in returning to London without discussing it with him first.

She'd had time to think and she knew that she wanted Bernard on any terms. She could be happy with him without them marrying or having a child of their own. Philippe felt like her own child already and if Bernard didn't want more children, neither did she. But did he want her? Had the short-term affair been enough for him to decide to go back to his independent lifestyle?

She moved towards him. 'Which room would you prefer?'

'I'd like to install myself back in my bedroom so let's go there. I need to shave and everything is in my bathroom. We can talk while I'm in there before I arrange my schedule at the hospital for today. I plan to go in for a couple of hours this morning. I've arranged for a nurse to come out from the hospital to be with Philippe, and Marianne and Gaston will be in charge here.'

She followed behind him. This wasn't how she'd planned to discuss her change of heart—in a bathroom!

He held the tray in one hand and pushed open his door with the other, walking swiftly over to the small round table by the window. She sank down into one of the armchairs and watched as he poured the coffee into the cups. He took a sip and swallowed. 'Mmm, that first coffee taste of the morning. Nothing like it!'

She watched, mesmerised, as he began to walk towards the bathroom, the cup firmly clenched in his fingers.

'Bernard! You're not really going to shave while we have the most important discussion of our lives!'

He turned, a half-smile again on his face. 'Ah, so you do have something to tell me? Don said you might have.'

He moved swiftly back to the table and stretched his long legs out in the armchair across from her.

'Don?'

'Who else knows you almost as well as I do? Well, professionally anyway. He phoned me last night to check how Philippe was but also to fill me in about your discussions. He said he thought you would be staying in France and conceded that his loss was my gain. He'd hoped to guide you up the career ladder in London until his retirement and he was sad to lose you.'

'So you were simply talking professionally?'

'What else?'

She was beginning to feel alarmed. The two men who'd been most influential in her career had been discussing her.

'He didn't touch on anything…er…well, personal?'

He feigned surprise at her question. 'Such as?'

'Oh, Bernard, you can be so infuriating at times!'

She leapt out of her seat and went across so she would have the advantage of looking down at him. 'Such as whether our relationship was over or not?'

'Ah, that.' He half rose from his seat and pulled her down onto his lap. 'Well, he might have mentioned it.'

She turned her head and looked up at him. He had the advantage now and she'd really wanted a discussion. She needed to convince him that she'd come to the right decision at last.

'I've had time to think over the last few days,' she said quietly. 'I know you don't want another child but I've realised that I can live as a surgeon so long as I have you…and Philippe, of course…in my life. I don't need a baby any more.'

'But I do,' he replied gently, drawing her so close that she could feel his heart beating. 'I've known for some time now that, contrary to how I used to feel, I would love to have a baby…but only with you. I've watched you caring for Philippe and I realised that you would be the most wonderful mother to our baby.'

'So why didn't you tell me you'd had a change of heart?'

'I wanted to be sure you wouldn't choose to have a baby with me just because I could fulfil one of your dearest wishes. I had to be sure that you loved me as much as I love you.'

'But I thought that was obvious!' She put her hands against his cheeks and drew his lips against hers.

She felt his response deepening, his hands gently caressing her body. Gently, he lifted her up into his arms and carried her over to the bed.

'Can I make my love any more obvious?' she whispered as they both lay back, exhausted by their lovemaking and panting for breath.

She turned her head on the pillow to look at him as she curled her toes against his, one of the positions she loved to adopt after they'd made love.

He smiled. 'I think you've convinced me... But, then again, I just might be having doubts.'

He rested on his elbow, looking down into her eyes. 'I'll need convincing often if we're going to stay together for the rest of our lives.'

She gazed up into his face. 'And are we going to stay together for the rest of our lives?'

Before she realised what he was doing he was on his knees beside the bed, looking up at her with those devastatingly sexy eyes that were expressing the love he felt for her.

'Julia, will you marry me?'

His voice was husky, full of emotion as he asked her the question she'd thought he might never ask. She'd had her doubts before but now that they'd sorted out the problems that had been holding them back she was free to commit herself.

She leaned forward and put her hands over his. 'Of course I will.'

He was in bed beside her, drawing her into his arms. 'Oh, Julia, my love...'

'Bernard, the nurse is here to look after Philippe.'

Julia struggled up through the tangle of sheets as she heard Marianne's voice outside in the corridor. She swung her legs over the side of the bed.

Bernard put out a restraining hand. 'I'll go,' he whispered. 'Stay here and rest. There's no hurry. Take your time before you come downstairs.'

He was smiling fondly down at her. 'As soon as Marianne hears our news, you'll need all your energy to cope with her. She'll be thinking ahead to the wedding and all the plans that will be needed.'

'Please don't tell her till I come downstairs.'

His smile broadened. 'I won't need to. That woman is psychic, I'm sure. She's been expecting an announcement ever since you stayed that first night here.'

It was only as she climbed out of the bath and reached for a towel a little later that she realised the enormity of the tasks ahead of her. There were phone calls to make to her parents—that must be a priority. How would her mother take it? Last time she'd announced she was going to be married her mother had been very unsure. She'd gone ahead with it defiantly and had lived to regret it. But this time she was absolutely sure of her man.

But the practicalities had to be dealt with. Where would they have the wedding? France? England? There'd have to be a long list of guests. How much easier if would be if they could just sneak away, the three of them.

As she thought of the three of them making a real family unit at last she felt a great longing to see her soon-to-be stepchild as soon as possible.

Hurrying along to his room, she slowed down to check that she was presentable. It was still early but so much had happened, so much had been resolved and so much needed to be sorted out. As her mother would say, she should gather her wits about her.

Yes, there would be a nurse from the hospital taking care of Philippe and she didn't want to look as if she'd been rolling about in Bernard's bed all night. It had only been this morning when she'd given herself completely to the joy of being finally sure that their future was well and truly together.

She smiled as she recognised one of the nurses from Paediatrics. 'Hello, Florence.'

'Julia!' Philippe's voice was croaky and weak but his happiness at seeing her again was expressed in the way he held out his thin little arms towards her.

She leaned down and clasped him against her. 'Oh, Philippe, it's good to see you looking so much better.'

'Can I come down and have breakfast with you and Papa? I'm feeling hungry now.'

'You said you didn't want to eat anything,' Florence said gently. 'Let me bring something up from the kitchen for you. I don't think you're strong enough to go downstairs yet.'

As if on cue, Bernard chose that moment to come in. 'What's this about breakfast, Philippe?'

He reached down and picked up his small son in his arms. Julia grabbed a blanket from the end of the bed and wrapped it round him. He snuggled happily against his father.

'Take a break, Florence,' Bernard said. 'Come down and have some breakfast with us. The more the merrier around the table today!'

Marianne was waiting for them in the kitchen, cafetière in her hand. The delicious smell of coffee had wafted up the stairs as Julia had walked behind Bernard, followed by Florence. Julia sat down beside Bernard, as close as she could to Philippe so that she could make sure he was comfortable in Bernard's arms. She doubted he would eat much, if anything, after the ordeal he'd been through, but it was the experience of being once more part of the family that he needed.

Their family! Her heart seemed to turn over at the implications of what was happening.

What a momentous occasion. Was Bernard going to make an announcement here at the breakfast table? With Florence here the news would spread like wildfire at the hospital. Was that what he wanted?

She glanced up at him as he cleared his throat. He was looking oh, so pleased with himself, happiness oozing from every fibre of his muscular, athletic, tantalisingly sexy body. His happiness was infectious. There was a feeling of total unreality about the situation but she'd never felt as happy as she did at that moment. Yes, she wanted to tell the whole world that she was soon to be married to the most wonderful man on the planet.

'Come and sit down, Marianne,' Bernard said. 'I want everybody here because I've got an announcement to make. Where's Gaston?'

'He's just finished the milking. He's going to take a shower as soon as—'

'Ask him to come in here, Marianne, if he's still out there, taking off his boots.'

Gaston glanced around the table as he walked in, treading carefully across the room in his socks to sit next to his wife.

'I haven't even washed my hands,' he complained to his wife before looking across at Bernard. 'What's this all about? I need to clean up.'

'Julia has just consented to become my wife. I want you all to share in our happiness.'

'And about time too,' Gaston said, now grinning from ear to ear. 'Creeping around in the middle of the night when the two of you—'

'Gaston!' his wife hissed at him. 'Be quiet.'

'No, I won't be quiet. This is the best news we've had in this house since I came to work here and told you that Marianne had set a date for our wedding.'

'And that was a long time ago, wasn't it, Gaston? I was much younger but I remember it well because my father opened one of his special bottles of champagne so we could drink a toast. I haven't been down to the cellar recently. Do you know if there's still a bottle of that vintage?'

Gaston struggled to his feet. 'I checked a few weeks ago because I was hoping you'd get a move on, Bernard. Shall I put a bottle on ice?'

'Bring a couple. We'll have a glass now and drink

some more this evening when we can all relax at the end of the day.'

'Julia, are you going to be my new mother?' Philippe asked shyly.

She swallowed hard. 'I'm going to be Papa's wife. You can carry on calling me Julia because I'll never replace your real mother, will I?'

'I suppose not. Well, you can be my second mother, then, but I'd like to still call you Julia.'

Gaston arrived with the champagne. 'It's freezing cold down there in the cellar. I've brought the ice bucket but we don't really need it. And it needs polishing. Hasn't been used for years. I cleared away the cobwebs but…'

He glanced across at his wife, who was already holding a duster.

Julia gathered Philippe into her arms as Bernard stood to do the honours. The cork was expertly removed with barely a hiss, the champagne was poured, the glasses raised.

Marianne was in tears now that she'd got the situation she'd hoped for. It was almost too much for her as she raised her glass to the happy pair.

'Congratulations!' she said, through her tears.

Florence was overwhelmed at being the first to acknowledge that there was some truth in the rumours that had been circulating in the hospital. Just wait until she got back there at the end of the week!

'Well, that all went very well today,' Bernard said, as he climbed into bed. 'Do you think you could put that list down and give me some attention? There can't be that much to do when you're organising a wedding, can there?'

'You must be joking! Not for the groom perhaps. So long as you write a good speech and…'

'Oh, do I have to give a speech? I'd better start now, then. Just lend me that notepad you're still scribbling in.'

He reached across and grabbed it from her, glancing down as he did so. 'Oh, how did your mother take the news?'

'Very well, actually. I gathered that you'd phoned Don this morning and he'd phoned Mum to prepare her for the news. They're old friends from way back at medical school. He'd also given you a very good character reference, I believe, because she said she was looking forward to meeting you.'

'And did you agree on where the wedding should take place?'

'The church where my grandmother and my mother were married in Montreuil sur Mer. I was baptised there because my mother insisted on keeping our French family connection going.'

'So, a very interesting family choice.'

'And do you approve?'

'Absolutely!' He drew her into his arms. 'Is that all the business for the day completed? The night nurse has taken over from Florence in Philippe's room so we're free to go to sleep or…'

As she gave herself up to the delights of their lovemaking she knew she was going to be the happiest bride ever.

EPILOGUE

THE day of the wedding dawned with a flurry of snow-flakes drifting outside the window. Julia had spent the night in a hotel in the village with her parents in line with the tradition of not seeing her groom before the wedding. It had been hard to be separated from Bernard but as he'd reminded her when he kissed her goodnight it was only one night apart and then they would be to-gether for the rest of their lives.

After Julia had eaten breakfast in bed, her mother arrived with Claudine, the dressmaker, and Monique, a hairdresser who was going to shampoo and arrange her long blonde hair so that it would fall over her shoulders underneath the delicate lace veil.

Claudine was going to dress her and make sure that the stunning silk dress they'd designed between them was shown off to perfection. The dressmaker held out the stiff petticoat and Julia stepped into it, one hand on Claudine's shoulder to steady herself. It looked gor-geous!

The ladies in the room asked for her to give them a twirl. She obliged. It didn't feel at all stiff and starchy as she'd thought it might.

Finally, she stood in front of the mirror fully dressed

in the superbly beautiful dress while her mother, Claudine and Monique stood around to admire her. Behind her reflection she could see her mother wiping away a tear. She turned and hugged her.

Her mother hugged her back, but gently. 'Careful of your dress, darling. I'm so happy for you. This time you're going to be very happy.'

And as she walked into the church on her father's arm she knew she really was going to be happy for the rest of her life. She'd chosen and been chosen by the most wonderful man in the world.

Walking down the aisle, she felt like a fairy-tale princess on her way to marry her prince. He was there in front of the altar, her own Prince Charming. He turned as she was nearing him, his eyes shining with love and admiration at this vision of perfection, his soon-to-be wife.

As she reached his side she realised there was someone else with her in front of the altar. Glancing down, she saw Philippe smiling up at her. He'd left his place in the procession of bridesmaids behind her and come to join her and his father. He looked adorable in his tailor-made suit.

'Let him stay with us,' she whispered to Bernard, who smiled and nodded in agreement.

The organist stopped playing. The congregation fell silent. The marriage service began.

There was another flurry of snowflakes as they came out of the church and stood on the steps for the photographs. Julia and Bernard smiled for the cameras. Her parents joined them with her brothers and their families. Philippe joined them and then agreed to leave the bridal

pair to join Julia's parents, who were going to take him
back to the farm. The photo shoot would have gone on
longer but the descending snow put an end to that.

'The kiss!' everyone was calling out.

Bernard took her in his arms and they kissed to loud
shouts of approval.

'Encore! Another kiss!'

'Just one more,' Bernard whispered. 'I want you all
to myself now.'

As soon as they could get away into the car, they did
so.

'See you back at the farm,' Bernard called out to
everybody as he drove away. He'd insisted on going
against tradition by driving his own car over to the
church so that they could be really alone on the way
back home.

'I wanted you to myself for the first few minutes of
our marriage,' he said, pulling the car in behind a tractor on the narrow country lane. 'I'm taking a short cut,
which should be quicker than the main road so we'll be
back at the farm before our guests arrive, I hope. We'll
have to be sociable for the rest of the day.'

She smiled. 'It's been such a whirlwind of organisa-
tion for the last few weeks. I'll be so glad to have some
normal married life.'

'Do you think we'll ever have a normal married life,
whatever that is?'

'I know we're both continuing with our careers but
as we both understand what the other's going through
we can pull together, help each other...until we have a
baby, when it might get a bit harder.'

She glanced across at him. His eyes were on the narrow road ahead. The tractor had turned into a gate and left the road clear at last. The snowflakes had stopped now and the pale wintry sun was peeping out from behind a cloud.

He changed gear as they went down into the valley where he could see smoke spiralling from the farm chimneys. 'I wonder when that will be?'

'Well, it could be sooner than we expected. I promised I would tell you if…well, don't get too excited but I'm seven days late.'

'My darling! Why didn't you tell me?'

'I'm telling you now! But it could just be the excitement of the wedding and all the preparations. Don't, for heaven's sake, start getting your hopes up.'

He pulled into the farmyard and switched the engine off.

'Come here, you gorgeous girl, my wonderful bride.'

He kissed her gently on the lips. As his kiss deepened she moved in his arms.

'Later, darling. Our guests are arriving.'

'Keep me informed, won't you?' he whispered as a car pulled in behind them.

'Of course.' She smiled happily as Gaston opened a door for her to climb out. A long strip of red carpet had been laid in front of her leading to the kitchen door. Bernard was already there for her holding out his hand to guide her indoors.

Bernard's speech was hilarious. Everybody was still laughing as they raised their glasses for another toast. They were all crowded into the dining room, the food spread out as a buffet.

'There's more food in the kitchen, Julia,' Marianne said quietly. 'Shall I bring the desserts yet?'

'I'll tell everybody the desserts are in the kitchen when they would like to help themselves. Nobody's standing on ceremony here. Everybody seems to be getting on well.'

'I should think so,' Gaston said, topping up her wine glass. 'Good thing we've got plenty of bottles in the cellar.'

She moved through the guests, trying to have a word with everybody. They all complimented her on her dress, especially her cousin Chantal. They'd been great friends as children and nothing ever changed when they met up again.

'Your dress is absolutely gorgeous, Julia! It fits you perfectly.'

'I had it made in Montreuil by the daughter of the dressmaker who made the wedding dresses of our grandmother and my mother, who's over there looking very happy to be the mother of the bride, don't you think?'

'She's also happy to be chatting to my mother. You can tell they're twins. They're so alike, aren't they? And they don't see enough of each other nowadays so they never stop talking when they do meet!'

'Just like we do!'

They both laughed.

Chantal turned back to admire Julia again. 'You're so slim. That dress fits you like a glove.'

'I suppose I am…at the moment.' Now, why had she said that? Was it because Chantal had always been more like a sister when they'd been small? The antidote to all those brothers bossing her around?

Chantal moved nearer and put a hand on her arm, guiding her through the throng of guests to a small window seat where they could whisper together. 'You're not…? Are you?'

Julia smiled. 'Maybe. Too early to say but I hope so.'

'So do I! Please remember me when you're choosing godparents.'

'Chantal, you would be my first choice! I'm so glad we're going to see more of each other now that I'm going to be living in France. It's easy for you to come over from Paris by train, isn't it?'

'I may be coming back to this area sooner than you think. I've split up with Jacques.'

'No! But I thought you two had the most perfect relationship.'

'So did I. He's gone back to his wife. He'd managed to fool me completely for a whole year. I didn't realise I was his mistress. I felt such a fool when he told me.'

'So are you thinking of leaving the hospital?'

'I've left! Couldn't stand working alongside him when all the time—'

Chantal broke off as Bernard arrived.

'Not interrupting anything, am I?'

'No! Well, actually Chantal was just telling me she's leaving Paris and moving back to this area.'

'I'll be looking for a job, Bernard. Any vacancies for a well-qualified and experienced doctor?'

'Send me your CV and I'll see what I can do, Chantal.'

'I'll do that!'

Philippe came running across the room to join them. 'Papa, I've got an idea. You see my friend Jules over there with his parents? Well, he got a little brother during the summer. Now that Julia and you are married, does that mean I can have a baby brother or sister? Maybe as a Christmas present?'

He was looking up beseechingly now at Julia.

She looked across at Bernard, who was smiling happily. 'We'll have to see what happens, won't we?' he told his son. 'These things take time.'

Philippe looked pleased. Papa hadn't ruled the idea out. He ran back to his friend Jules to say he might get a baby brother or sister but probably not for Christmas.

'These things take time,' he told Jules airily.

'I didn't think they would stay so late,' Julia said as she slipped into bed beside Bernard.

'Sign of a good party! I'd say it was a huge success.'

'It was wonderful to see my parents and all three of my brothers again but I'm glad they're staying at the hotel in the village, otherwise we'd still be downstairs, having supper.'

'Today has been a wonderful day!' he said, drawing her against him.

'It's been the happiest day of my life. Wasn't Philippe sweet when he asked for a baby brother? I don't know about Christmas but he might get one for his birthday!'

'Wonder woman!'

She laughed.

Bernard drew her closer. 'Just one request.'

'Yes?'

'You're not going to leave me in the early morning and go to the guest room, are you?'

'Not now that you've made an honest woman of me.'

'Any regrets?'

She sighed as she felt his arms drawing her even closer.

'Only that we didn't get together like this sooner.'

'You mean like this…or like this…or like this…?'

She laughed. 'You know what I mean.'

'I certainly do…'

*****